Sources, In Order of Importance

The Chalice and the Blade
Riane Eisler, HarperOne, 1988

Native Son
Richard Wright, Harper, 1940

The Spiral Dance
Starhawk, HarperOne, 1999

The Time Falling Bodies Take To Light
William Irwin Thompson, St. Martin's Press, 1991

The Civilization of the Goddess
Marija Gimbutas, HarperSanFrancisco, 1991

Life tomorrow
the flower of today.
Stars 'round the center
piroette and play.
Life not found
but of blossoms made.

—From the *Ringsongs*

Kaja

10,000 Years Ago

By

Tom Bast

Dedicated to

Red Tara, Eihei, Patty, Lieu, Melissa, Dylan and AliMae

Cover Art By

https://facebook.com/bachduong.artist/

The Gift

Drenched in frigid darkness, Kaja belly crawled up the stony shore. His body felt like loose meat hanging from sodden bones. He could barely drag his elbows and push his knees. His boots were gone, and his parka. And the ship. And the others on the ship.

Ahead, gusts of glowing mist licked sharp boulders pointing at a starless sky. He fixed his focus upon the closest ones and kept it there until he pulled himself into them, as high as he could. Wedged between two, he hung limply. The ocean hissed.

"Where am I?"

His words vanished in the night and depleted his mind. He awoke suddenly at the blush of dawn. His salt-scarred lungs smelled of blood. Saliva collected in his mouth, and his throat went down. Brine shot up and out, spattering on his arm. Panting, he waited, and the next heaves squeezed sour spit through his teeth.

Thirst forced him to stir. Low gray clouds slithered landward. His legs were numb, and he studied the shore while the pain sizzled. Boulders were strewn ahead for a thousand paces, where the land lifted a strange, gray-green, velvety brush unlike anything he knew. He saw no evidence of people. But in the cleft of a distant hillside, he saw trees standing into mist.

There. I'll find a stream.

A wave exploded behind him, and its flow went under him through the stones. The tide was coming in. He wondered how quickly. He wondered how far. He lowered himself and found his footing. He felt for his pouch—yes, it was still with him. It was all he had.

He made halting progress over slicing rocks as the tide flowed past the boulders where he slept. A wave crashed, and frigid seawater rose above his knees before the ebb pulled him into the foam. He locked his gaze on the strange brush climbing from the rocky shore. His body worked without his spirit, and he fought the waves until he could climb above them.

Scanning the brush to find where he could press in, he stopped to stare. A slanted rock hid a nest cradling five eggs.

Ma? Is this you? Why?

The eggs meant he would live. He cracked them into his mouth, and slimy moisture flowed from them, followed by the plop of a tiny embryo, which he gratefully chewed.

Shoes. I will make shoes.

In his pouch, he found his flint eating knife and a length of sinew wound around a wooden spool. The spool was made from a stick from a tree by his childhood home. When he touched it, his mind awakened with the memory of a world that no longer existed. He could smell the aroma of his homeland, and he clung to it, but only for a moment. Recollections from before the invaders came could take his sanity just as surely as the elements could take his life. He scanned the trees.

Shoes. Water. Before darkness.

He cut lengths from the legs of his trousers and tied one end over his toes, and the other snug to his ankle. The eggs sustained him for the task, but now thirst was a need so great it could not be acknowledged. He did not examine what was left in his pouch. He simply tied it closed again, and then opened it, to stuff the bird's nest inside, because it was dry and fine and would make good tender.

He could walk over broken sticks more easily with his feet wrapped. The brush grew as high as his waist, thickly covering the shallow slope. He pushed his way through, towards the clouds flowing over the distant trees.

Am I dead?

He heard birds, and shuffling animals, and insects. But no smoke rose from a distant fire, no shout came in the wind, and there were no trails. He studied the lay of the land and gained an eye for the terrain. The brush's minty fragrance calmed his lungs. He came upon orange flowers with thick petaled cups open to the sky, and from them he drank drops of pollen-filled dew.

The day was short, and his progress slow. In a depression, he saw an open patch of tiny clovers covering a small spring bubbling from an underground stream. *Why, Ma?* Kaja knelt and filled his hands over and over. He ate the clover and scoured the area for more eggs but found none. Before he realized he had moved, his body caught a bird, a dove of some sort, by snatching its feet when he startled it where it slept. He held it as it beat his face with its wings, until his groping hand found its head. With a quick snap, the meat was his. He gutted it with his eating knife and cleaned the bloody blade in his mouth.

When he made it to the forest, he found it peopled by the same trees as his homeland. But as he climbed, he saw no paths, no bench, no foot stones, no cairns. *Is this the world, or not?* He heard water singing, and his body took over. He got to it quickly, drank from it deeply, and walked up it. The trees were ancient, wise and quiet. For generations, they had stood under the grey clouds, smelling the distant sea, fondling the animals in their branches and their roots.

He placed his hand on one, a massive oak whose first branches were larger than some of the full-grown yew. *Ma, is this a realm between life and the Spirit World? Will I have some time to regain myself? I once knew who I was. But...they came and took it. And I...*

They had stripped him of so much. He could not think about what he had done to prevent them from stripping everything. He pressed his head against the tree the way his grandmother had taught him and uttered the blessing and the wish. Thrillingly, Knowledge flowed into him, as certain as a tree that speaks: *Ma has put you here to prove that you still know how to be good. Then, she will let you move on.*

He held the oak until the sensation subsided. Alive long before he was born, it would live long after he was gone. He watched its branches stroke the wind roiling the clouds.

Not far beyond it, he came to two boulders facing a yew burned by lightning. There was enough room to curl up in the black scar, and a fire before the rocks would keep his shelter warm and his embers alive. He sat inside, and swallowed slivers he cut from his bird. He gnawed it clean of every tissue and cracked its bones for morsels of marrow.

When it was gone, he emptied his pouch. The bird's nest was soaked, useless, and bits of it were stuck to everything. *What was I thinking?* The spool of sinew, his flint eating knife.

And, at the bottom, wedged in a corner, a tiny sitting goddess made of clay that his sister, Nana, had sculpted as a little child. When she gave it to him, she said it was a lucky amulet. One of her knees had broken off, and her face was worn nearly smooth. He hugged his treasure to his chest and wept.

⟨∿⟩

Finding dry wood in the damp forest took hours, as did whittling a drill. His sinew snapped when he made a bow with it, so he wove a cord from reeds that were ill-suited. Still, he managed to make a fire kit, and got a blaze going.

He sat next to the flames through the night, for he had not felt warmth in so long. He let it turn his skin red. He let the smoke stroke his face. Wind rustled the forest canopy, and a cold drizzle pattered on the ferns and stones. His fire gathered strength anyway.

He destroyed his pouch to create a sling, and before dawn, he left a pile of embers and a stack of sticks and climbed into an oak that reached across the stream. He brained a tired fox trudging home carelessly. Tied in a loose knot, the tail made a perfect pillow. He roasted the meat on a pole leaned against the rock and balanced its position and the structure of the fire until he could smell it.

He ate the entire animal, and it warmed him from within. He rested his head on his pillow with his feet by his fire.

I should scout. Tomorrow, go to the top of the hill and look around.

An owl hooted sagely.

⟨∿⟩

At dawn, drifting rain caressed the forest. He was cold. His salt-soaked leathers were cracking and did not hold his warmth. But during his sleep, his curiosity about where he was had become a great need to explore. He would not risk much—he would go only to a vantage point. If the land was as uninhabited as it seemed, then he would know he had washed ashore in a mystical place beyond the world. He tended his fire intimately, leaving it roasting new coals.

Gigantic cypress gripped the earth to arc over the gurgling stream. Alder grew thin and tall, racing to the light. Laurels filled the high banks, and their yellow trunks held a liquid glow in the ravine. Ferns spread across the dark soil and swift water alike, allowing access to thirsty hands only near little falls or miniature rapids. Birds chattered continuously, many landing on branches not far from him, where they cocked their heads. They seemed unaccustomed to people, and so they enchanted the forest.

This is not the world. It is like the world, but it couldn't be real. I could not have survived such a shipwreck. Surely, I drowned, and Ma has put me here.

The climb was steep, and his pace slowed as his weak breath deepened. He looked backwards frequently, so he would know how to return. In the drizzle, he could not see his fire's smoke, and the wind carried its aroma away.

He lifted himself onto a high rock and froze. He crouched upon a worn trail. Fear flooded him. Like everywhere else, this place would become dangerous. Like everywhere else, he would be ripped from himself. He began to pant. *People will come. Maybe on horses. I must hide.*

He heard a voice behind him and, snatching his knife like a claw and a rock in his fist, he bared his teeth and snarled as he spun.

It was a boy, twenty paces away. His face widened in terror and he stumbled to the ground. He began running before he regained his footing, and flew back from whence he came, shrieking. Kaja stood, dumbfounded. He scrambled to where the boy had fallen, took his felt hat, and hurried back to his home.

He built up his fire and trembled despite its warmth. *I need weapons. Weapons to kill people. A spear with my knife blade. A sharpened stick.* Yet all he could do was hug his sister's amulet, and softly weep.

The Ringfolk

Dogen and Regis sat on the fur carpets of Regis's home. They had the wooden door ajar, letting in air and light. Dogen's bow leaned against the jamb, his quiver nearby. Their morning hunt had been unsuccessful, but that was mostly because, when they found that Regis' mother had caught a great many songbirds in a net she had strung between two trees, they didn't bother to continue it. Regis had them boiling in a clay pot, with mushrooms and herbs, and he hummed a dance tune. The pot was encircled by a ring of hot stones, and they radiated a gentle warmth into the strange but well-made room.

Regis lived with his mother, Hypp, and they had a funny house. It was not round, as almost everyone else's was, but it had once been round. By way of adding space and rooms, Regis, and his father before him, had created a free-form structure that swelled out from the original circle like a pile of bubbles.

The interior of the great room, where Dogen and Regis sat, matched the strangeness of the structure itself. On one wall, a shelf, of sorts, slanted from roof to floor. Affixed with carved stops, Hypp's cookware seemed to pause while rolling downhill. Even their oven was different. Everywhere else, they were built in a half-bechive shape, but theirs was flat on the sides and had a square opening and a rounded top, which Hypp believed gave her bread a more satisfying crust.

Hypp and Regis had a greater profusion of stuff hanging from their walls and ceiling than most people collected in a lifetime. There were the expected items in great quantities—herbs and flowers drying in bundles tied to the rafters, bows and quivers and slings hanging from hooks, clothing draped on pegs, and stacks of wooden boxes full of mysterious medicines and treasures from distant lands. The walls were covered with insulating firs, and almost anywhere there was a space, little shelves held small sculptures such as fully feathered clay birds or elaborately carved and painted whales, barnacles, starfish, or octopus, one of which hung from the edge. Also on the shelves were dozens of oil lamps of many different designs. For gatherings, they were usually all lit. Making the place even more engaging, absolutely everything—shelves, strings, thongs, structural beams, pegs, knobs, all of it—was painted in an overwhelmingly chaotic complexity of color.

Their home was a natural gathering spot for celebrations, and people showed up expecting to have a good time. The porch out front and the little rooms billowing from the main one made it possible to be part of the general conviviality and to be intimate with just a few others at the same time. There was even a small patio atop one of the rooms, snuggled between two roofs and with a compact fireplace built against the wind.

Thanks to their prodigious oddity, Hypp and Regis were well loved in town. Hypp was a respected herbalist, and Regis was a Ringfolk who took it upon himself to wander farther afield than most. He carried news to and from other villages, and he kept an eye on the Nok, a troublesome tribe living farther inland.

Dogen, on the other hand, lived alone in a small house just past the edge of the village. He kept it immaculately clean, and nearly empty. His few possessions had their assigned places and were always in them. Each morning, he shaved his head and his beard and built his embers into a neat pyramid at the back of his oven. Each evening, he brushed the firs on his walls and swept the floor. People respected his piercing intelligence and his rigorous self-discipline and visited him for advice.

"Man it was cold out there this morning," Regis said.

"Good thing we let the game have a day off. Have to find the roe in their dens—they're too smart to wander around on a morning like this. Course now we'll have to go again tomorrow."

"No matter."

"Wonder how the Yuffs are doing today? Out on the far northern pastures right now. All they have is a tent."

"They're tough people. Village life would bore them."

"Like following the hoofed folk is so fascinating."

"Their teachers are out there with them."

"Hmmm. How'd they learn to talk to the falcons and the wind, that's what I'd like to know."

"Practice," Dogen said.

Trim went running full speed past their door, and they both startled at the intensity of his movement.

"Musta forgot something," Regis said.

"He was white as a cloud."

"Good kid, that Trim. Responsible. Little wild, but responsible. We should initiate him soon. Don't want his pecker to cause him any trouble, you know."

"He'd be a good apprentice for you, Regis. He likes to wander."

"That's the truth. Coming back from Bumblebee Hill last moon and came across him nearly a day away from here. Spear fishing in a stream. Standing so still I thought he was a tree till I noticed his towhead. We had a merry ol' conversation about his love life on the way home. Strong as an ox—not easy keeping up with him."

"Yeah, I remember seeing you two coming down the trail. Seemed like you were telling secrets."

"Everything's a secret to a ten year old."

Yowlif swung into the doorway abruptly. "Regis! Dogen! Come quick, to the Hall!" He ran off.

"Ah, well. Got my spot all warmed up," Regis said.

"I told you he was as white as a cloud."

"Hope it's nothin' about the Nok. Stupid folk probably set fire to the pastures again. Too lazy to find rocks for a fire ring."

"That was six years ago, Regis."

"Still amazes me."

Regis gathered embers from his fire into a clay brazier, and Dogen hefted firewood. Walking to the Hall they saw that Yowlif had gathered just about all the ranking Ringfolk and Talon.

The Hall was a long, straight building where no one lived. It was covered by a mound of earth, which meant that a fire inside quickly heated the room and it stayed warm. It was used for meetings and ceremonies, and for gatherings of the women's and men's lodges. No one else had thought to bring a fire, so Regis and Dogen were roundly commended as they lit one in the central pit.

They all sat in an oblong crowd around the fire and the two huge pillars supporting the roof. Ogden the Liege and High Hingemen Sekh made their entrance last and sat at the head of the room. Trip came with them and sat between.

Ogden was old, older than almost anyone else in the village. His long, white beard hung down to his belly, and his bearskin cloak rounded his once-powerful shoulders and dropped to thick folds around his crossed legs. Upon his head, he wore a ring of gold.

His brother, Sekh, was slightly younger, but far more mysterious. A wizard of great renown, he kept his black woolen hood pulled over his face, so only his grey eyes shone out through the shadow. He rocked gently throughout the meeting and made not a sound.

"Well, everyone," Ogden said. "We have a fine young man here, Trip, who, as many of you know, likes to go wandering far from town. He is not yet initiated, but is ripe for it, and so we shall listen to his story in all earnestness. I doubt he tells this tale for fun, but rather because he believes it himself. Trip, my boy, speak slowly so we can hear. Tell us what you saw this morning."

Several different emotions pulled on Trip. On the one hand, he was very pleased to be called "ripe for initiation" by Ogden, and he wanted to carry himself like a man. He was also pleased to be the center of attention, especially as a great adventurer who was returning from distant lands with amazing tales to tell. That was the presence he tried to project, anyway. But his efforts were severely undermined by his complete amazement and fear. There were still many things in the world he had not seen or experienced. This thing, though, this experience, he felt certain, was something that no one, not even Sekh, had ever seen before.

"Well, a-um." He paused and cleared his throat because his voice cracked. Beginning again, he held his head up and tried mightily to keep his hands still. "This morning I awoke well before dawn, for I planned to go to the shore and collect shellfish for my sister's birthday feast. It was very cold, and the mist blew heavily across the meadow. I knew it would be even colder in the forest, so I walked fast to get the shaman warmth within. Then I went down Raven Wood, heading out to the rocky shore where it's usually best to collect. Minn, the fisherman, told me the tide would be low early in the day, so I had in mind getting through the forest and down to the coast as quickly as I could."

The intent way the men were listening to him made him nervous. He would be able to pull off the air of bravado more easily around people his own age and took courage when he thought of how his exploits would impress them. He resolved to speak slowly, but the moment he uttered a sound, he couldn't control it, and the rest of the story spilled out in a flood.

"By the time I had traveled some distance the mist had lifted some, and I saw the ravine below, and I could tell that with the water so heavy in the branches, it would be drizzling in the wood. So I put on my rain hat and worked the pitch on my walking staff to be sure footed through the muddy forest. I must confess my thoughts were on the coast, and I wondered more about the shellfish I would find than I did about the place where I stood. No one lives in Raven Wood, for it is so cold and wet all the time out there. I expected to see no one at all the whole day.

"You can imagine my surprise when I smelled smoke on the wind. There had been no lightning or thunder all night, and none as I hiked, so I couldn't imagine the forest was burning. I thought it was a trick of my imagination, but then I smelled it again. In the mist I could see no column of smoke, but I definitely smelled it. This brought my thoughts more to the present. How strange to smell smoke from a wet and drizzling forest. I did not slow my pace, but I swept my gaze along the forest and the trail more carefully.

"As you know, the Raven Wood trail descends by switchbacks, since the country there is so steep, and cuts across it at the middle before climbing again and dropping to the coast on the far side. I had just come around the last switch, where the trail opens up and crosses the forest. I was walking quickly, seeking the fire. But I did not see fire.

"No, I tell you and I swear it is not a lie or some child's story, I saw a creature of some sort, unlike anything I have ever seen before. A wild man, I think, but even more destitute, filthy, and insane than Cowry Hermit. He was standing on the trail with his back to me when I came around, but he heard me right off, and spun around. He had claws like a bear, and he showed his teeth and growled and screeched at me.

"Never have I seen a face like his, never on any animal. His hair was matted and filthy, and he wore rags on his body and his feet, but his legs were bare. He threw at me the energy one throws at a mortal enemy. I had no doubt he would kill me if he caught me. But I was unarmed, save for a little barbed harpoon, and I was shocked and terrified by his strange looks. In an instant I ran as fast as I could. I lost my hat, I lost my staff, and my shock and fear were so great I ran all the way back here before they even began to wear off. Even now, telling you this story, I tremble at the thought of ever going through Raven Wood again.

"That is all, dear Ogden, wise Sekh, my uncles. I tell you exactly what I saw and what happened. Make of it what you will, but I stake my honor on its truth."

Now children are always staking their honor on things, for they hear the grown-ups saying it on important occasions. Having eaten honey and even while chewing the wax a child will sake his honor on the lie he didn't touch the honey. But then there comes a time when the child begins to understand what honor is, and they bandy about the word less lightly. After initiation, they understand it fully, and hardly ever talk of honor again, except when they really mean it.

The room was quiet for a while, as everyone seemed to independently conclude that Trip had used it in this grown-up sense. He was just a boy. But he hadn't seen a nightmare or a trick of the light. He had seen something. Wild man, monster, they couldn't tell. But he saw something.

Ogden spoke: "Young Trip, you were wise to run back to us. You acted honorably, and I thank you for being a true young man who cares about his people."

Trip swelled with pride. Ogden's words would have been perfect if he had said "man" rather than "young man," but "young man" was pretty good. He contemplated changing it to "man" in the retelling, but then thought better of it. Getting caught in a lie like that would cheapen the whole thing. Better to be a "young man" now, and eagerly await the night when the men would sneak into his house and tie a hood over his head to lead him into the mysteries of manhood.

Ogden sat pensively appraising the fire, for he knew what would happen next.

"Yo, Ogden, Sekh, good men. I'll go and take a look around. Not saying I'll find the beast Trip saw, but I might find evidence of him. Besides, if there's a fire in there we ought to go take a look at that, too. Head out right now and bring a roll, come back tomorrow sometime and let you all know what's up. Sound good to you?" Regis was so excited he could barely sit still. No matter what Ogden said, he was going to go look for the monster.

One of the main reasons he wandered around all the time was to find strange and unusual things, and to meet people who lived far different lives from his.

Dogen could feel his friend's excitement, and he loved being around him when he was full of life. "I'll go with him."

The others ran worried eyes over them before checking Ogden. He shifted, and scratched his bearded cheek with a thick, cracked thumbnail, watching the fire. He knew Regis and Dogen were going no matter what. But he also knew there was something out there they did not understand. He worried that their eagerness to go would end with their not coming back. He searched for what to say by wondering which foolish deed Regis was most likely to commit. He was a leader because he knew how to use silence. He used it for a while now.

"Regis, Dogen, we are grateful for your offer. However, I wonder if you have considered it fully. Some unknown beast with claws like a bear lurks there. An animal wearing ragged clothes, who does not speak but growls and screeches. I fear you are curious. I fear you are not afraid. What do you say?"

Regis piped up way too quickly, not knowing how to use silence or, truth be told, even be silent. "Well someone has to go out and take a look. What else are we going to do? Never go to the coast that way again? We'll be safe, don't worry. We'll bring arms and treat it like quarry."

Ogden remained silent, still staring at the fire. After a long while, he said, "Regis, you and Dogen are skilled hunters. But we hunt our brothers and sisters. We know their ways, we know their spirits. They know us. This beast, whatever it is—we cannot expect to hunt it like a brother spirit. We know nothing about it. Can it fly? Can it rise up out of the ground? Can it appear out of nothing, to set upon you before you have seen or heard it? I am afraid of this beast, Regis, because I do not know it. Why are you not afraid?"

Regis stammered, so Dogen spoke for them both. "We are curious, Ogden. But in our Hall, a familiar place by a warm fire, with people we know and trust, it is easy for us to be curious. I can assure you that as we approach the woods, the fear will rise up in us. We will heighten our awareness as we approach and use our fear to protect ourselves. We will follow Trip's example and will run willfully away if we feel danger. Indeed, Ogden, we will remember your questions most clearly when we are closing in."

Ogden remained silent, as if waiting for the fire to speak. Dogen nudged Regis. "Oh, yes, My Liege. Yes indeed. We'll be very careful."

Ogden raised an eyebrow at Regis, taking him on fully. "You may go, Regis, on one condition. Bring no hunting arms with you. Neither of you. Lurk like shadows between the trees. Enter the forest and leave it unseen even by the birds. Do not confront this thing. Do not attempt to bring it down. Look at it and see what you can learn about it. Then, perhaps, when we know something of its nature, we will hunt it."

"Yeah, definitely, Ogden, definitely. We'll do that. Not a problem," Regis nodded nervously. He just wanted to get going, confident that Dogen would know the details. He cracked a grin at Ogden and nodded with a wink.

His expression crumbled when another voice rumbled across the room, threatening like a distant avalanche. "Dogen." Sekh lifted his star-like gaze to his, transfixing him.

Dogen felt that Sekh was not really of this world. His countenance was weird, and the discourses in his mind flowed through the Spirit World as easily as through this one. When he spoke, which was rarely, his words referred to both worlds at once.

"Remember his face, Dogen. His face."

Dogen nodded.

Ash

The fever had come. Kaja knew he would die soon. His ragged shoes had worn through, and his cold-stiffened feet had slipped on mossy rocks. His head had hit a stone, and when he woke up, he found one of his toenails torn off. It festered quickly, for he was too weak to heal. He had been cold and wet since the sea coughed him up, and his strength had declined steadily, despite the fire. Despite the fox. Despite everything he had accomplished, he could not sustain himself any longer.

Slouched against the wall of his tree, he rasped like a fawn drowning in mud. His breath burned. "Nana, Nana," he murmured. No one answered. His flickering thoughts were phrases: *Nothing left. Everything lost. Who was the boy? Was he alive? Is this the world?*

He had nothing to eat. His sling had snapped. He could not repair it, for his fingers no longer worked delicately. His fire was dying, and he knew that when it was gone, he would be gone, too.

He had not had time to understand his life. He had not had time to become himself. He had not been good. *I failed the tree. Failed Ma.* The silence around him extended to the edge of the cosmos. "Nana, Nana…"

He was too tired to weep. Yet, death was too searing to pull into himself.

❧

"You smell anything?" Regis asked.

"No. Not yet. Is that smoke or mist in the trees?"

"Could be both."

"Could be."

"Sort of grey for mist."

"Yeah, a little."

"Natural fire might have died by now."

"Yeah, probably. Maybe a smoldering log down there, somewhere."

They approached the forest slowly, rounding the same bend where Trip had seen the beast.

"Would you look at that!" Dogen said.

"What?"

"There, in the trail. See? Footprints."

"You're sure they're not Trip's?"

"No, these are Trip's—the boot prints over here and there. But not that one, " Dogen pointed with his staff, "and that one there. Like a man's foot, maybe wrapped in something."

"Ma's mystery. It's not Trip, that's for sure."

"He's not too big, either."

"Nor heavy. Can you see which way he went?" Regis asked.

"Yes. Look." Dogen pointed with his staff. Below the rock, a sapling had been snapped, and a smear in the mud had been made by a sliding foot.

"You want to stick together or go down opposite sides of the creek?"

Dogen thought for a moment. "My gut tells me we should stay together, but that's probably not the smartest plan."

"I'm going with your gut."

"Yeah, let's." They climbed down the rock and followed a deer path. Birds chirped to each other, and little four-footed creatures squealed and scampered out of the way. The huge trees stood solidly, impassively observing the drama below. Mist drifted in the treetops.

"You smell that?" Regis asked.

"No."

"Hold up and sniff the wind. It's fire."

"Yeah, maybe. Yeah, I do smell it."

They came together. The fear was clear to them now. Who was this wild man with claws and an animal's growl, burning a fire? Did he already know of their approach? Were they about to be speared or shot through with an arrow? The unknown abruptly terrified them. They crouched down together, hiding under the brush. "Now what?" Regis asked.

"I don't know. What if he's already seen us?"

"Oh, he's seen us alright. How could he not have seen us? He's just playing with us. Trying to draw us to him, I bet. We're in a trap, Dogen. We better go back, and I mean now."

"Hold on, hold on. Calm down. Let's just think for a moment. He knows we know he's here. Alright. So what will he do next? Will he follow us back to the village? What if that's his plan? If we're not drawn in, maybe we'll just end up drawing him out. And then it will be too late."

"Where are our weapons? Ogden, I swear, sometimes… He doesn't always know what's best. We should be armed to the teeth and should just kill this thing. What do we need it for? We can see its face after it's dead. Ma's luck, Dogen, all we have are knives!"

"Alright, alright. Footprints and a fire. When was the last time anyone came through here? Do you remember?"

"I don't know. Didn't Mimm go fishing last full moon? What's that, nine days ago or something?"

"Then it's probably only been here for nine days."

"Oh come on, Dogen. Mimm? He could've walked through here without seeing the trees. What does that mean, nine days?"

"I don't know. What if it's not a beast? What if it's just a man?"

"With claws like a bear? We should just kill it. So what if it's just a man. Where did it come from? This trail leads to the shore, nothing else. You think he's a Nok taking the longest possible way to get to our village? Cross country? No way."

"Alright. So what do we do?"

"Lets find him," Regis declared clearly. "We have to now. I'll go high, you go down the crease. Stay low under the brush. I'll be a finch, you be a linnet, we'll call every five steps. Good?"

Regis changed abruptly all the time, and it never ceased to amaze Dogen how clearly he could think sometimes. He nodded, "That's good. Let's head for the fire first. If you see anything, call twice in a row for down and three times for up. If it's time to run, just yell. Plan?"

"Yeah. No bloody weapons. I can't believe it." Regis scrambled off through the brush, knife in hand. He whistled after five steps, even though he was still right in view. Dogen scrambled off downstream, chirping too.

Regis got a good look at Kaja's make-shift shelter first, with a weak little trail of smoke rising from dying embers. He called two times in a row, and Dogen answered. Dogen wasn't able to see the tree and boulders until he was almost right under them. He stayed hidden behind a fallen log, straddling a little waterfall, and scanned the trees in the area. He hoped Regis was doing the same. A dangerous beast who could climb would be high, ready to kill from above. He saw nothing. Then he studied the tree and the boulders for a while, with the little stream of smoke curling upward. Regis called, and he called back.

Then he heard a voice. It startled him, and he cowered down by the log. His hearing became twice as sensitive with the shot of fear. It was a voice. Saying some strange word he had never heard before.

Slowly, Dogen rose up. He found Regis on the bank above and signaled. Regis nodded, and held his knife high to throw if anything came out from where the fire was.

His heart pounding, Dogen stealthily moved towards the burned-out tree and boulders. The voice repeated the word over and over. Slowly, carefully, he pushed himself against the tree itself, and came around to the burned-out edge. Regis's wide-eyed gaze was fixed upon him. His arm, wielding his knife, hovered like a falcon with its claws sprung, ready to deal an instant death throw.

Dogen peeked into Kaja's den. His mouth dropped. He turned his back on Regis, and stood over Kaja in utter disbelief.

Regis came up behind. "Dear Ma," he said.

"Who could this possibly be?"

"I have no idea. But he'll be dead soon. I can almost smell it."

"He's exhausted."

"Look at his foot."

"He's filthy." Dogen knelt next to Kaja. "Where did he come from?"

"I've never even heard of someone like him before."

"Do you think we can save him?"

"Where do we start?"

"Let's clean that foot."

They stretched Kaja out on the ground, as he murmured deep in his hallucinations. They cleaned his foot and slathered it in healing ointment. Realizing that, with their supplies, there was little they could do to save him, they took his poles and rigged one of their bed rolls as a sling. If they could climb up out of the forest before nightfall, they ought to be able to see well enough by starlight to make it home. The healers could work their Magic then.

They hurriedly searched the den for his possessions, and found only the hat, the crude sling and the knife. These they laid on his chest and shouldered the poles to head back. He weighed almost nothing.

But wrapped in the thick furs, with healing ointment on his infection, and caring people nearby, he stopped murmuring, and fell asleep.

◄Ʌ►

"Ma's children," said Hypp, Regis's mother, as they carried him to the hearth. "Do you have any idea at all?"

"No, Ma, not a clue. He was living in a hollowed tree in the woods. He'd built a fire. He had no tools, and these rags his only clothes."

They laid Kaja on a bearskin, and Regis built up a large fire on the hearth, filling the room with penetrating warmth. Kaja didn't move, but he breathed. Hypp felt the water until it was warm enough. Using a large wad of wool, she started washing him. He was famished and filthy and was covered with scratches and pimples and bruises. There were several small infections in addition to his swollen and oozing foot.

Jinn arrived first, carrying a large sack of medicinals, and right behind her was Trawill, also packing supplies. They said that Dogen had sent them, but he had yet to appear.

"Where is he?" Regis muttered, but no one answered.

The women worked as though they were one mind with three bodies, dressing Kaja's wounds and sealing them with a sticky goo of sap and herbs before wrapping them with woolen felt. Under his nose and on his chin they smeared an aromatic ointment that would help with his fever. He was too weak to put through treatments that would heal him more quickly. They dressed him in some of her hiking clothes, for Regis' things were too loose, and they made a dozen braids of his unusual hair so he would not shed into his dressings.

Hypp sang to him all night. Kaja awoke briefly, before dawn, and looked around, helplessly lost. "Nana?" he said, gazing up at her. But he could not comprehend her response. He sipped the broth she offered him and fell back asleep.

Dogen arrived at dawn. Regis was about to launch into a long complaint when he spied his unshaven beard and Sekh behind him. The two friends exchanged a knowing glance, and then all present trained their attention on the great wizard.

The moment Sekh saw Kaja's face, he threw back his hood and knelt, staring in amazement. He removed a small vase from his cloak and, uncorking it, he poured a blue liquid on Kaja's forehead, using his bare fingers to work it into his skin. He chanted in the ancient language, the True Words Ma had used to sing the world into existence, until the liquid disappeared.

Sekh took Kaja's hand into his own, examining it closely. Kaja stirred from that, murmured the word again, "Nana," and drew his hand away to curl up in a ball with his head in Hypp's lap.

Sekh rocked back and sat upon the ground, deep in thought. The only sound was the crackling fire, and the soft rasping of Kaja's breathing. Dogen watched his face, for it was seldom one saw it, especially while he was thinking. What mysteries lie there, in the course of his thoughts? What Knowledge did he bring to this strange man from the sea? What was it like, to gaze upon Kaja and to have something more than astonishment fill one's mind?

Dogen desperately wanted to know. Since he was little, he had tried to distinguish himself as one worthy of the secret Knowledge. He practiced as a spiritual man should, he lived as one should. Others in the village spoke to him on matters of the spirit and mind—he had a reputation for wisdom and good advice.

Yet when the Hingemen chose his apprentice, he chose Bwain, a mere boy, who had done nothing to deserve it. And when Dogen had gone to get him from his windowless home, the wizard had listened to his story, and then left him sitting on his porch, not so much as telling him how long he would be, much less asking his opinion or pursuing his thoughts.

If another man had treated him like that, Dogen would have stalked off. But Sekh was different, so he meditated on his porch all night. When he looked at the old wizard, Dogen felt he saw a kinship, an affinity. And Sekh would look at Dogen, far more often than others, and let Dogen look back at him. Dogen had a feeling—perhaps a wish, perhaps an intuition—that he was also Sekh's apprentice, but in a separate way.

As if stirred from slumber, Sekh suddenly shook himself back to the room. "Ah, good people," he said, his quiet deep voice rumbling like rolling boulders. "We are fortunate this man found his way into your home. He is battered, in body, but more so in mind, and even more in spirit.

"I would like to talk to him. Bring him around and teach him our language. Let him have free rein of Squirrel Wood, but nowhere else. Let him be alone when he wants to be alone and keep him company when he wants company.

"The stars sent him to us, that is clear. And—" Sekh fell silent again, wagging his head slightly. They waited. Throwing his hood over his head, he said, "Soon I will have a clearer understanding." As he rose to leave, he slid his leaden gaze across Dogen's.

⟨ᐯ⟩

Kaja slept for seven days, raising his head only to drink the thick broth of boiled birds, mashed grain and herbed honey that the women prepared for him. His fever broke on the third day, and on the fifth, his wounds began to show signs of healing. They kept him quiet and very warm and sang to him often. The children of the village gathered around and jumped to peek through the high windows, and the adults, too, brought gifts of food and favorite remedies in the hopes of glimpsing the man from the sea.

Believing that anyone's intuition about remedies was valid under such circumstances, Hypp kept everything that was brought to Kaja. Carefully cooled in pots lowered to the bottom of a deep shaft beneath her home, she would see to it that Kaja consumed all of them.

On the seventh day, Kaja sat up on his own. Trawill placed a bowl of broth in his hands, and he bowed his head and prayed before drinking it. Hypp stroked his face and sang a Ringsong of health for him. He smiled then, for the first time, and fell once again into a deep, healing sleep.

"Did ja see that?!" Regis exclaimed. "He smiled! I saw him smile. Did ya see him, Ma? He smiled at you!" Hypp nodded, the ecstasy of motherly Magic playing her expression. "I gotta go find Dogen. He won't believe this." He slammed the door behind him enthusiastically, romping through the village wide-eyed. In no time he was surrounded.

"What happened, Regis?" the children clamored. "Come on, Regis, tell us!"

Adults, too gathered around, asking, "Regis! He is well? Why are you so happy?"

"He smiled, I tell ya!" Regis told them all. "The Sea Man sat up, prayed over his food, and then smiled at my mom. First thing he's done on his own since we found him. What do you know?"

From then on, Kaja's body healed itself and regained its vigor. But the experience of coming back to life was not pleasant for his mind and was not entirely welcomed by his spirit.

He had no idea where he was. Even the captain of the ship was uncertain of the coast they coursed towards before they wrecked. The circumstances under which they had fled—the fire, the confusion, the blood rage—did not lend themselves to careful navigation.

He had known none of his shipmates, but they had been like him, at least; they were Rishi. They had shared enough of his history to see him knowingly, and they had shared enough of his feelings to take off across the waters on the slim chance of survival, rather than tolerate what was on the land.

But here, he was a freak. It was a role that he could not warm to easily. Especially now, so soon after his time as a fugitive. For so long, he had hid himself from others, and had lived in the shadows and on the margins. He had lived from moment to moment, concealed in his homeland's forests, acutely aware of even slight smells or minute flashes of light through the trees. He could no longer behave like a normal person in a safe place and squirmed under the attention heaped on him by the kind folk of this town called Ash.

What sustained him, and when he pondered this he could not believe it was so simple, was his desire to be polite to his hosts. They had gone to such lengths to help him, he felt obligated to return their kindness, first by getting better, and then by working for them in some way. Those were the thoughts that got him out of bed on the thirteenth day, and those were the thoughts that had him speaking simple sentences in their language on his twenty-first day. When they took him out for sun, the children would gather around him, and they would give him things—children's gifts of woven reeds and feathers and little stones—which they thought would make him feel better. This helped him tremendously, because it was a situation he knew how to handle.

His people knew of spirits in all things, and to them, no phenomenon in Nature was bereft of life. Within the wind, within the aroma of the sea, within every creature and every person was a spirit. They loved the spirits, and they feared them as well. Sometimes, the spirits were beneficent, and, at other times, they were indifferent, but, often enough, they were openly hostile.

Kaja's folk had no grand scheme describing how these spirits related to one another, or how they were ordered. Instead, they had innumerable stories. If you were to hear them one after another, you would think they were inconsistent, perhaps even incoherent. But they were not told one after another. They were told one at a time, when the occasion presented itself, and so over the course of years they served to teach the young that the world was full of Magic and wonder, and to remind the old that that Magic and wonder sprang from love.

To call this to mind, Kaja's folk would say "Ma." Ma was the gorgeous and inscrutable truth dancing before us all.

When the children brought Kaja gifts, he saw that the children were Ma, as pure as a blossom, and he knew how to properly accept gifts from Ma. Holding one in his cupped hands, he would examine it thoughtfully, and then he would press it between his palms, hold it by his heart, and bow deeply. In this way, he came to know their natures, and they came to know his. He and Trip, the boy who had seen him first, shared a special, fraternal bond.

But the weapons disturbed him. In Regis' house, in Dogen's house, hanging from the rafters and leaning against the walls, were not only hunting weapons. There were also stiff flint knives with bone guards, hammered swords of copper or tin, and long-handled axes. These were weapons that were meant to kill other people.

Kaja's own folk had never made weapons like these. They had never even dreamed of them. And they learned of them a woefully short time before they saw them and felt them.

How could my hosts be so kind and gentle, and yet wield these things?

In his old world—as he came to call it, *my old world*—there were his folk, whom he loved, and there were the invaders who had the weapons of war, whom he hated. The people of his "new world," here in the hills by the sea, were somehow a blend of the two. He had to love them, for they had shown their love to him. And he had to fear them, for only demonic beasts would build weapons to kill other people.

Illusions

As time went on, he took to walking in the woods. Regis and Dogen often accompanied him and taught him where he was allowed to go. Dogen's meditation gazebo was included within his boundaries. Kaja retired there whenever he felt he could go off alone without being rude, and he gazed out at the sea. He did not know which direction faced home.

The land loved him, too, in Ma's inscrutable combination of beneficence and indifference. But the land was strange. The wide thick meadow leading to the edge of the sea, which his hosts called the "moor," was especially odd. Nowhere in his experience did a meadow grow so deep and thick as the moor did. The trees in the forest, too, were mostly familiar. But they grew differently—thicker, and squatter, and holding their branches more jauntily.

He knew he still walked the Earth, though a different Earth than had birthed him. A different place, a different time. He had left his homeland in the summer, but here it was Fall, or seemed to be, and for all he knew it would always be Fall.

He never wandered past his boundaries, but he would cast his gaze far down the misty trails when he was alone. As a man born from the womb of his loving mother into the womb of his loving community, his isolation from his people was a palpable taste in his mouth. His grief was a throbbing within his brow, his loneliness a heaviness in his breath.

᙮

For two Moons this did not change. He learned their language readily enough—the third he had known in his life. His body sustained him with only tacit cooperation from his spirit. He proved himself a capable hunter, and it relieved him that the animals acted the same here as they did at home, and that they recognized his benediction when he came to their corpses to be witnessed by their spirits. The hunt could focus him, but often his thoughts drifted powerfully away, and he could not collect them. Sometimes, he could only stare blankly, enveloped in an impenetrable melancholy.

His hosts treated him with unwavering generosity. He lived with Regis, and Hypp never tired of caring for him. Over time, she tended to his material well-being less than to his wounded spirit. She encouraged him in his own rites, and in his own practice. He did what he could remember, but these things had been torn from him just as he began to taste their power.

She filled the void with gentle suggestions, teaching him songs and Gathas from her own tradition, ones so ancient they had the ring of universality about them. And Kaja seemed to hear an echo of his mother and his grandmother in her voice. His love for her grew and grew, until, one day, he found himself living because he loved her, and because she loved him. This mystery gave him hope. Not all was lost.

❧

Throughout that time, Sekh lurked in the shadows. Kaja knew who he was, but he never saw the man about the village. His mysterious life and ways hid him from Kaja's view, and while others spoke of him with a reverential familiarity, his absence became more and more present for Kaja.

He knew, though he did not know how he knew, that his survival was because of the wizard. It is not natural for a war-like people to let strangers live in their midst, unless they served some purpose. In Kaja's experience, this meant slavery, but he was not a slave, nor did he see slaves—not that that that that meant they weren't there. He had no way of knowing what horrors might lie beyond the mists, for there was no road to his old world, and no wanderer came to share stories.

His experiences had destroyed his sleep. The best he could do was rest, without ever losing track of the smells and sounds around him. In the middle of a moonless, frigid night, Kaja awoke to footsteps. He discerned the click of two poles on the ground, and the knocking of a stick on a wooden box. From where the sounds came, he could not determine. At first, he held perfectly still, trying to locate it. It began far away and approached from all directions. He rose noiselessly and pressed himself into the shadows where his door would shield him when it opened. Too experienced to panic, he listened calmly, and did not move or make a sound. He wondered if he still had the strength to leap out the window and roll up from the impact into a full run.

Then, something in him changed. *I know about footsteps in the night. Hypp does not.* He would not flee into the darkness. He would protect Hypp. He had no weapons, for he had not asked to make any, and no one had offered to put one into his possession. He slid through the door along the floor and waited near the lid to the pit where Hypp kept her cold jars.

The knocking box, the poles on the ground and the footfalls resonated louder now, maybe ten paces away, maybe less. They still seemed to approach from all sides. An eerie presence manifest through the sounds. Kaja knew it. He remembered it. He crouched next to Hypp's bedroll and reached out to shake her shoulder.

She was not there. Fear stabbed him, but passed through him, like a poorly shot arrow through a deer's guts. The blood that filled the wound was rage.

Where is she? I will kill the force that took her.

Light was little more than silver lines on the edges of objects. But he knew where a flint blade hung, and as quietly as possible, he reached for it. Back and forth he groped in the spot— where was it? With both hands now, the footsteps closing in, he could find no weapon.

His heart raced. *So this is how it ends. This place is an illusion, after all. So be it. Surprise is all I have now.* His need to save Hypp threw him at the door, feet first. He hit it with such force that it tore from its hide hinges and slammed into the damp ground. He landed some way beyond it, a war cry he learned from his hated enemies tearing his vocal cords. It soared into silence. He searched one way, then the other. No one was there. Not a knock, not a footfall, not a sound, not a creature. Hypp was gone. Regis was gone. The weapons were gone—he could see it by starlight now. He was alone.

Alone where? This is not the world. The logic and flow of life could evaporate into dream, and leave him washed upon another shore, or standing by an empty home, with no past and no future. He did not know how to fight for his life, and he did not know how to surrender to death. He remained motionless. Sea fog drifted high over the trees.

Suddenly, a red light appeared in the house. Kaja watched it wearily. It floated in the darkness, supported by a shadow. Kaja's breath came in long plumes that wicked red from the ember and curled it into the fog above.

He did not move, but he spoke low and quietly in his own language. "Who are you?"

The light swung and came forward. The form holding it took the shape of a robed spirit, and the light became a clay lamp, hanging from a braid.

The form stood upon the fallen door, and it slowly changed shape. A bulge flowed up its height. When the bulge reached the top, it billowed out and cascaded down. A man's head appeared, lit from below, his long white beard tucked into the cloak in the front, his wild eyebrows spun to points, like tusks. His eyes, grey almost to being white all across, were heavy and still.

"Kaja, it is I," Sekh said, in the local tongue, the only one he knew.

Kaja did not respond. *Has he been inside this whole time? If not, then how did he get there? How did he cause the sounds to come from all directions?*

Kaja had seen much Magic as a boy—true Magic, healing Magic that played upon the soul and guided the heart and mind. He had seen other Magic, too—evil Magic that tore and scattered the self like a dog scatters bones, here the heart, there the mind, off in the distance the spirit, with only fear and confusion left to guide the hands and words.

But never had he witnessed Magic like this. Magic that seemed to change the world, to call sound out of nothing, to place Sekh where he could not be, and to vanish Hypp into the void.

This cannot be the world. In his own language, Kaja asked, "Where is Nana?"

Sekh did not move. When he grinned, deep in his hood, his yellow teeth bled red light.

"Where is Nana?" Kaja repeated, so Sekh could understand.

"I do not know who that is, Kaja, nor where they are."

"Where is Hypp?"

"She and your friends are safe."

"What are you?"

"A wizard."

"You lie."

"I believe you shall see."

"Why do this?"

"You possess something I need."

"What?"

"Knowledge."

Kaja's heart raced. *I know exactly what this wicked wizard is after.* He had to say something. He wanted to be bold. Instead, he was cunning: "Why not ask?"

"Why would a wizard of your stature speak to one who had not shown himself?"

"I am not wizard."

"Call yourself what you will. Now you know that I am."

"As you wish."

Sekh didn't move, except for the pendulating lantern. Quietly, he asked, "You have spoken with Tiss, have you not?"

"No. Who is Tiss?"

"Kaja, come now. Let us not be petty. Tiss was my master, as you surely know."

"I do not know."

"Give me the secret."

"I do not know."

"He sent you with secret knowledge. Enough of this. Give it to me now."

Sekh's lamp rocked in its small arc. He had always known his master would communicate with him from beyond the grave. He had always known that, once Tiss was in the realm of the dead, he would finally realize what a worthy student he was. And he knew that Kaja was his emissary. He must be. Kaja carried the secret that would ignite his Magic and his rites with a power so forceful, they would all feel it. They would all fear it. They would all obey it. And he alone would have it. His bleeding teeth dripped.

Kaja smelled foul death slithering about them. *He wants to know how they did it. He wants to know how to put a demon in a man. He wants to know the one secret that I will never tell to a single soul.* "I have no secret."

"You lie."

"No, I never lie."

"That is a lie!" Sekh screamed.

The sound pierced Kaja like a hornet's sting. He could feel the depth of Sekh's anger, the depth of his desperation, and the depth of his desire. He spoke evenly, trying to calm the wizard with his voice, "High Hingemen, you mistake. I not wizard. I not know Tiss. I not have secret."

The odor became a thick, sticky rot on Kaja's tongue. Sekh did not move, but he appeared to become larger. "You wish to know my powers, Kaja, and so I will show them to you!"

"I man, only, child of Ma."

"Ma," Sekh sneered. "Ma is dead."

Then the tree told the truth! Ma is testing me...

"If you will not act honorably, Kaja, then you dishonor me. So, as you deserve. I shall test you."

"I cannot win test. I not wizard."

Sekh snorted a sinister sneer that froze Kaja's blood. "Then tell me why you came."

"I not come. Ma went me to here."

"Ma!" He spat on the door. "Tiss sent you. I know it. And now you know that I know."

"I not sent."

Sekh took a step forward, his gray gaze boring over his twisted mouth. "Shall I command you taken out to sea to be returned from whence you came?"

Through long practice, Kaja did not react to his threat. *And perhaps that is all there is to it...I refuse him, and he kills me, and then, maybe, Ma will take me back.* His expression did not change, and neither did the tone of his voice, as he said, "You do that what you will."

"Only a wizard has no fear of death." Sekh's head began to float upward. His cloak widened as he became taller, and yet the lantern hung to the same height above the ground. The wizard arced above him and said, "I will win your secrets, Kaja, whether you want to give them to me or not."

He swung the lamp and inked a red circle into Kaja's vision, vanishing through it.

Nana

When they returned at dawn, Regis and Hypp found him sitting on the door, perfectly still, hugging his knees and watching the trail.

"Ma's boy," Regis said, dropping a leather roll full of weapons to lay his hand on Kaja's back. "What happened?"

Hypp kneeled before him and took his face into her hands. "Kaja, did he hurt you?"

Kaja shook his head.

"He told us he just wanted to talk to you alone!" Regis said.

"Oh, Kaja, what have we done?"

"No, Hypp," Kaja said. "Sekh has done."

Regis helped him up and they went inside.

"He frightened you," Hypp said, tucking Kaja to recline in his favorite spot, with his head against the wall and his feet at the hearth.

"He say, 'Tiss send me to here.'"

"Tiss? He would say that." Hypp scowled as she revived the hearth.

"He should've told us!" Regis said. "Then we'd a known he was flapping over a fire." He positioned the door, propping it to repair later.

"That's why he didn't. He shows us no honor."

"Getting real tired of that."

Hypp pointed at Kaja with the tea paddle. "Did he say why Tiss sent you?"

"He say, 'Give me the secret.'"

"What secret?"

Kaja paused. *Ma, do I lie to her, too? But, of course, I should. The test is to be good, which means to tell no one. The secret must die with me and never live in this strange land.* "I do not know. He say, he test me until I tell."

"And you don't know what to tell him?" Regis said, "That's a nice bind."

"He lied to us, Regis."

"He thinks his Magic excuses him from everything."

"This cannot continue." Hypp snugged the wool felt blanket around Kaja's feet and gave him the first hot cup of broth. She trapped his hands around it. "Kaja, forgive me," she said.

"Me too," Regis said. "It won't happen again."

"Of that, you can be certain."

Kaja nodded, and the broth put him to sleep.

❧

On a cold morning not long after, Kaja and Dogen perched on the edge of Dogen's gazebo, watching the sea's breast rise and fall. The sky was an even cloud from horizon to horizon, lit grey-white by the morning sun. The land dropped gently, one side spilling into a forest following a stream, and the other, sloping into a pasture for deer and sheep. Beyond the pasture, the breeze petted the moor's thick fur, and white waves slowly drifted towards them.

Dogen had taken his friend away to give him time to recover his mind in quietude. A skin of fruited water sat on the floor near them, with a pouch of seeded honey balls next to it.

Whenever Kaja spoke, trying to deflect him, Dogen answered quietly and thoughtfully, using few words. Kaja ascended into silence. Dogen listened to his even breath, showing good habits of mindful practice. But even there, he grasped the world too fiercely, always ready to suspect.

Dogen tried to flow serenely. He sat still, watched the sea, and generated in his heart the calmest, steadiest energy he could project. Kaja had lost too much. He would regain but a fraction of what he once had. Dogen could sense what that might be like. He waited for an opening, knowing intuitively that only silence could break the writhing trauma that pinned Kaja in such a contorted bind.

When his gaze finally rested upon one spot, Dogen, too, held steady. When he lifted his head, Dogen waited a moment, and followed suit. "Be here, Kaja, be here and nowhere else," he whispered. "Be aware of Ma, and she will speak."

Kaja began to breathe more deeply, and more quickly. Dogen did not match this, but his awareness of his friend rose even higher. He stilled himself and waited. Kaja made a gesture with his hand and opened his mouth. No sound came out, but the action was the opening. He ran his hand through his locks and licked thick saliva from his teeth. He tried to speak again, again with no success.

Dogen glanced at him, and then away. Just enough to let him see that he wanted to know, and that he would listen. Kaja took another deep breath, and his posture switched from crouched to proud. A tear rolled down his cheek.

"Nana," he said, trembling, "Nana was my sister."

⟨∿⟩

"Look at this nutcase," Regis said, days later, gesturing at Dogen with one of his fat paws. Kaja filled with play and knew something was new. Dogen was sitting on the floor of his little house, cross-legged on his bearskin bedroll, still as a stone. They saw him through the open door as they walked up his path. He had already shaved his beard and his head, and his golden-brown eyes twinkled merrily at them. "Poor guy's trying to remember if he crapped this morning. Sits like that for hours. Yo! Dogen!" Regis pitched a mushroom cap at Dogen, who reached out and caught it without changing his posture. He made a slight motion of benediction, and then began to eat it.

"So you seem real busy today," Regis said, by way of greeting.

"And you are especially cordial," Dogen said.

"That was an exceptional mushroom, wasn't it?"

"With a delicious dirt crust."

"Aids in digestion. So what have you got planned, anyway? I got something on my mind."

"Congratulations! We should celebrate. Come now! Mead for everyone!"

"Get up, you weirdo."

"What do you want to do?"

"Thinkin' of—I'm with Kaja, Dogen. Have you met my friend Kaja? Standing right there. Can't miss him."

"My apologies, Kaja. So good to see you," Dogen said. Kaja grinned and nodded, enjoying his friends' teasing. "You were thinking! Go on, please, go on."

"You remember a certain meeting with Ogden. Lots of Ringfolk. While ago? I was thinking we ought to do a little traveling."

"I see," Dogen smiled and glanced at Kaja happily. Kaja knew what "traveling" was, and the thought of moving outside his boundaries enticed him.

"Makes sense, don't you think? Hear what the word is out and about. What people actually know and what they say they know. Could be a valuable use of our time. Gotta admit that. Sort of thing we ought to do."

"Have you discussed this with Kaja?"

"Well. No. No, not really."

"Anyone else?"

"Might'a mentioned it to Ma."

"Come on inside, both of you. Let me pack."

Kaja and Regis went inside, and sat on the floor, leaning against posts with their legs stretched out. Kaja admired the austerity of Dogen's place—he had exactly what he needed, and nothing more. Dogen lifted his fine wood-frame pack from a peg and began packing food and equipment for the cold.

"Kaja," he said, "we had a meeting the night before..." He stopped, and checked Regis, who swung away. "Well, it was the night before Sekh visited you."

"Yeah, I guess it was the day before Sekh scared the living light out of—I mean, yeah, the night before he 'visited' you," Regis said. "We had this very important meeting and came up to some very important responsibilities. Didn't we, Dogen?"

Dogen grinned knowingly at Kaja. Kaja smirked quizzically, sensing that Regis was becoming oddly anxious.

"Indeed we did," Dogen replied,"There's been some trouble up North with some of the grazing lands, Kaja. We're not sure what to do about it. The damage has been done for this year, but we have to come to agreement before next."

"Stupid Noks will set the pasture on fire again," spat Regis.

"The trouble's with the Nok, Kaja. The Nok are people who live inland from us. They stole some grazing—grazing that's been shared by our people for generations. We can't understand why they did such a thing. They weren't supposed to come through there until late in the Summer, but they came through early."

"So what we gotta do is find out what we can about the whole situation. Right, Dogen?"

"What else is there to know?"

"Well. Why they did it..."

"Ah, I see," Dogen said, smiling again at Kaja. "And the people of Windhollow will have this secret Knowledge?"

"Why not Windhollow? They're knowledgeable folk."

"Why not, indeed!" chimed Dogen, releasing his friend from his teasing gaze and smiling, yet again, at Kaja.

It occurred to Kaja that Regis wanted to go to Windhollow for some other reason, one that had nothing to do with the Nok, and everything to do with something that would make him anxious. He grinned merrily, and eyed Dogen. "Are the Windhollow folk can be beautiful?"

Dogen burst into hysterics, and Regis became bright red. Kaja had never seen a person change color like that before. He'd seen his own people blush, but Regis' spotted skin, above his orange beard, turned absolutely red. Which Kaja found funny. He laughed, truly laughed, for the first time among his new friends. The two Ringfolk exchanged a happy glance and laughed with the man from the sea.

Hypp insisted on preparing their packs, and the whole time she worked she scolded Regis and Dogen over and over to take care of Kaja: "Now you listen to me, Regis, and you, too, Dogen. Kaja hasn't done a trip like this since he came here, and you need to go slow especially at first so he doesn't hurt himself. Do you understand me? And come here, both of you. See this ointment? If his foot starts to hurt you rub this into his foot from the bottom to the ankle. Do you see? It's this one. And I've got one of my special soaked moss pads here, you use this wool strap to hold it onto the bottom of his foot, and as soon as he can walk comfortably you bring him back here right away. Do you hear me Regis? You come right back. And take it slow. Regis, I'm putting this all in your pack. Drink plenty of water, too—I've finally got him back up to where he belongs and I don't want you boys rushing over streams, do you hear me, Regis? Drink at every one and be sure the water is clean first. And if the sun comes out you stay in the shade, do you understand? I don't want him to get too hot. And for Ma's sake wear your gear at night. Put your scarves on first, do you hear me Regis? Keep his neck and chest warm at night," she carried on and on, and Kaja leaned against the doorjamb, listening. His heart swelled with her.

When she was done she came over and held his face in her hands. "Now you be careful, young man. You come right back here, to this house. And walk light on your feet."

"That'll be a challenge," Regis said, "his pack weighs as much as I do."

Hypp smiled at this, and so did Kaja, now mother and son. Hypp reached out for a hug, which Kaja gave her generously.

❧

They took a trail that did not lead into Squirrel Wood. Kaja had never walked along it before. He was strong now, and able to walk with his gaze held proudly. He liked the design of his pack, though it was different from what he had grown up knowing. Similar to the ones from his old world, this one was made of hides affixed to a wooden frame. But where his people were always searching for branches curved to fit their bodies, here they took larger branches and carved them into the correct shape. And where his people used leather thongs to attach the supports, so the pack would give and bend to their motions, these people carved perfectly fitting notches into the branches, and tied them with wet thongs, so they dried rigid. It took time to get used to the solidity of the pack, but Kaja noticed how it held its weight higher, making it easier to walk upright. Kaja's walking staff was Hypp's walking staff, beautifully carved and painted and affixed with a blossom of feathers at the top. It was a woman's staff, and Kaja could feel Hypp's hand on it. It felt as though she was holding his hand and guiding him along.

Dogen and Regis made themselves aware of Kaja's gait and strength for some distance, measuring his ability, and surmising he was good. Clearly, he was eager to go forth to Windhollow. Regis hoped that, along the way, they would learn some of Kaja's stories. Dogen knew one name already.

Kaja took in the scenery. The terrain flowed gently into the distance, with neither mountains nor flatlands. It was well saturated with rain and water, and he appreciated the fine seal-skin boots Trawill had made for him. Their soles wrapped around up the sides of his feet, affixed to the uppers with a multitude of tiny sinew stitches. When they became wet, the skin expanded and sealed even the stitching to moisture. Within was a thick matted pad of woolen felt that did not slip or ball up under his feet, which were kept warm and dry by a lining of rabbit hide, the fur facing inward, even on the bottom. They were the finest boots he had ever owned.

And they opened the land before him, for he could walk with confidence and not examine the trail for hazards. He kept his gaze upon the horizon, admiring the little forests in the clefts of the rolling hills, and the open marshes in the valleys, and the grazing lands smoothed over the exposed rounds of the hills, many of them peopled by small herds of roe deer. The grey sky was "high," as the locals said, meaning the cloud cover was high and didn't threaten rain. He had yet to see a perfectly clear day in this land, though he had seen patches of blue sky now and then.

The trail followed the driest land to the North, and along the way there seemed to be no other towns or settlements. The three men walked in silence for some time, which meant nothing to Dogen and Kaja but which made Regis a little nervous. Kaja experienced feelings of a new beginning, and that Hypp's motherly love was finally being augmented by a manly acceptance as well.

He realized, clearly, that his only hope was to become part of the community here—there was no other community to which he could belong, and so he had to find a place in this one, as though born into it. These thoughts occupied his mind as he walked, even though he also remembered walking with his Uncle Cinn and having the same sorts of thoughts—but then, he was a boy, wondering what kind of a man he would become. Now, he was a man, though no ceremony had initiated him.

And where in this society would he fit? In his old world, he was becoming quite good in his chosen trade, which was making musical instruments. But what of musical instruments here? He had seen some in Regis' home, and had heard many in the evening air. These people had complex flutes which he admired, and they had bells and rattles and drums. But he had not seen any stringed instruments, though perhaps he had heard some now and then.

His Uncle Cinn had been an instrument maker, and he had taught Kaja how to make a bellows for a lyre. He had only made a few instrument on his own, and always with Cinn's guidance. Kaja thought he could remember enough, and invent the rest, to build one here. That would be a fine gift, and perhaps that could be his trade as well. An enlightening way, too, to bring his old world into this one.

It was in the midst of these forward, positive thoughts that he saw another trail that led to an unusual ring of trees at the top of a hill. He gazed up at them curiously, because he had not seen anything like it in Squirrel Wood. Dogen watched Kaja examine the hilltop. He was impressed that Kaja would notice it was different. And he was impressed that Kaja's gaze seemed to soften some as it played over the Ring. It seemed familial, and less suspicious.

When Regis saw what Kaja was looking at, he began talking immediately. "Couldn't ask for a better day to walk to Windhollow, I tell you. Not too hot, not too cold, ain't raining, though it probably will on our way back. Wonder where the Yuffs are—should be able to see them out here with the herds somewheres, or no, actually, they won't be this close in till later this Moon I think. Gonna love Windhollow, Kaja, tell ya they got the sweetest water in the whole land. Wait till you see the creek there, we're gonna walk right down her, sacred place since the beginning of time, never touched a tree or a fern or even a mushroom in there. Like going back to the beginning of the world. So about this place you came from, you know you really haven't said much about it, I wonder if it looked like this or not?" Regis grinned nervously.

Kaja understood far more of the language than he could speak, but his skill with their words was increasing daily. He waited for his mind to put together his thoughts in their words, and then he spoke quietly. "No, Regis, the land not too much like this. No moors there. The ocean came to the sea where a swamp. The trees, some same, but stood open. The land steep, and the valleys big, big oaks. Beautiful, like this. No trees in rings on hilltops."

"Really? That's odd. Big oaks in the valleys, too—now in some places a little farther inland you'll see that, too, around here. And way inland it gets a bit steeper, but not much. Heard of mountainous regions across the waters, though, but never seen 'em. Other parts of the island have massive white cliffs dropping into the ocean, that's something to see."

"Island?" Kaja asked.

Regis checked Dogen briefly, but Dogen didn't respond. "Yeah, this is an island, Kaja. A big island, but an island—you know, with water all around it. You can follow trails for days and days across the land, but you'll always come to the ocean again. You can follow trails that go around the whole thing and walk in a giant loop without ever losing the smell of the sea. Not everywhere's like that, though. We know of places where the land goes on forever. But you have to cross the waters from here to get to them. Was your land an island, too?"

"No. My land went on forever, one way to go. Visit other worlds, even. We live not far from sea. Maybe your people have been to my land? You sail the waters?"

"Oh sure, some do. Mostly up and down the coasts, but some will go straight out and drop over the horizon. Nuts if you ask me. But then they come back, you know, with things to trade and stories to tell. Never done it myself. Usually you're born to it."

"Where are the ships? None are at your town?"

"Naw, it's no good for ships by our town. They find places where the water is deep right up to the edge of the land. Around here there's no place like that. Instead we have these shallow, rocky coasts. Tough to even fish over most of it, though some do. The rocks are full of food, Ma's gifts, never get tired of eating the mussels and crab and seaweeds from out there. Great stuff."

Kaja remembered his ordeal over the rocks. *If we had floundered where the water was deep by the coast, I would be dead.* "Great stuff, yes. Your foods delicious. Different to my foods. Very, very good."

"Why thank you, Kaja. I rather enjoy it myself," Regis patted his large belly and they chuckled at him.

The ring of trees inched out of sight as they walked down. Below was a wet valley floor, stuffed with reeds, alder and birch, and a dozen aurochs stood in it placidly, chewing their cud.

"Your homeland sounds beautiful, Kaja. Will you tell us more about it? And who showed it to you as a boy?" Dogen said.

He casually surveyed the horizon, so there wasn't too much energy in his question or his curiosity. Kaja began to nod, and inwardly he reached out to hold hands with his grief. *To belong here, I will have to tell them about where I once was.* Memories of his old world filled him with longing, and were hard to put into words, for they were so immediate, so huge, so complete. He remained silent for a long while, lonely while with them, finding a spot where he could begin.

"Yes, yes, very beautiful, Dogen," he began. "My mother's brother, Cinn, was my special to show me land. Wherever he went he came me, from when I walked. Fine, strong man, very kind gentle. From my village, small to your town, we go hunting or mining. Cinn was great miner. In stream he would find good metal where I saw rocks. Or in hillside, he see copper vein where I see grass. We collected much metal. In pit he make special with fire, the metal would collect and pure. Cinn make rings wire beads great skill. He loved metal. But swords and big axes, never. We do not know in my village. Tools only, and beautiful things to wear. Many days we walk together on lands, looking to metal talking. He hold my hand. Sometimes say nothing for whole day, but we still we talk. You see? Kind with me always," Kaja kept nodding his head, up and down.

"I wish I could meet him, Kaja," Dogen said gently.

"Yes. You would like; Cinn would like. But no. Once in dream he come to me. One more time together. Now, gone." His nodding became more pronounced before he began watching a falcon over the marsh at the end of the valley, waiting for a duck to take flight.

"So how was the hunting around your town, Kaja? Anything like what you've seen in Squirrel Wood?" Regis asked.

"Yes, like Squirrel Wood. The animals here see my prayer too. Very happy they to know my people. Here, over waters, same animals born everywhere. Good hunting my town, most year. Cinn and I go together, spear hunting. I young small to take big game, but Cinn show me. I take pig and rabbit myself. Cinn help me gut, I carry to village. Little boy, come to village with pig, Cinn with pig, too. Me little man. At the feast he would ask question, and I tell hunting story everyone eating my pig. See? Kind man. Care for me, always, my mind too."

"I've noticed that about you, Kaja," Dogen said, "You have a practice for your mind, don't you? Did Cinn teach you your practice?"

"Some, yes, Dogen," Kaja said. Dogen saw into him, though he was only a few years older. He wondered if Dogen could teach him to practice the proper way, willfully, in peace, and without fear. Even if it was different from his people's practice, he wanted to have a practice, so he could move back into his life. "Yes. He taught me practice, but I little. Not all practice, see? He taught me first in hunting. Clear mind, open all the world. There was more, there was practice alone, like you Dogen. I did not learn. Later, alone I used the hunting practice in many ways. Is what you see?"

"Oh, Ma, another nutcase," Regis said playfully, pushing Kaja and grinning. "So you're telling me you want to sit like a rock? Thought you had more sense than that. Better to eat, don't you think?"

"Good to eat, definitely," Kaja said, smiling.

"Glad you brought it up. Why don't we stop awhile and have some lunch? No sense in carrying all this food on our backs, hey?"

The feast Hypp had prepared was impressive. There was bread soaked with honey, plenty of jerky, a sturdy basket full of berries, a wide variety of boiled tubers and roots, and a skin of broth flavored with spearmint, so it tasted wonderful even though it was cold. They didn't even touch Dogen's food, and the three of them were so stuffed they decided to sleep for a while before continuing their walk.

Kaja awoke first. Through the trees he thought he saw a flash of light, and a shadow move. He sniffed the air, and smelled some living thing caught. His heart quickened, and his mind raced to calm it, repeating that there was no danger, telling himself that it would be alright.

I have nothing of my own. The clay amulet Nana made for me—didn't I have it in my shelter between the rocks and the tree? Or was it just a fevered dream? Is this a fevered dream?

Kaja held his knees and rocked side to side. Dogen found him that way and offered his hand to pull him back to the present.

Windhollow

They hefted their packs and continued to Windhollow. As they got closer, Regis got more and more nervous, which greatly amused Dogen.

"Well, you can never tell what they'll know about this Nok situation, you know, can never tell," Regis said.

"So true, Regis. We have no possible way of knowing what they know. Unless we think about it, of course."

"I'm serious, Dogen, really. Maybe a trader's come back in the last couple weeks or so and they have some crucial bit of information that we should know back at the Court or something."

What is the "Court?"

" Or some herders come through with more news of other trespass or something. No way to tell. Any one of the families here could know something. So, doesn't matter where we start really. Maybe we should have taken the other trail into town and started over there. More I think about it, that's what we should have done, definitely. Ma's tears. Over there's closer to the trade route, they'd be the ones to talk to. What do you say we just head over in that direction anyway to find out?"

"It's almost dusk, Regis. We'll go this way."

"Ma's claws! How are my teeth?" Regis spun around and pulled his lips back so hard his neck became a hide taught between two cords.

"Oh brother, Regis, that's lovely," Dogen said. "You look like you just stepped in a steaming pile."

Kaja laughed aloud at this, and his two friends were so surprised they blinked before laughing with him.

"Your teeth are fine, Regis," Dogen said as they settled down. "But don't exhale near their hearth—your wind will catch fire."

"Ma's guts!" Regis said, and he clamored at one of his pouches in a near panic, shoving so much spearmint into his mouth he couldn't close his lips while he chewed. Dogen handed Kaja a few leaves, too, and chewed some himself. They washed it down with water as the trail dropped gently into the ancient grove of which Regis had spoken.

It was incredibly lovely. Some of the laurels there were as far through as Kaja was tall, with branches outstretched as though offering their leaves to the sky on an open palm. The aroma was fabulous, as periwinkle grew up the trees like vines, and wild roses blanketed the stream's banks. There was nothing like this in

Squirrel Wood, and nothing like this in his own land. Kaja felt the tremendous ceaseless flow of life through the grove, sensing that the trees had been there for thousands of years, untouched and well loved by all. The deep green moss on the rocks, fed by fog and the spray of little waterfalls, was dotted with tiny white and purple flowers. Multitudes of birds fluttered about, singing and calling to each other as the light began to fade, checking with their friends before snuggling into their evening rest.

"Dear Ma," Kaja said. "Blessed be." The force of the grove's beauty drew him out of himself and relaxed him. Regis, on the other hand, fussed about his equipment, arranging and smoothing things and wiping his face and neck with a moss felt. A picturesque wooden bridge crossed over the creek, and the trail dropped through the forest further, before turning to the North, circling around. Kaja could see that Windhollow would have a perfect southern exposure. The trees thinned some, and off in the distance Kaja saw a house, and a beautiful garden. In the garden a man and a woman worked peacefully. When the woman saw them, she ran off suddenly, and the man gently rose to come greet them.

"She's not there," Regis said.

"I thought I saw her," Dogen said.

"She'd be in the garden with Martin. She's not there," Regis couldn't decide if he was relieved or disappointed.

"I thought I saw a woman too," Kaja said.

"She's not there. Oh well. Too good to be true anyhow. What was I thinking? Why would a girl like her want a fat old

Ringfolk like me." Kaja crooked his head—another strange word, "Ringfolk," he had not heard before.

"Well, we can't just turn around. Let's go on and tend to our 'official' business. Martin could always use company now, you know."

"Martin is Morgaine's dad," Regis said for Kaja's benefit. "Morgaine's the girl who lives in that house. She died three years ago. I mean her mother died, in childbirth. She and her son went together. Very sad. Martin's never been the same, never will be the same. So everyone always visits him." He fidgeted with his staff. He had decided he was disappointed.

"And Morgaine?" Kaja asked.

"Morgaine? Well. She's different. You'll see. Someday, anyhow. But not today. She's probably off being courted by someone else. Someone from Windhollow most likely. She deserves the best, you know. A steady fellow, not a wanderer."

"Get off your own back, my friend. You know she likes you. You've been courting her so long, and she's always receptive. Besides, I'm pretty sure I saw her, right Kaja?"

"I think I saw woman, yes."

Martin came out onto the trail ahead of them. His mouth dropped open and his hoe clattered to the ground at the sight of Kaja, but then he regained his sense of propriety and waved, smiling, as he recovered his tool. All three of them waved back.

"Hey, Kaja, one thing we should tell you," Dogen said cryptically, "You have to let Regis and I decide who gets to see you." Then he greeted the man, "Martin! How are you, old friend?"

"Well, well, Dogen. This is a pleasant surprise, very good to see you."

"Hello Martin, sir. How are you?" Regis' hands started working around his staff in a jerky way.

"Fine Regis, very well. Good to see you, too. And so soon! Yes. Well. And this would be..."

"Kaja, sir," Dogen said, "Kaja of the Rishi. He comes from across the sea and is a guest of Sekh's at the Court."

"A guest of Sekh did you say? Well Kaja, it is an honor to meet you. Indeed. Yes," Martin examined Kaja with a multitude of short glances to various parts of him, for it was impolite among these folk to stare at someone. Kaja's heart raced, for Martin was the first person from outside his village he had met, and because he had been introduced as a "guest of Sekh's." He didn't like being appraised like a strange piece of foreign merchandise, under the protection of an even stranger wizard, but what could he really expect? He could tell Martin was ready to accept him, if not exactly as a man, then at least as a welcome creature from another world. It would have to do.

"Thank you, sir. Pleasure meet you fine Windhollow." Suddenly it occurred to Kaja that imitation of all his host's ways might not serve him best. So he pressed his palms together before his heart, and bowed to Martin in the same way he bowed to the children who brought him gifts when he was first recovering. It was the way he had been taught to acknowledge the fantastic occurrence that you and this other soul in the whirlwind of the universe had met—or, even more fantastically, had met again.

Dogen watched his friend closely, pleased with this action. He nodded and tried to put a sage expression on his face, should Kaja turn to him—which he did, as he rose from his bow.

"Ah. Yes. First time here no doubt, Kaja of the Rishi. Welcome to Windhollow. Indeed. Well. I'd take you to the Oak but it's getting late. Perhaps tomorrow. Now please come, come, I made far too much berry juice this afternoon. If we don't drink it, it will spoil," Martin said.

They followed him up the hillside to his house. Kaja was behind Regis, whose hands were still working around his staff, and whose mouth was now working around words that weren't there. Martin had built a beautiful wooden porch between his house and a giant beech tree. Hanging from the beech's first branch was a swing big enough for two or three people to sit upon. Kaja admired the fact that the entire estate—house, porch, garden, all of it, had been built around the spot the beech naturally placed this swing.

He was even more impressed when they got to the deck and he discovered that its southern view was a stunning panorama of the entire Windhollow valley. Its floor drained east to west, and its perimeter grew so profusely with flowers and herbs it seemed likely that these were tended, as clearly was the rest of the valley. The eastern side was heavily seeded with grain, and alternate rows were neatly mowed or left to fallow. The western side was marshy, and here they mowed reeds in the same way. He saw a hunting blind farther down, too, for goose and duck. Through the trees on the hillside he could see more houses, and trails of smoke rose from many evening hearths. Picturesque beyond description, Kaja watched it as though gazing into the face of a person. He could feel the peaceful serenity of the folk, and their complete confidence that nothing would approach over the hillsides, and that no menace lurked beyond the horizon.

Dogen noticed that Martin brought five cups to the little table. He cocked his brow at Regis, assuming his friend had taken in this welcome clue. But Regis was staring at the swing as though moved to some sort of aesthetic rapture. Dogen whacked him on the arm, but this only partially snapped him out of it.

"Dogen, sit, sit. Kaja of the Rishi, please come sit by me. Regis—there you go." Martin put Dogen and Kaja on chairs, and Regis on the swing, all arranged so they could see the view easily, and then he began filling the cups and passing them out. "So, Kaja," Martin said, still casting examining glances every couple of seconds, "What is this Rishi of yours?"

"My people and my river, sir. No longer mine, sad say. I lived in small town on river."

"You don't say? Good fishing?"

"Yes. Very good. Near my house salmon trout great many. And in beach cod as large as Regis." For some reason Dogen found this hilarious and laughed so hard he spilled his drink.

Martin grinned widely, too, as he refilled it. Regis searched their faces, having missed the joke completely.

"Cod! Now there's a good eating fish," Martin said.

"Salmon too. Remember once as a boy went on one Spirit Walk where we caught salmon with our bare hands. Not too hard to do when the stream's choked with them. But we'd bash their brains out on a rock and eat 'em raw right then and there. Best fish I ever had. Hey, Regis?"

"Yes, sir. Bash their brains out."

"Hum. Well. Indeed. So. What brings you here, Kaja?"

Dogen answered quickly, "We are interested in any news you have about the Nok—" when Kaja saw the woman come from behind the house.

She was captivatingly beautiful. Her skin was white, as were all the people—though this still seemed incredible to Kaja—but her's was white like the crest of an ocean wave. Her thick hair, almost golden in color, hung down past her waist, and was braided with tiny white flowers in it. Around her head she wore a narrow purple sash which made her bright blue eyes shine brilliantly. Her rosy cheeks flushed red when she saw Kaja, and her silky gait, beneath her comfortably flowing hemp gown with a fox fur collar, bobbled a moment at the sight of him. Kaja stood.

"Morgaine, my dear!" Martin said, "There you are."

Regis stared at her, enthralled. Kaja didn't know too much about these people's mating rites, except that they seemed to choose one partner for life, like birds of prey. It was clear who

Regis wished to choose. But he couldn't tell right off what Morgaine was up to.

"Come, come," Martin said. "You know Regis and Dogen. This fine man is a guest of Sekh's at Court. Kaja of the Rishi, I present my daughter, Morgaine."

"Morgaine I honor to meet you," Kaja said, bowing to her in his own way.

"Kaja of the Rishi, the honor is mine. Welcome to our humble home."

"I admire it is built surrounding swing."

"Oh! Yes! You noticed that! Indeed. Very good," Martin said, smiling widely and nodding. "My wife's idea, rest her soul. Very good. Hung the swing first, then built the porch, and then the house and garden. Very good, Kaja. Thank you."

"There is nothing so sweet as to sit here on a warm evening and watch the colors change as the sun sets," Morgaine said. "Please, sit, sit, Dogen, it is so good to see you again."

"And you, too, Morgaine. How is Charlene?"

"Oh very well, very well," Morgaine smiled and blushed a little again. Then she said, "Regis."

"You look very beautiful Morgaine," Regis said, standing like a poorly carved piece of wood, tilting a little. She sat on the swing next to him.

Later that evening, after they had eaten, and around the time they switched from drinking juice to drinking warm fermented honey, Martin and Kaja built a fire in the porch's fireplace, and placed the clay pitcher of mead near it, so their drinks would be as warm as their company. Dogen had clearly led them away from asking too many questions about Kaja's childhood or homeland and had steadfastly interrupted any mention of how he came to be among them in the first place.

Still, a closeness arose among them that Kaja had not felt before. It included Regis, who never really relaxed completely, even though Morgaine stayed near him the whole evening. It was adult camaraderie, for camaraderie's sake, and nothing like it had been part of his life. Somehow here, away from Ash, where everyone had seen him so near death, he could hold himself. He could be a little freer, a little prouder, and he could be the freak who was also a man. Martin made a point of making Kaja feel comfortable. He asked him to help him with the fire and he engaged him in a long conversation about what he remembered of squash farming from his home village.

The fire and the drink brought them further into intimacy, and after a long silence that was full of sweet anticipation that friendship would last and suppress the isolation that encases us all, Kaja spoke first. "Morgaine, your mother. How she was?"

Morgaine gazed at him—not his face, not his hair, but his eyes. She could see why he asked. She could feel that they shared a kinship. "She was wonderful, Kaja. Kind and good. And happy—that is what I remember most about her. She knew how to be happy. What is that, I wonder sometimes, how did she do it? But she was happy. She loved to garden and to take me for walks. She collected feathers. She sang all the time. We sang together all the time."

"Every day," Martin said. "The most beautiful sound I'll ever hear, wife and daughter singing together. Hmmm. Yes. Well. Yes," he nodded, and the now familiar emotion rose up in him. His heart felt like a chalice that held a delicious elixir he would never taste again.

"She loved us with all her heart, too," Morgaine said. "It was the way she was. When my little brother turned to go back, she didn't hesitate to take his hand and go with him, so he wouldn't be afraid. He needed her more than we did, and so she went with him. I can see it, you know, I can feel it. She just took his hand, and they walked back together."

"They walked."

"Yes. You will walk, too." She took his hand, and he wrapped his around hers.

The Hall

The next morning, Kaja was stretching on the porch while Dogen meditated on the swing. They heard men approaching quickly down the trail and stirred to the sound.

"Go inside," Dogen said. Kaja slipped through the door and watched through the window while the others crowded around him.

Two Hingemen strode into view, carrying bedrolls and spears. They wore heavy gray cloaks with long hoods that hid their faces, and their boots were dyed green. They spied Dogen and headed for him. The taller, thinner of the two called, "Where is he?"

"Who sent you?"

"You know who I am and you know who I represent. You answer me. Where is he?" The Hingemen strode up Martin's path to where Dogen stood.

"Sekh commanded us to bring him around. He needed to retreat from Ash to do that. We are here at Sekh's behest."

"Ma's tits," the shorter, heavier one sputtered. He threw back his hood, and sneered through thick, hanging jowls with his wild eyebrows bushy from sleep and his dark blue eyes spitting. He moved his hand around his spear.

"We'll have none of that, Dogen," said the tall one, staying within his hood. "He was not to go beyond Squirrel Wood."

"He was not to go beyond alone. He did not. He is with Ringfolk."

"So I see. But now, he's coming with us."

"Show me Ogden's insignia."

"The freak belongs to Sekh. We will take him if we have to."

Regis swiftly moved from the house to between Dogen and the Hingemen. "Phiop, Krev, come on now. You look like you got two hours of sleep on cold rocks. Why not have some breakfast, and then we'll all go back together?"

Kaja couldn't help but hear that Regis did not mean this as an invitation, but as a command. At some point, he had donned his stout flint sword, and it hung nonchalantly in his easy reach.

The tall one glanced at it briefly. "We will stay on the porch, and we will leave as soon as we are done. Sekh has commanded the freak's presence in the Hall tonight, to begin his duty."

"Alright, we can do that," Regis said. "You sit there, Phiop, and Krev, right here." They sat where he indicated, and Regis sat in Martin's accustomed spot, placing himself between the Hingemen and the door.

Morgaine and Martin were already busy preparing something to eat. Kaja tried to help.

"Father," Morgaine whispered, "I must go with them."

"No."

"I must. My presence will calm them, and I cannot leave Kaja alone."

Kaja paused to wonder at her, and he never thought of her the same again. "Thank you, Morgaine." He began packing his pack and Dogen's, which was the right place to put his energies.

Martin didn't say anything, and only glanced as Morgaine began preparing a pack for herself. "I'll be fine, father, and I'll return as soon as I can."

They brought bowls of steaming porridge, platters of lettuces and fruit, and cups of hot broth to the porch, and sat to eat glumly. Kaja had never felt more conspicuous, or less like a person. *This is it. They have this part of the secret. But they do not seem to understand it. Not fully. Not yet.*

The Hingemen consumed all that was served to them but said not a word. As soon as they were nearly done, the tall one said, "We have a long time to travel. You go first and keep a steady pace." He made motions to put his bowl and cup down and to rise. The others quickly finished, and silently donned their packs. Martin and Morgaine hugged for a long while, and then he bid farewell to them all.

The walk back to Ash was quiet, as none present could speak their minds without being heard by others they did not trust. This fact became the essence between them. Kaja sensed it was new to them, and that whatever Hingemen and Ringfolk balance had existed was now spilled.

Kaja's heart hammered as he walked with his friends to the Hall in Ash that night. Hypp was already inside, with her Coven.

The Hall was a magical space, used for ceremonies. Kaja had watched the Coven retire to it now and then, in sync with their moon. And he had seen the men retire to it now and then as well, often wearing strange regalia, and always in all seriousness. And once, when a trading party had come through from the far north, wearing outlandish headgear with long feathers standing up and trailing braids of cloth and leather and fur, they were taken into the Hall with the men, and they lived there for the few days that they stayed. Kaja had been hidden from them, and he saw them only from a distance. They were the first foreigners he had seen, besides himself, and he wished he could ask them about the lands through which they journeyed. But he was not allowed, and despite the kindness his hosts had shown him, he was twisted by the fact they wouldn't let him ask the travelers about his people.

The air was charged, waiting for the moment to storm forth and ravish the ground. Many townspeople, including some of the older children, walked to the low door at one end of the long building that was covered with earth. From the chimney heavy smoke arose, wandering off in lurking gusts.

At last, Kaja would see inside. He was attending at Sekh's request, and Dogen and Regis clearly knew something of the proceeding that was about to take place. They stayed close to Kaja so he would not feel alone. Or, at least, so he would feel less alone. Morgaine, too, stayed close to him, all but holding his hand as they came to the door.

They had to crawl through. Kaja took a moment to adapt to the light, and he scanned in stark amazement. His friends guided him forward to his seat, as the townsfolk arranged themselves in audiences along the long walls. A fire raged in the center of the room, tended by two naked children, painted red from head to toe.

Dogen and Regis sat on either side of Kaja, and Morgaine sat behind, with Martin next to her. Hypp, Jinn and Trawill wore bright yellow scarves about their heads and bowed to Kaja when he found them. He worked furiously just to take in the room itself. He tried to keep his gaze from sweeping back and forth, tried to focus it on details here and there. The first things that captured his attention were the pillars. Centered between the long walls and on either side of the fire, they were massive beams, trunks really, holding up the ceiling of cross beams like branching trees. They were carved more elaborately than anything Kaja had ever seen before. Depressions in the pillars were sconces, inlaid with gold or tin or copper, and the bowl at the bottom held oil and a small flame glowing from a wick, with the light reflecting off the metal behind and under it. Each pillar had a dozen of these, rising up from the floor in a spiral trail leading around the pillar to the ceiling.

The light they threw, combined with the flickering fire, made the pillars seem alive. Chasing the spiral of lamps was a great profusion of animals—fantastically carved, in relief, and vibrantly painted. They were running and fornicating and climbing and flying and swimming. Each animal flowed into the next. The otter swimming in a whirlpool, smiling with a fish in its mouth, was actually swimming in the curl of a squirrel's tail, who was happily wrestling with its partner, making more squirrels, on a tree branch that was actually the hind leg of a roe deer, who was running up the pillar, but whose brow and eye was actually a robin taking flight into a sky of billowing clouds, which were actually ocean waves in which a dolphin was leaping, whose swishing tail was actually the wings of a dragonfly, who was alighting on a wild rose. The carvings' variety seemed infinite. In every elaborately painted curl and meandering spiral another animal arose, as though materializing from the wind.

Kaja determined that the animals' eyes were inlaid with colored stones or jewels or balls of metal, which is why they had the appearance of life. Their expressions flickered with the flames, ready for the next moment of play. Kaja admired how the beams of the ceiling resembled the branches of a tree, as seen from below, so the pillars were the trunks, and somehow, deep in the distance beyond the branches, stars flickered.

The long walls were hung with thick furs, stitched together to hold in the warmth and to absorb sound and light. The townspeople's faces, some of which were painted, some of which were shaved, some of which were young and some of which were wrinkled, hovered before a dark and soundless void.

When everyone was quiet, save a few whispered words here and there—words which Kaja now largely knew—a single rattle began a rhythmic pulse from the back of the Hall. The musicians were robed in white, their faces painted blue, their hair combed back and matted to their skulls with a red paste. The red children tending the fire, one a boy and the other a girl, stood and held hands, facing each other and rocking their arms to and fro with the rattle. Other rattles joined in, played by the blue-faced musicians in their fantastic garb, adding tempos around the base beat.

Kaja noticed that behind them was another door, very low and small, hung with a sparkling material and leading into a perfectly dark chamber beyond. The audience opposite Kaja's side of the room began to rock back and forth to the rhythm, and then Kaja's side did the same, in the opposite direction. Dogen and Regis gently nudged Kaja's body into synch, and then the flutes began to play. At first there were long, low notes, soothing and gentle, changing little, and extending over long stretches of the meter. Other flutes then joined, like birdsong, quick and high and happily playing around the original rattle, which continued pulsing evenly and steadily.

Kaja tried to study the nature of the ritual. He had witnessed many in his lifetime. Some he wished he had never seen. Those were the ones that still troubled his dreams, the ones that made him question the possibility his hosts could be as they appeared to be. Those were the rituals that tore him from his soul.

He tried to settle into it, as he would have when he was a child, eager to place himself in the path of the rites, eager to feel their energy flow through him, eager to be changed and to be included. He rocked with his friends but could not help twitching his sight from spot to spot, seeking the unexpected, ready for the facade of peaceful contemplation to switch and sting him, like a handful of sand thrown into his eyes.

Dogen felt all this passing through Kaja. He could sense that his friend was making a sincere effort, but that he would not be able to relax into the flow of the rite. Not this first time.

When the singer called out, "Sisters and brothers are you there?" and the whole gathering sang back, "We are here, we are here, will you sing to us now?" Dogen placed his hand on Kaja's knee, as if to say, "You and I will just rock and listen tonight."

Kaja nodded, and Dogen could sense how much his friend trusted him now. And he could sense that Kaja and he were fellow travelers, driven to understand the mystical, and that Kaja wanted him to guide him through the strange and unique paths Dogen's people took to those realms. Dogen wanted to guide him, but more so, he wanted to be guided. No one had come forth to do this for him. Kaja grasped Dogen's hand for a moment, as though he understood his thoughts.

The singers sang a line, and then the people sang it back:

We shall sing of Summer, sing of Ma.
We shall sing of Winter, sing of Ma.
We shall sing of new Spring, sing of Ma.
We shall sing of old Fall, sing of Ma.
We shall sing of Newborn, sing of Ma.
We shall sing of Crone, sing of Ma.
We shall sing of Morning Star, sing of Ma.
We shall sing of Evening Star, sing of Ma.
Sing the animals...
Sing the trees...
Sing birds to the air...
Sing fish to the sea...
Sing Hingemen to the Hinge...
Sing child to her mother.
Ma and her children.
We are Ma, we are Ma.
We are children, we are children.

They hung on the last note, and the nasal consonant created an eerie insect presence that whirled around the Hall and settled slowly into the ground.

Kaja saw deep into the soul of Ash, more than they saw themselves: *Sekh spits at Ma, but the people sing of Her. They do not know. They do not know that he has changed, and they do not know what he has become. But, I know. They cannot imagine what he would do. But, I can. Ma's test for me is more difficult. To be good, I must stop him.*

The musicians allowed an instant of silence before one began to knock on a hollow branch with a hard stick.

Sekh pushed aside the iridescent covering of the small door behind the musicians and emerged from the dark chamber. He was followed by Ogden. Like the musicians, their hair was matted to their head with red paste. Their robes were pure black, though, and copious folds concealed their limbs and shape. They sat next to each other at the head of the room. A young woman, similarly attired, came out and sat behind Ogden. Everyone was silent. The knocking instrument made the only sound.

Then Ogden lifted his head and said, in his rumbling voice that wetted the "s" and drew you into confidence, "Greetings friends."

"Greetings, Ogden," the whole group replied. The knocking stopped. Everyone waited for Ogden to continue, and he let them hang on his words. He smoothed out his robe and grinned at the pillar closest to him for a while, and gave a special wink to the red children sitting by the fire. Sekh sat motionless next to Ogden, staring at the floor in front of him.

The ceremony had not snapped and become the other kind Kaja had seen. It was still serene, still true. Kaja's gaze twitched less. He watched Sekh, because if something would change, it would change through him.

"Well, my friends," Ogden said, "strange things have been happening lately, as many of you have heard. I apologize for allowing the rumors to grow, and for waiting so long before calling you together to discuss them. As always, I have followed the guidance of my brother Sekh, our beloved Hingemen. But now the waiting has come to an end.

"First, let me tell you about the Nok and the troubles in our pasturelands to the north. You know that the Nok moved through the Yuffs' grazing lands in advance of their turn, causing the Yuffs to exhaust their flocks by moving them too far, too fast, and this has cost them meat and fleece. You may not know that, recently, the troubles have deepened.

"The Yuffs, a fine tribe that has been part of our community for generations out of mind, a noble and proud family who are always just in their ways and their trade, were grazing their herds in strange pastureland a bit beyond our bounds. They had no reason to believe they were trespassing, and in fact we do not believe that they were. We believe the pasture was beyond our lands and beyond the lands of the Nok's as well.

"Well, as you know, a proper herdsman is equipped to hunt and to defend his flocks from the wolves. But a proper herdsman, in a just society where their lands and turns are clearly defined, do not carry weapons of war. Nor are they accompanied by Talon, even if, when the time does come to pass, they become Talon for the realm. It was in this innocent and proper state they encamped in this strange land and tended to their trade.

"But then, a party of Nok warriors came to them, fully armed and thick with days of drinking, their eyes red with the will to fight. They threatened the Yuffs and were rough with them, but the Yuffs were unprepared to meet such a show of arms and were forced to submit to the Nok's demands. The Nok took a portion of the Yuffs' herd, and claimed the pasture for themselves, not for that month, but for all months for all time.

"The Yuffs protested that they were on unclaimed land, and that the only reason they were there was because of the Nok's trespass in the first place. The warriors were angered by this and brandished their weapons as though to attack. And blood would have been spilt, if not for the intelligence and bravery of Kwill, the priestess and astronomer of the Yuffs' family. She was able to get the Nok to be satisfied with the flocks they were stealing, and to leave the Yuffs to themselves with time enough to move their herds into pasture lands that are clearly our own.

"So though the number of the Yuffs did not decrease, the number of their herds did, and that has angered the Yuffs deeply and justifiably. They appealed to the Court for help, and we are beholden to provide it. They moved their herds back to closer pasture, and slaughtered a greater portion, in order to end up with the nearly same amount of winter stores of meat, wool and hides. They will be alright this winter, but they may not recover properly next summer, even if we are able to sort out this problem and again agree with the Nok on grazing rights.

"And so, those rumors that have been passed among you are true. The northern reaches of our community are not at peace. And, if we do not act, we risk losing our lands, and our herds, and the wool we need to live in comfort and prosperity.

"However, we have not decided what to do. No one is to act alone, no matter how strong your kinship may be with the Yuffs, for I know in this room and in this town there are relatives and tradespeople who love the Yuffs dearly, and who will feel this transgression against them more strongly than they would feel a transgression against themselves. Soon, we will share with you the plan we have devised."

Ogden paused dramatically, and Kaja discovered deep anger in the hearts of many present. Thievery of any kind rises blood rage. But thievery like this—thievery by a band of so-called warriors as opposed to disfigured misfits—well, that was far worse. Kaja could feel the lust for revenge, and he could tell by the way Ogden told the story, and by the admonishment with which he ended it, that he fully intended to use those feelings towards his own ends. It was a device of leadership Kaja had witnessed before. A device of leadership he did not trust.

A few grumbles were heard, but Ogden silenced them with his steely gaze. He was an old man, but beneath his black robe were the shoulders of a fighter who had once been more powerful than any other. Ogden had drawn that strength and power into his presence, and he could subdue a man with a glare more easily than most others could with clubs and rope. Ogden took a slow sip from his cup and continued.

"The trouble with the Nok is not the only strange thing that has happened this year, my friends." He cast a glance to Kaja, and it seemed that everyone else did, too. "But this other realm is beyond me and my understanding. For that reason, our beloved wizard, the High Hingemen Sekh, will speak upon this strangeness."

Kneel

K aja did not appreciate the juxtaposition of himself with the trouble with the Nok. Many of the gazes that fell upon him were hostile, as though feelings towards the Nok carried over to him as well. Some seemed to wonder if, in a magical way, he had brought a curse of sorts on the people and perhaps he was somehow responsible for the Yuffs' misfortune. Kaja's breathing quickened and his face sweat. Dogen and Regis could feel it, but Morgaine was the one who reached out and gently placed her hand on his back.

He openly stared at Sekh as he slowly took a pipe and a small vase from within his cape. He uncorked the vase and tapped some of its contents into the bowl. One of the red children ran over, carrying an ember in a thick piece of leather, and held it while Sekh drew in smoke. He nodded to the child, who ran back to his spot by the fire. Sekh smoked for a while and the dusty aroma of it filled the room. The silence extended to the point that

Kaja began to wonder if he was going to speak. All attention was focused upon the old Hingemen, save a few glances in Kaja's direction.

"My friends," Sekh said at last, his voice higher and thinner than Ogden's, but still carrying the weight of dominance, "I must reveal to you things that my master Tiss, rest his soul, would never have revealed. I have not come to this conclusion lightly, for the mysteries of my art work best when they remain mysteries. The simplicity of soothsaying deceives many who attempt to learn it, for the method itself is but a small part of the art. However, I must trust you with this one secret. I can see no other way. My apprentice Bwain, who would usually sit by my side tonight, I have left behind, for I could not bear to have him watch, and because he must do for me the work he tends as I speak. Yet you will go forth from this room with Knowledge that properly belongs to him alone. I have begged his forgiveness, and he has granted it. But now I must beg for your forgiveness as well and know that you have granted it." He fell silent at this point, smoking placidly while contemplating the floor.

No one moved, not a sound was heard. It was some time before the young woman behind Ogden gave him a sharp nudge.

Ogden understood immediately, and his face rounded.

"Dear brother," he began, gesturing outwardly with his hand, "High Hingemen Sekh. You have shown your love for us more times that I or anyone present can count. You toil daily at your Magic and have predicted with great accuracy drought and flood and heavy snow.

"And what have you asked of us in return? Nothing. We will always hold you in the highest honor, even if you err and err again. We forgive you. All present, if you forgive Sekh and honor his ways, say 'Aye.'"

Instantly a loud "Aye" went up from the gathering—too loud, and too suddenly. It had a ring to it that Kaja recognized from the evil rituals he had seen. Devoid of thought, devoid of understanding. It hung in the air like the clap of an ax.

Sekh nodded his head, and drew again from his pipe, "I thank you, dear Ogden, for your kind words. And so I tell you this story.

"There are many ways to read the stars' intent, my brethren. Some are simple. We call the simplest ones 'knowing Ma,' and many possess that basic Knowledge. The gardener watches the insects and birds and knows of Ma's intent. The hunter watches the horizon and the migrations, and knows Ma's intent, as well.

"But there are higher arts. More powerful arts. Bwain and I, we watch the motions of the stars and the planets. We know their wanderings, and their moods, and we know their intent.

"Then there are arts that are higher still. Arts that are true Magic. True Magic must be tended to for centuries before it works and must be passed down through life-long training, until you can witness it in dream, or in solitude, or through the use of sacred substances. Tiss passed them to me, and I shall pass them Bwain, who will surely, someday, surpass my skill and understanding."

Kaja felt Dogen shift.

"And one of them, my friends, one of the very highest arts, I must reveal to you, so you can understand." He pulled a small pouch from his robe, hanging from a thin strap. "This pouch has been with us longer than any living person can tell. Tiss received it from Upu, who received it from Grif, who received it from Mijj, and so on back to the very first wizards who walked this land. But the pouch is mere tradition, with little power of its own. The Magic I have here, next to my heart at all times, is inside the pouch.

"What is it? Power from the stars. Magic that makes power, Magic that would let us have sway over the Nok, over anyone. You know the usual tools of power. The blade. The ax. The sling.

"The secret in this pouch brings us a much greater power than that. Tonight, the power in this pouch has brought us to the brink of a new Magic. Nearly, though not fully, to a new way of existing in this world. It is up to me to make it real."

He shifted forward dramatically, as tough lifted by the eerie cadence of his discourse. The red children jumped visibly as some of the audience startled and some gasped. He held out the pouch and hung it in front of them, and moved it in circles, dangling from its thong, to expose it to every part of the room.

Sekh waited for everyone to become transfixed upon it. Afraid of it. Kaja watched him do it.

"Just seeds, my friends," Sekh said quietly.

Seeds had never seemed so terrifying before. They were seeds that could sprout into monsters. Seeds that could give birth to warriors, and to weapons, and to war cries, and to screams.

"Just seeds. Mustard. The land is blonde with it in the spring. It grows from rock and dirt and duff. For generations, that is all this pouch has held. A sacred number are planted on a sacred day, a sacred number are collected on another sacred day. For centuries.

"These seeds can speak. When they bloom, they speak. Only I know their language. I can hear, and so I listen. They come to me in my dreams, and in my thoughts. But, when they feel things deeply, they may choose other ways to speak.

Sekh stopped. The room was so still, Kaja heard his teeth click the stem of his pipe as he drew in more smoke. He heard his lips part when he began again.

"It was seventeen years ago when my teacher, Tiss, left us to return to Ma. Those of you who remember know the sadness we felt at our loss, for Tiss loved us, and he guided us through many, many fine years of happiness and plenty. None, perhaps, knew the magnitude of our loss as keenly as did I. I remember going alone that year to plant the seeds. I wept bitterly upon their ground, so they would know how I felt. How sad I was that the stars had done their work and taken him.

"There were fewer flowers in the spring, and I knew the seeds felt our loss, too. I collected their children, carried them with me, followed the rites. The next year, again, there were fewer flowers. I knew the seeds still mourned, and the year after that, my friends, fewer still did bloom. My troubled thoughts turned to them often, as I practiced as Tiss had taught me. I worried for them. I worried they were passing from us, as had Tiss. I worried we had lost another old friend. Each and every year, their numbers diminished. Eight, nine, ten. Fewer still. Eleven, twelve. So few I needed to collect nearly every seed they gave, just to have the sacred number in my pouch.

"But then, my friends. Then. On the thirteenth year they began to speak in a language clearer than I had ever known before. More clearly than any magical language I know. Upon their petals were lines. Black lines, thin and chaotic, down near the base of their petals, near the center. I dreamed upon it.

"The fourteenth year, the lines spread further up the petals, and began to take on some sort of form. Was it a spider infecting my sacred garden? I searched the plants every day, removing any spiders. That winter I cleared away the snow from the spot and dug into the frozen ground to search for the cause of this strange happening. I could find none. It was Magic. It was the flowers' Magic, the Magic we have all asked of them from time out of mind.

"The fifteenth year, the lines covered still more of the flowers, now clearly tracing forms and shapes. I searched the prairies and fields for others similarly marked. I traveled far afield, so disturbed I was by this odd message. The sixteenth year the lines nearly reached the edge of the flowers' faces. I was driven mad by my inability to understand their words. They fairly shouted at me, and still I could not hear. I practiced desperate rites. I ripped one from the ground and carried it with me, roaming across the moors and far cliffs. I held it to my ear, I talked to it, I begged of it. And there it sat, clutched in my hand, speaking as clearly as it could. But I did not hear.

"The seventeenth year, my friends. This year. The flowers bloomed again. And upon their faces, to the edges of their petals, were lines, lines in spirals and in waves, in curls and in swirls. Lines, my friends.

"Lines like his." With this he pointed straight at Kaja. All eyes fell on him, gasping in fear.

For tattooed across Kaja's face, and around his neck, and over his shoulders, and down his spine, were the stories of his people, told in lines.

❧

Everything in his world dropped away, save Morgaine's hand on his back and Sekh's two grey stars, stabbing across the abyss. Hostility breathed around him, thick and hot. He wanted to abandon this place. He wanted to hold Nana's amulet and drift off to Ma, her lullaby in his ears.

How audacious of his kin to wear their stories on their bodies. Wherever he was, he was the emissary of his people's philosophy. He could not conceal his ontology. He could not deceive. He could not deny who he was. No one else, in his new world, carried this burden.

His body knew how to live. It held him high and tracked the leering Hingemen across the abyss. The wizard acted slowly, caressing and pulling his drama as though drawing a drum skin over its hoop. Now he tightened it, then he smoothed it, now he tightened it again. The pouch of mustard seeds had disappeared. He drew from within his cloak a string laced through a hundred leaves, fresh from the forest. Then, the skeleton of a bird, dangling from a string with the skull in the center. It had garish red eyes that seared Kaja, as though Sekh had trapped a demon. He held the loops in silence, holding Kaja too.

"Which one is it?" he asked.

"The albatross," Kaja heard himself say, though he did not know why. He didn't even consciously realize that the skull was of an albatross. He watched Sekh steadily, and a thin smile crawled across his yellow teeth.

Sekh placed the loops on the floor in front of him and picked up his pipe again. "Kaja of the Rishi," he said before drawing slowly from his pipe and letting go a plume of purple smoke, "You were born seventeen years ago, were you not?"

"Yes, High Hingemen Sekh, I was born seventeen years ago."

A gasp went up from the crowd. Kaja understood power. He realized that Sekh's intent was to draw power to himself, and to make the people want it there. *How could he have known my age? Was it a guess? Or was there some method to it? Did I tell him in my delirium when I first arrived? Or could it be that the flowers told him, somehow?* Kaja leaned into Morgaine's hand, as a way of touching back. She held steady. She had seen her mother walk off into Ma's womb without hesitation, and she brought that lesson to her life now.

"Kaja of the Rishi," Sekh continued, "these lines upon your face and upon your body—they were put there by your people, were they not?"

"Yes, High Hingemen, they were."

"And they have meaning to your people, do they not?"

"Yes, High Hingemen, they do."

"And they were drawn upon you to initiate you, were they not?"

"Yes, High Hingemen, they were."

"And the people who did this loved you, did they not?"

"Yes, High Hingemen, they did."

"And the stories in these lines are not about you, are they?"

Kaja hesitated for a moment. The question was imprecise. They were about his people's history, and so they were about him. They were about his beliefs, and so they were about him. But rather than quibble, he realized that assisting Sekh in this drama was his wisest course of action. Anything else might anger him, and that may put a quick end to his journey. So he said, "No, High Hingemen, they are not about me alone."

"They are about your people, are they not?"

"Yes, High Hingemen, they are."

"And about where your people come from?"

"Yes, High Hingemen."

"And about your people's place in the stars?"

"Yes, High Hingemen."

"Your tattoos are not complete, are they Kaja?"

"No, High Hingemen, they are not."

Sekh stared and smoked for some time. Then he leaned over and whispered something in Ogden's ear, and Ogden nodded.

"Kaja of the Rishi," Sekh began again, quietly, almost gently, "you would like to live among us, is this true?"

"Yes, High Hingemen Sekh. I would."

"Have you seen other foreigners living among us, Kaja?"

"No, High Hingemen, I have not."

"There are reasons for that." He drew from his pipe, relishing his power over all present. And by enjoying it, he increased it. "But for you, Kaja, for you we might make an exception. Since the flowers announced your arrival. Would you like that?"

"Yes, High Hingemen, I would be very thankful."

"Indeed, indeed. For where could you go?" Sekh nodded and drew his audience together. "We may let you stay," he paused, and smoked, "if you prove yourself worthy."

Kaja hung in the pause, but he had not been asked a question, so he remained silent. *This, at least, I can control.*

"Kaja, the winter is nearly upon us. It will be mild, with rain but little snow, though very cold and dark. We will need you for other work in the spring, but for the winter, we shall hear your story. To understand why the stars brought you here, we should know where you come from. On winter nights in this Hall, you shall tell us the story of your people, and the story of how you came to be among us."

Kaja had been so long without freedom, that the anger he felt at being told that he had to share his life, publicly, burned in him, deep where he could keep it. *Yet again...I have no choice. Either do it or die.* He thought for a long while, and finally decided that Ma needed him to stop Sekh, and that, perversely, the first step on that path was to submit to him.

The quiet in the hall slunk around like a cold wind. Kaja broke it by saying, as strongly and as steadily as he could, "Yes, High Hingemen, I tell my story. To hope you accept me here. To hope your town is my home."

Then Regis's voice rang out, loud and clear. "I'll vouch for him, Sekh, come on."

Dogen put his hand on Kaja's knee, as if to say, "let Regis go."

Regis continued, "He's a fine hunter and you know he's stayed in his boundaries the whole time. He's a good guy, been through the underworld seems to me, just wants a peaceful life now. Never asked for a weapon, even though he's hunted for us, and brings his kills to my mother. I'll vouch for him to the Court. He's already living in my house."

Sekh disdained Regis crossly. He'd blown the oppressive secrecy and mystery wide open, because, suddenly, what Kaja wanted, and who he was, seemed obvious. He was a lost man who wanted a place to live. Nothing more.

Ogden spoke, "Regis, my friend, your generosity is well known among us. And you and Hypp know Kaja better than any."

Kaja saw Sekh's gray glare twitch to Dogen for an instant.

"So the court listens when you tell us he is a 'good guy.'"
A chuckle flitted through the room. "But Sekh sees more than you
do, Regis. He sees more than I do. You may vouch for him if you
wish, but Sekh will decide how Kaja may come to take up
residence among us. Surely you understand."

Regis shuffled, a little confused. "Yeah, sure, that's not
what I was talking about, really. But Kaja here's a friend of mine.
So. He's a good hunter, too. You know where to find him. So
does anybody. Right?"

"Yes, Regis. And we know you will bring him here at
Sekh's bidding, so we may listen to what he has to tell."

"Yeah, yeah, sure I will. That's all." Regis seemed a little
worried.

Sekh said. "All present, the story I have told you is yours
alone. Yours alone." With that he rocked forward, swept up the
leaves and the albatross, and crawled through the door at the back
of the room.

"Enough, good friends," Ogden said. "The rain has come.
Walk carefully. We shall call you again soon. Good night!" He
went after Sekh.

The young woman behind Ogden paused before following
them. She turned to Dogen, and then Kaja, and then Regis. She
did not smile openly, but there was something warm and perhaps
even merry in her look. She disappeared through the glistening
fabric, and the two red children followed last.

None of the people moved, save the musicians, who filled the air with strumming drums, and then with flowing flutes. Murmuring quietly, the people began to crawl back outside.

Kaja leaned to Dogen and asked, "Who is young woman?"

"Quinn," Dogen said. "She is Ogden's daughter, and his heir apparent."

"His what?"

"She will become our leader when Ogden dies."

Kaja nodded and followed him through the low door and into the rain.

Rishi

There was a woman in town, younger than Kaja, though not by much. He saw her from time to time but had not spoken to her. He had brought her into his dreams, gently, to think of talking to her, or walking with her.

Kaja let his dream fill with her a little. Just enough, so thinking of talking to her made his heart race. Just enough to wonder if she would dream with him. Just enough to believe that she wanted him to go on dreaming of her. But he would do nothing, for he wanted to keep the dream. If he so much as spoke of her, its bloom could wilt on its ethereal stem, curling and fading in a moment.

She was there in the Hall, on the same side as Kaja, but down towards the door. He found a way to see her through the crowd, and when she saw him looking, she looked right back, restraining her grin, and curved her hand towards him. A tiny gesture, nearly concealed in her lap, but it consumed him.

She knows. She likes knowing. He did not hold her gaze, though he realized that this dream, this dream with her in it, had become dangerously important to him. *That's weakness. That's what they use.*

He watched the others sing and sway. *They dream together. They keep the dream going and help each other when one loses the thread.* In the Between, he had been thrown into a world without a dream, where he scraped against reality like a fang on bone. Now he wanted back in. He wanted to learn Ash's dream, to immerse himself in it and take refuge in it. *Ma, I could be a good man here.*

He snapped to Sekh, whose glowering gaze hovered in the darkness of his hood, trained on him. Steady. Still. Rapacious. He watched as the wizard filled his pipe, tracking him without pause. The red child who lit it moved into and out of the way, but his gaze never wavered.

Kaja heard Ogden say his name, and he left Sekh. It took a moment to find his way into their language. He glanced towards the girl, but the line of sight had closed. With an outstretched hand and a shake of his black mane, he said, "It is hard to begin. I not be hero. I not am traveler. My story not to be adventure. Yet the mustard flower wants to hear. So I speak to you.

"I do not brag when I tell you my land, my home people were the most beautiful I have seen, and different kinds of people I have seen then I came to your world. We were good true folk. We come out of cave in the hills long ago, and cave is still there. In the ground you can see the footprints of first the Rishi, walking from Ma to the light.

"The land always loved us, from the beginning, and we loved the land. It was not much different than here, but different some. Deep forest like here and by beautiful Windhollow, but steeper hillsides, like the Squirrel Wood. But no moor like here. The meadow turned to sand, to cliff, the sea met the sand. Like you, we lived in village together one family, together for feast and festival and rites. My people loved the children most, and I loved being a child there in them. Yes I did. And they loved me. Yes, they did. I would not have left. No, I did not leave. No. I would not have left, ever.

"Cinn was my uncle, my mother's brother. A very good man. He loved me and I loved him. He was quiet, and wise. He was miner, and hunter. He took me with him, and when I could barely walk a little boy. Anywhere he could find metal. But most of the time we would walk, and look at the world, and to look at the world he taught me how. It was deep Magic. I never finished learning it. He taught me patiently, quietly, by showing me how. From Cinn I learned much, yes I did.

"Also in my house was my mother and my sister, Nana. My mother was beloved to me, as all mothers are to their sons. She was like her brother, very wise and knowing. And she was not like her brother, since she talked much the time. She loved to tell stories and she made silly stories for children, to make me and sister laugh. Funny silly things about talking animals and adventures in the sea and in the trees. We love her stories and would help her make them. Silly questions we would ask and she would answer with silly answers. Very much fun being with my mother and my sister on those days, yes.

"And my sister, Nana. Nana shared with me a very special love, which others around us could feel right. Very good friends, but we did not spend every time together. I would be with Cinn, and she with Mother. Still, when we were together we could read our thoughts. I am not a singer, but Nana was. And she was not an instrument player, but I am. I would make instruments and play, and she would make songs and sing. Many in our village loved to listen to our music. We would eat with friends and family and sing together, sometimes only Nana, sometimes everyone, sometimes just the women or just the men.

"You see how we were? We made music, we walked in the world, we loved one another. That is all. That is who I am, in my heart. Please believe, please let me show. For the rest of my story, it does not sound like this.

"My village very small, close from the coast, in the hills. But to the East from us a much larger town, maybe one day walk away, in bad weather, two days. That town was called Riversmouth, and a mighty river flowed past her. Riversmouth was on the sea on the river, and on good ground. I heard many stories about Riversmouth. Ships came from the sea—ships from your land, maybe, though I have not heard. Ships from towns on the edge of the sea, up and down the coast. And many ships from the river too, come down from far to the South and East to Riversmouth to trade. A road, too, went along the river from Riversmouth to the edge of the Earth, they said, though never I did meet a traveler who went so far.

"Now people of Riversmouth were Rishi like me.
Language a little different, but many tattoos very same. Many
ways the same, many rites and prayers. We trusted them and when
Cinn went to Riversmouth with gold tin copper the traders treated
him respect, trade him goods from far off lands, beautiful things.
Cinn told me he would take me to Riversmouth when I am
initiated. I was excited to go, to see. When Cinn would go he
would go and back. I want to go and back. Not stay there, either.
Thought of travel farther never in my mind. I did not want to
leave. See Riversmouth with Cinn, someday, but no more.

"But it was not to be. For in the Fall of my thirteenth year,
when I was full of anticipation to be initiated soon, strange news
came to us. We did not know what to think. For, news a person
brings is one thing, the words. But then there is the eyes as well.
And when the words go from one to another, sometimes the story
is lost, or meaning is lost. But when the eyes are passed along too,
more than the story comes to you. And so it was this time.

"His name was Traq, a good, upright man who loved the
trade more than we did. He sometimes took metal from Cinn to
Riversmouth, taking some as his own for the trip, and always very
honest with the return, even bringing the metal back if there was
no good trade. Sometimes he went in bad weather, or in Fall or
early spring before people from distant lands had traveled so far as
Riversmouth from their home. Then there would not be so much
for him to find. It was like that in Fall when he came back from
Riversmouth. We had sent with Traq tin and copper, hoping to
trade nice clear flint.

"But Traq came back with nothing instead. Even his pack,
bedroll, hat, staff, was not with him when he came back. We ran

to him when we saw him on the trail, for there are robbers sometimes but very rare, very few. In my life, only stories. Until Traq came back, and we saw he had nothing with him. Some men pulled his arms over their shoulders and help him to walk. Stay close to him to make him warm and took him to his mother's house. But we had seen his face, too, seen the fear in him, and we were afraid. Our mothers took us children back home, and the others gathered with Traq to hear the story, to see if there were robbers about and what to do.

"Now since I was ten I thought I was already a man, even though I had not been initiated, and I did not like going back home with my mother. I wanted to stay and listen to Traq's story. But I could not. I had to wait for Cinn to come home. Which he did, very late at night. We waiting. It was then that I saw the eyes had been passed along, from Traq to my uncle. I remember watching his eyes he spoke. Voice familiar, Cinn, but eyes not Cinn. We were afraid, because Cinn was afraid, because Traq was afraid.

"Traq had been robbed in Riversmouth. Not by men. He had been robbed by beasts he had never seen before. Men with four legs. Men with two heads. That is what Traq saw, and that is all he saw. He threw his pack and ran away, back to us.

"That was how it began. The fear came to us that way. The fear took our life away. Nothing the same again. Ever."

Kaja sat nodding his head, up and down. No tears rained, but his body racked.

❧

Sitting in the gazebo the next morning, early, staring into the fog, Kaja thought about the young woman, and her curled hand. She had long red hair, and it was wavy and thick. She had blue eyes. She had a purple, hemp blouse with an otter fur collar that showed the shape of what was underneath. She had braided her hair and had woven small blue flowers into it. He had seen these things about her.

But the curled hand captivated him. Would she let him hold her hand? Would there come a day when it was her hand that reached out for his, and not this other hand, this clawed demon?

❧

While Kaja waited there, Regis and Dogen were gathered with the Talon in the Hall with Ogden. Sekh was not present. Weapons lined the walls—knives and axes, hammers and clubs, bows and arrows, spears and spear throwers. The weapons were in attendance and hovered over the gathering as a force of will. They were included now in expectation they would be included later.

Ogden understood their use in both arenas, better than anyone else present save, perhaps, Dogen, who sat by Regis and surveyed the faces of the other men present. Most of their faces were set in violence, for the problem before them seemed simple enough: the Nok had stolen pasture, had stolen livestock, had threatened the Yuffs with bloodshed. They had to be put in their place. Order had to be re-established, and fear would enforce it.

Dogen could tell which Talon had seen battle before. There were those who lusted for the heat of the fight, for in that heat they felt alive as never before. The fight itself was beautiful to them, for when battle arose within them, the world was pure. To see clearly is glorious, and it is possible to attain it through the fight.

To attain clear sight in other ways is a far more difficult struggle. Few comprehend it, and fewer still emerge victorious. The Ringsong went:

A warrior may conquer a thousand in battle
Wielding his ax and sword
A warrior may conquer a thousand more
Vanquish his enemy and over him lord
Save his people from tribulation
Watch them dancing, hear them drum...

Another warrior may confront himself
On a field with no ground
He fights without weapons
Save his Will, his Intent, his Sacred Sound
Let this warrior win his battle
Conquer himself, become his own lord
He saves his people, the animals, the wind and the sea
The stars in heaven, and the living at the Rings.

Among the Talon who had witnessed battle, Dogen could see the few who realized the second battle was the more honorable of the two. Dogen could also see that the Yuffs had been violated, and that something had to be done. His weapons rested against the wall behind him.

"Well it's pretty bloody clear to me we need to put together a posse and go find the Nok and take their whole bloody herd back to the Yuffs. They don't like it, we'll leave their guts for the vultures and foxes."

"Bloody right, Toot, I'm with you on that one. Maybe spear a couple of them so-called warriors on the way in just to make the point clear to 'em. Too bloody stupid to honor a simple grazing agreement, we gotta speak a language they understand," Yet said.

"The Yuffs will know where to find them. Probably one or two wouldn't mind going with us. Bring 'em weapons first and head straight to the Nok. Be good for the Nok smart enough to run to see a few Yuffs working 'em over," Bal said.

"And if they burn the graze again we'll pay a little visit to their court and express ourselves," Toot scoffed.

A rowdy laughter went up, not just from Toot, Bal and Yet but from the other Talon itching to roam across the land rolling fear ahead of them like mean children whipping a hoop. Dogen and Regis smirked gamely, as did Ogden, but they did not laugh. Ogden, in fact, had said almost nothing at all.

"Timing's perfect, too," chimed in Bal, "got a full moon comin' up, we could make good time to the Yuffs and get in close to the Nok at night. Wish 'em a good morning then explain to 'em how we feel about their treatment of our folk. 'Mornin' Nok, sorry about the spear stickin' out your ass.'" The laughter rose even meaner.

Ogden needed this. Dogen could tell. Regis could tell, too, though for him the proceedings were alarming in a different way. He didn't want to fight anyone. His distaste for conflict was profound, and any time he saw power accruing he tried to undo the process. He lived in a chaotic house crammed full of things so anyone who walked in would find something intriguing—and perhaps the most intriguing thing was that there was something intriguing for everyone. People gathered around he and Hypp because there was no possibility of ranking in their household—only chaos, happy chaos exalting the nonsensical in Nature and the comic in existence. He had been born into the warrior class, as had Dogen, but he didn't know why he had been initiated. Not that he was incompetent, it was just that he didn't have the passion or the skill or the inclination to fight.

But Ogden needed him, too.

The cruel banter continued for a while, and as it degenerated further into wicked humor, Ogden found an opening to stop it, and to call everyone back to the real issue at hand. The Talon had not developed a plan, but a fantasy, and Ogden would guide them into his own conclusion slowly.

"Well, well, my friends," he began. "There's no question the Nok have crossed the wrong tribe, heh?" To this a universal and enthusiastic "Aye!" went up.

"And," Ogden continued, "there's no question we will handle this situation and set things right for the Yuffs, hey?" Again, everyone agreed.

"And since you men can handle these buffoons at any time, in any weather, if there's a full moon or not, we already know who's going to graze on our lands, and who's going to return a few sheep, don't we?"

"Bloody right we do!"

"And who's not going to bother the Yuffs again for many years to come, hey?"

"Forever!" The men were drooling.

"That's right... That's right... But you know what gets me? You know what I don't understand? You know what makes my blood boil?"

"Hey! Tell us, Ogden!"

"Here's what I want to know: Why are a bunch of so-called warriors wandering around, drunk off their asses, threatening the Yuffs? Huh?"

"Yeah!"

"What the Ma is going on in the Nok's court that they've got a bunch of drunk idiots wandering around the countryside carrying the insignia of Nok warriors?"

"Yeah!"

"You want to know what I want to know?"

"Yeah!"

"I want to know what's going on in their Court. And you know why?"

"Why!"

"Because I wonder, I just wonder—why go after a few drunks and a herd of sheep, when there might be more out there for us? Huh?"

At this, everyone's expression widened. Immediately they were in Ogden's camp. They didn't know why. But they knew what Ogden had in mind was bigger than what they had in mind, so they wanted to be on the same side as the big idea. And besides, being on Ogden's team meant they were all on the same team, and when the heat rises it's important to have others around, for it usually takes a team to remember the one idea that started the whole thing and that justifies it. What was Ogden talking about?

"That's what I wonder. What's going on in the Nok court, that there's these drunks carrying around insignia and acting like thieves? Huh? What does that mean to us? Huh? What do you think that means? Yet?"

Yet swelled and swung back and forth at his comrades. He had no idea what Ogden was talking about but acting as though he knew just what he was getting at, he said, "Yeah. What does that mean?"

"You see where I'm going with this, Bal?" Ogden said, quietly, letting a brothers-in-arms emotion rise up strong and hard.

"Yeah. I do..." Bal said.

"Are you with me on this, Toot?"

"Thievin' drunks," Toot said.

"Alright. Now we're getting somewhere. We're going to need more weapons. You can see that, right? I want you three to work on that. Compound bows for the initial attack. But we're gonna need more flint swords, more metal axes. Can I trust you three with that? We need them before the end of Winter. That's not much time. But if we don't have them, we won't be able to do anything. You understand? I need you men to supervise. Get the smiths to work on the axes. Get the help you need to make the bows, and plenty of arrows. If you say you'll do it, I can work on the rest of the plan. But I have to know you have the weapons under control. Yet, are you in?"

"Bloody aim, I am."

"Toot? I need your eye for detail here."

"By the end of winter, huh?" Toot shook his head, acting as though it would be a superhuman feat for him to pull this off, even with his eye for detail.

"By the end of winter, Bal. You tell me if we can do it."

Bal admired his leader and nodded once. "We can."

"Toot. I need to know Bal can count on you."

"Oh yeah. We will get it done!"

"Alright," Ogden sat up a little, and then leaned in. "Men. Listen to me. This plan cannot go beyond the walls of this room. No one can know what we are doing. Before anyone leaves this room, we must swear ourselves to secrecy." Ogden took each man's eyes in his, dramatically, seriously. Then he put out his hand, and the men put their hands in on top of it. "Secrecy then,"

Ogden said. "We discuss this only with each other. Aye!" he yelled, and they yelled after him.

"Very well," Ogden said, leaning back as though relieved he had this crucial part of the plan taken care of. "Dogen, Regis, you and I will go to the Nok's court next week, to take a look around. In the meantime. Yet, Toot, Bal, it all depends on you."

Divination

The time had come, as it did regularly, for Hypp to retire with some of the other Crones to the Hall for women's Moon Rites. She believed the timing was a good omen—as her beloved Regis traveled off to a distant, hostile town, she would grace his ways with the power and force of her Coven's Magic.

Kaja could not be left alone, so it was arranged that he would travel with Regis, Dogen & Ogden as far as Windhollow, where Morgaine and Martin would keep him while they traveled to the Nok.

Hypp busied herself with every conceivable detail involved in packing for her sons, as she now considered Kaja her adopted kin, and she watched over him with the fierce and absolute love a mother reserves for her strangest offspring. She would never fully forgive Sekh for asking her—convincing her, really, with tales about Kaja's greater good being served—to participate in the horrid theater that scared Kaja witless. After they took care of him and he had fallen asleep, she and Regis noticed how he had disheveled her bedding. Sekh believed Kaja was some sort of magical being conjured up by his flowers. But seeing the fear Kaja experienced, and the protective love he felt for her, Hypp knew that Sekh was wrong.

He was a lost boy. Her boy. He did not know it, but he had an ally in her more formidable than the Hingemen or the Talon could imagine. The women in her Coven helped her in secret.

And so, laden with food and clothing and medicine, the Court's posse set off down the trail for Windhollow. All but Kaja wore wooden plaques on their chests which showed that they were fully initiated Ringfolk. Regis had one with a carving of a wasp over a mushroom. Ogden's showed a roaring lion who had wings like an eagle. And Dogen's showed a falcon folded into a full dive, plunging from nothing but heading directly for something. They wore feathers in their hats, too, dyed green to show their rank. For weapons, they used long axes as walking staves, and had bows slung over their shoulders, a quiver on one hip and a stout flint sword on the other. Kaja had only his walking staff—and it was his now, for Hypp had given it to him on the fifth moon anniversary of his discovery in Raven Wood.

The sky was a brooding dark blue, and a quick breeze of frozen air zipped past them as they walked. Kaja worried about his friends' journey into the distance. It would be difficult to travel in this weather, which would almost certainly get worse. If they were to walk. He knew they would not let him see how they went to the Nok. Perhaps they would just vanish into thin air, or fly off like insects, or burrow into the earth like rodents. He had no way of knowing if anything was impossible for them.

They came up the rise by the hilltop that had the ring of trees, and Kaja pointedly admired them. Dogen and Ogden were behind him, and Kaja could not see Ogden's reaction. Surely there was something significant about the ring. It had been planted centuries ago, judging by the size of the oaks. Was it rude for him to look? Or was he only showing that he was observant, and would notice and examine the unusual?

No one offered a word. The path curved around the base of the hill, and Kaja noticed a trail leading up to the ring that he hadn't seen before. He pointed lazily, almost begging for a comment or a reaction. Still nothing, not even a grunt, though Regis seemed oppressed by the silence, perhaps thinking it would be Ogden's place to speak, if anything was to be said.

The path arced downhill, and they walked away from the Ring in silence. Just as Kaja decided that probably nothing would be said, he heard a fast seven-note tune played on a flute, then played again.

It was Ogden. He held a small clay pipe, glazed forest green with russet rings around the holes. He played the tune again. He arched his bushy white eyebrows at Kaja. Again. Dogen flashed Kaja his secret smile.

"Kaja, can you learn to play that while we are gone?" Ogden asked.

"Yes, Ogden. I will."

"Very good. Here, have this flute." He offered it to Kaja, who paused before taking it. *What does this gift cost?*

"Thank you, Ogden," Kaja said. He placed it between his palms and bowed.

"Come, let me show you," Ogden said, and then gently arranged Kaja's fingers where they belonged for the first note. "Puff into it to get a sharp sound," he said. "Later you can experiment with longer blows. Try."

Kaja knew how to play a flute, and he puffed into it so the first note sang clear and true. Dogen's grin widened. "Very good. Now lift this finger, and puff again." Kaja did so. The second note. "And now this finger." The third note. "And now this finger." The fourth note. "Now lift this finger and put this one back down. Do you see the pattern?" Kaja nodded and puffed out the next three notes. Kaja played the tune again, and Ogden nodded, pleased. "Ask Morgaine to help you. She is a wonderful flutist. Isn't she, Regis?"

Ogden's abrupt intimacy felt good and like a mild command to chuckle. They did.

"Oh yeah, Ogden. Sure is. In fact, I remember one time, Ma knows, it was almost a year ago now I came out to Windhollow on my own, you know, to see what was going on, and I ended up at Morgaine's house. We were sitting on the swing together, a fond memory indeed, and a little linnet came and landed on the porch to eat some of the mites or whatever it is linnets eat. So we were sitting there and we got real quiet watching this little bird when, all the sudden, it looked up at us like it just noticed us for the first time. And it sang a little tune, and cocked its head real cute, looking right at us. As if it said hello or something. So Morgaine pulls this tiny flute out of nowhere, and plays a quick melody back. So the little bird hops toward us a few times and I swear it had a smile on its face, like Morgaine had made a joke or like she'd invited it to play, and it lets go another little tune, sweetest ditty you ever heard, looking straight at Morgaine. So she plays another one back, and I swear I'm not making this up, the little bird hops around in a circle, faces Morgaine again, and sings another one. Morgaine sings back. This goes on for five or six times. She's talking to this bird, and the bird is having a merry old time, but then it sees something and flies up to a branch in the leaves. But before it flies away it sings one last little song, and Morgaine answers. Like they said goodbye or something. Most amazing thing I ever saw."

"Morgaine is a good soul," Ogden said, his growling voice rumbling over the word "soul" as if it were an object.

"Do all the music talk in some way?" Kaja asked. He remembered his people believed music was a story, and that sometimes the story came first and was made into music, and sometimes the music came first and later revealed its story.

"Oh sure, definitely, in some way or another. Good group of musicians can tell stories about the whole universe all night long. Sometimes at the Ring…" Regis paused nervously and began again. "I mean, well, sometimes when good musicians really get going, it's amazing to hear, just carries you away. Gotta love it when that happens, it's quite a pleasure."

Kaja was getting worn by the half sentences that corralled what was said in his presence. *What is the Ring? And why won't they tell me?* Rather than ask, he brought the flute to his lips and played the tune, loudly and perfectly. "And this song—what is its story?" he asked.

"That's a Ringsong, Kaja, and one of the oldest," Regis said before considering his words.

Ogden squinted down the trail, into the gathering forest. He would not defy his brother's declaration of secrecy but indicated that he wouldn't protest if they did. "Ringsongs, Kaja, are for the Ring of Trees," Dogen explained quietly. "Our people have planted rings of trees for generations. And we gather at them to celebrate and sing their songs. At least, some of the time."

A sullen melancholy passed through his golden eyes, reflecting an unwelcome change. Kaja thought of Sekh immediately.

But Dogen went on, "Play that tune over and over, Kaja, and see what meaning you can find in it. It is ancient, and close to the hearts of our people. When we return, perhaps you will tell me the story in the music. There's more than one. I will tell you others then." Without thinking, Kaja bowed to his friend.

Regis broke in loudly, "You know, Hypp is going to love hearing you play that tune. She's awful fond of you, Kaja. She'll know by listening how much of the story you know, even if you can't put it into words. Or our words, anyway. It's gonna make her real happy to hear you play that," Regis grinned.

"Yes, Hypp is Ma to me. Yes, I would like to make her happy. Dogen do you promise?"

Without checking Ogden, and without hesitating, Dogen said, "Yes, Kaja, I promise."

Rather than being held in Martin and Morgaine's house, so he could not see them leave for the Nok village, Morgaine concealed that secret by taking him to their sacred Oak. He couldn't watch them from there, either. But, by walking openly to it, he learned that he would no longer be hidden from the people of Windhollow.

The Oak was massive, so ancient that it commanded reverence. It seemed to observe those who came near, in some deep way beyond words or sense. Indeed, it had known the company of generations of people in this land, from the first who wandered by, to the first who settled in, to the first who gathered in a ring around her to sing and pray. Kaja could feel this history in her presence immediately, and without hesitation, he greeted the great tree as his Grandmother had taught him. Touching her trunk, he spoke in his own language. He felt the tree understood. As the animals knew his hunting rites, the tree knew his benediction. *At least, in some ways, I am home, among familiar spirits.*

But there was something new about the tree he had never seen before. He admired it openly. Hanging from the branches was a profusion of gifts. Most were small colorful pouches containing wishes and dreams and hopes. Others were small wooden plaques with symbols upon them, or intricate carvings, or little statues. Still others were loops of string laced through different kinds of leaves, sometimes hundreds of them, drying slowly and crumbling in the breeze. Morgaine and Martin watched Kaja as he walked around the tree, admiring it. When he came back to their side, he took Ogden's flute from his pocket and played the tune for the tree three times, noticing that the squirrels and voles and birds in its branches scampered about as though recognizing the music.

Kaja shared a grin with Morgaine, and then he played the tune a few more times. Each time, the animals seemed to respond to it—perhaps because they knew the Ringsong, perhaps because they liked flutes in general. But it made Kaja happy. He had played too little in his life and had played not at all in the Between.

Kaja smiled up into the tree. "Many animals and birds."

"Yes. We love this old tree."

"How long your people in Windhollow by this tree?"

"Oh, Ma knows, Kaja, many many generations. The story goes that this tree was here when the first of us arrived and has been part of our lives forever."

"It is wonderful tree, indeed."

"She has been very good to us," Morgaine said. The happiness in Kaja's expression shone like a bright blossom floating upon vast, dark lake of sadness. "Kaja?"

"Yes, Morgaine?"

"I have a friend here in town I would like you to meet."

"Yes?"

"She is my teacher. She practices a very old art that I think you might find interesting."

"Old art?"

"Divination."

"Yes?"

"Can you say it?" Kaja tried, and they practiced a few times until he got it right. "Come, let's walk and talk." Morgaine led Kaja back along the path to her home, very slowly.

"Divination, Kaja. How to explain. It is the art of seeing what cannot be seen. The art of learning things without being taught."

"What does your friend do?"

"It is called the Tarot. Twenty-one patches of stiff leather, painted with images. She lays them out in a pattern, and then turns them over in order to see what story the images tell. Does that make any sense? I have been studying it for some time, but I do not even begin to approach Charlene's Knowledge. She's been practicing since she was my age, and she is quite old now."

"Charlene?"

"Yes. You will like her, Kaja, she is very kind, but very powerful. In her mind, like you."

Kaja swiped aside involuntarily, as though to spit out the notion that his mind was powerful. *It is not power. You sense my secret. I will not tell you, either.* His mouth grimaced sourly, but he regained himself by examining his flute. He said, "Divination. Yes, I know it. My people we used dice made of bone taken from hoofed-one ankle. Like a box, dried, symbol carved painted on each side. Nine, she would toss and read the 'divination.' High art, difficult to know."

"Yes, Kaja, that's the exact same sort of thing. And so, Charlene offered —"

"Did not work. Not for us."

Morgaine implored him quietly and gently. "How do you mean?"

"Divination to see what can't be seen. We did not see what could not be seen. What could not be seen remained hidden, until it was too late. For us. Maybe your divination is better. Maybe it is not."

Morgaine was taken aback. When he made statements, they were so intense, and so certain, and so undeniably true, she understood how important integrity was to him, and why.

She said, "I'm sure ours is no better than yours, Kaja. If the Tarot works at all, it works for a person, one person at a time. It cannot work for the whole world. It can't predict the future of our village, or even the weather this year. It can only point in a direction, just for you. It might be able to show you things about yourself, or maybe about those who are closest to you. Nothing more."

She saw that this calmed Kaja somewhat, but she was curious to learn more. She asked, "Did your divination tell the story of the world?"

Kaja sighed and said sadly, "I do not know. As a child, the divination was not used much near me. Not for children, not playing."

"The Tarot cannot see the whole world. But Charlene wondered if you wanted her to throw a deck for you. For you, personally. She invited us to spend the night at her house tonight, if you are interested."

That sparked Kaja's curiosity. "Yes, thank you, that would be wonderful, Morgaine. I would like to meet your teacher. Charlene, a beautiful name."

"She is a beautiful person, Kaja, I am lucky to have her."

"That is good, Morgaine, good for you to know that. I would like to hunt to bring Charlene a gift. May I use Martin's weapons? May I go into the forest here?"

Morgaine dodged his gaze self-consciously. She did not like the limits placed upon Kaja. But there were many things in her world that she did not control. "Perhaps you could hunt up and north of our home. Please don't go into the forest you walked through on your way into town."

"Regis told me that the forest there is sacred, untouched. A wonderful place, yes."

❧

There was something about Charlene's house that reminded Kaja of Hypp's. The door was blue, which was different, and painted upon it were red stars and a white crescent moon. The door jam was decorated with broken pieces of colored clay tiles affixed so the pattern trailed off onto the walls like the tendrils of a jellyfish. Otherwise, the house was normal, round, and well made, with a thick-thatched roof and a trail of smoke curling from under a tent of leather at the top.

Kaja was loaded with their bedrolls and with the clean carcass of a pig. Morgaine shifted their pack and rapped on the moon. A tiny voice trilled from inside. When Charlene pulled open her door, a fragrant aroma billowed forth that Kaja couldn't place, and the entire interior seemed to glow the color of red embers.

Kaja stood away, almost shocked. Charlene was the tiniest woman he had ever seen. She stood no taller than his belly, and he was shorter than most of the men in Ash. She was simply a miniature person, with the figure of a well-fed, elderly lady. Her eyes were bright green and shone from within powdered lobes of white skin. She wore a yellow cloth wound about her head, with a giant knot at the top, and from her shoulders fell a full-length robe of mink.

"Why, Morgaine, come here, my love." Her voice chirped like a cricket. Charlene reached out and Morgaine dipped down to hug her.

"Hello Charlene, you look wonderful," Morgaine said.

"Thank you, my dear."

"And this is my dear friend Kaja."

"Kaja! Of the Rishi! I have heard so much about you, and now I meet you, at last. Please, come inside!"

"It is pleasure to meet you, Charlene," Kaja said. "Do you want I to spit pig your hearth?"

"Oh, you didn't have to do that, Kaja. My goodness, look at that. It's too much. Well, I suppose you have to then. Go on, now, so it doesn't spoil. The spit's hanging over there. I'll have to have the whole town over for breakfast. You are so kind, Kaja."

Kaja walked in ahead of Morgaine, placed the bed rolls on the floor, and carried the pig over to the fire. Charlene's expression glistened as he moved into the light. He stood on the far side of the fire and he could marvel at Charlene while she marveled at him. Their glances fell into each other's with a sudden spark of humor.

"Ah, ha! Kaja, you have finally found someone who gets stares the same way you do, haven't you?"

"Yes, Charlene, we are like in that, perhaps."

"Perhaps! Come on now, good man, you are tattooed like a well-carved roof post. From a distance you look like a wet tree with legs. Where can you go without drawing stares?"

Kaja's grin spread ear to ear. "Nowhere, Charlene."

"Of course not! And how many grown people have you seen small enough to hide in a berry basket?"

"None, Charlene."

"Well then, I'd say we're a couple of freaks, wouldn't you? There, that's better. Never did understand all this tiptoeing around the obvious. Nothing wrong with being a little different. In fact, sometimes makes life more interesting. Wouldn't you say, Kaja?"

"Different, yes. Interesting, maybe not."

"Oh, come on now, Kaja. Think about it. I know a little about you without you opening your mouth. You're sad all the time, for one thing, the light's been put out of you. And you were driven from your home against your will—any woman can tell you're the perfect marrying type, solid, loyal, you'd never have left on your own. And you're not from the island, that's for sure, not if you're that color and drawn all over. So, however you got here, there's probably no going back. You can see this yourself, no news to you, only thing is you can't trust the future because of what you've seen so far. Hey? 'Course, Morgaine tells me you're Sekh's guest, so lord knows that complicates things. My goodness what a wonderful pig! Nice fat one you got there, Kaja, and you hung it my way, too, legs together so you don't lose the juices. Won't those ribs be tasty in the morning?"

Kaja finished decoding all she had said a few seconds after she stopped talking, and said, "Yes, I hope so."

"So what do you think about what I've said so far? On the mark or not? Of course, I am. Well I'll just have to have a word or two with Sekh—don't tell him I told you that. So we need to help you with the future, somehow, and we have to turn your mind and spirit around. Your body's not going to let you go, that's clear. It's the only reason you're here in the first place. Let's see, let's see. Tea! Shall we have some tea? My my, the whole house was full of it before you put up that wonderful pig. Kaja, you sit there."

She pointed, and Kaja dutifully sat on a spotted fawn skin. Morgaine sat on one next to him. From a pot of boiling lavender nestled in the fire, Charlene drew ladle-fulls and filled cups.

"So you know what, Kaja, sometimes the thing that makes us most sad is just one little question we can't answer. We think about the reasons we have to be sad, and the thoughts always end up seeming like there's a whole pattern in our life that makes us sad. That's a tough situation to get out of, because once you see mostly sadness with glimmers of light here and there, well, you can't just disprove that way of seeing things. You know? There's truth in that. There's also truth in seeing the good in life all the time, with glimmers of sadness here and there. Kaja, do you like being sad all the time?"

"It is better than fear."

"Better than fear." Charlene arrested Kaja's gaze. She changed her voice completely, from a rapid-fire grandma to an almost sultry deepness, "If you could have anything in the world, what would it be, Kaja?"

"A different life." He found himself fascinated by the depth of her attention.

"If you could be with anyone alive, who would it be?"

"My sister Nana. I don't know if she lives." There was something about being with Charlene that made existence clearer. He did not choke on the statement as he would normally. It was simply a fact.

"Perhaps I can help you there," Charlene said, her voice transitioning back to the grandmotherly one. She looked down, and Kaja followed her gaze. On the thickly knotted wool rug between them was an array of leather cards, each just a little larger than Charlene's child-sized hand. One card was in the center, with Charlene and Kaja at either end. Radiating from it were four others. Morgaine moved closer to the reading. In the red light, her complexion twinkled like a tide pool in moonlight.

"Kaja have you ever seen a reading like this before?"

"No."

"I didn't think so. It's very simple, really. The cards are very sensitive to people, and, if I do my part well, I can usually expose them to something deep in your mind. I lay out this pattern, or actually there are several possible patterns, and the images on the cards will tell a story, of sorts, related to whatever was on your mind when I threw the Tarot. Do you see?"

"I didn't see you move."

"Well, that's good, then, isn't it? Because it means the cards passed through the air when it was full of the questions I asked and the answers you gave. Understand?"

Kaja nodded slowly. He had never heard anyone speak like that, of the air being full, but there was a truth there. "How does it work?"

"Oh, the deck is Magic, is all. Made by my grandma, this one. The pictures aren't really attached to the cards. They flow around and the right ones come up on the cards I throw."

"Really? How's that done?"

"Can't tell you. But I can tell you this: if you want to destroy a Tarot deck, just turn all the cards face up at the same time. If they're ever all face up at the same time, then the images get stuck, and they can't move anymore."

"That's amazing."

"That's just the start. Let's see what we have here… Morgaine, we're going to begin in the center and then work around." Charlene gave a sideways glance at her student, who seemed worried. She flipped the card, revealing waves of water that flowed in all directions off the edges.

Morgaine gasped, and her fingers went to her lips as her cheeks spilled with tears. Kaja looked from her to Charlene. The expression on the tiny witch's face enthralled him and thrilled him. She was capable of being more people than just herself.

"She lives, Kaja," the Charlene who was there at the moment chirped. She rubbed her hands together over the cards, as though washing them with rising smoke. "Your sister is alive."

The Nok

When they returned to Ash, Kaja stayed with Hypp
while the travelers went to tell Sekh what they
had learned of the Nok. In the Hall, they sat in a
quiet circle with the wizard. Ogden's daughter, Quinn, and Sekh's
apprentice, Bwain, also attended, but they sat behind and did not
speak.

Dogen watched Sekh's eyes as best he could. Grey, almost
white, and impossible to fathom, like a sonorous wind moaning
across snow-covered desolation and slipping into icy mists.

"My brother, it is stranger and worse than we expected,"
Ogden said, stroking his long, white beard.

Sekh nodded, "How so?"

"The Nok Court is in disarray. Our old friend Bit is no
longer there."

"And?"

"Those who remain have little control over themselves. The energies that an honorable man directs and contains, they let run wild, pulling them along like a stone tied to a dog's tail."

"Yes, I can feel it in you," Sekh said, cutting his brother off. "Forgive me, but I would like to hear Dogen tell the story."

Dogen's shaved head and azure, brushed wool shirt gleamed in the firelight.

"And so you shall. Dogen saw all and said little. As always, he carried himself well. Dogen."

"Thank you Ogden. High Hingemen," Dogen nodded at Sekh—was this his opening with the old wizard? Was this how his acceptance, perhaps even his apprenticeship, would finally begin? He tried to focus on what Sekh would want to know. The Hingemen did not move nor lift his gaze above his pipe. "Our pass over the hills forewarned of what we were to see at the Nok village. The ravens swooped low across our way, screeching. The animals carried the news to us first, hiding in the forest as though in fear. The forest itself did not sing with the twitter and murmurings as usual but held silence in the thick webs that arced from branch to branch. Often the only sounds we heard were our own footfalls, as though we were not in the world but in a room with ourselves alone.

"We came upon a house in the woods, one we remembered was the home of a wise, old recluse, an herbalist and healer and mushroom seer. No smoke rose from the chimney, but we approached nonetheless, hoping for a kind word if she would give us one. But the house was abandoned, Sekh. Worse, it had been defiled. Her jars were broken, her instruments smashed, her winter clothes cut to shreds. The furs had been pulled from her walls, and the sacred images beneath attacked with axes and hammers, crumbling the plaster and exposing the sticks. It stank of urine. This made us afraid, for who would do such a thing?

"We drew together and conferred as to what to do. We wondered aloud if we should go back, heed the ravens' warnings, and enter upon this path again only with a large posse, prepared to fight. But something compelled us forward. We armed ourselves, we walked with loaded slings over our shoulders, and our spears and spear throwers at the ready.

"We came around to another home. I have heard of fine welcomes laid out by the Nok for posses of ours in the past. One would expect the family we saw to at least wave, if they would not come forth and greet us normally. And yet, at the sight of us, they went inside, quickly and deliberately. There was a mother and two children, and an old man, too old to be her brother. He looked at us briefly and I felt—I felt —"

"Use whatever words come to your mind, Dogen, and I shall see through you," Sekh said.

"I felt he was protecting them, and not from us. I felt that he did as he did because, not to, would put them at risk. That's what I felt. In some ways, though, this strikes me most—for some reason, he was the one directing them, it was his perception that caused them to act. Strange. And she had a child, too.

"We heard shouts, vacant yells that landed on the ground like clods of dirt. But no moving about—we walked into town unobserved and were discovered only when a giant man with a pimply red face staggered to a wall, where he leaned heavily and peed prodigiously on his feet. When he spied us, he let out a shout that wasn't even a word—for their dialect is not so different from our own—and he didn't even put himself away.

"A few other similarly red-faced men came around. They were very drunk. They weren't sure how to react to our presence, but, thankfully, Regis stepped up. With big, happy gestures and loud, simple words, he befriended them right away. And explained that we had come to pay our respects to King Bit. It was then that we realized we had a much bigger problem on our hands than we realized. 'Bit!' the men roared, as if to attack us. They spit on the ground and cursed. 'No Bit!' And Regis, bless his soul, smiles and says something like, 'Well you have someone better now, we want to pay our respects to him.'"

"Truly an inspired piece of statesmanship," interjected Ogden.

"I wish it were," Regis said, shaking his huge head and bushy red beard. "But when your feet are in the fire, you know."

"So these drunks start saying 'Better!' and a few slurred exchanges we didn't understand when Regis pipes up again. 'Let us honor the new man!' and immediately the drunks think we're the best friends they ever had. So they form a procession of sorts.

"The town was miserable, Sekh. There was no spirit left in it, no pride, no art. No one seemed to be there, either. It was as if a scourge had swept through.

"They took us to the Hall. We expected it to be empty, because there had not been any time for them to gather to receive us. And we expected it to be dark, and cold, with probably no fire, for the same reason. We expected a cool reception, and a cool conversation, but one with a rational man.

"You cannot imagine our shock when we crawled through the door. The Hall was packed full of the men of town. They had been there for days, if not weeks. The smell was unbelievable— barf, urine, sweat, rot—and every part of it seemed to be covered by a drunk, groaning man snoozing or mouthing over the cup in his hand. There was a fire of sorts burning in the center—it too was a mess, smokey and disordered, more like a pile than a hearth. As we entered, someone yelled, 'Look at Swak—his pecker's sticking out!' and the portion of the crowd that was awake laughed rudely.

"But then a few present perceived that we were there, and a rumble sent around the room quieted the laughter. At the far end of the hall one man slouched on a squat chair, the only chair in the hall, and a thin man with a long nose shook him awake and whispered in his ear. There were weapons leaning everywhere, including a number of knives and scabbards stabbed through the firs on the walls, and some spears stabbed into the ceiling.

"I heard the Raven caw, as if to warn us again. The feeling in the air was a hum of unquiet ready to roar into viscous anger. Regis and Ogden saved our lives—there is no question in my mind. The man who led us in, apparently called Swak, yelled out fiercely—far more fiercely than I would have expected, given his demeanor—something to the effect that since we were so lightly armed he brought us to the court rather than killing us and leaving us by the road.

"The crowd growled and shifted as those awake hit those asleep to rouse them. Then, the man in the chair at the front gave an even more fierce yell in return, saying, 'Go play with your dick by yourself, you sniveling drunk,' followed by a command to bring us forward.

"Now, where we stood was by the door. If we walked to the other end of the Hall—that would have been a much different picture. Again, Regis' genius saved us. He called out, 'Oh, sorry to bother you, sir, but we wanted to meet the new ruler of the Nok. But the King of the Nok never asked King Ogden and Dogen and I to the front of the Hall. If you could tell us where to find him, we'll be on our way.'

"This man in the chair at the front of the Hall, wearing a ridiculous display of gold jewelry and a leather hat with gold studs all over it, became nervous, as did the long nosed man, who was obviously his counselor or something along those lines. After a moment of hesitation, the man in the chair called out to us, 'King Ogden, hey? I've heard of you. You can't come to the front of my Hall, either!' and he sniggered a bit, as did the rest of the men present, the way a flock of vultures will approach a lion's kill only after one leads the way. So Ogden took a step backwards, as if to demure, and Regis speaks again, saying, 'Good King of the Nok, what is your venerable name? For somehow your fame has not spread to our humble county.'

"'Net!' he nearly screamed at us. 'And what do you want?'

"Regis explained about the Yuff, and asked what Net had done about it. Net was confused by this, but the long nose man whispered something into his ear. Net says, 'Those sheep were tribute. They were grazed on our lands, so we levied a fee of some of the meat. Fair trade, as anyone could see.' The thin man leaned forward again, and Net added, 'Did you come all this way to discover that?'

"Now, at the time, there was no way for us to even to feel anger. We needed a way out of the Hall, but it was Ogden who spoke up now. 'King Net, the King who came before you, who I knew as King Bit—surely you and he discussed your reign before you took the throne?' A loud sniggering spread through the Hall at this, a dangerous and ignorant sound, but Net set his gaze on Ogden menacingly.

"'Do you see Bit here now?'

"'I didn't ask where he was, I asked if you and he had discussed your reign.'

"'I said, do you see Bit here now?' Ogden remained silent."

Sekh interrupted, "You can be a fool, Ogden."

Ogden said, "A man must not relinquish all his pride, Sekh."

"You are not a man, Ogden, but a leader."

"I was not alone."

"You worry me. Do not trust Bwain and I so dearly. There are limits. We cannot protect you from blows when you are in a room full of warriors. Forgive me, Dogen. Please continue."

138

"Well, Regis again managed to disarm the situation with some ingenious banter. But as he did that, I noticed one of the men tracking me steadily. I tried to acknowledge him without being conspicuous, and he made this motion—" Dogen showed Sekh, who was astonished at the sight. "What does that mean?"

"Distress," Sekh said, brushing his woolen robe and reaching for his pipe. "It's a sign. The man either was a Hingemen, or some Hingemen taught it to him, for just such a moment."

"Is that so," Ogden said. "Then there's no question we were right. The Court will dissolve as soon as we emerge from the trees."

"It's hard to say, Ogden—we cannot imagine their present way of being, but it is possible more men than just Net and the long-nosed man are pleased with the order of things as they are now," Sekh said. He surveyed that space only he could see. "We will know more soon."

Dogen paused a while, not sure if he was to go on. The silence grew, until he felt he was expected to fill it: "Well, now that Net had yelled at us, and we had not yelled back, things were uncomfortable. Regis just kept going, though, and somehow got Net to explode, 'They are not your pasturelands! Do you understand? Now get out of my sight!'

"And that was a stroke of luck we hadn't anticipated. Net himself seemed surprised that he'd said it. But in no time, and without another word, we were out the door and heading across town mighty fast. We heard laughter behind us, and just hoped to Ma they decided to enjoy their drink rather than try to catch us."

"Why in the name of Ma's did you not just come home?" Sekh demanded of his brother.

"We had to take a look around, Sekh—you should have seen that place," Ogden said, "They weren't even taking care of themselves. No beauty left in the town, no smiles on their faces. That strange sign from the man in the Hall. We had to —"

"Ogden, you truly scare me. There are limits, my brother, there are limits."

"You put those words into his mouth," Ogden protested.

"Yes, and you should have used them to escape."

"Well," Ogden said, "however it happened, we were able to leave the way we came, and then we bushwhacked through the forest back around to the Western side of town. The next day, a posse went out to find us, or so it seemed, since they were armed to the teeth and loaded with skins of drink. We stayed in the trees, drank dew, spoke with hand signals, and peed down our legs for two days. You won't believe what we saw. After the posse left — "

"Please, brother. I need Dogen's sight."

Dogen shifted and let a respectful pause go past. "Well, after the posse left —"

"The forest first, Dogen, tell me of the forest first."

Dogen recollected his thoughts, and his memory. He checked Regis, who sat with a sad pout on his face, trying to enjoy his broth, but lost in dark thoughts.

"The forest seemed like any other, to look at, High Hingemen. But there was something odd about it. Usually, the trees—it is hard to say. In the crooks of the lower branches the duff was piled too high, too delicately, as though no child's foot had planted itself there to climb in a long, long time. And the same with the fallen logs—their bark was not rubbed down, nor the sharp bases of twigs torn off, to make a comfortable place to sit. There were no lost strings, no toy arrows, no forgotten dolls— nothing.

"As Ogden says, we climbed trees and hid in them where we could watch part of the town. We saw a man stagger up to one of the homes under us. I saw his face for a moment—loose, red skin draped over mad boar's eyes. Shortly after he went in, an old man and woman and two children came out. The children were crying hysterically—especially the younger one, a boy, who reached towards the house and wailed for his mother. The mad man emerged a while later—not happy, mind you, but seemingly even more enraged. The boy child, who couldn't have been more than four or five, broke free from his elders and charged him with a passionate rage. But the man did no more than send the child flying with a single blow to his head. There was nothing for them to do except kill the man, which they apparently could not— probably because the result would have been even worse punishment."

"And to think, there's nothing we can do till spring," Regis said, working his hands around his moon stick now, rubbing the image of an osprey with his thumb. "What a winter that family will have. I hope the bastard freezes to death."

"They are not our kin, Regis," Sekh said.

Regis reacted with shock. "You shoulda seen the little boy! Looking after his father from the ground."

"Yes, Regis, I am sure it was disturbing. But they are not our kin. You need to remember that. Especially in the winter."

Regis rubbed his stick and pouted his lip.

"The Nok are out of control. Would you agree, Dogen?" Ogden said.

Firelight mottled Dogen's smooth head, and his golden eyes deepened as he cast an empathetic gaze to Regis. But he agreed, "Yes, Ogden. They are lost."

The old ruler continued, "They are dangerous. There's no telling what they will do, and there is no reason to believe they will honor their agreements with us. Besides..." He went on for some time, molding thoughts into words and plans.

Dogen watched Sekh. When he described it to Kaja later, the strangeness of the wizard's response struck him even more. His mind was fixed outside this world. When Ogden solicited his thoughts, he only bobbed his head, as though he had not heard.

Thurgans

T he fear changed us, in a way it is hard to say. There was nothing we could do. Nothing we could react. We felt danger, but we were not like you. We never made weapons of war. We have weapons for to hunt—but to kill people? We did not know what 'enemy' was. No one who come to us like the Nok went to the Yuffs. That was unknown to us. So we could not understand what was to happen."

Rain thrummed the roof, and a hundred lamps lit the Hall. The animals on the pillars paused their play to listen.

"It was late in winter, and was only mud and bare trees and grey clouds in sky. Weather like that, to me beautiful, but most others wanted to turn spring. I go walking in the mud, which most people hate to do. I had fine equipment there at home, not as fine as what Hypp given to me here. Still, good equipment for walking in rain. I was out one day, hunting for a buck or a pig maybe, anything so long as it wasn't pregnant, but mostly just to walk about and enjoy the views, which were completely different when the trees were bare.

"And I saw in the distance, on the trail that led to Riversmouth, the thing we had feared the most. The very thing we were unable to be prepared. The very thing in our nightmares, that had changed us without us wanting, without it even appearing before us. I never seen anything like it before. There were the monsters, yes—men it seemed, in the distance, with four legs and two heads. One head a man's and one head a horse. And with them was something else I had never seen before—a moving building. It was long and narrow and made of wood, with four corner posts holding up wall and roof of skins or canvas. My heart raced, as did my mind. They were moving down the trail very fast, despite the mud. There were many of them, six monsters.

"So what could I do about it? There was nothing I could do. Or everything I could do wasn't nearly enough. I ran back home as fast as I run and told the elders and my parents what I seen. None knew what to do, either. But something we had to do. So Lille, who the leader of the elders, made a plan that helped us so we did not do nothing. She told the mothers to take the children together into her home and to stay there. And she told the women to go home and to arm themselves and stay inside, unseen and listening and watching. And she told the young men to go get simple gifts to give to the monsters and told the men to go put on arms and to go to the Cypress and meet there. For she remembered the story, that the two-headed monsters were men. It was a deep intuition from her, to know the men, and not the women, should greet them.

144

"But nothing could have prepared us for what to happen. I was just boy. We knew the hills and the animals and the music. We knew tattooing and instrument making, and festivals and feasts. That is all we wanted to know, and so was all we knew.

"Cinn was afraid. He gathered into sack ore we had—good ore, one of gold, one of tin, one of copper. Nana and my mother gathered arrows together, readied the spears, and prepared to charge out from the house to attack the monsters if they needed. I have not seen too many women here hunting, but among my people, women knew how to hunt, and would hunt, except when have children. So my mother and Nana were good with weapons, especially Nana. Then Cinn and I went with our sack to the Cypress.

"Lille and the other elders were there, and so were the other men, holding thing to give to the monsters. We were afraid. One my friends, Jom, said, some of us should go to spy on them as they approached, and he and some other boys ran off to hide behind trees where the forest thinned before our town. I stayed with Cinn, because he was afraid. We waited, there was nothing we could do but to wait. These monsters, they came to us first in story, and changed us, and now they came again, and we stand in fear, waiting for more fear. You see how evil? It is hard to say, and you will not believe it, but I swear I tell you what I remember with my own eyes and hearing my own ears. Yes. This is what I saw, I will tell you for the mustard, for Sekh. I will."

There was no sound, save the crackle of the fire. The audience was riveted on him.

"For first came the sound, yes, a sound I will not forget.

The monster's footsteps in mud, hitting hard ground below, like banging the Earth with a stick heavier than tree. Feel it through the ground, feel it come into you from the ground. Evil, wicked sound. Not like the sound of deer or bison or horses, but the sound of evil. The sound of hatred, from people who hated everything, who had no love in life—only lust, impure and grotesque. For they were people. People of some sort.

"But then came another sound, one that caused us to think to flee—and we would have, if not for Lille, who put up her hand and showed us to stand behind the Cypress, together, and not to leave. Though we could see the fear in her face, too. This sound was like thunder, it rolled across the Earth and through us, too, but it pulsed like a drumbeat, a rhythmic thunder. It getting louder, and closer, and we trembled in fear, and we looked at each other to see if we stay or run. We manage to stay. That we did. We held together with our gazes that time and managed to stay.

"First two monsters. They were not four-legged men with two heads. They were men on the back of horses. The way a baby rides mother's back. They tied up the horse's head and held straps that they could pull the horse's head from side to side. On their boots were sharp points from their heels, and they would stab the horse with these to make it do their bidding. They wore terrible clothes, leather and metal plates. Every metal plate had the same image, of a fierce and blazing sun, all over them in the metal. And upon their heads were helmets—I learned later this is the name— 'helmet,' like hat but, too, made of metal and leather. And top, sticking straight up, the tail of a horse, so the tail flowed behind them as they rode, and they evil, violent grins.

"They rode the horses to us, and we back away at fear. Some did run off, too afraid to face men who would tie the beasts and make them slaves. To kill, to eat, yes—but to make a slave in this way, we had never seen, never wanted to see before. We were afraid, but now, like see death, unable to turn away. It was spell, powerful Magic that worked into the middle of spirit. Still there for me, always now.

"Then moving building, pulled by two horse-men and two horse-men behind. The thunder sound came from behind the building's walls made of skins. It is louder and louder, as the building sat still before our Cypress, and the horse-men prowled around, and we stood together still with fear, staring while the evil worked its way into us, deep into us from the outside. Then the walls began to raise up, pulled up by rigging from inside, and then we saw what was there, where the sound came from. More of the men, but these even worse than the ones on the horses. Four of them, each with a huge metal double-edged ax, on a heavy pole longer than I tall, holding upright, beating the bottom with it. Each wearing the same metal clothes of the horse-men, but these with helmet not one horse tail, but two.

"And their faces were starburst scars, horrid thick scars from the center of forehead cut across face, healed poorly around mouth, twisting the lips. And smell from them—they had not bathed and smelled of puke and strong drink.

"But that was not worst. No, not at all. Not even close to the worst. For they did not look out from within their eyes. They were not of this world. Their gaze was not fixed here, they did not see here, they did not see us.

"They saw some other world, trapped into the sight of some evil demon who had their soul. The demon in the sun, the sun on their clothes, everywhere a sun burning like their evil eyes. No souls in them, but out, in the hot sun, not here with Ma. We in terror."

Sekh gleamed as he watched Kaja. He now knew that tattooed freak possessed magnificent Knowledge. He knew it must be true. He knew he had it right. Through his clenched teeth he hissed, "Tiss!"—but none heard. None, save his apprentice Bwain, behind him, who startled at his master's voice.

"So terror, we could not move. We were their mercy. There was nothing could do to help ourselves. It is too late. We no longer same people, we would not be same people again. Over, all of it from before.

"One man in building paint his face scars red, and he yell out ugly word, sound like sickness. And, instantly, the pounding stopped, the thunder over. He did not move, though. The others did not move. The silence was bad like thunder. Then he called out another word, and, instantly, they beat the cart again. We tremble. Never we see one man who was four men that way. He called out the first word again and again all stopped, instantly. He look down at us, and none of the men moved now, not even the ones on the horses.

"Then he yelled out another word, and more, and one of the horse-men got off his horse, and went to Ipa, my friend's father, a good man, very funny to listen to stories, seemed every silly thing that could happen always happen to him so he could tell a story. Ipa had the goat to the men for a gift, and the horse-man took the goat from him without a word and brought it to the cart. The goat struggled to get away so the horse-man held it by its horn, up off the ground so it could not kick or even cry out. We watched the animal suffer, Ipa loved his goats, he did, he was good man Ipa yes. Yes. But then another word from the red star face, and the man behind him stood up and hit the goat with an ax blow so fast and so hard his head came off in the hand of the one holding the horn, and the body writhed around on the ground, so shocked to be dead now.

"And blood was spilled at the foot of the Cypress for the first time then. We gasp at this, we are even more terrified, for now the Cypress has blood in it, evil Magic. The red-faced man liked we were afraid even more now, and he laughed, a wicked laugh from his demon world, world better never know, but now too late, known by me forever now.

"He yell again, and the man on the ground toss the head at us, and we back away in fear, and he pick up the goat and throw it into the cart without word, without blessing, without kindness or respect. The red-faced man laugh more. And still, worse thing, the other three in the cart and the other horse-man do nothing, nothing at all, they just wait and remain still. The man who killed the goat sits down and looks straight ahead again, nothing more. Dead, a dead soul.

"The red faced man yells out another command, and the horse-man turns on us. He point to one of us, yells a word, and he throws out the basket he is carrying. The horse-man yells the word again, and we throw out our things into a pile. We do not even know his words and we do exactly what he says. Terrible Magic, more powerful than any we ever see, and evil, bad, horrible feeling Magic.

"The horse man leans down to the things. He throws the baskets and pots out, throws out wood carvings. He tosses to the same man who slaughtered the goat a pot of honey, and he tells the red-faced man what it is. Throws out statue, throws out hat. Then he comes to my bag, the bag my uncle and I gave to them. He opens it. He takes it to the red-faced man. He looks inside. He takes out the metal. He looks carefully. He looks at us. He smiles. That was even worse than nothing, worse than dead gaze. For now the demon soul was happy. What could be more terrible? Happy demon. Metal. They want metal.

"The red faced demon with the metal in his hand yell a word of his language. We say nothing, terrified still. He says word again, and again, louder and louder. We do understand but we say nothing, we do nothing. The demon looks at us. I can see he is thinking of what to do. I can see he is thinking, wondering what else we have.

"Somehow I change at that moment, even more. I think now I live only because of the way I change. I change, and now I be here to tell.

"I step forward to them. I point to the red scar man. I yell at him. But not in my language. I yell at him the same word he said to make the thunder stop. He looks at me with amaze shock. So do my brothers. I yell a word again. This time, word he said to made the thunder start up again. I think I am saying, 'Stop. Go.' He says to me a sentence in his language. Again I say 'stop, go.'

Then I say all the words the man in the cart said to him, 'honey,' 'beer,' 'metal,' and again 'stop, go.' He is amaze.

"Somehow we have some strength now, something more than nothing a moment before. The red face man look at us again, maybe see the weapons, just wood and flint. But strong wood and sharp flint. Yes. So he thinks again, and says something to his men. One lowers the walls of the moving building. The horse-men ride ahead of the cart. The cart move off down the trail. They leave.

"What do we do? What is there to do? We gather together by Lille's house. We do not know anything about the world now. So we can do nothing. Our world, gone. That is all. Yes. Gone now."

Kaja pitched forward and scrambled for the door, trying to conceal his face as he hurried over those near him. Dogen saw Sekh throw back his hood, and track Kaja with a fierce, desirous leer. He followed his friend.

Kaja did not look at the girl in his dreams, but she looked at him.

Enslaved

The next time Kaja was to speak, the entire town came to the Hall. Its earthen walls and heavy timbers could not hold back the howling wind prowling town. Kaja's felt-like locks, his strange face, and his swirling tattoos captivated them.

"In confusion we lived. None knew what to do. None knew rites to take blood out from the Cypress. Should we go to where? Should we go to Riversmouth? What should we do? So we did nothing. My uncle and I went on walks together, but we could not go along with peace as before. We had to worry, 'had they come back to town?' We all felt that—we needed to be together always. To be alone was worrying about the others. But being together always—that is difficult, for free man and woman need to roam. We quarrel more, we say things, and later say we are sorry. It goes on like this.

"The night comes when it is too late now. We have done nothing, and so we have nothing to show for the time. Nana hears them first, off in the distance. No moon, cold wind shifting and moaning in the trees. She hear horses, horses running. She wakes me, we wake us. Cinn so scared he begins to cry. Mother says to pack, we run away, so we pack. Hunting packs, and bedrolls, and all the food. She takes the statue of Ma from the hearth—our home is over.

"Suddenly it seems the horses are much, much closer. We run from our house, strong and fast, into the forest away from the sound of the horses. No garden now, no hearth, no spirit dishes. Into night. But the wind has fooled us. They used the wind, I know now. The wind will carry sound this way and that, in itself. A steady wind, a steady sound—a shifting wind, a shifting sound.

"I do not remember all that happened. My townspeople running. Then the horses were among us, with the evil demon-men riding them and swinging their axes. In the starlight I see a Thurgan jump from his horse onto my sister and tackle her to the ground. I turn to her, when I see a long ax hack into my Mother's back, just ahead of me, and she falls to the ground. I turn to go to her, and then everything stops. I know no more about that night. It was the end of my first world, the end of my first life. That is all."

Kaja was silent for some time, gaining control of his breath. The girl in his dream tried to catch his eye, but he did not see her.

"Later I awake because of pain. Slowly, I understand where. I am tied with rope, my hands my feet, and I on my side. I am in moving building, on the wooden floor. Soon I see there are others with me, others of my people. One or two I recognize from home, others, I do not. I try to move my head but the pain is so great I lie still, and breathe only. We are not moving. I begin to hear sounds —more of Thurgan words, horses. Then again I go into blackness.

"Next I awake they have thrown water onto me. Soon I know it is salt water, for the pain stings. One grabs my shoulder and lifts me up. Now I can see. I think in Riversmouth, because buildings look much like my village, made by my people. One woman like us, sees, and it hurts her like a blow, but not a blow, so she keeps walking.

"Then demon-man in front of me, yelling with man holding me. I learn later he was one of who came first to my village. He came to get me because of the words I spoke. The man holding me up lifts me off the cart and puts me on the ground. I look back to the cart. Rom lying there, his mouth open, his eyes wide and gaping. Does not see, because dead. Dead, and lying next to me. I not know until then.

"How to go on? I tell you, it is not your thought to decide. Something deep in you draws you. So I stand and look into face of demon, who look back like I am object made of wood, a tool or equipment. Nothing more. I fear him, but see he is to keep me alive, and so both with hatred and hope I go with him. That is how, with hatred and hope. Nothing else, no life, no knowing, no prayer, no rite."

Kaja paused a moment, the silence around him deep and dense, clear as darkness. He remembered standing by the demon-man and feeling in his pocket the little clay amulet his sister made for him, and realizing he still had a treasure. That gave him hope then, and will. But he would not speak of it here. For he had lost it, and he did not know what that meant.

"He took me to a house in the town of Riversmouth, where I was a slave of the rulers there for a year. They trapped me in a small cell by the big room. They called themselves 'Thurgan.'

"The things I saw there, such a horror has no place in the world, but in the world it was. I would try to leave the world in my thoughts, in my dreams, but I could not. In thoughts and dreams there is no path out of the world, though if I found it I would take it. We have no other place to be but here, in the world. To see the horrors, to see the beauty, we are here only.

"The Thurgans did not have women among them, or only one that I ever saw. She was the slave of the King, and one of the Thurgan tribe. Once she was there in the house, but I did not see her more than that time. The Thurgan would take the girls from my sisters and cousins and would make them slaves. They trapped them in rooms in the big house so they could not get away. They would go into the rooms whenever they wanted. The girls I could hear in my cell. Early before dawn their families would come when the Thurgan were asleep from drink. They would call to their daughters from outside, and the daughters would answer, wail and cry and beg for death, until the day came they could not even answer.

"They would take a man and would kill him in the town center. Sometimes, make his brothers kill him, make them sling stones at him until he was dead, or to dig a hole and to throw him in tied and alive, and then make his family bury him.

"There was nothing we could do. You not believe, but it is so. I will tell you what happened to me, for that is all I know. I learned to speak the Thurgan language quickly. This was my place in their evil.

"From my people would come some of the elders to try to speak reason. And when my elders came, I would try to speak what they said in the Thurgan tongue, and then, too, back to my people from the Thurgan."

Sekh drew his pipe and poked the bowl with a carved bone.

This is where the secret begins, wizard, but you do not hear. You are not as intelligent as you seem. You are waiting for a gift from Tiss, because you cannot create a gift for yourself.

"The elders ask that the children go wash to the river, but the answer was no, the children chip ore and pump furnace. The elders ask if daughters could visit family on one day, and the answer would be evil laughter, no, no. Thurgan would rise, laughing, and go right then, to show the elders how they used their daughters.

"I was kept in the house in the small cell and the door held fast so I could not escape. I was outside only a few times for all those moons. But I never sleep. Instead, first with my fingers and then, with a flint knife I stole from the floor, I chew away at the corner of the room behind the door where they would not see. For night after night I do this, to make a passage out. Finally, I can break off pieces of the floor and then put them back afterwards to hide my work. Then I work at digging under the wall. They hardly feed me, though, so as I work I get weaker, with no sleep and no food. Maybe twice in three days I am given something to eat. And never enough water to drink. Still I work.

"At last, one night, the hole is big enough, and I am thin, and through it I go into the cold darkness outside. I run into the forest. I know nothing of where I am, or where I go. That is what I did. Into Ma, to join my family, so I thought. I wanted to be with my family, to go out of this world at last. Instead, as before, that part deeper than thought makes me live."

Morgaine rubbed his back, and Dogen pressed against him. No one made a sound.

"Hunted now, I knew it. For it did not matter I was one boy. What mattered was I escaped. For them the power is everything. I went under the power and was away. So I knew they come, and not to bring me back, but to kill me.

"It was in this time, the time Between, that I did not think like a man. It was in this time I learned to think like a Thurgan. I became a thief. Not a path in life, but a way into being lost.

"I did not go far into forest but instead I went up into tree. I could not run into the forest like the deer and live. That was not possible. So into a tree instead, to wait. I remember being in the tree. It is first time I am free from them. First time I am free and know am free. As a child, free always, everyone free, so how do you know what free is? Now, I know. It was cold in the tree, but still I wait. The dawn comes, but there is nothing, for the Thurgans do not wake from stupor until longer.

"In morning light, I hear them. Shouts first. Then horse sounds. They come. I hold tight the branch near at top of the tree. I am more afraid now than ever before, because I know what they are, and I have felt free. To lose freedom to them would be worse. They ride under me—maybe ten of them, on horses, weapons drawn. I cannot see where they go. Not long from there, they excited again, like they caught something, and in short time they go by under me again. Tied up and laid across one horse is a boy, older and bigger than me, but like me. My heart comes out throat. For they must know that boy is not me, but it does not matter, I see. Only that matters is to kill someone, with any reason why. Only that matters to say, 'See, this boy ran, and we caught him, and now watch what we do to him.' It does not matter which boy they kill.

"So I stay in the tree for the day, until my body is tired sore I must move. I hear no one, I see no one. So in the late light I climb down, and run uphill into the forest. After a ways I come to a meadow and stop there. I eat mushrooms and leaves and insects until I am stuffed with them. I find water at the edge of the meadow and drink of that.

"I have idea. I climb up into top of another tree. This time I study at the lay of the land. Yes, this must be Riversmouth. For there is river, and there is sea. And I find a road.

"I go to it. I find a spot near where I to hide, and then wait. All night I waiting. For I know the Thurgan, I know his weakness. I do. I wait by the road. And soon comes the Thurgans, these ones going away from Riversmouth. Three on horses. They pass by me, going at a slow pace for a horse, but a fast pace for me. Unseen in the forest I follow them away from Riversmouth. For the whole day I follow them unseen, silent. I hear them speak sometimes and know their words. They are heading to 'salt mines,' of I have heard but know nothing. Then when the day begins to fade still I watch. They stop and let their horses go to pasture.

They take their things and make a camp by the side of the road. I climb into a tree watch them gather wood for fire.

"I have no fear, I have no thoughts. I wait. They get out their skins and begin to drink. This is their weakness. Yes. They become loud and vicious. I listen to their words, they make less sense as time goes by, they speak of nonsense, of other Thurgans and of their way with women. They fall asleep from the drink at last, and still I wait.

"The horses are asleep in the meadow, I know where. Their fire is low, there is little light. In the darkness I go to the men. I cannot see their faces. I take a long ax, and I become a Thurgan. Without mercy, without pause, I hack at their necks. I do not stop. No. I steal food, clothes, equipment, all I can carry. When I pull off the pants off one, I see around his penis a golden sheath. A sheath of gold for his penis. For this, my family is dead? For this, I am slave? What sense can I make of it? Many times since, I wonder at it. I leave the metal they are carrying on the ground, in their blood, but take the sacks. Yes. I took the sacks. And coat pants heavy boots I took, stained with blood. Into forest.

"How long until they are found? I cannot know. What will Thurgan do then? I do not know. They kill boy walking in forest for what I did, to run away and no more. They will hunt me, too, no doubt. I climb up and up. I leave deep boot prints in the duff, there is no way to help it. Perhaps I am dead. But again, like in the tree, I am free. In the forest, near the top of the ridge, boulders show through the soil spilling around them. These I search, and soon I find a small cave, not deep, but deep enough, more a space between two boulders with ground over the top. Into this I put the things I have stolen. Into it I put myself, to eat.

"But then I hear the horses, in the blush of dawn. I cannot see them but I can feel they are in distress. What to do? I am moved by the sounds of the horses. I follow the sound, I come to them in the forest. The Thurgans had tied the two together, their heads together, with strap. The strap is wrapped around one horse's neck and a tree. The horse is dying, its throat crushed against the tree. The other horse has horror in its face and it struggles to get away, but its fierce strength makes the strap tighter. I run up with the long ax over my head, and before they see me with a great swing I cut the strap and stick the ax head into wood. The struggling horse runs away. The other continues to pull his head and the strap begins to give. It falls away from the tree, and the horse gets up. Then it falls to the ground, and let go its last breath, dead now. I go to the horse and sing to it as my grand uncle taught me. I go to get from the ax. I know what now to do to save myself.

"Back to the cave, I go through the equipment carefully. I make lighter, but still keep the best. I make a pack, and I keep straps and ropes and knives and skins, all the food. Through the forest then I go back towards Riversmouth. I stay away from the road a long distance, but listen carefully, all day. I move through the light for the last time in a long time. I did not know it then, but many times after I would think about walking in the light that last time.

"I did not hear the Thurgan moving on the road that day, and indeed never discovered what happened about the dead. I find a spot in a steep ravine not too far from Riversmouth, where I think I can survive winter. From there I scout terrain everywhere, before dawn and in twilight. I know where the roads, and how my crevice looks from above and all sides. I know how to sit in it during the bright light so I could not be seen unless someone walked right upon me. And for this I had a bow and arrow always at my side. For I soon to learn more about what had happened to my people, to the spirit of my people."

He fell silent, head hanging.

Dogen nudged him, at which his friend shook. In the expressions of some of the townspeople, he thought he saw understanding dawn, and care arise. But not all.

Genu

Here you go, Kaja, try this on for me," Hypp said. Kaja couldn't believe it. Regis and Dogen and Morgaine grinned merrily at his complete surprise. Kaja had never seen a piece of equipment as well made as the parka Hypp held out to him. He took it from her gently, but before putting it on he admired it and explored it. The outer was paneled with shark and seal. They had been so skillfully cut, and the stitching so skillfully angled, he could see that water would run off it as it runs off a rock. Inside the waterproof outer was a liner with the fur still attached, sewn so the fur was between the outer and the inner surfaces, forming an insulating space. Kaja marveled at the workmanship and did not fully realize just how warm the parka would keep him, even in driving snow.

He pulled it over his head. It hung below his buttocks, and he pulled the drawstring, affixing it with an ivory tightener that all but sealed it off around the top of his legs. The neck was high, and when he pulled the hood over his head he noticed that when he tightened its drawstring, it covered his head completely, except for his eyes. The ends of the sleeves, too, were long and could be drawn closed over the hand by pulling on a thong within. Kaja had never seen a piece of equipment like this before. Coupled with his boots, which had not worn out at all despite considerable punishment, he was now nearly impervious to weather.

With the drawstrings tight so he didn't seem to have hands or a face, he made his customary bow of gratitude to Hypp. His muffled voice came from within: "Thank you Hypp. I have never owned equipment as good as what you make. Excellent, amazing." The word "amazing" sounded especially funny, emanating it seemed from a bulging sack, and Morgaine laughed, which spread to the others. Kaja quickly loosened everything and popped his head out, laughing too.

Winter was upon them. The rains had gotten harder, and colder, and the days had become shorter. Outside Regis' odd home the wind blew a spattering of rain, and the clouds were dark. "May I go hunting, Hypp?" Kaja asked. "Regis? May I borrow a spear set? I would like to bring a feast to you in thanks for this amazing parka." He mimicked his muffled sound when he said "amazing," and they chuckled again. Kaja didn't expect anyone to go with him, because Regis would want to stay with Morgaine, and because Dogen had mentioned he would be visiting his friend.

"Good luck, old man," Regis said, "This wind shifts enough to make it impossible to stay upwind. But, knowing you, you'll bring back something. Never seen a man as patient as you with a hunt. Don't forget we got plenty of food for dinner. So you come back before Hypp makes me go find ya, alright?"

Regis handed Kaja two spears and a spear thrower. Kaja went to Hypp. She and he had developed a custom, from the first time he went to Windhollow. "You come back here, to our house," she said.

Kaja nodded, and quickly shut the door behind him, so the warm air wouldn't float away.

⟨∧⟩

It was freezing outside. In his other parka, Kaja would simply grit his teeth and find the shaman warmth within that had sustained him so many nights in the Between. This time, he tightened the drawstring at the bottom of the parka and pulled the hood loosely over his head. By the fifteenth step, he was so hot he had to open both, making the neck loose so his chest was open to the rain. *Remarkable!* He practiced throwing the spear, making the motions and marveling at how well the parka flowed over his movements. Clearly, generations of wisdom had gone into its construction.

His boundaries had not changed, so he headed off to Squirrel Wood, along a different path than the one that led to the porch, but one that would offer an alternate route up there later. At first, he stalked like a hunter, for it never ceased to amaze him how often he would bag excellent game right near town, but then the wind and the spattering rain caught his attention. The air felt different and smelled different—neither forest nor sea but both, and more intensely of each. The roiling storm clouds overhead

164

contemplated when and how they would unleash their fury. The trees were illuminated by a precise and diffuse light. Without knowing it, he picked up speed, and strode through the forest looking about as though he had never seen it before. The canopy was open to the sky, dripping and flashing, capturing light in the air. It was strange and thrilling.

As he came toward the trail that crossed his own and led to the porch, he saw another person coming up from below. This did not surprise him—remarkable weather like this deserves a good walk. There were those who would gather around a warm hearth on such a day and relish the weather outside because of the space it created inside. And there were those who had to go out and taste it. Kaja looked openly at the other person, who was drawn into their parka completely, and waved. The person waved back and slowed down to meet him.

"Don't you think, remarkable weather?" Kaja said, as a way of greeting. His face exposed, he knew the other person would recognize him, and since there were still townspeople with whom he had not spoken individually, he tried to be forthright with his greetings, to ease the other person's trepidation.

"Indeed, it is," the other person said, coming up to Kaja. Kaja could tell from the voice that it was a woman, and as soon as he saw into her hood, his heart flooded his throat, and he had no idea how to carry himself, or what to do, or what to say. *It's her!*

Kaja stood arrested by the reality of her presence, amazed that the event he had dreamed about—speaking to her—had come to pass, in the forest, in such strange light and aromatic air. She, too, seemed stunned by his chance presence, and certainly more so by the fact that he had recognized her immediately, despite her hood.

For so long now she had imagined being with him, and she had imagined him telling her his secrets, his fantastic adventures—especially the parts that he told to no one else. She had imagined being the woman this amazing man from a distant world had chosen to take as his own. And here he was before her, clearly in the grip of deep feelings himself. She now knew that she was right—he *had* looked for her in the Hall, he had wanted to know she was there, and he had wanted to know she cared. She loosened her hood and pulled it down so he could see her face. She watched him watch her as she did it. She saw the response she'd hoped for—upon seeing her up close for the first time, he wanted her even more.

They stood transfixed on each other, each marveling at the unspoken exchange. Something passed between them, each knew it, each acknowledged the sincerity of their part, and each marveled that it could actually be true.

Kaja spoke first. "Please tell me your name."

"Genu."

"Genu. Genu. Genu. Yes. Thank you for your gesture in the Hall the night. It meant greatly to me."

"You are welcome, Kaja of the Rishi." She looked at him slyly. Her teeth curled in a bit, and her long lashes stroked her arresting, sea-blue eyes. Kaja's face lit. He had never heard his name sound so lovely.

"Are you going up to the porch?" Kaja asked.

"I thought, if it didn't get much colder, I would go take a look."

"May I go with you?"

"I would like that."

"Do you like my parka?"

"It is very nice."

"Hypp made it for me and gave today. I hunt for her to thank her."

"Hypp is a wonderful person."

"Yes. I love her. She has been so good to me. She and Regis and Dogen."

"You have made excellent friends."

"Yes, I have," Kaja said. He moved to her, and she came to him. "How do you know Hypp?"

"She is one of the leaders of the Coven. I have so much respect for her."

"Coven?"

"Women's lodge. Not for you or any man. Some things are for our lodges alone. You'll see, I'm sure."

Kaja nodded. He just wanted her to talk; specifics about the lodge were irrelevant. He took a different tack. "Do you walk up here often?"

"Pretty often."

"How often do you see weather like this?" The big splattering droplets had become more frequent as the charged air toyed with the concept of rain.

"Not often enough. It is glorious, isn't it?"

"Yes, I love it—I haven't seen it before."

"Not even in your own land?"

"Oh, maybe as a boy. But for so long, I couldn't walk about while the day. I never notice weather, not in normal sense like now."

"In what sense did you notice it?"

"Survival. Always survival. It was very grim, Genu. Not the man I want to be now."

"What kind of man do you want to be now?"

"A good man, a trusted man." He warmed to the smile that spread across her freckled face. "I would like to live here with you. With all of you. Safe. I make instruments—some you have never heard before but might like."

"Oh? What kind of instruments?"

"You have heard when you pluck a bow string it makes a sound? I can make the sound into music—not with a bow, but with an instrument with strings and a hollow wooden part we called 'bellows.' Do you make instruments like that but I have not seen them?"

"No, I don't think so, Kaja. That would be interesting to listen to. Maybe you can make one over the winter?"

"Yes. I will try. But you know, it takes a long time to do it well. And, so. There is plenty of time to talk while you are working. Do you have work like that?"

"Oh, of course. I love to weave. I spend all summer making thread and all winter weaving. It's the same sort of thing—a lot of work, to do it well, and plenty of time to talk."

"Maybe you would honor me to come to Hypp's house and weaving while I work on instrument? We could talk then, if you would. And Hypp, who you respect, is there too, and Regis, and Dogen often. Maybe you would like that? I would like the honor of your company."

Genu bumped herself against Kaja's arm. Her face flushed with cold, or happiness, or both. To Kaja, it felt like the world shifted under his feet. "I would like that a lot, Kaja," she said. "It would be very nice to spend time that way."

After a while, they came to the porch, and sat down together. Kaja noticed the quality of Genu's equipment was as good as his—he had to respect a people who had moved into their climate so well. The view was stunning—clear under the clouds to the horizon, where the storm mixed with the sea. In the deep, dim light, the ocean waves were crystalline, each droplet of luminescent foam visible even from this height. And the sound was different, too, because somehow it carried clearly and perfectly up the hillside to their ears, so they sat above the coast and yet listened to it as if perched on a rock at the shore.

"Genu?"

"Yes, Kaja?"

"I must mention again. I hope is alright."

"Ma's word."

"That night, in the Hall, when I saw you and you waved back, just a little?"

"Yes."

"That was a very beautiful thing to do, Genu. Very kind to me. My heart was moved. Yes. Very kind." He rocked forward and back, looking off into the distance. "Thank you, Genu. Yes."

Genu watched him, but he did not look back. He rocked instead and nodded a bit. His hand was on his knee, so she undid her sleeve, and put hers on his. To both of them, it seemed like they had known each other, in some way, since before they were born.

"You're welcome, Kaja," she said quietly.

He nodded; he could not speak. He turned his hand over and held hers. The energy that flowed through took them far beyond anywhere words could reach.

≪∧≫

By the time Kaja got back to Hypp's house, it was late afternoon and pouring rain. He had a roe deer. He hung it from the rafters outside the door and worked quickly to skin it, putting

170

such accurate and wholehearted force into every motion he had a beautiful pelt ready in no time. Regis came out to see what he was up to, and could tell immediately that more, much more, than just a successful hunt had transpired that day.

"Kaja, old man. Lots of times when you come home you say 'hello' to the people inside. Strange custom, I know, but we're a strange people."

"Sorry Regis."

"No problem. That's a nice deer you got there. Ought to make a good dinner for —"

"Can I invite a guest?"

"A guest? Sure, I can't see why not. What's with you —"

"Can I take a flank to give a gift?"

"If you don't it'll go to waste. So who's the —" Kaja took the hatchet from the peg and whacked the carcass so hard he nearly tore the flank off with one blow. "Slow down Kaja before you cut your hand off. You gonna tell me what's going on here? I never seen you like this before."

Kaja caught his eye. "How are my teeth?" he said, and pulled his neck back.

"Ho ho!" Regis said. "Now, I didn't see this one coming. Who is she?"

"Genu."

"Genu! Oh, she's a fine one, alright. Don't know her too well. When did this happen?"

"I met her in the forest."

"That's odd. What's she doing in the forest?"

"Looking at the weather."

"Looking at the weather, hey? She happens to go out just then. What do you know. Never ceases to amaze me. Absolutely never ceases to amaze me."

Regis peeked inside at Hypp, who, sure enough, glanced at him briefly, with a secretive smile on her face, before going back to chatting with Morgaine.

"Can I go get her now?"

"Go, my friend."

"Is Dogen back?"

"No, he's spending the night with his friend."

"I see. Will you tell Hypp?"

"That it worked? Sure. And the meat here—we'll spit that up too."

Kaja took the flank and the pelt and walked off across town. He'd already taken Genu home earlier, before hiking back out to hunt, so he knew where she was, and he knew that her family was expecting him.

They welcomed him with wonder, graciously accepting his gift. He felt comfortable in their home—in some ways, even more so than in Hypp and Regis' home. It was simple, and plain—not the aesthetic simplicity of Dogen's, but the simplicity that comes with exact expectations from life. Simplicity that comes from contentment and acceptance. Simplicity much like the simplicity of the home he knew as a boy. They chatted openly together about the unusually beautiful weather that afternoon, and about the chance meeting in the forest, and about the stringed instrument Kaja knew how to make.

"So, Kaja," Genu's father, Paw, said after a while, "Quite a journey you've taken, hey? Your stories are the talk of Ash."

"Yes, sir. Difficult journey."

"Does it bother you that Sekh asked you to tell it to us?" asked Genu's mother, Rimm.

Kaja did not answer with words, but he immediately began nodding. Speaking of Sekh always had an air of danger. *I can't get them in trouble with him. And, I want them in my life.* "Yes, Rimm," he said. "It is hard for me to go back. Especially in the beautiful Hall, with everyone around. Many things I did I am not proud to tell."

"But what could you have done about it, Kaja?" Paw said.

"Really now, my boy. You called yourself a thief—did you steal from the Thurgans or did you just find a way to save yourself? To my mind, a thief steals because his soul is warped. What you did was clear to me."

"Me, too," Genu said.

"The people I've talked to all approve, Kaja," Rimm said. "No one thinks you are a thief, or a killer." She shook her head sweetly.

"Oh, don't even say that word, mother. He fought for his survival."

Kaja worked his hands. They had wielded the long ax, and they had hacked at living men to separate them from their possessions. He had done that. And now these gentle folks chatted with him over broth, pleased to see his affection for their daughter. *How could this be?*

"Yes, certainly," Rinn said, "That is how we all see it, Kaja."

"So how did you get here, anyway?" Paw asked.

With that, Kaja knew that Sekh had not given them instructions about him. He scowled. *Why, Ma, does he have this power over me, even here? I wish I could speak freely, but if I did, I would entangle them with him.* So, instead, he gave them a different kind of truth. "Sekh forbid me to say."

Rimm shook her head, and there was a personal anger in her gesture, "Aw, Sekh. I suppose the drama will be more to his liking if you reveal it in the Hall. So be it. But tell us a little about your people, Kaja. Were you betrothed or intended for anyone?"

"Forgive me, Rimm, I do not know 'betrothed.'"

"Did you have a girl at home, Kaja?" Paw said.

Genu blushed. Kaja glanced at her and could tell there was more significance to his answer than he understood.

"Oh, no, sir," he said, "I was too young for that."

"Was there a girl who was to be yours?" Rimm asked.

"No. My people did not join with one person as the custom here. Love, yes, often and always. But more like village one family. At Spring Rites, many men and women together. And many souls come to women. But one special the woman for me, no."

"So at these Spring Rites, what did a young boy do?" Rimm asked.

Genu blushed even deeper. Kaja glanced at her again, but he answered honestly and fully, so they would know he was hiding nothing. "I played with friends, and some of the Crones and Elders tell us stories all night. In the day, play in the forest and run through everyone's house, eating everything we find. In the night, by lamplight, they told us story after story. First funny, then scary. Using puppets and toys. We stay awake as long as we can, and then we sleep in pile, like kittens. I did love the Spring Rites, yes. But like a grown man, no. Like a boy, yes."

"Is that so! Is that so!" Rimm simultaneously deflated with relief and inflated with cheer. "Well, that does sound like fun. Doesn't it Genu?"

Genu righted herself, and her strength and her youth overpowered the presence of her parents. She held Kaja's attention in a way that aroused him to the core. While looking towards him, she talked to her mother. "Are you through, Mother? May we go to Hypp's house now? They're expecting us."

"Oh, child!" Rimm said.

"Well, don't keep them waiting, now!" Paw said. "Kaja, you are welcome here any time. You remember that, hey?"

"Yes sir. Thank you, sir."

Hypp's house was only a short distance away. Genu's parents had put a strain between them, and Kaja had no idea what to do about it. But Genu did. She pulled him behind a tree where neither house could see them, if anyone was watching.

"I saw you walking in the forest once," she said.

"You did?"

"Yes. A while ago. You walk like a lion."

"I do?"

"Yes, you do. I was very impressed."

"You were?"

"Mmmm hmmm."

"Before I knew your name I thought about you," Kaja said.

"You did?"

"Yes. To meet you I wanted very much."

"I wanted to meet you, too."

"Good. Yes. Genu?"

"What?"

"When you are not there, I will think of you. May I?"

"You better," she smiled, fixed on Kaja. She did not waver, or turn away, or wonder. Kaja admired her.

"How did this happen?"

"Magic."

"How could I be so lucky?"

"How could we be so lucky, you mean."

"Yes."

"Does it matter?"

"No."

Genu stood close in front of him. In the dusk, her eyes flickered a wet blue, set off by her clear white complexion and her auburn hair.

"Genu," he said.

"Yes?"

"May I kiss you?"

"You better."

He took her in his arms, and she held him, and they kissed. Something opened in Kaja he did not know was closed. His body flooded with it. He could barely control it.

"Genu?"

"Mmmmm?"

"May I hold your hand?"

"Only if you make me a promise."
"Promise what?"

"Promise you won't let go."

"I will not let go."

She moved into his embrace again, and Kaja seemed to lose track of himself, unsure where his "self" had flowed to. All that existed was her kiss, her body, her presence. Genu was the entire cosmos.

Then she took his hand and led him from behind the tree. A quick rustle arose from every porch within eyesight, but neither of them heard it. They had solved life's greatest problem, without knowing what it was, or that they had solved it.

Alliance

When Kaja opened Hypp's door, it seemed like everyone had just taken their positions. The air inside was a little cold, considering there was a fire and several people around it. They wore goofy smiles. Regis and Morgaine were nearly one body, cuddled under a wool blanket and leaning against the wall. Hypp was next to the hearth, stirring the pot, and her sitting spot was waiting for her under a purple blanket with her friends Jinn and Trawill.

"Children!" Hypp said, "There you are. Just in time. I think the soup is ready. And can you believe what a fine deer Kaja brought us?"

Hypp smiled way too radiantly for it to be about the food. Their gazes tracked Kaja and Genu's every move. They didn't notice. The Magic prevented thought in words. Kaja helped Genu take off her parka, and she helped him. When Genu caught the blanket that Morgaine tossed to her, she and Morgaine exchanged a womanly glance. That little toss meant they were allies now, and friends.

Genu's family was simple, without a Ringfolk to its name, and it had a strange, deviant, and sadly shameful secret lurking in it. Yet, Genu took to the company of clairvoyants and Ringfolk as though born to it. She felt herself equal to them, and they were happy to have a strong spirit added to their circle. Kaja put his arm around her as though he always had and guided her to recline with him in his accustomed space.

A lurking, dark cold coiled about the house, but the hearth made them impervious. Genu and Kaja held hands under their crimson blanket, embroidered with an owl, and Morgaine leaned against Regis, and the three Crones cuddled, too.

Trawill spoke first, after a comfortable quiet had opened them to one another. "Morgaine, tell me more about your mother. I wish I had known her better."

"Oh, I miss her every day. Her and my little brother. Every day, I wonder what it would be like to have a mother still. The Coven guides me and teaches me, and I have Charlene. But no one ever really knows you the way your mother does. No one ever knew me the way she did. When I was little and we would play together, I knew she could read my thoughts. I just knew it. When I was troubled, she knew it, and she would help me. Sometimes in the gentlest ways, just coming to me when I sat alone—you know how things are when you are eleven or so, on the verge of your time, when everything is profound. And maybe she would sing, or maybe she would hold me, or would test my Knowledge of weaving or the Tarot. She would always make me feel better. Always. I miss her."

"Aye, child," Jinn said, "I remember being with her when we shared rites at the Ring."

Kaja's mind flashed open with the way she said the word, "Ring." *Surely, she means the Ring of Trees I saw along the trail to Windhollow...*

He pulled Genu closer and listened to Jinn's melodic voice.

"Your mother was quiet and gentle, Morgaine, but her presence was always known. She had a clear mind. I never heard an unkind word about her—aye, when one spoke of her, it was always with respect. She carried her own mystery. Her absence was felt by all at the Ring, it was, my dear. How long has it been now?"

"Almost two years."

"Aye, not long enough yet, for you. Carry her spirit, child, for she is with you. I can see her with you."

"Indeed, Morgaine," Trawill said, "She knows of you. She will stay with you as long as you wish. She will guide a spirit to your womb, I believe, and guide it into the world. Pain you shall know, as all do, but fear—less than most, thanks to her. She gave you some of her secrets, did she not?"

"How do you mean?"

"Her ways, her means. Each woman has her own and passes on the ones she used the most."

"Secrets of the Rings, or the Tarot?"

"No, no, child. Personal ones. Secrets of love. Secrets of practice. No two people are the same in this."

"Oh, those secrets. Yes, a few she passed to me. Especially after the first time Regis came to our house."

Regis perked up at this, "What do you mean? What did she say? When was that, anyway?"

"Well, if I told you, they wouldn't be secrets."

"Aw come on, you can tell me one. Just one? Come on, pretty please? Tell me one little secret. Did she like me?"

"Oh yes, she liked you quite a lot. You don't remember what happened? What you did?"

"What did I do? I didn't make a fool of myself did I? Did I eat too much? Spill something?"

"Oh no, you were quite well-behaved."

"When was that? Was that the time I brought you the rotten honey?"

"No."

"No? That's it? Just 'No'? Come on, gimme a hint."

"You had just become a Ringfolk."

"I had just become a Ringfolk... So I was wandering around and came to your house. Oh come on, Morgaine, what did I do?"

"You left your breast plate and your hat. Remember? Martin caught up to you on the trail?"

"Oh yeah! Now I remember. That was embarrassing. Imagine that, get this great honor from the Court and then forget the stuff. Ma, what an imbecile I can be sometimes. And Martin, I'm trying to impress him and end up acting like a dolt instead. I remember that. I'd managed to forget that, actually. Thank you for reminding me, Morgaine."

Morgaine laughed merrily, and to Trawill she said, "Those secrets?"

The old clairvoyant smirked and nodded. Kaja and Regis shared a friendly glance. Outnumbered five to two, they were getting a precious glimpse into female conversation.

"I remember when I first met Choud," Jinn said, the sweet memory shining on her rosy cheeks, "He was so big and strong and gentle. I had an insatiable desire for him the moment I saw him."

"So did everyone else, dear," Trawill trilled.

"Yes, I suppose they did. But I was the one. I knew it right from the start."

"Your mother's secret ways, you did use them?" Kaja asked.

"Well, of course, Kaja. They aren't for nothing you know. Choud was such a fine young man. He knew everyone admired him, but he was so kind and gentle he didn't know what to do about it. So mostly he just went hunting. With his guy friends, you know." All the women laughed and laughed, as though this was a joke, and Kaja and Regis exchanging a perplexed shrug.

"Oh, but I brought him around. I remember the first time —"

"You can't just skip over that part, Jinn," complained Regis comically, "What did ya do to 'bring him around'? You gotta tell us. You brought it up."

"Oh, Regis, you're so funny. But alright, I'll tell you a little. I used to think about him when he wasn't there," Jinn winked at Morgaine, as though she had said something mysterious.

Regis gaped at Morgaine, then at Kaja, who shrugged again, and back to Jinn. "That's it? You thought about him? I thought about Morgaine for years and she didn't even know my name. How come it works for you and not for us? Come on, Jinn, what did you really do?"

"Regis, Regis, Regis, I do love you, my boy. But I can't tell you. I can't explain it to you. Choud could just see it in me, and I knew he would. That's all."

She paused sheepishly. "Go on, Jinn," Genu said, "Tell us about the first time."

Jinn's face flared brightly for an instant. "Well, pretty soon, I knew he had noticed me, and I saw he was noticing the other girls a little less. So I ignored him completely, in just a way to let him know he was being ignored. It was so funny to watch him from the corner of my eye. He would stare at me openly, and I wouldn't even look in his direction.

"In no time he showed up on my porch with a little bunch of flowers. This giant man with shoulders like a bear standing there with a little bunch of flowers. My mother opened the door, and then shut it behind her, trapping him on the porch with her. She made him stand there and answer her questions for a long time. Obviously, I was spying and listening. He was so nervous he couldn't say two words in a row without saying 'ma'am'. She had a merry old time with him, asking him the most personal questions.

"Then she came back inside and closed the door again. We were giggling so hard we thought for sure he could hear. Then finally I came outside, and I knew—and he knew—in that first look, we both knew that we would grow old together. I'll never forget the expression on his face that day. Never. He and my mother joked about that time on the porch for years and years afterwards." She folded her hands and both Hypp and Trawill reached over to hold them.

"Oh, Jinn, that is such a lovely story," Trawill said. "I do wonder how the flame never died between the two of you. With me and Jooq things were like that at first. Really, they were. But like a dry twig, we burned brightly and then there was nothing left. It just died away, and we were both perfectly aware of it. The most painful thing was to see him go, especially since my girls cried so, but what could we do? He didn't want to be there, he didn't belong with us.

"So cold and strange. He left in the morning, and none of us could believe how clammy and still the house was that night. My daughters and I huddled by the hearth, a cold slippery film seeming to coat every surface. Silence that became louder with every word spoken. It was awful. For so long we had to work against that feeling.

"And you know what's oddest? What I would never have expected? He's traveled through several times since, and each time, we're so glad to see each other. Like good, old friends. It's odd, isn't it? But you know what, it's not his fault. It really isn't. It isn't my fault, either. There's no use in asking why. None at all."

"Do you think you will love again?" Morgaine asked.

"We do!" Hypp said merrily. "See?" she held up the ball made of hers and Jinn's and Trawill's hands. "We love again. In a new way."

"Yes, a new way," Trawill said, smiling, but shy.

"Our own way," Jinn said.

"Father would be real happy to see it, too—I know he would," Regis said.

"Do you think so, son? He would be, wouldn't he?"

"Sure would. You remember what a cad he was. He'd make fun of you morning, noon, and night if he was here. But since he's not, I bet he's wearing that famous smirk in the Spirit World. He never tired of teasing you about the Coven, but you know, that was his way of showing respect."

"He did make awful fun of us, didn't he?"

"Never rested. Amazing man, dad was—everything was funny to him. Especially things like the Coven, and Sekh. And all."

Sekh's name seeped into the room like an odor. Kaja and Genu could smell it, and they knew the others could smell it.

"Your father, Regis, how long since he passed?" Kaja asked.

Regis sighed, checking his mother gently. "He didn't 'pass,' Kaja. I don't think he ever would have died if he'd been left to his own devices. Didn't believe in death. Having too much fun here. But he was a Ringfolk, you know. Probably only reason I'm a Ringfolk is he was a Ringfolk. Ogden loved him. But, oh, about six years ago now, we had some trouble with robbers on the eastern trails. Just some vagabonds raiding traders over the summer. So Sekh gets out his bowls and discovers there's three of them, they live in the forest, blah blah blah. Ogden put together a posse of ten men and sent them out. My dad was with 'em. Turns out there were fifteen robbers, and they lived in the rocks. Ambushed the posse, and my dad took an arrow through his gut. Dragged him here. Managed to live long enough to die by his hearth. That was before my Ringfolk initiation, even, so dad never knew I got it. I tell you, though, I miss the ol' bugger."

Regis' face was red, and he pulled a taught smile through his beard.

Hypp's hand worked within the ball, and her face twitched in a way Kaja had not seen before. His instinct was to leave it at that, but Genu was not afraid. "What of it, Hypp?" she asked.

Hypp tried to speak but couldn't find her first word. Jinn answered for her, "Child, child. There is no divination that can find unknown people in an unknown hiding place. Perhaps you can find one you love, if your love is pure enough, and if you try from there. But to locate three robbers in a certain spot—only an idiot would make such a claim. And Ogden trusts his brother so much, he didn't even think about what he was doing. Didn't even send out spies. It was a travesty. There, there, dear,"

She and Trawill pet Hypp's flowing grey mane. Kaja watched her crying.

Are her tears of sadness? Or rage?

Trapped

The flickering flames in the pillar's sconces fluttered faces before the darkness.

"Alone in the forest but not alone, never alone. With me always first the thought of my family and my people and my town. Always first, and still there was no time, no way to have the grief. But with me always too were the Thurgan, always there. I live with the fear, I live in the very moment, in myself, for to loosen the moment in dream or distraction was a danger that could end my life, yes. And I did not know it then, but I was to live, to come here and to sit with you and admire your Hall and your fine faces. Yes.

"But then in deep fear I lived by the day. I could not make fire, and never once for the time in the forest was I warm. For I could not go out by day, either. Nor set traps. So I learned to hunt at night, in a dishonorable fashion, for there was no sense of honor possible for me then. I stood like the stone or the tree and took small prey from above and ate them raw. Many mushrooms and insects. Like an animal I did live then, for the winter, which was thick with rain and mud and snow. The thing that kept me warm was the thought of killing more Thurgan. I am ashamed to say that to you, but the mustard did not call to me to lie. I would have died there in the winter if I had not taken those Thurgan's lives. It was that alone that let me hold my head to the dawn, let me drink from the waters, and to pray to the trees.

"By the spring I knew the forest around Riversmouth perfect, and had more than one place to stay. I knew best trees for climbing, I knew where the Thurgan went and where did not go. For the forest was not visited as a normal people would visit, no. Not visited or loved or known—not even the children would go. It was fearful to think the people now lived in the town and did not leave, did not go to wander and think. No. As the sprays thickened, I could hide in them for the day, if I could stay perfectly awake, which I did learn to do, though I was hungry. I search for the weak spots, the places I could place myself. There was in me great passion.

"Only the old of the people there had their tattoos complete, and they were beautiful to behold beyond measure. But what could they do? They counseled their young to learn to live with the Thurgan, for they did not see any other way. This power from the outside that came to them entered them in this way. They did not tattoo. They did not go to the trees and sing, they did not paint themselves and dance, they did not sit together and chant. For toys the children had horses made of tied straw, and carts made of clay. They would tie to their head a bundle of grass to look like a horse tail. How could this be? Such a thing. It angered me more, but I was but a boy in a tree. What could I do? My people became the Thurgan, and what could I do? Just to know, nothing more.

"And, too, I watched the Thurgan. What was it they wanted? I remembered my time in the court, and now and then would see one of the Thurgans who would be sometimes there. I wished greatly to shoot them with my bow, but I could not, for surely, I would be caught and killed. To be in their prison for one moment again was unthinkable for me. So I held the tree with my leg and took full aim and held the bow steady and true but did not release the arrow. Not once in that time.

"I thought of my grandfather, a good and kindly man who always told stories about things he had done himself that made him look like a fool. For a wise man will always tell you about what a fool he is. You see then, I am not wise. I tell you my story like I did the right thing, or the only thing. Not wise.

"I watched, too, the ships in the river. Most were rafts. And these with the poles the men would push up the river and would float back down. But I felt true that up the river was more land the Thurgan control. So I did not desire to go there. Instead, I watched the other craft, the ships with reed hulls and sails, that went out to the sea and sailed away from Thurgan land forever. To myself, many times watching the ships upon the waters, I thought that no other escape was possible. But how to get upon a ship? I knew nothing of the art. And the ships, they landed at the same place, where the traders came and went from Riversmouth, and never from any other place.

"So in the spring I took my equipment, which was worn but which still served me well, and moved it to another hiding place, this one nearer the river so I could watch the ships coming and going. I knew there would be more of them as the weather warm, for that is when traders move about, and I thought I might learn of how to get aboard one by watching them.

"And so that was how I spent my days. Up in tree, cold in the wind, watching ships come and go. I learned to see the different ships. And I observed that they always, without fail, went to the port at Riversmouth and to nowhere else. I do not know to this day how the Thurgan Magic worked, that the ships would all go to that one spot. But they did."

Sekh straightened his back abruptly, and many others besides Kaja's shifted to him. He lifted his pipe, and one of the red children brought him an ember. With a slight gesture, he indicated Kaja should continue.

"And then it was the full moon and I thought that I would stay in my tree and watch to see what happened by night, if anything. And it was then that I made a great discovery. For below me, in the deepest part of the night, I heard footsteps. But not Thurgan footsteps, not violent daring footsteps. Footsteps of thieves, like me. Footsteps of people who knew how to move unseen and unheard by any but their fellow ghosts. I watch. I listen. I see nothing, but I follow the sound. In whispers I hear my own language—music to my ears, for so time I had no one to talk to. There are three of them, perhaps four. They move upriver some distance. I listen carefully, but finally they fall out of earshot. I wonder should I follow them? But the danger is too great, so I remain still and unseen. After a long while, but well before dawn, they come back. Still silent, still gliding like a breeze between the trees. This I respect, for only a true thief knows to be the ghost on the way back as well.

"I strain to see, to follow the sound in the forest, but it is too dark. Still, I hear whispers in my own tongue. I believe they are my kin. Back to Riversmouth they travel. Still I do not move. Not until they have passed long away. In the darkness I go to my hiding place, and in the daylight I stay still and silent, not even warm in the sun but cramped beneath a cold rock.

"When the darkness returns I go back, but now I walk where before I heard the sounds. Up a deer path along the water's edge, through thick brush and soft dirt. Still I can see cut and broken branches—a sign that my kin went this way before. I search. Under the trees it is darker even though the moon shines. Under giant banyan I walk in mud. Their branches hang over the water a long way.

"Then I see freedom and hope and happiness. I see ship. Under the branches, a reed ship, an ocean-going ship, is tied.

"I begin to cry, I did. Yes. So joy. For what could it be? My kin were planning to escape. I would escape with them. I had found my way out of that place. So I believed. I did not know it then, I could not know it. But there, too, in the reeds of that ship and in the sacks tied down under tarps and in the hemp ropes and rigging and in the pitch below, even there, was the Thurgan spirit. Even there. It was everywhere in the world. I see that now. It is everywhere in the world, along with the happiness and freedom, it too is there.

"So then, what to do? I do not know. How to make myself known but not to be killed by them? How to ask of them, what do I have to give? I reflect for a short while, then I know, I have quite a lot to give.

"Suddenly, I heard my kin approaching from behind. I do wonder if they heard me cry and exclaim, for they come quickly. In the dark under the great tree I climbed aboard their ship. Then I remember I am wearing head to foot in Thurgan clothes. If they are armed they will kill me on sight. So I call to them, quietly, but clearly, in our own language.

"'Kindred, kindred. Do not be afraid. I am kin of yours. I have killed Thurgan soldiers and am wearing their clothes. I am kin of yours. Come look at me, I am in your ship. Do you hear?'

"'Damage that ship and I'll cut your throat,' one growls, now all of them in a full run through the deep mud. They appear at the edge of the dome of banyan branches. Three of them, all men. They are ragged and exhausted, not sleeping but working always. I can see their eyes shining. They hate me, yes, they hate me through. They would have killed me right then, but none of them had a bow or a spear. Each had a knife in his hand, though. If they could have gotten to me they would have cut me without stopping. But drawn back and ready I held a Thurgan spear, and they could see that one of them would die if they did not treat me with respect. And how could they tell which one? So for moments they stood and see me, and I them.

"'I am kin of yours,' I say again, and they say nothing. 'Take me with you away from here.' I say, 'I have equipment. I can guard your ship in the day.'

"One asks how I found the ship. And so I tell them a little of my story, that my town was destroyed and I was made a slave, but that I escaped and killed Thurgans in the road. I could tell their hearts softened a bit towards me, so I asked them to tell me of themselves something. But they say there is no time, they must put their load into the ship and leave before discovered by dawn. They ask if I would I go get the equipment I say I have for them. I say yes I will.

"But then what happens? They begin to walk through the water toward the ship, their knives still in hand. 'So you will take me with you?' I ask. They grumble. Then the one says, 'You bring us equipment and we will take you.'

"I do not know if to believe him. I fear they will take my equipment and leave without me. 'Then first put your knives away, and I will stash my spear.' This they do, and so do I. It is then I see on the floor of the ship a great hide roll, carefully tied with much line. This I know what it is. So I say, 'You wait there. For I will give you some food and equipment now.' I lower my own pack to the deck, which was most valuable to me. And then I raise up the roll, which I knew was their sail, and sling it over my back. 'And I shall take this to keep it safe for you. When do we depart?' For you see, even without trying, I then think like a Thurgan—how to make the other desperate, but unable to fight.

"The one curses and says if I take the sail he will kill me. I say the sail will be safe, for I am his kin. With the sail I know they cannot leave without me. I tell him he needs me because I have spears to fish and sacks and good skins for water. He will be safer at sea with me along. Not worry. I too want to escape. Then again I ask, when do we depart? Again they grumble together, and a different one says, 'In four nights.' I can see what he wants will be to leave at the time the Thurgans will be drinking, and that the moon will just be rising then, and we will be far at sea before dawn. 'Good, brother. Good. I will leave things in the boat, and in four nights will be here waiting for you again. Now please stay there. I will see you in four nights. Tomorrow when you return, you will see I do not lie. Some of my treasure will be in your boat. I trust you, brother. We depart together. Yes?' As I speak I climb up into the banyan, and disappear with their sail into the forest away from them."

"So then for the next three days I have great hope. I believe I will finally get away from this place. And I keep my word— indeed, I risk everything on these men. I take my weapons, my skins, my bedroll, everything I take to the boat. I sleep in the boat during the day. I study it, seeing how the mast is held up, guessing how rigging work, seeing how oars go. At night I climb into the tree and hide silently while my brothers come and unload their goods. I listen to them, and they speak of me. Who is this man? Where did he come from? How did he get these Thurgan things? They do not want to take me, for they are afraid the boat is not big enough, but I do not hear them plotting to kill me. Though I suspect they might.

"Their sail I have hidden in my closest cave. On third night I bring back, just before dawn, and lie down in the boat to sleep through the day. But I cannot. I watch the light in the trees. I listen to every sound. When the dusk comes, I fill the water skins. I tie them down in the back of the boat. I do good work, for I have spent much time studying the way the boat is made. I wear my heavy Thurgan coat, and I know where my knife is but do not hold it, and I am standing in the boat when they come.

"Without pause they come right up to the boat and climb in, all three of them. 'Good, you have the sail,' they say, 'Good, you have tied things down.' One of them, Uoop, told me that another, Link, was the captain, and that we had to do what he said, for safety. I do not answer that. I say only that I have brought as much equipment as all of them put together. I see they have only one skin for water, and I have brought six. Link and the third man, Rit, are busy with the mast and the line. They lay the mast down over the bow, and lace lines through a ring at its top and other rings attached to the reed hull. The sail, too, which was rolled up, full of lines, they position and tie here and there.

"'We are ready', says Link, 'Rit, Uoop, to the oars. Kaja, get into the banyan and untie the rope.' I do not move. I see now that, even with all I have brought to them, they intend to leave me behind. Rit and Uoop have the long oars over the side, wedged in mud, ready to push the boat out from under the branches and into the current. Again Link says, 'Obey your captain, Kaja. If you want to come, get into the banyan and untie the rope.' When he turns to me he sees I have my long, metal, Thurgan knife in my hand. With this I saw the good heavy rope, and it drops away from the ship. 'You are captain so long as we sail together,' I say. I do not move. Uoop and Rit look at each other. Rit gives a nod, and Link says to go. They push the ship through the branches into the open river. Link scan black water ahead. Rit and Uoop pull the oars to get us to deep. I stand in the back, and they face me. I slide my knife into my boot and watch the way we go.

"I see in the distance a great light on the edge of the river. Our ship moves into the center of current and begins to go very fast. As we approach Riversmouth I see they have lit it on fire. I cannot tell, but I do think the house they kept me in was leaping flames now. Many other houses burning, too, and we hear the screams of the people. The fire and shouts like Thurgan demon made real. Many ships they had lit on fire, too.

"How could three men do this so quickly? I wondered. Indeed, I think back on it now, and that is what I thought. Not feelings for the people burning. No. Only thinking, 'How did they do it?'

"See how much I become Thurgan? For my next thought was then to draw my knife, for when I turned back to shipmates, indeed Link facing me, with fire in his mind. He stop, though. For I was careful to tie the water skins at the back of the boat, and I stood before them. They would drink only if they took me with them.

"Link could see right off that I did not have feelings. Uoop and Rit rowed hard, even in the fast-flowing water, and Riversmouth was soon behind us. Link did know what to do, for he kept us in the center of the deepest current, and we glided past many small islands—some of them where I could see campfires through the trees—and then, into a vast and empty darkness.

"The moon had not yet risen, and the stars were hidden behind a high fog. Link then called, and Uoop and Rit put the oars away, and they three worked on raising the mast and tying it firmly up, and then tying the sail to catch the wind. Now, going even faster, we were swept with the current to the West, and by the wind to the North. I wanted to turn back and see my land for one last time, but I could not. I could not turn away from my shipmates. For even then, just as when I escaped, only deep within me, for a small moment, could I feel free. To live now, I had to make my shipmates fear me. So, too, for only a small moment could I feel sadness, wishing that I did not have to live like this, wishing I with my sister and my mother in my town. For all around me now was cold darkness, empty.

"We sail for another day. Never did the men speak of their plot against me, and never did I pass out a full skin of water. We were together in the ship, but together-in-spirit did not rise among us. For with us we brought the Thurgan Magic, stronger than the words we shared."

Sekh tracked Kaja's story as a fox tracks a shrew, and Kaja knew it. *He missed the moment when he could have found my secret. He missed the moment, and he still does not know he did. He will think I have told my whole story, but I have not.* He hoped he had done as the tree told him he should.

"The morning of the third day, we saw land in the distance, and headed straight for it. What was this place? We wondered. But we did not know. Perhaps fresh water, perhaps fire and warmth. We went forward to it because it was there, not because we hoped to live on and ever be happy. For all we wanted had been stripped from us. At the sight of the land, we did not know why we left. We did not know why we had not burned our lives fighting back against the Thurgan. We knew only that the wind would carry us to shore, and that the current would carry us past the shore. So we plied the sail, worked the oars, and we searched the shore for a good place to land.

"The current fought us for the whole day, but closer we did come. No excitement arose with us. Instead, we spoke of the work, or not at all.

"I do not know what happened to the ship, High Hingemen Sekh, Honorable Ogden. From below, some force hit us, and the ship broke in many places. Into the water we were thrown, I wearing the Thurgan coat with metal sewn in. This I struggled to get off, and my boots too, and when I did, I came up next to a big piece of wood that held the reed hull in shape. This I grabbed hold of, with what strength, I do not know.

"It was afternoon and in the sunlight I saw two of the others way off, struggling to swim and to find something to hold onto. I shouted to them and did try to push my wood to the man closest. Who he was, I could not tell. But the current was too strong, and I could not move the wood against it. I heard him yelling to me, and trying to swim to me, and I saw him go under and not come back up. The other two I did not see die.

"Alone in the ocean then, I held the wood. That is what I remember. For the sea chose to keep me alive, by giving me the wood, and chose to wash me ashore here, on your land, so I could know your kindness.

"That is my story, High Hingemen Sekh, Honorable Ogden. That is all I know. If Magic, there it is."

Deceived

Hypp had taken Kaja aside to explain some customs to him, about courting, about waiting, about marriage. Kaja did not know the sense of it, but he knew that he wanted to obey, so Genu and her family would respect him.

Rain washed the air, and Kaja invited Genu to go romping in it. They ran together in the charged wind, holding hands in the rain. Genu asked simple questions that went deep into Kaja: *What's your favorite song? Where was your favorite place to play? Did you have a special spot when you were little? Wanna see mine?*

He began to feel it was possible to leave his old world behind. He began to feel the awful demon loosen its grip on his heart, and he hoped that Genu could grab hold of it instead. He tried to be with her this afternoon, in this rain, now, and nowhere else. He chased her, and she chased him, and they played.

Dogen and Regis teased him as an equal, as a man—and as nothing other than that. His freakishness faded for them. They did not need to see one just like themselves to see one worthy of praise and admiration and friendship. They needed to see only a noble soul desiring a noble life.

Through Kaja, they saw themselves relative to Ma, and that went deeper than seeing themselves compared to Sekh or to society. Life was good for them, and they took the goodness thoughtfully. To be truly satisfied, one must stoop to the rill and drink steadily of its trickle.

Danger lurked far off in the distance, or so they came to believe.

⟨∿⟩

Kaja walked off one day alone to bow hunt. He wanted a pig. Fat and tender, he wanted to feed it to Genu, to touch her lips and her tongue. True, she had no tattoos. There were no serpents suckling at her breasts, there was no bird flying from her womb, no water flowing around her neck—yet still, she was more beautiful to him than any woman he had ever seen. He walked lightly, holding the bow with an arrow in one hand, his parka and boots protecting him perfectly from the cold rain flying in the wind— rain that he loved to taste and push himself into.

He came around a blind bend near the spot where he first met Genu, a spot that was sacred to him now, a spot where he always gasshoed to no one but Ma—and when he saw the spot, the very spot, in that spot there stood a Thurgan.

Tall and fierce, wearing a heavy black cloak with metal sewn in, wearing a horsetail helmet, his face concealed in a black scarf, his presence a putrid stain upon the Earth. Kaja's eye fell on his enemy one moment, and the next an arrow with the full force of Kaja's spirit flew through the Thurgan's throat.

The demon-man collapsed like a frame of sticks. In an instant, before thought, Kaja had killed again.

He ran. Not back home—how could he? *There are no Thurgan here, only traders, only people like Genu's family, like Dogen's family, who traded for Thurgan clothes because they were heavy and warm. I have killed one of my countrymen.*

He would find no home here, after all. He would not feed dripping meat to Genu. He would not disrobe her on a fire lit bearskin and know her within, he would not have children, he would not have a trade in instruments, no home. He could not live among the fine, the gentle, the honorable in Ash. There was no place in this world for him.

I have failed, Ma. The Thurgan made me. Not my people. Not these people. I am a Thurgan demon.

He ran to the Ring of Trees—for why not? He had nothing to lose now. He charged up the hillside and burst into the Ring— nothing there, nothing more than planted trees. He spun around in the middle of it, dropping to his knees and pounding the ground, screaming in his mother's language, "Why? Why?"

All was lost, again. He ran down the opposite hillside, away to the North, away from home, away from Ash, away from Windhollow, away away away.

❧

Hypp flew up the trail to Sekh's windowless hut and threw open his door. Sekh stood stunned. His woolen nightshirt was stained, and his unbrushed cloak hung limply from his shoulders. He whipped it closed and tied it with a sash of rope.

"Where is he?" Hypp said, ice in her voice.

"How dare you!"

"Where is he?"

"Get out of here."

"Where is he?"

"I told you —"

"I know where your mother's bones are buried." Hypp's presence was steady and dangerous and completely devoid of fear.

Sekh lost his composure. "You would threaten me?" he snarled, and curled his lip in a sneer.

"Your Hingemen Magic will do nothing."

"Perhaps I should teach you."

"One of us shall learn."

"Get out."

"Tell me where he is or I go to your mother's bones."

"You don't understand."

"I will find him, Sekh, and then I will have nothing to lose."

"You will not find him."

"Cast your shrouds, Sekh, poison me. You cannot keep me away."

"I can destroy you with a bowl and a wand."

"You have nothing to use against me."

"What of this?" Sekh reached behind a fold in his wall fur and showed Hypp her staff.

"Thief."

"He is mine. The mustard gave him to me."

"No one belongs to you."

"He defied me! I gave him his chance, and he eluded me!"

"What do you mean? He told you all he knows to tell."

"You are so easily misled, woman. Now, take your weeping ways and get out of my sight."

"Where is he?"

"Woman! Get out!"

"Genu is your cousin's niece."

"Get out!"

"What are you doing to us?"

"He is mine! Mine! Get away before I use force."

"You do not know what force is." Hypp stared at him hard and fierce.

"Your art is but a part of mine. You know not of what you speak. Get away. I shall not harm him."

"So long as you need him."

"And you—what do you need him for?"

"You will never know."

"Get out! Out! Out, now!"

Hypp stepped up to him and held her finger right before his face. "Your mother was a good woman. She never trusted you, and that pains you still. For now, I will leave her bones where they lie. You keep your word. Do not bring him harm. If you lie to me, you will learn from me. Do you understand, Sekh?"

"Mad woman. Get out, for the last time, get out!"

"You would call me mad? You think your mustard brought you Kaja so you could torture him? So you could drive him to his wits end? And what will you accomplish by doing this, Sekh? If you are not mad, explain yourself to me."

"I will not listen to this, Hypp. There are things of which you know nothing. There are reasons for what I do that you could not understand." He spun away from her.

"Your Magic does not contain mine, Sekh. You may have powers here and there. But if you think some great mystery justifies what you are doing, then your understanding is thin and weak. Mark my words Sekh, power without understanding is evil—"

"Enough! I have been patient, Hypp. Your boy-girl tricks are nice. Do not vex me or your Coven shall celebrate under the protection of Talon in arms. Do you understand, woman?"

Hypp stared hard at the wizard's back. He would do it, she knew.

"Now go," he muttered dismissively, "I must tend to my work."

Hypp walked past Sekh and took Kaja's staff from where it leaned. Without a word, she strode through his door, leaving it open. He slammed it at her back.

❧

Morgaine and Genu were at Hypp's house, waiting for her return. Both were worried sick, and Genu had been in tears for over a day.

"I just want him back, to tell him it will be alright," Genu cried.

"He'll return, don't worry. I know he will. He's been through so much—what can you expect? He loves you, Genu, you know he does."

Hypp came through the door and moved into their midst with the presence of a predator. The girls sensed her and watched her spirit without speaking. So angry and insulted, Hypp merely paced back and forth before them, holding Kaja's walking staff but not letting it touch the ground. Her walk became a dance, conjuring the essence of what she felt.

"Sekh," she said, "has him."

Genu's hands went to her face, her heart nearly broken with fear. It was worse. For he was not merely gone away. He was taken away.

"He took him. I don't know how, and I don't know where."

"What else?" Morgaine asked.

"He is a sky worshiper, Morgaine. He insults our Magic."

She wiped her cheeks, though her voice remained steady. "First, he threw us out of our own home, so he could toy with Kaja's mind. Now this. He believes there is some grand reason I cannot understand that justifies it."

Suddenly she shouted, "*Ma! Where is my boy!*" and Kaja's staff flew with such force that it blasted a thick pot on the slanted shelf. Heightened silence followed.

On the floor before Morgaine sat a circle of eight cards, radiating like petals from the ninth in the center. Even Genu, who was sitting right next to her, had not seen her move. Hypp came over, fixated, and sat directly across from her young friend.

Wordlessly, Morgaine began with the card before Hypp. A slender root tip pointed at the Crone, the two baby leaves that begin any plant at the other end. Next, she flipped the opposite card, directly in front of herself, showing the North star at the center of a spiral. Then the two cards at the other cardinal points. To Hypp's left, flowing water off the edges of the card, to her right, a meander extending the length of the card, beginning off one edge and continuing off the other. Hypp said nothing, and Genu studied them intently. Morgaine continued, now with the card between water and the North star. It was a line topped with a bird's head, the ancient symbol for heightened consciousness through holy practice. Opposite this card, Morgaine revealed the Ring of Trees, beautifully painted. Then the card between the meander and the North star, which was of a sacred tree, like the Windhollow Oak. Opposite of it, she revealed the world mountain.

Morgaine trapped the center card and paused. Before she turned it over, she knew what it had to be—and so it was. Ma was seated, with a child at her breast.

"Sekh doesn't want to kill him. Not now," Morgaine said.

"Kaja's to the North, and will have a transformative experience there. He wants to return, but he thinks he can't. That must be the trick Sekh played on him."

"He must be with the hermit," Genu said. She sat up with her disheveled hair sticking to her tear-stained face. The hermit. She wondered if either of them knew.

"Of course," Hypp said, "If he doesn't want to kill him, what better place for him to be? What better place to continue this gross theater, than in Elrik's miserable cave?"

"Why do you suppose Sekh chose the hermit?" Genu asked, staring off into space.

"To prepare him for the Hinge, perhaps," Morgaine said.

"But why the hermit?" Genu insisted.

"Far off, lonely, trustworthy, but insane," ruminated Hypp.

"Indebted to Sekh, no doubt, and deathly afraid of him," added Morgaine.

"The hermit. Elrik. Could Sekh not know?" Genu said quietly.

"Not know what, child?" Hypp asked.

"Yes, what?" Morgaine asked.

"Elrik is my kin."

The two women were shocked. "Surely you are mistaken, child," Hypp said, "Elrik has no kin. No one knows where he came from." She was thoroughly taken aback, for she believed she knew the secrets of the village. How had this escaped discussion in the Coven? It didn't seem possible.

"No, Hypp, he is kin. My great-grandmother's brother. It is not something we speak of, for we do not wish to frighten our townsfolk. Or carry the shame of it. But it is true. He left home as a young man to hunt, and he never returned. Most gave him up for dead, but his mother, my great-great grandmother, did not believe it, and she traveled far and wide until she found him. Living like an animal, in a cave. He has dedicated himself to the path of the plant guides. He eats the mushroom, he smokes the herbs, he brews the tubers. He is never without one of them. And there is nothing else in his life."

"Have you ever met him?"

"No, never."

"And he, you?" Hypp asked.

"They say, the night I was born, in the shadows around the house, there was a presence, a spirit. My great-grandmother believed it was her brother, but she was so pained by his loss, especially in her advanced age, that she often thought he was about to return to her. But he never did."

"What shall we do?" Morgaine asked. "His Magic must be fierce, to have lived this long out there, alone. And Sekh—shall we defy him?"

Hypp thought in silence. "To defy…"

Genu, though, knew what she would do. She interrupted the Crone, "Kaja has lost too much already. He will not lose me."

❮◠❯

Dogen and Regis returned well after dusk, clearly exhausted.

"We went everywhere. Absolutely everywhere. Up the hills, down the hills, into the forest, out of the forest, bushwhacking into ravines, combing through spider webs in caves. Calling for him. He is not in Raven Wood, and he's not in Squirrel Wood, either. I swear to Ma, Mother, he isn't there. Now I'm not saying we won't go again tomorrow. I'm just telling you where he's not. So we'll head out towards Windhollow in the morning and comb through the forests there. Who knows, mighta got lost or something out that way. I worry about him, too, but he can take care of himself, Mother, and he's got that fine equipment—maybe he just needed a little time alone? You can relate to that. Little impolite to just disappear —"

"Regis."

211

"Now I'm serious mother, there's no way we can keep searching now. There's no moon yet. We were stumbling along from Raven Wood, just to get home, and usually, you know, people take a whole day just to get there and back. We got nothing but starlight now, pitch black in the trees. It's not that cold out, Mother, just a little drizzly, nothing a strong man needs to worry about. But of course, if you want I'll get up with the moon and go —"

"Regis."

"Ma's luck, we'll go back out now. I got a feeling about the Living Ring. So just let me first —"

"Regis, you have to go to the hermit Elrik. Genu is going with you. And you, Dogen, will you go, too?"

Dogen and Regis swung to Hypp, and then to the young girl, whose bright blue eyes shone between her flushed cheeks and focused brow.

Hallucinations

Kaja met Elrik in the open, off trail, in a rocky meadow on a blustery hillside above the moor. He wore a tattered coat that had once been fine, and he offered a place to spend the night. *If this is the real world, then why does it keep shifting like a dream before my eyes?*

He had begun to think in the words of what he hoped would be his last language, but his thoughts reverted to his native tongue, incomprehensible to all but himself. He followed Elrik to his tiny, filthy cave. The hermit sat in silence, poking at the embers of dung in his crude stone fire pit. He was in no rush to do anything, for in fact, there was nothing for him to do. Kaja jabbed at the cave's floor with a stick.

Here is a man who managed to create his spot alone, apart, to contemplate rather than live. Here is a man who succeeded in doing what I failed to do for Ma.

"So you have come a long way, hey?" Elrik asked.

"I did not 'come,' but I am here," Kaja said. He also had nothing to do.

"Very good. Very good."

In Elrik's part of the island, there were long moors stretching from rocky hills to the sea. The weather of the ocean blew over them without hindrance, and Elrik's cave faced the sea directly, so the weather blew straight into it. Across its crooked opening was a skin door, poorly made—as was most everything Elrik had—but since the narrow cave, more like a crack, angled back and down, it was possible to get away from the blasts of wind that passed straight through the skins. Elrik ate mostly plants and insects, though he strung nets in the nearby forest to catch birds. He was grotesquely thin and unkempt. His teeth were rotted, his hair long and unwashed, his fingernails caked with dirt and cracked. His coat and boots were once fine, though through disrepair and disregard, they were falling apart.

"You need to see the horizon," Elrik said.

"Do you think I am blind?"

"Do you truly see the horizon? Go look."

"I don't need to go look. I know how the horizon is."

"You walk in this world, do you?"

Kaja glanced at the hermit. He was insane, clearly beyond the boundaries. "You think you know what this world is?"

"Ah! Very good. No, I do not. But I have seen the horizon."

"So have I."

"You have seen where the sky meets the water?"

"You babble."

"You have seen that the sky meets the water?"

"I have seen an ax blade disappear into my mother's back. What have you seen?"

"I have seen my mother cry because of me."

"Then you are evil."

"Everyone cries."

"Then why add to it?"

"What is adding or taking away? Everyone cries, that is all."

"Even you?"

"Oh yes."

"Why live like this?"

"No reason."

Elrik took a handful of ground bark, crumbled leaves and dried mushrooms from a pot, and gave it to Kaja on a slat of wood. "Here, eat."

Kaja was not hungry, but he took the mixture to his nose. The smell was strong and strange. "What is this? I have never smelled it before."

"Eat, eat."

Kaja ate, and so did Elrik.

"Come on," Elrik said, "Let us walk together." Kaja reached for his bow and quiver, but Elrik said, "Not now, Kaja. Let us just walk. You can hunt later, if you want."

Since nothing really mattered anymore, Kaja left the weapon behind. They walked along a thin trail above the cave, following along the top of the lazy ridge of low hills, with the occasional boulder protruding from the rounded earth. At one such boulder, Elrik invited Kaja to sit, and to take in the magnificent view of the moor and the ocean beyond.

Kaja began to feel a strange, quiet, insistent alteration in the flow of his thoughts.

"This is the Magic Mushroom?" he asked Elrik.

"She is beautiful, Kaja, so beautiful. She is with her allies in what you ate. They will come to you. Let them come to you. Lie with them, walk with them, talk with them, see with them. Anything you want."

"And look at the horizon," Kaja said.

"Later, the horizon will appear before you. Some horizon."

Kaja nodded. He could let it come to him now. There was no reason not to. Driven and exiled from everywhere, his remaining abode was the present. Here, at the edge, was a strange peace. There was no more hatred, no more hope. Just a little time to spend before returning to Ma. *I have failed.* He settled in, resigned to that, and the mushroom began to permeate his mind.

The sea charged the air with an aroma he knew well but had never smelled before. The clouds became material—just clouds, not clouds about to rain, or clouds that would not rain. Clouds alone. An approaching ocean wave paused, its sound disappearing, presenting to Kaja a long moment when there was a still, silent wave upon the ocean. The ground, the ocean, the clouds came closer to him, containing him in the space in which he existed at that moment.

He forgot to describe the world and his place to himself. He simply witnessed instead. Twenty pelicans flew together over the waves, and he grunted a single laugh. Then the lines where images met began to radiate rainbow colors, and these became part of the world—somehow, the vision felt so familiar, even though he had never seen it before. Huge undulating lines waved across the sky—once more, a feature of Ma he knew was there, but had never witnessed. Within the distant waves he heard deep clicking sounds. The drug continued to build in his consciousness, and the rainbow lines filled his vision, until he became oddly drowsy.

And there, for the first time since the Thurgan owned him, the darkness that led to sleep did not lead first through the hell realm of his secret. When it came, it was not sleep—a part of him remained alert, fascinated, as though watching the spectacle unfolding in his mind. In the darkness came shapes and flowing lines and patterns of black and red and yellow and orange. They arose endlessly from some churning center, some distant source. Before the kaleidoscopic patterns, a statuette of Ma, like Nana's but glowing green, tumbled from a great distance towards him, forever approaching though never arriving. Yet even as this appeared to him, he wondered cogently if he felt like lying down or not. He decided not to. He held himself erect and watched the hallucinations within his mind. They were not dreams, for no familiar dreamscape coalesced. They created a place, perhaps the Spirit World itself, and the radiating patterns hung in an immense void where he, too, hovered, visiting before his time. How long had he witnessed this before the dazzling hallucinations began to subside? He did not know. Perhaps an eternity. Perhaps an instant.

He found that he was inside his body, seeing the world as though peering at it from within a cave. Inside his body, it smelled like the herbs and bark and mushroom. His mind was no longer only his—now it was his and the mushroom's, as though the mushroom came to life in him, as though it was thrilled to be eaten so it could see through his eyes and hear through his ears. Kaja could see every blade of grass at his feet and every brush of heather in the moor below. He could see every droplet of water, every fold in the foam of the waves. He looked at his own hands, and they appeared huge and magnified. He wanted to walk around and experience the world like this. He stood, and Elrik stood with him. He had momentarily forgotten about Elrik. So he said, in Elrik's language, clearly and effortlessly, "Let's go for a walk."

Elrik merely nodded and led the way farther along the path they had taken. The view from standing was significantly different than it had been sitting down, and Kaja was once again enthralled by it. He saw Elrik in a new light. *Power. Defiance and fortitude, to insist upon this life, to exit society and to enter into this realm, this other world revealed by the mushroom. What did anything matter, other than to witness the world in this way? What a glorious feast was this mushroom—everything drops away, except the aroma and spectacle of the Earth. A pure perception, a perfect perception.*

They wandered farther along the trail, Kaja watching intently. Language began to fill his mind again. He had found a place where he could be. He had found a way that he could continue to live. Since the company of others was denied him, stripped from him by the Thurgan, he could abandon normal consciousness as well. He could abandon the entanglements of life. He could abandon desires—all save one, and that he could fulfill simply by eating the mushroom. He could change the world that he occupied. He resolved to do so. He was a freak already— why not be the freak murderer, the freak repelled by human society, the freak hermit? He followed Elrik. All he needed from this man was to know where to find the mushroom, and the other plants that helped it.

He heard the wind in his ears. The sublimity of it was the silence surrounding the gentle whispers. There was no clatter in his mind. There was no internal discourse. The only distraction was noting no distraction perturbed him. He listened to the wind. He listened to his footfalls. He tasted the air and relished the musty mushroom flavor in his mouth. The ragged hermit picked his way carefully, tapping the Earth with his staff. A bird—did it matter what kind?—landed on the trail before him, and Kaja could see that it was happy. He saw through its little bird eye into bird consciousness—a realm harshly limited in some ways, and in others, completely open to the clear one-ness of Ma and her children. The bird pitched forward, chirped at him as though to welcome him into this new world, and then fluttered away.

Kaja could hear the language of Ma of which Dogen had spoken. Why search any farther? The mushroom was the perfect conduit, most perfectly enjoyed in solitude where the endless distractions and demands of society and other people were irrelevant. All that mattered to him on the trail, slowly advancing to nowhere, was the sight of a flower, or a dragonfly, or the light in the air. Kaja felt happy, happy in a mysterious way unlike any happiness he had ever known. This was a freedom greater even than the freedom he knew for that instant after escaping the Thurgan. A freedom relative only to the panoply of Ma's endless fecundity and creative genius.

This is good, very good.

Elrik led him along the trail. They did not cover great distances but expended much time. The trail revealed beauty upon beauty. They saw the moors from the level of the brush tops. They saw the hills from the lapping ocean. They saw the tide-pool rocks, black and slipping with endless living things grasping them and sliding under them and crawling over them. They saw the distant forests and the golden grasses on the wind-burned, boulder-strewn pastures. They saw the sky from the low meadows behind the first crest of the hills.

The drug faded slowly, or seemed to. At times it felt as though it had passed, but then the sound of an animal in the duff would elevate it again, or the sight of the sailing clouds would transfix him in wordless awe.

His memory opened. For a man accustomed to fearing his memory, to welcome it was, itself, a new experience. The quality of his recollections was immensely heightened. Clear as yesterday, with fragrance and touch fully recalled, he remembered walking with Cinn up a rocky creek bend, picking through the rough stones to find the occasional bit of ore. So much made sense to him now. He felt at peace with his life, understanding, in an inexpressible way, that all was well, all was as it should be, all that had happened added up to something meaningful and proper and appropriate to him. He knew his sister as never before. He could intuit her, he could hold in his mind this sense of knowing her that transcended mere explanation.

And still, through it all, some part of him observed what was happening. Some part of him caught him when he stumbled. Some part of him checked to make sure he had not lost his knife. Some part of him observed the phenomenon opening in his mushroom mind, and wondered at its endless incomprehensibility, framed in the most intimate clarity.

❧

Kaja awoke on the floor of Elrik's cave. He lifted his head from the dirt and found the hermit balled in the crook of the crack, so still as to seem dead. A deep shudder passed through him, and his teeth began to chatter. He wanted to sleep more and deliberated for a moment if he could fall back into the dreamless void from which he had just emerged. He lay his head down to try, but the cold within him would not subside. With great effort, he pulled his feet from the dampness by the door and scooted in the dirt to a sitting position. He reached into a ragged basket by the hearth and drew out handfuls of dry dung which he placed on the weak embers. These released a thick, acrid smoke that filled the cave, one trickle escaping from the top of the crack and wisping into the sky.

Little heat emerged from the fire, and Kaja shifted to sit closer to what it could give. He held his hands over the sputtering flames and tried to force blood into his numb feet. His mind resisted thought. No sublime wordlessness, nor awareness of sublime wordlessness, accompanied his perusal of the filthy cave. There was a pot on the hearth with some water and chopped insects in it. Had it boiled and been stirred, it would have become a nutritious gruel. Kaja dipped a crude clay cup into it and drank it as it was, cold and discrete. The moisture froze his parched throat, and he gagged on the pieces in it. Then he filled the cup again. A shudder passed through him. He tried to breathe, but the smoke in the cave caused him to cough violently.

Elrik's body was little more than a skeleton covered with a once-fine coat strewn with poorly-sewn patches. His abode held nothing more than the equipment needed by one who found his physical existence distracting. Kaja vaguely determined what could be done to make it more tolerable. He thought vaguely about the plans he and Genu had begun to make, plans to create a home in the world among others. Kaja's mind bifurcated. One part wondered why he could not feel the pain, the other part looked to the mushroom for an answer. Not an answer; a respite.

Elrik stirred, and when he rolled over he saw Kaja sitting with the pot of mushrooms in his lap, beginning to eat.

"You wish to go back?" he asked.

Kaja nodded.

"Good, good, that is good. You see now what I do?"

Kaja nodded again.

"It is a difficult path, Kaja, but one you can take."

Kaja's cheeks were wet. *Who is this insane man with a bowl of mushrooms and a dung fire?* But the question did not interest him much. He did not dwell upon it.

He would not "take" this path. This path was the only one left for him. *I have failed, and Ma will see to it that I know I have.* The mushroom was the only beauty possible for him now. And he didn't care. That would do. He would rather be dead, he assumed, but since he could not be dead, he would trod this path to his death.

Elrik came to the hearth and took a cup of the uncooked gruel for himself. He took a skin from a peg on the wall and drank from it, handing it to Kaja after he had finished. Kaja took the skin, which impressed him for a moment as a sign of concern and caring from his demented partner.

"This will help," he said simply.

Kaja sipped and recoiled from the sharp taste that seared his tongue.

"Drink it all. She helps to teach."

"What is it?"

"Another guide."

Kaja drank the rest. He ate a handful of the mushroom mixture while Elrik poked at smoldering dung with a stick.

When the alteration began to arise in his mind again, Kaja put the pot where Elrik could reach it. A defeated peace came over him, and he waited for the hallucinations to arrive. He breathed short, for the dung smoke choked the room. The hallucinations would come first, and then the beautiful state of mind, and then the experience of memory. He waited, expecting the process to repeat itself, expecting the far side of the hallucinations to give him the energy to stand and walk outside.

But something was different. The drug rose in him like a fire howling through a tunnel. His heart began to pound, which had not happened before. It seemed unnatural. It seemed to be an error. He blinked and felt he was falling forward. He jerked back but found he had not moved. The part of him that would observe the drug's effects acknowledged there was nothing he could do about the onrushing experience. It seemed that he was panting, and it seemed that the physical world about him was changing into a hallucination.

He was no longer confident the cave existed. He was no longer confident his feet were cold, or that he was sitting, or that he was breathing, or living. Fear began to rise in him, and the observer part of him tried to combat that but was unsure if it could—or if it was supposed to. The mushroom was a teacher, a ruthless one, and it had its own ideas about what to do with the mind it occupied.

Abruptly and without warning, in place of the dung fire and the sooty floor, an intensely detailed image of one of the Thurgan he had hacked to death leaped forward and took his full attention. The first hack had opened the man's jugular but did not kill him. His eyes flashed open, and his mouth began to move, when the second blow fell, the full weight of the man's own ax splitting his spine. When he yanked the blade out to move on to the next, a great gush of blood spurted across him. The man stared at him as his life expired. The image was so vivid, it was as if he had knelt over the man to relish every detail of his violent death. And there were no words to understand it, no interpretation, no justification, no explanation, no forgiveness—just the fact, and blood dripping from his brow and jaw.

He launched himself into one wall and crashed into the other. He tried to scream, he tried to shake the memory from his vision, but he could not. He could see the cave and the man's death throes at the same time. He staggered to the skin door, his feet blocks of stone, and collapsed through it to stumble until he fell into dirt and sprouts of grass. White stones gleamed so brilliantly they seared him, and Kaja clutched his face with his hands, rolling over on his stomach to find darkness in the ground. Still the man's face was there, but now the blood no longer flowed, and a vulture ate his eye.

Kaja managed to emit a low scream at this, and he stumbled to his feet only to collapse onto his buttocks, where he sat on the damp ground, his clothing bunched and twisted. The mushroom wanted to know him, and it had no sense of propriety. It explored his mind as an insect explores a carcass, without revulsion or regard. What Kaja experienced because of it was pure and uninterpreted.

Dread gripped him.

No, not that…

But the moment he begged himself not to remember his secret, not to review the Magic Sekh wanted, it began to play in his mind.

No, stop…

It was not a memory; he was there. It became his world. He could smell it. He could see it. He buried his face in his hands, and that made it worse. The memory proceeded slowly, meanly, as though to be as ugly as it possibly could be. So much worse than killing. So much worse than killing could ever be.

He slammed his head against the ground. The taste of blood on his teeth made the smells and sounds more acute.

Without a single detail omitted, his secret passed through his mind. He heard himself screaming. He felt himself flinging his body. It did not stop.

※

Elrik leaned in the opening of his cave, watching Kaja dispassionately. It was beginning to work. The drugs would open the freak from afar. The drugs would bring him the secret Sekh wanted. It was only a matter of time.

He filled a pouch with more of his mixture, and a sack with more of his brew. Kneeling to place a hand on Kaja's shoulder, he suggested that they walk a short distance, to a spot where they could sit out of the wind.

Defiance

Genu was unaccustomed to acting outside of what was proper and expected. When she told her parents where she was going, they were afraid for her. When she finished the whole story, including how they intended to un-do Sekh's plans, the context of their fear shifted from the untrammeled Northern wilderness to the fierce and starless wilderness within.

Their daughter had fallen in love with a strange and powerful man—a man who commanded the attention of High Hingemen Sekh. A man who should have died a dozen times but did not. That this noble spirit from far away loved her in return confirmed a deep intuition they had had about her since she was small—namely, that she was a strange and powerful person in her own right.

They had hoped her nature would manifest itself in some benign and simple way—since they were simple folk and pleased with that—but her path had led, inexorably, to extreme wanderings of the soul. She trekked an endless beach of solitude, contemplating the vast ocean, deep with the mysteries of life, while passing all the paths inland, towards other people. There was nothing they could do to change her, and, wisely, they made no attempt.

She had met this boy Kaja on that lonely beach, and so, solemnly, her father gave her his hunting amulet, and her mother blessed the hearth Ma with a shower of ashes. Genu kissed them, hefted her pack, and left.

When she arrived at Hypp's house, Regis was saying, "I still think we oughta told Ogden what we were going to do. I mean, he's a reasonable guy, and it's pretty clear to me that Sekh has lost his mind over Kaja. The daffy old fart told us himself that he was running all over the place yelling at a flower. I mean, when you think about it, even a wizard's gotta have some sense, sometimes. If Ogden knew what we were doing, I'd sure feel a lot more comfortable about it."

"He would have told us not to go, and he would have told us to let Sekh do his work. How would that make you feel?" Dogen didn't look at his friend. His anger at Sekh smoldered in his heart. So did pride at the way Ash's finest had asked him him to help, when their wizard had lost his way.

"Yeah, you're right. Then we'd be in direct defiance, instead of going to collect our tattooed brother from a loon. But then again, if we'd told Ogden, maybe we'd know where we were going. 'North' is not really the sort of directions a guy needs when he's trying to find a hermit living in a cave. And while traveling through a storm." He checked Genu, who was holding Kaja's staff as though mesmerized.

"You're sure you never saw him before? Never once, in all the travels you've made?" Dogen asked.

"Well you know how it goes. I don't make any attempt to be secretive, and Ma knows it's not too hard to see me from a distance. Everywhere I go, people tell me about mysterious hermits living in the wilderness—if you believed the folk, there's more hermits out there than goats. Anyway, I never saw one of them, nor a cave of one."

"He can see the ocean," Genu said.

"Then again I usually stick to the trails, which get mighty thin if you're just on some herder's path. I mean the main trails you can almost socialize on them when the weather's warm, there's so many folk coming and going. But the herder's trails can be desolate, especially in the rain like this. Don't usually travel out too far in the rain, but I do occasionally, especially if the Yuffs or some folk are late or if they sent a few ahead to town and they're worrying. You know, can make a world of difference to them if I just go off to meet their people coming into town. In fact one time— what do you mean, he can see the ocean?" Regis landed his attention on Genu, and so did Dogen.

"Kaja can see the ocean," Genu said, "He can see the horizon, and it is the ocean."

"You can tell?" Dogen asked.

"Did Hypp take this staff into the Coven with her?" Genu asked.

"Yes."

"I can tell." She examined Kaja's staff thoughtfully. When Hypp threw it, the pot that burst gouged out a groove rounding the top. They had replaced it with a hard pitch that they dyed a radiant blue. It purposefully disrupted the artful oiling on the knob of the staff, acting as a physical testament to the moment of Hypp's question. Genu rubbed the blue and twitched her nose near the loop of leather. It smelled like Kaja's hand.

"So, how can you tell?" Dogen asked again.

Genu arrested him. "What separates you from this world, Dogen?"

He was thrown. He perceived the essence of something he had yet to understand, nodded to her, and said nothing.

"That's enough deep stuff for now. So, Kaja can see the ocean. That gives a much more precise meaning to the word 'north.' Now we have, north, by the sea. Excellent. On the bright side, now the sleet from the storm will get to us while it's still fresh. Nothing worse than stale sleet that's been losing force blowing across the ground. Better to get bit by it when it's good and fast and happy. Don't you think?"

⟨∧⟩

Elrik and Kaja had begun to work together on certain things, such as the cold tea they drank when they roused from the mushroom, which allowed for rest before eating more. They pooled the dung and scraps of wood they gathered for Elrik's crude hearth, which filled the little cave with foul curls that took the shape of demons.

Over time, the visions within the darkness of Kaja's torment were followed with other piercing memories that were more vivid than hallucinations, and more pure than daydreams. He would catch a glimpse of Cinn's reaction when he answered a question correctly about some obscure geological fact known only to miners. He would go back and actually be with his people's Elders in the house at the Spring Rites, feeling the fun-filled fear of a child enthralled by a puppet show, diving with his friends under the blankets to peer out, like a fawn watching a lion, at the evil monster puppet threatening to eat the baby bird puppet. Then the violence of his loss, and the ghosts of the people he had been with, would sear his mind, and he would take refuge in the dirt and sky around him.

Memories of Genu were the worst. They were thin sacks of blood, hanging from his heart, and when he thought of her, they burst, and sloshed their hot sadness through his guts. They were the slow, miserable, and certain death of his soul, one impossible kiss at a time. He no longer had any use for sanity or propriety.

Elrik grinned. He found the process fascinating, and went through it himself, over and over again. Nothing could rush it, nothing could hinder it. Always, it would happen. And now, it was happening to Kaja. He was certain he would learn Kaja's secret. He would soon know who Kaja truly was. He would soon know how Kaja truly came to them, and he would know the dark, powerful, incredible Magic of the Thurgan.

He watched the young freak, who was now braced on all fours, trembling and weeping. He smiled to himself and tried to suck the aroma of his drugs into his soul, to become them. He had done his work. He had succeeded.

Or, almost. He would succeed. He could tell that now. Sekh would be pleased. He would get the reward promised to him. Twenty skins of strong mead. New clothes. And a nubile Nok slave, all his own, for seven days. Just for Kaja's secret. He practiced posing his face, to appear weird, or sage, or ancient, or spiritual, and stirred his drugs.

❧

Genu was relentless. She fed upon something unseen, and the men could barely keep up. Walking so erect and striding so gracefully, she wasted not an ounce of energy. Her mind did not wander, and neither did her gaze.

Dogen and, finally, even Regis, gave up talking altogether. All they could do was follow her. She did not search the ground for paths—she scanned the rocks for caves, and then headed for them. When darkness came, she lay down on her bedroll and with few words and no ceremony she would eat and immediately pass into a deep motionless slumber. At first light she arose again, and with a word awoke her comrades and began her search, her thumb rubbing the blue repair on Kaja's walking staff.

The rain fell steadily, and the leaden clouds progressed northward in a giant arc across the sky. The sea was blown high, and gigantic, irregularly shaped waves slammed meanly onto the shore, their booming sound sweeping through them like wet wind through a net. On occasion a bird would chirp in the underbrush, or an osprey would appear, hovering over the waves. Otherwise, they saw no animal life.

Genu examined the piling hills. No detail escaped her. And then, suddenly, she stood frozen, focused intently on a rock formation. Dogen followed her gaze as Regis huffed his way up to them.

"What is it?" Dogen asked.

"There," she said, pointing with the knob of Kaja's staff.

"Ma's mood. More rocks. You see that, Dogen?" Regis said, bent with his hands on his knees and puffing at the ground.

"Smoke?" Dogen said.

"I think so."

"What?" Regis said.

"Look."

"Hard to tell in the rain."

"Could be though," Dogen said.

"Lets go," Regis said.

But Genu was already pressing herself through the brush. Indeed, black smoke seeped out from the point of a cave opening, to be sucked by the storm into the slithering sky. She dropped her pack and went faster.

"Maybe it's time you talk a little, Kaja," Elrik said,

"Sometimes the guides can show too much all at once. Can you talk?"

For a long time Kaja did not move or respond. Finally, he shook his head. He did not want to talk. Putting it into words would accomplish nothing. The work he was doing inside, with the mushroom—that was what he needed. Elrik, he did not need. He managed to stand, steadying himself against the wall of the cave as the now familiar falling-forward sensation disbursed into the sound of his breath. He reached for his parka.

"Don't go out, Kaja. You will get cold and not know it. And when you come back in, the cave will chill because of you and we will have to wait for it to warm. Sit."

Kaja ignored him totally and struggled to get his parka over his head without letting go of the cave wall. When his head popped through the top, he bent his attention to the first sleeve, and then the other. Carefully, he walked to the skins and slid through the edge, kicking the stone weight back into place as the first blast of clear air filled him.

He heard someone call his name, but only noted how much it sounded like it did not come from within his mind. He took a step away from the support of the rock, and breathed consciousness back into himself. He looked to the horizon. Deep gray clouds flowed up and over the edge of the black ocean, and huge droplets splattered against his face. Again he heard his name, and his head jerked toward the sound. He saw Genu walking up

the hillside towards him. To see her once again, even in fantasy—
he welcomed it. Soon, he would eat some more. Now, he would
watch Genu. And Regis, and Dogen, farther off in the distance.
He expected them to come as his mother had, as Cinn had, and as
his sister Nana had —intense visions, to gaze at him sagely. He
expected them to become another apparition that would soon
morph into something else.

Strangely, the vision of Genu continued to approach, too
accurately proportioned for the mushroom. And, she was not
changing. If his attention strayed from her, his wandering thoughts
did not cause her to vanish.

*How strange! Could this be one of the "allies" Elrik had
spoken of? One of the strange, mystical beings who can only be
seen with the gift of the mushroom? Perhaps they have come to
show me the way to the Spirit World.*

He took a step towards her, and again, she called his name.
He could see her, drenched and dirty from hard rain and hard
travel. Her face was tear stained, and she called his name again.
He gasshoed to the ally. Still she approached. He took a lurching
step towards her, just as she freed herself from the brush and ran to
him. She seemed so real.

When he felt her arms around him, and smelled her hair,
and felt the squirms of her body against his—he held her, and it
was as if she was really there. *Take me now, Ma. Let my last
moment here be holding her.*

"Kaja, oh, Kaja," Genu said. "Shhhhh, Kaja. Shhhh. Don't
say anything. It's really me." She stroked his hair and his cheeks
and pulled him into her arms again. "Dogen and Regis are coming.
We're going to take you home."

"They will kill me," Kaja said.

"Shhhhh, Kaja, no. It's us. We have you now. No one will kill you."

She felt how thin he was. She stroked his dirty dreadlocks, full of duff and filth, and combed them with her fingers, and washed them with rain. She could feel the strength the plant guides had given him, and the strength they had taken away.

"Kaja! Ol' boy! Lovely weather we're having, hey?" Kaja looked up at Regis, dumbfounded and blank, and the red bearded Ringfolk could see what had happened to him, too.

"Kaja, thank Ma you're alright," Dogen said. He held Kaja's face in his hands. "Kaja, Kaja, it's really me, my friend. We're going to take you home. Come here, Kaja, come here."

Dogen embraced him, and Kaja held onto him the way he held onto the wood in the sea.

"Think I'll go have a word with Elrik," Regis said.

"I'll go with you." Genu said.

Dogen stayed with Kaja, rocking him.

A few steps away, Regis drew his copper saber, and Genu drew her stout flint knife.

⟨∿⟩

"Get out of here!" Elrik screeched as Regis entered his cave.

For a large man, Regis was unusually nimble, and without touching Elrik, he rose the hermit to his feet and pinned him against the back of the cave, his saber at arm's length, its point at his throat.

"Not a problem, Elrik. We'll leave in just a minute," he said. Genu quickly searched the pots in the cave and found the one holding his hallucinogenic mixture. She stood by the fire where Elrik could see her.

"No no no no no no no!" Elrik screeched, clearly twisted by his fear, and by the fact Genu had just tossed a handful of his drug into the fire.

"Will you listen, uncle?" Genu said.

"No no no no, please, no, I beg you, no…"

Genu tossed in another handful. "Will you listen? *Uncle,*" she said again, hitting him with the word as though wielding a club. She held the next handful over the weak flames.

"What do you want! He came to me!"

"I don't believe you, uncle," she dropped the handful, and it sputtered before flaming. She held more over the fire.

"What do you want? Who are you? Why are you here?"

"I am your niece, Elrik. Didn't you know?"

"Leave me alone, I haven't done anything. Let me go." Elrik began to cry, and so crippled was he by his way of being, he was more than pathetic—it was dangerously pathetic.

Regis did not flinch, and showed him no mercy, whatsoever, so the hermit had to stay on his feet. Regis understood people well, and he knew how they worked. As usual, his understanding was functionally efficacious. Elrik calmed himself, and though he was still clearly in the midst of his drug, he managed to look at Regis. Regis stared back coldly, and Elrik realized that he had just tried his only hope for pity and lost it.

"Will you listen, uncle?" Genu asked again. She hardened herself to the sight of him. He was her own kin, dressed in rags, filthy, trembling and drooling at Regis with red-rimmed, bulging eyes.

"Yes."

"Very good. Did you know that the only thing your sister wanted for the last years of her life was to be with you, if only for a little while?"

"No—YES!" he screamed, but the drug had already fallen, and flamed, and more were in Genu's hand.

"You came to her, but then did not make your presence known."

"Yes."

"She died without her brother's love."

"Yes."

"Did Sekh come to you, or did Bwain?"

"Both."

"And you went and got Kaja?"

"Yes."

"Why does Kaja think the townsfolk will kill him?"

"Kaja thinks he killed a man wearing Thurgan clothes."

Genu considered this. It was probably true, even though she couldn't imagine how Sekh might have done it. She didn't drop the drug. "What does Sekh want you to do with Kaja?"

"Learn his secret."

"What is Kaja's secret?"

"I don't know." Genu let a pause pass. Elrik screamed, *"I swear to Ma I don't know!"* The folds of his face and his long, wet lips slid around the tip of Regis' saber like an octopus squirming upon a rock.

Genu did not drop the drug. She waited, and Elrik quickly realized that he had to provide details, or she would.

"Just today," he panted, "he was going to tell me, but you came before he could. Please believe me, oh please, oh please, please, no more, please...."

With a slight motion Regis caused Elrik to raise his head higher and pay attention.

"Would you like us to leave you here, Elrik, so you can continue your practice?" Genu asked.

"Yes."

"Well, we will. But you must make a promise. Will you do that?"

"Yes."

"What is my name, Elrik?"

Elrik scanned the cave, desperately searching his memory, snapping to the drug in Genu's hand, over and over. He was drenched in sweat and was beginning to shake uncontrollably. "Genu," he said at last.

"What is this Ringfolk's name?"

"I don't know."

"When you speak with Sekh or Bwain, Uncle Elrik, tell them that you found out what Kaja's secret was. Tell them you succeeded. You found out that Kaja came to us to bring a sound. That is Kaja's secret, Elrik. He came to us to bring a sound. Can you remember that, Uncle Elrik?"

"Yes."

"What is Kaja's secret?"

"He came to us to bring a sound."

"Again."

"He came to us to bring a sound."

"Very good. What do you think will happen to you if you do not tell them this?"

"You will kill me."

"Oh, no, uncle. Never that. We will come and bring you home."

Genu put the handful back into the pot, dramatically and slowly, so Elrik could see. She set the pot on the ground and left.

Regis did not move. When Elrik was alone with him, he flushed white, and a thin trail of foul urine ran down his leg.

"Again," Regis said.

"Kaja came to us to bring a sound."

Slowly, Regis lowered his saber. Without backing up, he slid it into its leather scabbard. As he did so, he held Elrik frozen with his gaze alone. He watched his writhing face and bloodshot eyes. When they flashed, Regis knew that Elrik understood he had harmed his friend, and that he would never be trusted.

"Remember me, Uncle Elrik," Regis said. He backed away calmly. "Remember me."

Elrik slid to the floor and sat in his piss.

Rebels

Dogen knocked on Charlene's wall just before the first blush of dawn, whispered to the witches within, and then disappeared. They waited for his return with giddy anticipation, and when his next knock came, Charlene heard her great-grandmother's gong calling celebrants to the Ring. "Dogen! Is he with you?"

"Yes." His legs were worn, having made it to Windhollow, back to his friends on the trail, and now to Windhollow again. As they returned from Elrik's altered space, they had revived Kaja, but he had slowed their progress through the long distance and freezing rains.

Now that they had succeeded in getting him out of Sekh's dominion and to the secret safety of Charlene's home, they could feel only relief. Worrying about how the wizard would respond could wait. When they stood in her warm, fur-lined home, Kaja could not remember ever feeling so accepted. The travelers poled their parkas and propped their boots before sagging against the walls, exhausted and happy.

"Hypp will be so jealous that I have you," the tiny witch whispered. "At dawn, I'll send messengers to her."

They tucked the felt blankets Charlene gave them around their aching feet, and gratefully ate the bread, jerky and berries she provided.

As Kaja revived from Poppy's drugs, he found himself enthralled before a vivid world, observing everything as though it was brand new. Charlene's home was the civilized opposite of the hermit's cave. Every detail thrilled him. Ma sat peacefully upon the hearth, and he saw every paintbrush stroke enlivening her contemplative smile, and each golden anther on the flowers set at her feet. He was moved to aesthetic rapture by steam rising from the mint tea in her pot, and by the yellow tower of wound fabric knotted atop her head.

Her glowing amber home let them wander to the solace of sleep. As they drifted off, one by one, they drew ever more closely together. The tiny Crone's magical presence was murmuring water, to the rhythm of little ticks she made while tending her cookware and studying her Tarot.

Sekh does not know we are here. And there is no place I would rather be hidden. He slept with Genu in his arms.

⟨∿⟩

In Ash the next night, Hypp invited Charlene's messengers to sit with her and her Coven in the Hall. They were arranged in an egg-shaped line around the fire and the two pillars, and they sang Ringsongs beneath the illusion of stars:

> *Yesterday's mind*
> *makes life today*
> *Wind blow hither*
> *wind blow away*
> *Life tomorrow*
> *the flower of today*
> *Stars round the center*
> *pirouette and play*
> *Life not found*
> *but of blossoms made*

Then Hypp rose, and began to walk before her sisters, embraced by their presence. Once, twice, she did not speak. Her Coven loved her, and let their silence lift her.

"The Ring of Trees that Kaja saw," she began, "by the trail to Windhollow. It is one of ours. And yet, even that I should say this, shows you what has become of us. How could a Ring 'belong' to anyone? The Ring of Trees is alive. It reaches into the ground, holds her, knows her. Our grandmother's bones are buried there. The bones of our children are with them.

"And yet, if the day is not designated, we must steal away to it, should we wish to visit it. Our grandmothers ate picnics there. Chased butterflies. Made love. And we must wait for a designated day. Assigned to us by the Hingemen. To sing Ringsongs to our own trees, in our own Ring. And our Ring is considered a weak Ring, an old Ring, a primitive Ring.

"We are to believe the Hingemen's Knowledge is greater than ours. Sekh's giant, dead Hinge. A Hinge of stars. No roots in the ground. And they trust it and believe it.

"How did this come to pass? That is the question I ask. How did this come to pass...? And what is passing now, that will mystify our daughters? What will our daughters say of what we do today?

"Sekh says Kaja is his. Those were his words. He believes the mustard gave Kaja to him. He believes Kaja holds some secret he needs, some Magic. He will not release Kaja from these tortures until he has Kaja's secret."

Hypp kept walking in slow circles. Her Coven sisters listened and contemplated the fire.

"But Kaja has no such secret. He is not Sekh's. He is one of us. His home is the Ring of Trees.

"Sekh tricked him. Made him think he killed a countryman wearing Thurgan clothes. Kaja ran away. Sekh did this even knowing that I love Kaja, Dogen loves him, Regis loves him, Morgaine of Windhollow loves him. Worse, he did it knowing his own niece loves him, Genu, who loves him as her life mate. Still, he caused this evil theater. He hoped this would crack Kaja open and make this secret spill out.

"But it did not. And I am indebted to you for that, for the walking staff we consecrated here went with Genu and Regis and Dogen as they searched for our beloved, gifted son. And Genu used it well. Found him, with her long-lost uncle, and brought him back.

"Ah yes. Elrik is Genu's kin. I did not know it either. Now we all know it. And one of you may slip and speak of it, and soon, Sekh will know too.

"What am I to do? For I have threatened the High Hingemen, and I have undone his plans, and I have the boy he believes is his. What shall I do? We do. I beseech you, what shall we do?" She circled back to her place and sat down.

The silence continued for a while.

Then, Trawill said, "I have an idea..."

❧

"That vile bitch!" screeched Sekh, hurling his clay cup. It burst to shards on impact.

Ogden leaned against a lantern post and waited—he had seen his brother lose his composure before. Bwain, though, was unable to adapt to it, and he stood wide-eyed near Ogden.

"Bitch!" Sekh screamed again. "She ruined it! It was perfect! Perfect! He had no way out! The drugs worked into him! Now he is gone! Our best chance! Vile bitch! I shall forbid Genu to see him again. I shall forbid Hypp from even passing the Hall, much less entering it. Where is that freak!" he screeched, advancing on Bwain as though to choke him.

"I—I—I don't know, High Hingemen, I told you."

"You followed them all the way to Elrik's cave, talked to the imbecile after they left, and that's all you know?"

"They found him, somehow, but he had already told the secret."

"And it didn't occur to you to ask any additional questions?" Sekh glared at him with contempt.

Bwain stammered and his toes curled. "I—I thought you should know right away."

"Ah!" Sekh exclaimed, throwing up a hand, "Go prepare the bowls. Perhaps we can divine more later." He spun from the boy and muttered, "A sound. What crap."

Bwain flushed, and with a quick glance to Ogden, ran from the room.

"Sekh, get control of yourself," Ogden said. "When was the last time you tried to talk with Elrik?"

"I know, I know, he's insane. I'm sure Bwain did the best he could. Should have sent Bal with him."

"Well, you're going to have to go to Hypp now. What are you going to say? This has to make sense, Sekh. If it's just fear, it will turn on you. They'll dance around behind your back, and soon you'll have no influence. Whatever it is you're trying to get, whatever Magic it is you and Tiss' spirit are after, you have to make sense. No more of this thuggishness. Kaja is yours, granted. But Hypp and Genu love him, and he has good friends. You have to use that, Sekh. You're working against it, and it's getting you nowhere."

Sekh scowled while Ogden scratched his neck thoughtfully. He wasn't sure what was going on. Sekh's careful, premeditated behavior seemed to be loosening. He perceived an element of disorder and decay but did not have confidence in his own ability to understand. Sekh had incredible powers—did he not predict the blood moon?—and he was reluctant to question his methods. Still… "Sekh, you will have to…"

"Alright, alright. I'll get her to help me. Somehow."

"You know what she wants."

Sekh's head jerked. "Surely you jest, Ogden. You would consider letting this freak live here? You expect me to let him have our niece? You want his blood in our line? Come on now."

"Genu's mother is our cousin. Her children would hardly be 'in our line'. Besides, there's Quinn."

"Still."

"Still what? Hold it out as a possibility. Gain Hypp's trust. When you get your secret, we'll send him out as a scout for the attack on the Nok. Tell him he'll be initiated and married when he comes back. When the Nok see him, he'll die a hero, he'll plant no seed, and we'll make a song out of him." Ogden watched Sekh closely. He seemed cowed.

"Sounds easy, but I'm the one who has to talk to Hypp," he muttered as he lifted a crimson cloth with a golden sun embroidered upon it to unfold a bundle of long wing bones and dried herbs on his workbench.

"Come now, Sekh. Her sweet little tunes about thoughts and trees? Lift your eyes. Your Magic must be far stronger than hers. I have confidence." He stood to leave, and then glanced over his shoulder. "Shouldn't I?"

⟨∿⟩

The Crones conferred one last time, standing in Hypp's house. Trawill did not direct much, but when she did, it mattered.

"Trawill, you found the medicine in the bark," Hypp said, taking her friend's hands in hers. "We shall celebrate in our own way if this works."

"That, we will," Jinn said, adjusting her bright yellow scarf, and tidying the deep yellow wind about Trawill's head. "Ma be with you."

She and Trawill made a long, elaborate show of leaving Hypp's house, making sure they were seen. Hypp closed the door behind them and steeled herself.

It did not take long. As soon as she was alone, there came a pounding on the door. Sekh stood between the angrily glaring Hingemen, Phiop and Krev. She was far more concerned with what was going on in Sekh's mind than she was about the weapons his men carried, or the malicious pause that he forced her to endure.

Without asking to be welcomed, he came through her door. She backed away, and made a calculated, fearful glance at the Hingemen. She shut them outside and faced Sekh alone.

"So Sekh, now you have come to me," she said.

The wizard threw back his hood. His thin white hair hung in tendrils to his long beard, so his ashen face floated in a plume of

249

smoke. He ignored what she said completely. "You would dare to defy me?"

"We did not know you caused him to run until after we had found him."

"You are so ignorant, Hypp. Do you think he would just randomly run away? You, of all the women in the Coven, should have known that I was behind it. You should have seen that great Magic was being practiced."

"Tormenting him is magic?"

"Testing him. You would not understand."

"Then, drugs are the extent of your 'Magic?'"

"Who are you to judge my methods? Enough of this. I am here to give you a choice." He rounded on her slightly, and Hypp appeared to shudder, even as she tracked him.

"Obviously, you do not understand the situation. Let me enlighten you."

"Kaja is just…"

"Enough, I said! Kaja is not 'just' anything. Do you know what the Hingemen think of him? The Talon? No. You do not. Everyone believes that he is a bad omen. He shows up, and the Nok become belligerent. They all make the connection."

"Of course, they do. You saw to that the first time you brought him to the Hall."

"And you think it's just a matter of me plotting. How could you be so daft? The flowers warned us that he would arrive, and that bad times would follow, as they did."

"Magic cannot divine such things."

"Mine can."

Hypp reared before she could stop herself. "Yours least of all, Sekh. You should know that by now."

"And this on your authority? Bah, don't be a silly woman. Three things happened in a tight series: flowers, Kaja, Nok. They must be connected. That's why they were discussed in the same gathering. Everyone made the obvious connection, except you."

Hypp realized that she needed to back down and to appear subdued, or she would fail. She said, "I have not heard these rumors."

"Of course, you haven't. You don't listen, for one thing. And for another, you protect Kaja like a wolf protects her cubs. No one would say such a thing to your face."

Hypp dropped her gaze.

"The Hingemen and Talon will never accept him as one of us because they don't know his family. On some level, even you must be able to comprehend this. Can you name a single person here whose family we can't trace for generations?"

"No…"

"And Kaja just washed ashore one day, or so it seems. He is no one, and he will always be no one."

"But…"

"But what? That is the situation. And now that he has disappeared, any Talon who sees him will kill him."

"Why? What has he done?"

"They make another obvious connection that is apparently beyond you. He brought the Nok to the Yuffs and put us in danger. So then. What other evil can he bring into our lives? Why wait to find out? Just kill him and be done with it."

Hypp pretended to dart around nervously. "You said, I have a choice?"

"Yes, you do. Right now, I am the only person in the realm who can save him. He lives only if I protect him."

Hypp appealed to him with trembling lips, trying to appear powerless. "What do you want?"

Sekh sneered and relished his moment of ascendance. "Either Kaja comes back to Ash to face me, alone, or he is killed."

"If he comes back, what happens to him?"

"I will tell you only this: he will be tested."

"He has already done his Spirit Walk."

"To the Hingemen and Talon, that might have proved he is not a boy. Now he must prove he is a man. It is the only possible way for him to live among us. I will give him one chance."

"What is this test?"

"I will not tell you, nor will anyone else. I have had enough of your meddling. He will complete this mission alone."

Trawill had foreseen that Kaja's only path to survival began with doing what Sekh demanded. Trawill's trick was to buy time by making him feel as if he was directing events.

"If he succeeds, you will initiate him, and let him live in peace?" She dropped her head, hoping that would be submissive enough.

The wizard's beard was beaded with spittle, and his face curled with distaste. "If he cooperates, and if he succeeds, then yes."

"Do I have your word?"

"My word? I would not deign to speak to you twice. You cannot hide him forever. Deal with me now, and he may be initiated. Defy me now, and he will be captured and brought to me. I will force Knowledge from him, and then throw him back into the sea, tied hand and foot."

Hypp watched Sekh quivering with rage and desire. His willingness to kill revolted her. His thirst for some kind of victory over Kaja washed any remaining humanity from his withered heart. There was no opening in him for further discussion, and no possibility for any thoughts other than the ones already throbbing in his mind. Hypp realized she had to make her choice now or lose it. "Very well, Sekh. I will bring Kaja to you."

"You will bring Kaja to your home. We will come get him when it pleases us."

"As you wish."

"I am not going to ask you for your word, Hypp, because I know, when it comes to Kaja, your word is worthless. Instead, give me your Tarot deck. If I get my secret, then I will return it to you."

Hypp felt triumph inwardly but managed to seem mortified. Trawill had foreseen this as well. Sekh could not return to Bwain and Ogden with words alone. He had to take something Magical from her. That was the way his mind worked.

She knew that Sekh would try to use her Tarot to divine what she was thinking, and what she was doing. And so, she could not risk giving him a living deck. She could not put Ma's Magic into a Hingemen's hands.

So, appearing sad and reflective, she sat on an otter-skin cushion before her low table. Slowly, she removed her Tarot from her cloak, and unwrapped it. Her grandmother had made it and had given it to her when she was just a girl. For decades, it had always been with her, next to her body. It had cured sickness of the mind, and had helped people through trepidation, and had alleviated their fears, and satisfied their longings.

Yet the deck was only a stack of painted and carved leathers. When her grandmother gave it to her, on the Full Moon, in the Living Ring, laced round with colored cloth and garlands, she said simply, "Serve others, serve love, serve Ma."

And so she would.

Slowly, as though contemplating the gravity of what she was doing, she unwrapped the deck. Sekh inflated triumphantly, fooled into feeling lordly since he towered over her and her Magic.

She looked up at him, as though fearful of putting such power into his hands. She set the deck on the table face up, and fanned out the cards, so they could both see all the images at once. She felt the Magic in them change immediately, as if an animal shuddered in mortal pain. The images could no longer travel. The deck became useless.

Sekh examined the artful variety greedily, as though a fantastic mystery had been revealed to him. Hypp stacked them together, kissed them, and set them in the wizard's bony, gray hand.

The Hinge of Stone

Charlene's messengers returned to Windhollow to tell of Trawill's prescience and Sekh's offer.

"Well, then, we've got to make a show of returning," Regis said.

"Ma's morning, yes" Charlene said. "Sekh will feel trusted if you do."

They prepared for the trip and set out the next day. Just before twilight, they came bounding down the trail into Ash as a boisterous group, laughing at Regis' banter.

Kaja had his staff in one hand and held Genu's in the other. Morgaine, her white cheeks crimson with laughter, careened under Regis' heavy arm. He was so lost in his own hilarity, he could say almost anything and they would all laugh.

Gan came running up to Dogen, and they staggered together before falling to the ground, much to everyone's delight.

Regis caused a drinking song to erupt again, as they regained their footing with his help, all loudly singing the gender they appreciated most:

> *Oh, I once knew a girl from Avalon*
> *Walked in her sleep with nothin' on.*
> *One night I saw her comin' along*
> *Thought to myself,*
>
> *"Oh there's nothing wrong,*
>
> *Walking along with nothin' on,*
> *If you're a girl from Avalon."*

And then Regis exclaimed, drawing it out, "Ohhhhhh," and they sang it again.

By the time they got to Hypp's house, many Ringfolk had joined, and it was clear that mead and food were amply called for, now that Kaja had returned.

Hypp grabbed her tattooed son, and Kaja let fall his staff and let go of Genu's hand to embrace her. "You come back here, to our home." Kaja drank her in. The celebration lasted into the wee hours of the morning, and Kaja thrived on it.

❧

The next day, Bal and Yet banged on the door of Hypp's house. Regis opened it, and tried to step outside, but they pushed him in. They wore thick leather cloaks and carried heavy tin swords in scabbards of engraved and painted leather. Bal wore a wooden plaque upon his chest, showing his family's roaring bear crest.

"What do you think you're doing? Bal? Yet? Come on now, none of this," Regis said.

"We've come for him."

"He's not leaving under arms," Dogen said flatly. "He will go of his own free will or not at all."

"He's coming, is all. Had enough of it, Dogen," Bal said. When he reached for Kaja, Dogen stepped forward and Regis swung in front of him.

"I said none of this!" Regis checked Kaja briefly, with a twinkle in his eye. Trawill had foreseen that if Talon came for him, then Ogden sent them, and not Sekh. It was as far as her foresight extended, but it meant Sekh had been corralled, at least for a while.

"I go," Kaja said, returning the twinkle. "We know I go. Now we know how." He moved around Regis, who retreated and let the Talon lead Kaja away.

They came to Sekh's small, windowless house on a steep meadow above town. The Talon knocked a secret knock and stood back, behind Kaja. He realized that they were not allowed inside. A child servant in a black wool robe with his head painted green opened the door, and Kaja entered the wizard's den for the first time. It was dark and smelled of dank rot. A fire burned bluish on the hearth before the oven, and atop three tall poles sat little oil lamps, throwing a wane light from above. It was cluttered with the apothecary's eerie apparatus, tied rolls of leather, and mysterious paintings on slabs of bark, scattered about short benches pressed against the curving wall. Bwain sat in the shadows behind the hearth, and quietly observed Kaja while working some unseen tool with his hands.

"Come, Kaja, sit down over here," Ogden said. "It's good to see you."

Silently, Kaja did as he was told.

Sekh gazed at him benignly, which appeared to Kaja a worse menace than a glare. *He is not going to acknowledge what he has done. He's not going to acknowledge that my friends defied him and won.*

Ogden took his seat opposite them, and the flames pawed at the dusty air hanging between them. When a blush of regret passed through the folds of his aged face, Kaja hoped he might say something about the ordeal Sekh had forced him through.

Instead, Sekh began. "Kaja, I happen to know that you were about to tell something to Elrik, just before your friends, um, found you."

I was not. I will never tell you or anyone else. Kaja shook his head. "No, High Hingemen. I do not remember. It was certainly fantasy. And you know why I think so, would you not?"

He glanced at Ogden, who turned away.

"And this sound Elrik spoke of?"

"I know how to make instrument unknown to your people. I will happy make many of them for you, if you would like me to."

"Really? What can you make that we lack?" Sekh snarled his lip, and Bwain looked up to him, flat eyed.

"Hard to explain. Easier to see. And to hear."

"Indeed, then, a new sound, quite literally," Ogden said, glancing sideways at Sekh, who pretended to be unimpressed. "A fine offer. Why don't you make one for Quinn? My daughter loves music."

"I would be honored."

"Very good. She will be intrigued."

Sekh shouldered away from his brother.

"I hope she is pleased, sir," Kaja said.

"Enough of this nonsense," Sekh snapped. "You are still testing me. So I will test you. Tell me, would you like to be a man, Kaja?"

An expression of disgust waved through Kaja's lips. Rage filled his mind. *You are to award me manhood? Why must it be like this? But, how else can I take my place in this land, in this world, without your permission? Ma, why must I always be powerless?* He said evenly, "Yes, High Hingemen. I would like to live here among your fine people, and to be considered a man."

"Good," Sekh said, like slime slowing to freeze. He put his fingertips together and held Kaja in his silence for a long while. "We might let you stay." Slowly, he bared his stained, burned teeth, as though to convey a normal emotion, and it chilled Kaja to the bone. "Many of the townspeople are fond of you." The expression, whatever it was, widened. "Some others...well..."

He fell silent for so long, Kaja felt he had to say something. "Yes, High Hingemen."

"Kaja, there are a few things you don't know," Ogden said. "Not everyone here likes having you around. It's an old tradition that we only initiate people whose family we know. And when I say, 'know,' I mean, we know you for generations. A lot of people here will never accept you because you were coughed up by the sea."

That's not true…

Ogden waited for Kaja to come back before continuing. "So, here's how it's going to go. We're going to initiate you anyway. That will give you some degree of protection."

Immediately, Kaja's gut told him, *I don't need your protection.* He tried not to betray his thoughts on his face.

"But the ceremony is only the first part. You still have to prove yourself. And for that, I have a special mission for you. When the time comes, in the Spring, I'll send for you. Until then, if you stay in your boundaries, we will leave you alone. Won't we, Sekh?"

Sekh glared at his brother, threw his hood over his face, and slouched back in his chair.

"I'll take that as a yes," Ogden said. "Kaja, will you abide?"

"Yes, High Hingemen Sekh, Honorable Ogden. I will stay in my boundaries."

"Very well," Ogden said. "You may go."

Kaja stood and bowed in the way his people did, and he backed to the door, watching the wizard.

As soon as he was gone, Sekh spun to Bwain. "Well?"

"Look at this," the boy said.

In neat rows on the ground before him were Hypp's Tarot cards, one dropped every few seconds for the duration of the conversation. Each one and every one showed a man hanging from a tree, upside down, from a rope tied to his left ankle. His right leg was crossed behind him, and his arms were crossed before his chest, and his eyes were closed.

"What do you suppose that means?" Bwain asked.
Ogden watched Sekh, who stared agape.

❧

"Talon!" Ogden shouted as he blew through the door.

"Aye!" went up the shout in return.

"I see your furnace is hot!" he shouted again.

"Aye!"

"But our blood is hotter, do you hear?"

"Aye!"

Ogden paused and surveyed the smithy, allowing slobber to drip from his open lips. "Ha ha! Look at this!" He walked around the furnace, a deep hole lined with rock, fed through a narrow trench that led to a small opening at the bottom. It sucked air so fiercely you could hear it. In a small rock-bottomed chamber above the fire was a sloping tray of hardened clay. Ore was placed into the tray, and the metal bled into a removable clay bowl. When removed, the metal would slowly harden, only to be melted again and again until it was pure, and then poured into a form, and then beaten into blades while warm.

Ogden passed close to each of his comrades in turn, but he kept his gaze fixed upon the completed weapons hanging from the ceiling. He stopped next to Toot, still slobbering and wide eyed. "Men!" he shouted. "Men! Do you know what you are doing!

You will earn us victory! We need more! More! More like these, more with this quality! Do you hear?"

They all cheered, "Aye!"

"We shall carve out a place in this land with these weapons, men. Your families shall honor your names for generations. My family shall honor your names forever! Forever!"

"Aye!"

"I am mightily impressed, men. Mightily impressed. I shall remember this well when we return with our just rewards. I shall remember it well. More!"

With a flourish, he left. Bal, Yet, and Toot, drunk with lust, worked fiercely.

⟨⌇⟩

Kaja and the men went hunting, mostly as an excuse to get outside and to feel their blood flow.

"So how come you get to bring Gan?" Regis asked.

"Because I'm smarter than you," Dogen said.

"Doubt that. I can count to a hundred."

"On your third or fourth try," Gan said, "on a good day."

"Today would be a good day," Kaja said.

"One, two, three, Morgaine—darn. One, two, Morgaine. Darn again. Three, five, Morgaine. Darn it. Maybe not so good after all," Regis joked.

"How did we get so lucky?" Dogen asked.

"Clean living. Anyone bring some mead?"

"Right here," Gan said, passing the skin to Regis.

"Where are we headed?" Dogen asked.

"Let go of his hand. It's not fair," Regis said.

Dogen kissed Gan on the cheek. "Now that's fair."

"I've had enough. Back to the girls."

"How about out towards Raven Wood?" Gan asked.

"Uphill on the way back," Regis pointed out.

"Like we're going to get anything," Gan grinned.

"Not smelling like that you won't," Regis said.

"Did you say something, Regis? I can't see you through your green cloud," Gan teased back.

"That's right. Pick on the big guy."

"Why not Raven Wood?" Dogen said. "Let's show Kaja where it's gonna be."

"Ah ha! Why don't we do that? It'll help you, Kaja, if you see it first." Regis said.

"See what?"

"Well, the Hinge," Regis winked at him.

"Won't Ogden be mad?" Gan asked.

"If we tell him, yeah."

"Let's formally swear to secrecy," Dogen said.

"Done."

"Done."

"What's a Hinge?" Kaja asked.

"A Hingemen Ring. The sky flows through it," Regis said.

"I will be initiated at the Hinge?"

"Yup. That's where Sekh does his public Magic. It's a pretty creepy place. You can feel how strong it is."

Kaja took out his flute and played the Living Ring's tune.

"Oh no, Kaja," Dogen said, "Not at the Hinge. That music is for the Ring of Trees. We don't do much at the Rings anymore."

"Hypp does," Regis said.

"Well, some people still go to the Rings a few times a year. But most of what we do is at the Hinge," Gan said.

"Why is that?" Kaja asked.

Dogen cast him a sage expression but said nothing. They trekked down the same trail they came up when they brought Kaja to Ash. As they neared the forest, Kaja began to remember. He did not say anything, but his heart quickened, and he held Hypp's staff tight. It seemed to get heavier, as though recoiling from the direction they traveled. Raven Wood had been out of bounds for him, so he had never been back to see his spot between the tree and the rocks. He had never been back to where Trip had seen him that first moment of his discovery.

"Well it's mostly because there's more room around the Hinge, I think," Gan said. "And because we have the poles there to set up shelters, in case a celebration is on a rainy day."

"I remember that one time a celebration wasn't on a rainy day," Regis said. "We usually stand around in our hoods freezing our butts off while Sekh does his thing."

They came to the spot where Trip had seen him, and Kaja inspected the ground. He wanted to see a footprint, or some remains of that day, when he still believed he was in Ma's care, given a chance to ponder life before falling into her embrace. But nothing was there. Washed by rain and covered with leaves, the forest bore no trace of his ordeal.

"You alright, Kaja?" Dogen asked.

"Yes. I'm fine," Kaja said, nodding to convince himself.

Then he saw it, laying on the ground in that exact spot. It was perfect. A fallen oak branch. A burl at the base of it had weakened it, causing it to drop in the wind. Kaja bent down and picked it up, mystified. *Ma has given me this. How else could it have appeared in this exact spot? Ma has given me this...*

"Hello, Kaja? You sure you're alright? You're staring at a hunk of wood. Kaja?" Regis said. For an instant he became alarmed that they had made a grave error bringing Kaja back down this trail.

"Perfect this is for Quinn's bellows," Kaja said quietly.

"What?" Regis asked.

"Perfect."

Dogen reached out and put his hand on his strange friend's arm. "Well then, give it to me and I'll carry it for you. What will you do with it, Kaja?"

"For my sound, for my instrument. Which I will give to Quinn. This is the perfect shape." He held it to his ear and knocked on it. "Hard to hear in the wet wood."

He saw Nana bringing a similar burl to him, exuberantly excited because she knew how happy he would be to have it. And he had been happy. For weeks, he worked the wood into a harp, and on the day he completed it, Nana had bled for the first time. When her rites were over in the Women's Lodge, he had played it for her for hours. All of his family and the families of Nana's friends were there, in a grand gathering about a roaring fire, celebrating Nana and listening to his music. He had even sung her a song, and she never forgot it, because Kaja was a poor singer and rarely sang. But he had put such feeling and love into it, his alliance with his sister was forever strengthened. Then he gave it to her, and she considered it precious. She rarely played it herself, but she often got it out and asked Kaja if he would play it. She kept it as her own, though, in a special bag of red fox fur, and she let her love for it show to all.

Kaja handed the branch to Dogen, and he and Gan cut off the twigs. Dogen balanced it in his pack, with the branch part sticking out high over his head, and they walked on.

"Ah, here's the secret trail!" Regis said, trying to color the mood. He had his hand on a post with a heavy iron arrow nailed to it, pointing up a well-worn trail.

"Good thing we have you with us, Regis," Gan said, "Or we'd be completely lost."

Kaja smirked and looked away, tearing himself from his memories. They hiked up steep switchbacks. As they reached the top of the hill, a monstrous, brooding structure rose from the horizon. Massive, stone pillars stood in a perfect circle, and thick wood beams stretched from the top of one to the other, forming a nine-sided ring pointing north. Smaller, wooden pillars stood in a ring within the larger one, and on the north side, between the rings, rose a stone platform. Situated at the very apex of the hill, the wind and rain blew through it fiercely, accentuating its formidable solidity. It remained impossibly still, hulking between the men and the dark clouds flowing overhead.

Kaja stayed close to his friends. The Hinge frightened him, and he did not want to approach it. They stopped to stare for a while, acknowledging its presence, unwilling to enter its dominion.

"Well, there it is," Regis said.

"Again, I thank you," Gan said, "I wasn't sure where we were."

"I told you to let go of his hand," Regis said.

"I ignored you, didn't I?"

Kaja saw Dogen's troubled brow, and the way he gripped Gan's hand with a need transcending companionship.

"Are you glad we brought you here?" Gan asked.

"Yes. Yes, this is much better. To see it for the first time when I for initiation would be fearful."

Kaja realized that his friends had undone a bit more of Sekh's Magic. *That's what they're really doing. Magic of their own.*

"It'll be a whole lot weirder at your initiation," Regis said. "Sometimes it can be downright scary. Sort of puts the fear of Ma into you, you know what I mean?"

"Fear of Ma?" Kaja said, "No. Fear of Sekh."

They nodded.

"Let's go back," Gan said.

"I'm outta here," Regis said.

They hiked down the hill. Kaja asked, quietly, though they all heard, "Is the Hinge part of your practice, Dogen?"

Dogen said, simply, "No."

They shook off the heavy, dead Hinge as they descended, and intentionally guided their conversation towards what awaited them at home.

Knowledge

The women were at Hypp's house, weaving on their upright looms. Hypp was a master, and Genu and Morgaine gladly accepted suggestions as they worked.

"Hypp, I've been to your house a thousand times, and I never get tired of looking at the things you have," Morgaine said.

"Me, too, Hypp," Genu said, "I have been here far less often, but I marvel at your collections every time."

"Oh, thank you, children," Hypp replied. "It has been many generations in the making."

"You got some of this from your family?"

"Oh, most of it, I'd say. Most people are visited by fire now and then, to help them clean house. But somehow, for a long time, it never happened to us. So I still have it all."

"Is that through some Magic spell?"

"Oh no, Genu. I wish it were—I could protect everyone from fire that way. It is just luck. Someday all of this will burn. And a good thing, too. Makes it more beautiful today, don't you think?"

"It is beautiful, Hypp. And curious too. Some of these things must be from very distant lands."

"You know what I like?" Morgaine said, "The feather collection. How long have you been adding to that?"

"Ah, my grandmother started it, Morgaine. And she had feathers from her mother as well." Hypp gazed lovingly at the fan of feathers on the wall behind the hearth, an ever-growing half-circle, pointing downward.

"They are not all from this island, are they?" Genu asked.

"Oh no, no. Some are from places whose names I don't even know. See that gangly one with a circle near the end of it? That one came from a place called 'India,' which is so far away that no one even knows where it is anymore."

"How did it get here?"

"Well. Things were different a few generations ago. Our grandmothers were practiced in the arts, and they would often travel huge distances to gather Knowledge. And what better treasure to carry back from distant lands than a feather?"

"Indeed! Did you ever know someone who went to India?" Morgaine asked.

"When I was a little girl, there was a woman named Breeno, who I remember well. She was very old, very old, much older than I am now. Dogen is her great, great, great grandson, as a matter of fact. I only met her a few times, but she left a powerful impression on me. She had been to India. She left on a Spirit Walk well before I was born, and the journey took her nine years. And then, a while later she left again, to go see the Basque and then the Cretans. That time she was gone seven years, if I am remembering the story correctly."

"She left her children behind to travel?" Genu asked.

"Oh, they were grown by then, dear. She didn't begin her travels until she was a Crone. They missed her, but they were very proud of her as well. Imagine going off on an adventure like that!"

"Why did she do it?"

"Knowledge, Genu. She left to visit the Spirit Masters of other tribes across the world. They say it was different then. They say a Crone could travel across the world and never worry about thieves or capture. Now you can't walk two towns away without being fearful. But Breeno, they say, was able to wander the world without fear. She would come to a village, introduce herself to the first person who greeted her, and the local Coven would take her in. She would teach them what she had learned, and they would increase her Knowledge as well."

"Imagine that," Genu said.

"Indeed, imagine it. Imagine it well, Genu, Morgaine. For it is true. These fetters on our freedom chafe at me. Think of our Ring! She is in disrepair, unloved and abandoned. It is shameful. Breeno would not have stood for it."

"Then why do we?"

Hypp thought for a long time before responding to Genu's question. "To live a life of Knowledge requires great freedom. A woman like Breeno cannot exist in a world where she must contend with others all the time. There were no wizards in her day that would torment a person the way Sekh has tormented Kaja. Now we must use our skills to protect our own. In her day, there was more agreement. It was that way when I was younger, too— or so it seemed. Men, women—all people—wanted to possess Knowledge, and they were happy to let others get it. Now we strive for different things, for different reasons."

"We should try to change it back." Genu's admonishment flowed through the weft of each of their looms.

Hypp smiled secretly. She *was* going to change it back, with Jinn and Trawill, and their plans were already mature. "Yes, child, we should find that path. Perhaps you would like to sit with my Coven sometime. We have discussed that many times. There are simple answers that seem to explain. Our grandmothers and grandfathers used to work together for the rites. They shared Knowledge freely among themselves. And within that Knowledge drifted the stars and the planets.

"Indeed, for many generations, we had watched the night skies. And we came to know our brothers and sisters there, the Morning Star, dancing with the seasons. The Red planet who ambled across the sky one way and then went back from whence it came before proceeding as it did before. The other planets, who moved like migrating animals. And, of course, the Moon, pulsing in our bodies and in the sky. All this lived amidst the unchanging constellations. We loved them, we painted them.

"But over time, the study of the sky began to change. We don't know when, because it did not happen suddenly. Over time, the wizards began to search for their Moon. They wanted to know what in the sky was theirs, as the Moon belonged to the witches. But there was no brother there, save perhaps the Red Star, who seemed to hunt.

"They began to believe that all of the sky was their brother, and that everything in it was theirs. When the gentle stories of the night were brushed aside by the glory of the sun, that was them. When the constellations moved across the horizon, that was them. When a shadow passed across the Moon, or when she flowed blood red, that was them.

"Knowledge of the movements in the sky became self knowledge for the men. A strange rigor came into it. That is why they built their first Hinges. The Hinge fits the sky, and fits it perfectly, and this makes it Magical to them. And, while the Hinges are like the Rings, they are not Rings. They stand atop the ground, and only reach up to the sky. Roots are forgotten.

"The Hinge blots out stories the same way the sun blots out stars. The stories do not matter. This makes the Hingemen's Magic as rootless as their Hinge. That is how we got to where we stand now."

"What of the flowers?" Genu asked. "How did that Magic become rootless, if it is?"

Hypp pointed her shuttle at Genu, pleased with the question. "The seeds began with our grandmothers' Magic, Genu. They helped predict the weather. This is what goes wrong, you see, they take something bred for one purpose, and without understanding it, they use it for something else. We never saw the flowers, and we have no reason to believe he's telling the truth about the lines. If they really are there, they're probably the flower's expression of revulsion towards Sekh. He cannot call forth signs, nor can he understand them. He cannot learn in the proper sense, and so he never accumulates true Knowledge."

"That's sad," Morgaine said.

"That's dangerous," added Genu.

"Indeed it is," Hypp said, evening a thread between her fingers.

"And what about me, Hypp? Why would I fall in love with this strange man from a distant land? Why do I care about him so deeply, even though I just met him?"

"Oh, Genu," sighed Morgaine, thinking of Regis.

"Genu, you are a noble soul," Hypp said. "Who can know how people fall in love? Kaja is a strong man. To have survived in mind the way he has—few men could retain themselves as he has, as they travel through the Hinge and back. To come through such horror, and to desire only love and a simple life—I find that remarkable. Ma brought him to us so we can learn from him."

"Hypp, Morgaine, may I tell you something?" Genu asked.

"Please, child."

"Well. I know this isn't proper, and you may think ill of me for it."

"That's not possible, Genu. We know your spirit now," Morgaine said, the casualness of her remark enhancing its power and meaning to Genu.

"Well. I have thoughts about Kaja. I want to lay with him. I want to know him as a woman knows a man. And I feel he wants that too. I want to be with him even if we are not betrothed. I love him so, I want to know him before Ma takes him away. I want to carry him inside me."

The women paused for a moment, quietly smiling. Morgaine spoke first, "I know how you feel, Genu. I have felt the same way about Regis."

"And?" Hypp asked.

"And I have known him, and he has known me. How could that be wrong? We have kept my father unaware of it, so he could adapt to the idea of giving me away. Having lost so much, we don't want him to think he will lose anything more. He is beginning to understand that he can never lose me."

"Now, is that really why you have kept it secret, Morgaine?" Hypp asked. "Surely Martin knows your love of him is too deep for anything to touch or change it."

Morgaine blushed, "Well, Hypp. You know that's not all."

Hypp laughed, "Of course I know. When Quip and I first fell in love, our desire was so great we could barely contain ourselves. We let it build and build. We toyed with it, and those around us could see. Then there came one night—my goodness, I was younger than you by a year or so, Genu—when we met at the Ring. Quip loved the Ring, and often we would picnic there. But that first time—it was as if every person in the world dropped away, and we had all of Ma and all of the Cosmos to ourselves. It was wonderful, simply wonderful."

Her words began to quiver. "When he lay here, in this very house, captured by infection and hovering before the veil, there was one moment when his fever left him suddenly. He took my hands in his and looked deep into my eyes. 'Remember the Ring?' he said. And I held him. That moment with me, when we were so young, was his parting thought. Who cares about 'proper'? That was the most beautiful gift we ever shared."

"You still miss him, Hypp?" Genu asked, very quietly.

"Every day. Every moment of every day. Our souls touched and then held fast for nearly twenty years. I believe he will come take my hand and pull me through the veil to be with him again. I believe he loves me that much, even still."

They heard the men singing about their favorite gender as they stomped down the trail.

It's an island
Drenched in rain
Covered in moss and slime
Don't matter to me

I'll hunt just the same
'Cause my girl's at home
And she's mine!

When they crashed into the house and loudly took over the space, they found the women wiping tears and smiling radiantly.

"Uh oh," Regis said, grinning lavishly at Morgaine.

Kaja fixed a consuming gaze on Genu, who returned it.

Gan immediately broke into fake tears, and, sobbing comically on Dogen's shoulder, exclaimed, "Oh, Dogen, I missed you so! Boo hoo hoo! By the way, did you kill anything I can eat?" That broke the room like snapping a twig, and they laughed hilariously—most of all Hypp, the fearless old Crone.

⊰∧⊱

It snowed. They had been spending so much time together, inside away from the rain, that the trees had lost their leaves without being watched day to day. Kaja had his bellows largely hollowed out, having worked at the burl with a small flint knife for hours on end, occasionally raising it to his ear to knock on it. His friends had watched with admiration as the strange instrument took shape. He did not explain what he was doing, and let them wonder, knowing full well they had no idea where he was going with the project.

One white day, Genu asked him to come, just the two of them, to walk through the forest as soft snow drifted slowly down, blanketing the world with silence. It was too cold to hold hands, so they walked side by side. After a visit to the gazebo, she said, "Kaja, let's go to my house rather than to Hypp's."

"Miss your parents a little?"

"Naw. I saw them just yesterday, silly. They're staying with friends," It was hard to tell, since her hood was drawn, but Kaja could not decipher her mischievous eyes.

They went into her home, and Kaja kindled a fire on the hearth. Soon, it was warm enough for them to take off their parkas. Genu brushed the bearskin by the fire and placed a pot of fermented berries near the embers. Kaja sprawled, his legs stretched out, leaning back on a rolled hide. He watched Genu toss her long red curls around her aquiline profile. She drew herself to kneeling before him. Her locks brushed over one shoulder, and she snuggled her face into them. No question now—that was a mischievous look.

"What's going on here, Kaja?" she asked.

Fixated on her incredible beauty, Kaja understood the question only glancingly. He answered, "I love you."

"You do?"

"More than anyone, Genu."

"Well. That's good. Why do you love me?"

Kaja shifted, confounded. There were the obvious answers, but he feared those would not satisfy the moment. "Because when we're together, I am very happy." She blushed, so Kaja kept going, "Because I feel I would do anything for you. I like to feel that way, and I feel it for you only."

Genu leaned forward onto her hands, letting Kaja see down her shirt before she kissed him. Then she backed away. His eyes were so dark in the firelight that she could not see the line between his deep brown iris and his black pupil. It was like looking into the night. A warm and inviting night…but in the distance, reaving ghosts and dangerous adventure prowled in a hot, swirling wind.

"Good," she said, smiling.

Her translucent, freckled skin glistened opalescent. To Kaja, she seemed impossibly divine. She was his Ma, his goddess. Her breath was the breath of Ma in a glade, her touch soft moss, her gaze, shining starlight. He leaned forward and wrapped his legs around her and kissed her again. He stroked her hair, and he slid his hands under her shirt, lifting it off her. His calloused palms traveled her like a cresting tide on some incredible, untested ocean.

The Ring of Trees

Hypp and her Coven manipulated Sekh skillfully, so when the New Moon came, everything was in place, and the Hingemen had no clue. Neither did Ogden, or his Talon.

Most importantly, Kaja was also in the dark. He spent a good while working on his instrument surrounded by goofy smiles, sly winks, and knowing twitches of the eyebrow, none of which he suspected had anything to do with him.

When the day came, Genu asked him to go for a walk. She did it innocently enough, and he gladly dropped what he was doing to don his parka and head out into the clear cold with her. There had been no snow or rain for a couple days, so the ground was muddy, but frozen, and it did not sink under their footfalls.

"I have a surprise for you, Kaja," she said, gripping his hand and striding elegantly.

"You do?"

"Mmmm himmm. A really good surprise."

"What is it?"

"If I told you, it wouldn't be a surprise, now would it?"

"You are a surprise, Genu. No other do I need."

She came closer to him and wrapped her arm around his. "But this is a really, really good surprise."

Kaja grinned widely, his tattoos stretching into a brighter pattern. "So will you take me to it, if you won't tell me what is it?"

"Sure."

"That's it? 'Sure' is all you will say?"

"Mmmm hmmm."

"Give me one hint."

"No."

"Just one?"

"Well..."

"Just little one?"

"Just a little one." She thought for a moment.

"What is it?"

"It's not at town."

"That's my hint?"

"Yup."

"Can I have another one? We are already not at town. You will let me have you again? Is that the surprise? Of the surprises, that would be my favorite."

"Well, you can kiss me." Right away he held her and kissed her until their faces were warm.

"Yes, that is the best surprise. Where shall we go?"

"Do you want another hint?"

"That wasn't my surprise?"

"That is part of it."

"Yes please, another hint."

"Hmmmm. I don't know if I want to give you another hint."

"But you said you would."

"I changed my mind."

"Oh."

"Let's go this way." At the fork in the trail she took the route to Windhollow. As they approached the Ring of Trees, Kaja heard voices.

"Is the surprise at the Ring of Trees?" he asked.

"Yup."

"A celebration at the Living Ring! I am to come, too?"

"Yup."

"For the women only, though? But I can come to see?"

"They're not always for the women only."

"Really? I did not know. Which men sometimes come?"

"You'll know who some of them are. But they will wear masks."

"What is the celebration for?"

"Oh, you'll see."

Again Kaja embraced her, holding her supple form, within her winter equipment, close to him. His allegiance to her animated his life. He did not fear it, though it was everything. He had lost so much, to now have this was beyond belief. He would die before losing it. He would die rather than lose it. Or, so he hoped.

She tried to snuggle into him, but his parka was too cold on her face. So she grabbed his hand and took off, and he followed alongside. They ran to the voices in the trees.

❦

"Oh ho, what a great face!" yelled a giant blue man with a green beard and red feathers fanning from his temples. "Good to see you!" It was Regis, and he crushed Kaja in a bear hug. "Hey, everybody! He's here!" he hollered towards the Ring. With an arm around Kaja he led him towards it.

The Ring of Trees had been made into a shelter of sorts, wrapped with a continuous wall of skins, with lean-tos and other encampments next to it. Genu disappeared before Kaja could see which way she went. In the center of the Ring roared a great fire, throwing a great warmth into the raggedly beautiful circle. Dozens were there, it seemed. All of Hypp's Coven from Ash, all of Morgaine's Coven from Windhollow, and many of their brothers and partners.

No face was unadorned—many were like Regis's. Others were painted purple, with masks tied over parts of them, making their noses into snouts of deer, pig, and lion. Some wore antlers on their heads and had artfully combed shapes of fur on their cheeks and foreheads.

In one spot a clutch of animals beat a swinging rhythm on a dozen drums so enticingly no one could stand still. Near them were flautists, some with their long yellow hair pasted into looping rings and swirls around their pink and coral faces. With them were several children, squirrels and rabbits and foxes, shaking rattles with varying levels of skill but with an unvarying height of laughter and enthusiasm. Roe and aurouch and dolphin and carp— and there, fairies and gibbons and griffins—danced around the fire.

Kaja stood under Regis' heavy arm and stared in amazement as his big friend laughing uproariously at his bug-eyed disbelief. Two white birds approached. They had long delicate wings flowing back from their cheeks, and a spray of feathers rising from atop their heads.

"Well, what do you think?" Dogen asked, giving Kaja a long embrace.

"Hey, Kaja, welcome home," Gan said, joining in.

"I thank you for having me," Kaja murmured.

"Ha ha! 'I thank you for having me!' Lighten up ol' man! It's time to just let it flow through you!" Regis pounded Kaja's back. "Shall we tell him?"

"Hypp said we could," Dogen said.

"You're in, Kaja. This is your initiation. The real one. We're gonna blow your tattooed mind here tonight, and then it's done. You're a man to us."

Kaja shifted from one face to another. "But what of Sekh?"

"Aw, forget that old geezer. He ain't here, though he's probably got Bwain dressed up like a pile of dung somewhere. Don't dance with the dung, got it Kaja?"

Kaja laughed and his friends led him into the swirling mass of color and music, introducing him to all variety of animals and dream creatures. They fed him some rude-tasting cake and gave him some mead, which combined to soften his mind and open his heart. He began to laugh and to play. He showed them some of his native dances, and his three friends stayed by his side to bring them out.

It was a while before Kaja thought to ask what had happened to Genu, and where Morgaine and Hypp were. Regis licked his lips and rubbed some of the green off his beard, saying,

"Oh, brother. No one knows where they go. But they'll be back. Don't you worry. They always come back."

Not much later, Kaja noticed that the children were gone, too. His friends grabbed his arms.

"Give me your parka," Regis said.

"Just stay right here," Dogen said.

They left him standing alone. Everyone had gathered around him. The fire was to his back, and he was facing south. The drumming rose to an even greater volume and passion, and the animals began to hoot and holler. Kaja slowly spun, taking in the spectacle when they started pounding the ground to the beat. Even the trees seemed to partake, their branches illuminated from below and waving in time, as shrews and squirrels ran up and down.

From nowhere a procession approached him. At its front strode a magnificent owl, its sharp beak nodding on a grey feathered face, with a huge half-circle of feathers fanned out behind it, quivering with other-worldly energy. Behind the owl were ten or so children, now without their rattles but instead each carrying a little bundle in both hands, giggling and doing their best to stay in line. Behind the children more birds fluttered—a hawk and a dove, an albatross and a raven.

And at the end of the line, he thought he saw by the firelight, was a woman from his native land. It was upon her he fixed his gaze. Her face was tattooed in a manner reminiscent of his own, but the patterns somehow changed as she moved, flowing from one composition into another, endlessly the same, but never exactly the same twice.

The owl stood before the fire, the raging light illuminating her crown of feathers from behind and hiding her face. The children walked up to him in turn and handed him the knotted end of a colorful ribbon of dyed wool. He tried to bow to each, but they pressed the cloth into his hands with such enthusiasm, and then dashed away, unfurling the ribbon, that he had to hold on tight and abandon propriety, laughing and nodding instead to show his thanks. The other birds lined up next to the owl, who let the drumming rise and the hooting peak before raising her staff high up into the air, whereupon everyone stopped and cheered.

Kaja stood in the middle of a circle of children, holding one end of a ribbon leading to each, within a larger circle of animals, within the circle of trees. The owl brought down her staff, and the cheering quieted. Kaja heard birdsong in the trees. He saw that the owl's staff was his staff, and when she spoke, he knew it was Hypp.

"Friends! Blessed be to Ma!" the owl said.

"Aye!" yelled the crowd.

"Before you, see Kaja of the Rishi—a man beloved by many, a man beloved by Genu, who shall have him, and a man beloved by Hypp, his Mother now. Do you see this man?"

"Aye!"

"Do you want this man?"

"Aye!"

"Children! For Ma, bring him to us!"

Instantly the drumming and the flutes exploded into a pounding rhythm, and the ring of animals swung and clapped to the beat. The children took off in different directions, jumping and ducking in a barely sensible pattern. Kaja just managed to get his elbows up as a woven macramé of colored ribbon approached him from all around, weaving a beautiful sheath around his body.

The children got closer and closer, laughing and squealing, and then little hands came up to him, tucking their ends of the ribbons into the weave in a happy crescendo of inclusion. They backed away into their circle and tried to clap to the beat, too, but they couldn't help but lean to each other and share admiration for their work.

The tattooed woman walked up to him, and took the ribbon's ends from his hands, pulling them over his shoulders and tucking them in to complete his garment. They held hands, and Kaja wanted to hold her for as long as this world lasted.

"I love you, Kaja," Genu said.

" I love you, Genu."

They embraced, and the rhythmic clapping broke into cheers.

Then the drums rounded a bend and swung into a dancing Ringsong. Genu grabbed Kaja's hand and they jumped in with the children. The birds joined them, and the animals, and the dream creatures. The fire warmed the Ring of Trees, and Regis and Dogen brought them mead and then more mead after that. The night swirled with carefree laughter and dancing bodies that could not get close enough to each other.

The woven garment came loose here and there, though it held snug around Kaja's heart.

Force

B wain was washing his hair and face with warm water and ash. Leaves and twigs came unstuck and fell to the floor.

"What do you mean, 'nothing?' Nothing? How could it be 'nothing?' You must have missed something. Come on, boy, think!" Sekh hovered over his apprentice, trying to control himself.

"High Hingemen, he didn't do anything. Please believe me, Master. I watched the whole thing. I didn't even go relieve myself. I swear, he just stood there with a grin on his face while they did their silly little theater."

"Bwain, my boy. Of course, he just stood there. What else under the stars could he do? Think about the people around him, Bwain. Think. How did he control them?"

"They just did the rites, is all."

"They must have bowed to him."

"They danced in a circle, master. I swear. Nothing more. The birds came."

"Birds! There's something. What did the birds do?"

"They sang."

"Of course they sang, you idiot! The stars make them sing! How did he use them?"

"I don't even know if he heard them."

"You just said he called them."

"No, master, they were just there."

"'They were just there.' Come on, Bwain! Think! Don't you understand what Tiss is doing for us here? Don't you realize what this could mean? WHAT DID HE DO!" This last came out as a shout in Bwain's ear, and the boy trembled.

"Master, don't yell at me! There was nothing there—just a simple Ringfolk rite!"

Sekh ran his hand through his hair and backed away from the boy. He couldn't use Bwain the way Tiss had used him. He couldn't figure out why. He had done the rites; he knew Bwain was born at the right time; he knew Bwain had the right birthmark. Still, he couldn't see through Bwain's eyes.

"Alright. Let's think together here. He got what he wanted, didn't he? Why would he use his secret powers there? He didn't have to do anything to get what he wanted. So there was nothing. Nothing you saw, anyway. Now he's got Genu, polluting our line. We'll deal with that later. What else to do?" Sekh paced around. Bwain tried to take refuge in the warm water and didn't look up from his washing.

"He almost cracked with Elrik. He responds to pressure. I ought to poison Hypp. But they'll know I did it. The women will, anyway. Her Coven. That will have to wait. We need to put the fear into him again. Then he'll give us his secret. Tiss will be proud."

"I'll help."

"You certainly will. You've got to do something right, eventually. Tiss came to me in a dream. He did. I was in the Ring of Trees, alone. Why am I telling you this? He walked out of the mists and stood there before me shaking his head. Like I was a failure. Like I couldn't accomplish this simple task. This is my test, Bwain. This is what will make me great. Greater than I am now. They will sit at my feet. You'll see. By stars, you will help."

Bwain snuck a glance at the old wizard. Sekh paced back and forth, a dribble of spit running from his lip into his beard, his attention leaping from one spot to another. Bwain strained his imagination to make up something that would please his master, but his ignorance was too great. How could he invent a lie if he had no idea what the old wizard wanted? Better to remain silent. Better to just do as he was told.

❧

Hypp's house was full again, and in the first full light of morning they rearranged their bedding into bolsters and prepared food and drink, according to their skill. In the lowest rank were Kaja and Regis, chopping. Dogen, Gen and the Crones added oils and seasonings, and made tea and warm mead. Morgaine was the artist, and Genu was her second. The two of them combined it into breakfast. Kaja passed his chopped walnuts, mushrooms and onions to Morgaine, and accepted a cup of tea from Trawill.

"Look out there," Regis said, "it's gonna be a beautiful day."

"Magic in the air," Genu said, casting a glance at Kaja.

At that moment, a violent pounding on the door crumbled their world. They cast glances around and resigned to it.

"Today is the day," Kaja said.

"I wish there was another way," Regis said, handing his tea to Morgaine as he stood.

"When we know what you have to do, we will find a way to help you," Morgaine said.

Kaja inhaled deeply and gazed into the bundles of herbs drying in the rafters. So often, they had spoken of how they would help him on his Spirit Walk. They wanted to believe that he would not be alone, now that he was one of them. They wanted to try to protect him. *No, Morgaine. You will not know where I am. I will not allow Sekh to draw any of you into this. You do not know his nature. I do.*

Genu pulled him into her arms from where she snuggled next to him. Hypp crawled over and joined them. "You come back here, to our house." Kaja held them tight.

When he stood, he donned his parka and his boots. Regis opened the door, and Bal walked in without greeting. He surveyed the room derisively, and said to Kaja, "Bring your instrument."

Kaja hefted the box and took no pack. With a wink at Genu, he followed Yet while Bal followed him.

When he walked into Sekh's den, it smelled strange. He couldn't place what was burning, or rotting, or fermenting, to create the odor. Sekh noticed his curious discomfort, and glistened. When he reached out for his instrument, the malevolence in his presence made Kaja worry that he would smash it against an owl's head. But he handed it over. Sekh took it in his hands with mock sincerity, though Ogden appraised it with wonder.

"This is very, very interesting, Kaja," Sekh said. He handled the bellows with tremulous hands and ran his fingers up its long neck. It was nearly complete. There were empty notches, holes and slots where the other pieces would fit. "So it will make a magical sound?"

"It will make music, High Hingemen."

Bwain was sitting on the floor, working his unseen tool again, and he leered at Kaja.

"Music! How lovely! Very clever. My, how clever your people were, before…well, you know."

"I'm sure Quinn will love it, Kaja," Ogden said, casting an annoyed glance at Sekh.

Kaja paused. *Was that kindness I heard in his voice? Or just gratitude, because this is a gift for his daughter?* "Thank you, My Liege."

"'My Liege'?" Sekh sneered. "Did you say, 'My Liege'?"

"Yes, High Hingemen, I did."

"No, no, no. You can't say 'My Liege' until after you are initiated. Have we initiated you yet?"

Kaja paused and let a moment of memory fill him with confidence. He saw the laughing children weaving his magical garment, with Hypp and Genu smiling over them, and his community dancing all around. *This is a great gift the Coven has given me. Powerful Magic.* He said, steadily and certainly, "No, High Hingemen."

"I didn't think so. My goodness, I'd hate to miss that party. Ha ha. It's Honorable Ogden for now. Do you understand?"

"Yes, High Hingemen."

"Listen, Kaja," Ogden said carefully, "we need you to do your initiation task long before your initiation ceremony. I'm really sorry it turned out this way. But..." Ogden cast a suspicious glance at Sekh. "It just worked out that way."

"Oh," Kaja said.

Desperation and desire crawled like insects in Bwain's face.

"But on the bright side, it's a much easier task than we originally intended. I mean, usually initiation is pretty dangerous. But for you, we have something else in mind," Ogden said.

He's lying. But Kaja said only, "Yes, Honorable Ogden."

Sekh nodded too fast.

"It's really nothing," Ogden continued, "We need to take advantage of the skills you picked up in the forests by Riversmouth. You got pretty good at moving around unseen and unheard, didn't you?"

"Yes, Honorable Ogden."

"And at spying. You learned a lot about the Thurgan just by spying from trees. Didn't you?"

"Yes, Honorable Ogden." Kaja felt the love of Genu and the love of his friends, even now, even here. He was not as afraid. He was not as abject as before. *Sekh does not know my secret. Am I succeeding? I might be...* There was trust in his life now—real trust. That made all the difference.

"Good, good," Ogden said, still acting falsely trustworthy. "Well, here's the situation. We know from an informant that the Nok are preparing some sort of battle with us. They've been making weapons and whipping their soldiers into a fury over this pasturelands problem. Do you know what I mean?"

"I believe I do, Honorable Ogden."

"Yes. I believe that you do. And, more than that, I believe you can find out all we should know. For your initiation mission, we want you to go to the Nok and watch them for a while. Unseen. Just spy on them, and catalog what kind of force they have prepared. Anything relevant to their abilities, so we can have an idea about their plans. I don't like surprises on the battlefield."

"You'll go alone," Sekh said, smiling cruelly with his wretched, stained teeth. "All you have to do is get there unseen, remain there unseen, and return unseen. No one will know where you are." He licked his lips and swept the air with his empty pipe. "It is typical for a young man to go on such a Walk before initiation. No one will think about it twice."

"Yes, High Hingemen Sekh, I see." *That's the opposite of what Ogden just said.*

Sekh chuckled coldly, which prompted Ogden to speak. "There will be no more of this funny business between you and Sekh, either, Kaja. I have his word on it. Don't I, Sekh?"

"I am satisfied," Sekh said.

"Your word Sekh, I do have it?" Kaja asked, holding his gaze steady.

Sekh frowned and glared back. "No one demands anything of me." He sneered and rolled off Kaja's eyes.

"I see. Honorable Ogden, I shall give this service to you."

"Excellent. That's the way. The north road, that leads to Windhollow, continues on to the land of the Nok. You will see cairns here and there to guide you through the mountains. Just keep your head up, and don't actually use the trail, and you'll be fine. Just when you think you are lost in the wilderness, you will come upon the notch that leads to the Nok's town. On the way down, you will see some ruined houses, and the forest is unused and wild. It is not a town like ours, mind you. The people live in fear, with no freedom. We'll leave it to your own devices to learn what you can for us."

"Yes, Honorable Ogden."

Ogden stood up suddenly, "Very well. We have prepared a special pack for you, with weapons and food. You are wearing your winter gear?"

"Yes, Honorable Ogden."

"Good. You are to leave immediately."

Kaja started, and looked at Bwain, whose insects bulged and slithered into his eyes. "But, my instrument. I must take it home."

"Bwain will carry it." Sekh ran his bony fingers along its delicate, arcing wood. "Do not think about it."

"May I bid my friends goodbye first?"

"No," Sekh said harshly, "That is not the normal way for a Spirit Walk. I collect the young men as I have collected you, and I send them away. Part of the Magic is to leave suddenly. Have no fear. Ogden himself will go to Hypp's home and announce your departure."

"In my tradition I must bid my people farewell first."

"But you are not being initiated by your people, are you?" Sekh sneered.

"Do I have your word, or not?" Kaja stared hard at the old wizard, who nearly launched at him in violence.

"Yes, you have his word," Ogden said quickly. "And I am your witness. Now, let us do this properly, according to our rites, so all will know you have been truly initiated when the time comes."

Ogden pulled a smile across his teeth and led Kaja to a pack. *They think I am powerless. They can not tell.* He shouldered it and took up the spear and spear-thrower that Ogden offered him. He slung the line of the bow across his chest, strapped a flint knife and scabbard around his thigh, and slung a quiver over his shoulder.

It occurred to him there was one thing he could do to show Ma he understood. Without asking or pausing, he pressed his hands together before his heart, and, in his own language, he recited a curse he knew from childhood:

> *Changes come*
> *Changes leave*
> *Serenity wakes*
> *Serenity sleeps*
> *Honor between us*
> *Honor weeps*

With that, he bowed and left.

When the door swung closed behind him, Bwain jumped back. Ogden palmed his golden crown and ran his hand through the long gray hair rimming his head. Sekh examined the cards on the floor. Each was identical again. This time, each was a cross, and nothing more.

The Demon

Kaja ran full speed through the forest towards Windhollow and the Nok beyond. At a bend, he climbed a tree to the very top and waited. In no time, Bwain passed by underneath, staying to the side of the trail. His pack was much lighter, and he carried only a bow.

Kaja stayed in the tree. *I will not endanger them. I will not let Sekh endanger them.*

What was Bwain's mission? To kill him? Kaja breathed deeply, and he allowed his mind to revert. He let his nature slide away from what it could be, when he was in the Ring of Trees, and let it become again what it had become after he escaped slavery. It tasted like blood and smelled like carrion. It was the freedom of a beast, the Knowledge of a predator. The Thurgan mind rose up in him. He went down to meet it. And, he waited. For hours.

Then, in the dead of night, when the trail was only a starlit ribbon of purple, two figures ran past, breathing in unison, striding in unison. They carried nothing and were firmly set in a rhythm for distance. Behind one trailed long golden waves, behind the other, long, red curls.

Morgaine and Genu. Running all night to Windhollow, to raise the alarm. She loves me. They love me. They must not find me. I will not lead them into Sekh's trap. I will go alone. I have no choice. Ma, help me…

He understood Bwain, but he could not easily predict what he would do. The floundering apprentice had to succeed at his mission, whatever it was. His need to impress Sekh would be his greatest weakness.

Kaja surveyed the starlit night from the treetop. He dropped quickly and silently to the ground and went through his pack. All the food he removed and buried beneath forest duff. He removed the rocks as well. He carefully sniffed the water, and then poured it upon the ground, but kept the skin. He examined the fire kit and found it to be sound. *Thank you, Ogden.* He stuffed his knife into the pack and shoved in the spear and spearthrower as well, tying the top around them. He tested his bow and felt a few arrows with his fingers and donned them again.

He darted cross-country for the Living Ring. Breathing in rhythm with his footfalls, his movements were punctuated by perfect silence, which he used to survey the forest sounds, just as he had in the forests outside of Riversmouth. He felt his thoughts slip away, as they had in his homeland. Nothing existed for him, save his trek.

In a moment of silence he heard breathing, and stopped short on his next foot, frozen motionless. Listening, he detected only a pig rutting in the roots of a tree. He began to run again. Gliding almost soundlessly in the near total darkness of the forest, he gained the top of the hill and the Living Ring. The Coven sisters had eradicated any trace of his initiation celebration. The duff seemed unmoved, the fire ring gone. Even spiders had been released, to form dust-covered webs between the trees. He broke through one and stopped at the center. His breath came in long, even swoons. He took Ogden's flute from his parka and played the Living Ring's music, low and quiet, before whispering almost inaudibly, "Come with me, all of you."

He stashed the flute and ran through the other side of the Ring, confident the animals and trees ran with him. The next range of hills was higher, and he found a good vantage at the first blush of dawn. Below, he could see Windhollow's Oak, with prayer ties blowing peacefully in the morning breeze. He examined the lay of the land and determined where the trail to the Nok must lie. Then he dropped down to the western side of the hill and headed for the mountains with an entire range between him and the trail.

At a creek he washed his mouth and face and drank copiously. From the mud he collected slugs and swallowed them. He rinsed his water skin over and over, and then filled it. No one, not even Hypp, would expect him to take such a widely ranging path. No one knew how to read the land as well as he.

He continued without pause through the day, heading into the rocky mountains. There he had to come closer, over the trail, to view the cairns from a distance, for there was no way to know where the notch to the Nok village was without them. In the light, he feared the ridge tops he needed, so he scanned the ground below fiercely and continuously, allowing it to slow him. He saw no sign of Bwain. But the trek through the mountains was tougher than he anticipated. At nightfall, he was forced into a small crevasse for protection from the mercilessly cold wind that whistled over the stones and swept even air from the sky. He could see the Milky Way through the crack.

He dozed fitfully until it subsided and the sky held the faintest dawn twilight. He felt for his equipment before pushing himself out into the open. Off again. There was only one pass through the ridge, and he decided to take it, even at the risk of having to come back and follow the cairns. He stayed high on the rocks and kept watching the ground below.

It was from that vantage that he saw Bwain in the distance, taking an unlikely path. Kaja watched him move across the mountainside, and after he had disappeared, he watched for a long time more, to see if he was lost and would come back. He did not. So Kaja made his way to where the apprentice had been, and, as the rock walls were too steep and the ridges too high, he followed the same hidden trail through the notch.

He stayed far enough behind to remain unseen, but close enough to watch where Bwain went. Bwain's ignorance was the glory of Ma. Bwain's clouded mind was the Hinge of fate. He stalked Bwain, wondering how best to consume him.

As they descended through the forest into the Nok town, Kaja began to understand Ma's test. He saw the Nok staggering. He saw how they abused their children and their wives. He witnessed what they had destroyed and defiled, for no other reason than that they could, while no one could stop them.

I know these people. I know what they have become. They are the dead souls who pounded the cart with their spears. They are the dead souls who obey their leader without thinking. They are the dead souls Sekh wants to create. Ma has brought me back to this.

As he tracked Bwain, he heard no music, no singing, and no visiting. It was a village of women, children, and elders—all the men, it seemed, were gathered in the Hall, as Dogen had told, certainly still drinking and making bladed tools of war.

I know what it is like in their minds. I know the demon who lives there, and I know how that demon got there, and I know what that demon can do.

He began to hate these weak, obedient men as he hated the Thurgan soldiers who had enslaved him and his people. As he circled the Nok town, following Bwain continuously, he analyzed how the Nok dead souls lived. He began to understand their greatest weakness. And he began to prepare to take advantage of it, creating a stash where he assembled the weapons he would use.

Early in the morning on the third day, Kaja was perched in a tree, watching Bwain squatting on the forest floor, shitting out the remains of whatever food he had managed to consume. Then he saw one of the warrior men emerge from a house—which was unusual—and head for the forest, with probably the same intent.

Kaja's heart raced as the man veered one way and then another, finally deciding to head for the same spot as Bwain. The man stopped, and tried to focus his gaze, disbelieving what he thought he saw.

Bwain was too intent on his bowels to notice. Kaja watched a dumb anger fill the man, who reached for his knife only to find it wasn't there. So he broke into a run, and took a flying leap at Bwain from behind, smashing him into the ground with a loud grunt, and, after a brief struggle, standing with the apprentice clutched to his chest.

Bwain fought back for an instant. But then, he stopped struggling. Kaja pitied him. He was so accustomed to being under the power of Sekh that, even now, he simply submitted.

How do I handle this?

But in his instant of hesitation, an arrow flew from the forest and plunged clear through the Nok's clothing, through his heart, till the flint blade stuck out his back.

Profoundly surprised, the man's bug-eyed gaze first scanned for his assailant, and then rotated to the sky, before he fell to the ground like a sack of rocks. Some of Bwain's hair had been plunged into the wound, so he was pulled down on top of the man, and had to yank himself free, which he did with a terrified gurgle. Bwain's eyes were popping, and it seemed like he might scream, but instead he just ran into the forest, leaving behind his weapons and pack, and pulling up his pants as he crashed through the trees.

Kaja did not move. Whoever shot the arrow did not move. The Nok's body did not move. Nothing moved. No one noticed what had happened.

But they will, and when they do, they will invade this forest and kill both Bwain and me. And, perhaps whomever shot the arrow. He marveled at the fact that whoever that was, they had eluded him completely. He had felt that he was totally aware of his surroundings, but he had not been. *All that matters now is stopping them while I still can. My only chance to protect Ash and Windhollow is right now. I will not fail again.*

He dropped to the ground and went to his stash. Two crude torches, and dry duff and kindling.

From the village he heard a scream, and then crying, and then other voices joining in, piercing the silent, bird-less morning with agony that added to an endless stream of agony.

There is no time left. Ma, I shall pass your test. But why must it be like this? Why does the world always force me to be like this?

He set up his fire kit, and as he began pumping the bow, he knew it was true. When a twirl of smoke rose from the fluff, he transferred it to a ball of grass and blew through it gently. He had to focus his whole attention, without fearing that another arrow might fly and cleave him from his body. He put the ball into a well of leaves and added twigs over the top.

He touched the whittled and flayed ends of the torches into the small fire. The fire sputtered for an instant, unsure of itself. Kaja blew gently, reestablishing his patience. He watched the ends of his torches. The thin curls began to burn, and the sap he had pressed into them began to pop. He heard gathering voices and sensed that very soon the men in the Hall would know.

The fire began to leap. He picked up his torches—how he wished he had oil—and at the end of each was a smoky, billowing flame that would last only a short while. He jogged through the forest as quickly as he could without putting them out. The fire he left behind began to spread through the duff. He did not pause.

If I am to leave this world now, then it will be in this attempt. Ma will witness.

He ran from the forest up the earth piled against the back of the Hall. He slowed as he approached the chimney and waited for the better of the two torches to recover its strength. Then, he tore off the rain hood, thrust the torch into the Hall, and threw it towards the entrance.

He went to the front and threw the other torch onto the thatched roof of a nearby house. It caught fire immediately. He glanced back at the chimney. Smoke began to billow from within the Hall.

People began to run into the area ahead of him. Kaja watched their faces as he drew his stout flint knife. *Are they really coming here for protection? They will run to these foul dead souls for help? I can't believe it.*

When they saw him, they froze, white with fear at the sight of him, tattooed face, dark skin, standing in fire.

Kaja screamed at them in Thurgan: "Vermin!" The people ran.

Beneath his feet, a commotion gathered panic. The men were piling on top of one another, fighting to get out of the one small, low door. And they were not getting out. One gagging soldier staggered away, while a second and a third plugged the door as they fought each other to get through it. Kaja leaped from the roof to the ground, and stabbed the one on top through his spine, and slit the throat of the one below. The commotion inside became a desperate tumble of screaming and punching.

He ran after the one who had got out, commanding him in Thurgan. He leaped on his back and thrust his knife clear through one of his biceps. *This one lives.* The man struggled at first, but he was either too choked with smoke to do more, or he gave up out of the same habit of mind that had caused Bwain to give up. Kaja pulled off his pouch and tied his hands with the strap. He pulled him to his feet by his hair and held the strap in one hand and his knife at the bottom of the man's skull with the other.

He marched the man across the town, screaming in Thurgan. Most of the people disappeared, but not all. From behind doors, and peering from around corners, a few trembling faces watched the demon and his prisoner.

Thick, oily smoke poured from the Hall where the warriors suffocated in the flames of their own filth.

The Savior

K aja took the trail this time. His prisoner retched, covering himself with hot, yellow puke. His arm was covered in blood, and the wound was surging. Kaja threw him to the ground, letting his face bounce off the dust. He cut a length of leather from the man's coat and used it as a tourniquet. The Nok screamed in pain, but Kaja didn't listen, and didn't care.

He marched him, without pause, through the day and into the darkness. This brought them to the narrow pass that fed into the rough mountains. Kaja threw the Nok to the ground again and cut another length from his coat. This he used to bind his legs to his hands where he lay. He left the Nok hogtied and walked off. His prisoner cried out, begging for water, but his voice hit the cliff and vanished into it.

The Nok managed to roll onto his side. His legs and back flamed in pain. He scanned the towering black walls of the pass, which tunneled upward to a star-filled slot. He felt as though he had never noticed the stars before. His heart rose into his throat at the beauty of it. He wept.

And, when a tiny figure approached him, he thought that he was dying. He prayed quietly, hoping that Ma would not deal with him as harshly as he deserved. But the tiny figure did not seem like a spirit. It did not seem like a hallucination. When it poured water into his mouth—real water—he thought she was Ma. But, also a real woman. His breath slowed, and the water let him drop from terror into unconsciousness.

❧

Deep in the night, Kaja leaned against the wall where the Nok could not hear him weep, nor see him shudder.

I have killed again. Ma, this is how I am to be good? Why?

He lay his head against the cold stone, watching the stars, and his breath come in long plumes. Then, from the darkness around him, a whisper came.

"Kaja?"

He slid his back up the rock and drew his bloody knife.

Again, "Kaja?"

He listened.

A flute played the tune of the Living Ring. "Kaja?"

Is that Nana? The question loosened the spell that bound him. *Could it be you? Have you come at last to take me from here? Will this illusion finally disappear? Will this forsaken*

310

world finally vanish? Will you hold my hand, and take me someplace safe? He replied, more a whimper than a word, "Nana?"

"Kaja…I am Charlene, Kaja. From Windhollow, Kaja. Morgaine's teacher. Your friend. Tarot. May I come close to you?"

He knew the voice. His body slumped. His knife fell with a cold clatter. He raised his hands to his face, "Nana? Nana?"

"Shhhhh, Kaja, shhhhh. I will take you back to Genu and Hypp and your friends. Do you know me?"

In the darkness, Kaja nodded, and Charlene approached him.

"It's safe, Kaja. It's me," she said, and Kaja dropped to sit against the wall.

She sat next to him, and took his hand, and snuggled close. He was cold. She rubbed his fingers and began talking in the darkness. "Do you know what we do in the Spring, Kaja? No? Well, let me tell you about it. It is a wonderful celebration. The air smells so sweet! All the flowers are blooming, why, it's so colorful you can't even believe it! The meadows and the creeks are full of color and baby animals and sweet little birds. So, you know what we do? We go to the Living Ring—the same place we initiated you, Kaja. Won't that be fun? We all go there, and we have a big feast."

Kaja's sobbing wracked his body dangerously.

"It's nice and warm, and everyone just wants to play. We dance and we sing and we laugh together. Oh, people fall in love all the time at the Spring celebration. They really do. That's my favorite part. Young people, old people—whoever has fallen so in love they want to make impossible promises and mean them with all their heart. I bet you and Genu will make promises there. I bet you will. I know she wants to make promises to you. That is true. And you'll kiss her in front of everybody, and everybody will cheer and make all sorts of jokes and things. Does that sound like fun, Kaja? Doesn't that sound like fun?..."

Charlene talked all night. It wasn't until dawn that Kaja responded, interrupting her in the middle of a story.

"...but Morgaine was only three then, so she thought the bunny had disappeared! I'll never forget her surprise! Then she —"

"I knew they would be trapped."

Charlene continued rubbing the back of his hand, and paused before responding, "Yes. But what if they had marched along this very trail, and came to Windhollow in violence?"

"What if. Never Knowledge. Just guesses."

"Yes. In this realm, only guesses."

"Let this one go." Kaja stood and walked away, leaving his knife and pack on the ground.

Charlene gathered them and followed. Then she heard movements in the notch. "Kaja —"

Kaja did not respond. He was standing, transfixed. Bwain stood over the miserable prisoner. The Nok was kneeling, and Bwain had tied him much more completely, with a noose around his neck. He stood holding the other end of it.

Kaja bored into the boy with his gaze alone.

"He's mine now, Kaja," Bwain said.

"Kill you where you stand."

"You will not."

"Let him go. There be no battle with Nok now."

"I'm taking him to Sekh."

"Why?"

"You could not understand."

Kaja spat, "What do you know, Bwain? You are Sekh's slave. To him, that is all you be."

Bwain's mouth quivered, "How dare you speak that way to a High Hingemen!"

"You came here to kill me."

"You know nothing."

"I know you ran through your own shit to get away from a Nok. That I saw, that I know." Kaja widened with astonishment as a realization drew him out of himself. He briefly glanced to Charlene. Clearly, she was the shooter whose arrow plugged Bwain's hair into his captor's chest.

"You saw me kill that Nok!" Bwain shouted. He pouted, like a little boy, but with the alarming addition of adult fortitude.

"Charlene saved your life…" Kaja said, half to confirm his realization to himself. Charlene stood no taller than the kneeling man.

Bwain's face contorted. "Freak!" he screamed. "Leave us alone! Go back to your homeland. No one wants you here!"

"Oh, that's not true, Bwain," Charlene said.

"Yes it is! The Talon will never accept him! Ogden wants to get rid of him! I heard him say so himself!"

"So you did come to kill me."

"You live because I let you live."

"Children, children, enough of this," Charlene walked to stand between the two, and the Nok pitched forward as if at her.

Bwain jerked to pull him back, but he had lost his grip on the rope. The man collapsed, his face in the dust. Bwain stood up taller, as though he had demonstrated power. He said, "I'm not letting him go."

"Then what will you do for Kaja when we get back to town?" Charlene asked. "You owe me Bwain. No one needs to know. But you know, and I know. And Kaja knows. Are you an honorable man, Bwain?"

"I am a loyal man, Charlene."

"Loyal to what, Bwain?"

"To the Hingemen—nothing else."

"What is the Hingemen's purpose, Bwain?"

"I cannot tell you. Nor will I."

"Is it Knowledge, Bwain?"

"I will not say."

"Knowledge must be part of it, Bwain. Why else build the Hinges? Why else learn the rites?"

Bwain said nothing. He shifted rapidly between Charlene and Kaja.

"Do you know why I saved your life, Bwain?"

"I didn't need your help."

"Perhaps not. But I helped you. You are not a prisoner of the Nok, now, are you?"

"I...I..."

"You want to do well. And, you want to impress your teacher, because you are loyal to him. That is good, Bwain. Sekh chose you—you did not choose Sekh. And you work very hard, don't you, Bwain."

"Yes, I do."

"That's very good, Bwain. Did Ogden really tell you to kill Kaja?"

"He. I..." Bwain could not look at her.

"Or did Sekh tell you to do that?"

"They thought the Nok would do it. Sekh just wanted. He sent me to..."

"Alright then. Things didn't work out that way. But look at what has happened. The Nok cannot attack us now. The Yuffs will be able to graze their herds. And, you have a prisoner. Will Sekh be pleased with this? What do you think?"

"I… He wants..."

"Will Ogden be pleased?"

"Yes."

"And Bal and the Talon? Will they be pleased to march here to see what has happened?"

"Yes, they will."

"And what will they think when they come here, knowing that you brought home the prisoner?"

Kaja understood what Charlene was doing. After a while, a grin spread across Bwain's face.

"And what will the townsfolk think, when the soldiers return with their stories?" Charlene continued.

"I see…"

"Will they think better of you if you kill Kaja, Bwain?"

"No. No. I get your point."

"Do you know what Kaja is supposed to be doing out here, Bwain?"

"Spying on the Nok."

"How easy would it be to find the Nok village, if you didn't know about this pass?"

"You probably couldn't"

"Probably not. That's what I'd say. So, what if, you followed Kaja, but then, you saw an opportunity to attack the Nok, all on your own?"

Kaja listened to Charlene's sweet voice, leading Bwain along. She had found a way out of this trap, but she must know that she was taking a path to a new one, a worse one for her people. *Will she really help this sniveling moron become a hero?*

"What if I did?"

"Yes, what if? What if Kaja took a long time to come home? What if he found the Nok village before he returned? What if, when he found it, he saw that it had burned to the ground?"

Bwain nodded slowly. "Yes?"

"And, what if, before he got back with that news, you had already brought your prisoner to Sekh and Ogden? What would the people think of you then?"

Bwain looked pleadingly at Kaja.

"I will do this, Bwain. If you to try so Sekh will let me stay. I want to live with Genu, that is all. We will go to Windhollow, to be with Martin, so you will not need to see me."

Bwain asked Charlene, "Will you do it, too?"

"Yes, Bwain. I would be happy to. We can live in peace, my friend Kaja with us. And you can be happy, too."

"What if…"

"Bwain," Charlene said, walking up to stand in front of him, with her back to Kaja. "Will you swear to me that you owe me your life?"

"I swear it, Charlene. If you do this for me, I will swear it every morning."

"Will you vouch for Kaja to the court, and gain him safe haven with us?"

"Yes, I will. If he does this, too." He cast a liquid glance at Kaja, who nodded reassuringly.

"Very good. Very good. There is one more thing I need from you, though. One more thing you must give me, and we will go our separate ways. Will you give it to me?"

"What is it?"

"The seeds in the pouch around your neck, Bwain. Your mustard. Give them to me, and on your way home, replace them with others. Sekh will never know."

Bwain hesitated for a moment. Then, with a casual cock of his head, he lifted the pouch off his neck and handed it to Charlene. She emptied the seeds into a small cloth, which she rolled and tied. This she held between her palms and bowed to Bwain, imitating Kaja's way.

The Beat

What a bowl of dung," Sekh snarled after Bwain left them alone.

"It could be true," Ogden said.

"You've got to be kidding. Bwain can't pick his nose without worrying he's got it wrong. How could he possibly take out the entire Nok contingent and bring home a prisoner? He'd never have the guts. Or any idea how. It must have been Kaja's Magic. There's more to this than Bwain is letting on, I tell you."

Ogden slid a stick down his shirt and scratched his back thoughtfully. Sekh thought everything was a plot. He always concluded that, no matter what happened, it was part of some conspiracy against him. "Kaja might've missed the trail to the Nok village. He's probably still out there wandering around blindly. Shall I send someone for him?"

"Why? They'd never find him. And if they killed him, the Coven would know." Sekh fumbled small bone jars on his workbench.

"Well then, we live with him."

"For now."

Ogden stopped scratching and a snarl climbed his nose. Did Sikh think he could kill at will? On his own authority? Was there any boundary to what he might do? He took his time with the stick, until his desire to confront his brother subsided. "That Nok in the hole is real enough. How did Bwain get a prisoner? Could it be, that you really did pick the right apprentice?"

"You seem pleased by all of this."

"Well, seems to me, Sekh, if there's a grain of truth in Bwain's story, I'm pretty happy about it."

"Happy? Bah."

"Sure, happy. We might avoid a battle. We might get the pasturelands uncontested. That's good, right?"

"When are you leaving?"

Ogden paused. Had his brother heard him? The old wizard was running his hands over the back of his chair, his gaze darting around, seeing little. "When the Talon are done pissing on the prisoner, the poor fool. Probably around dawn, we'll head out."

"Don't let them kill him. We'll use him later."

"I know, you told me."

"Are you taking Bwain?"

"I am," Ogden said, surprised by the question. "Everyone saw him lead the prisoner into town. The Talon are fascinated. He can lead the way through the notch to the Nok. Let the men follow him, and I'll take up the rear."

Sekh curled his lip and shuffled over to one of his wall posts. He pulled on a peg to open a secret chamber Ogden did not know was there. He could not see into it from where he sat, and his brother's strange behavior transfixed him. Sekh whispered into the chamber inaudibly and put up his ear to listen. Again he talked to it, and again he listened. He cursed and slammed the chamber closed. Flipping his hood over his head, he hissed, "Tiss!" With his back to Ogden, he muttered a dismissal, "I have work to do."

Ogden shut the door behind him quietly and listened through it. His brother muttered to himself, but he could not hear what he said.

❧

"It's nice being lost together, Kaja," Charlene said.

"Yes, Charlene. I like with you to be lost a while."

"I know a nice trail we can take from here to our Living Ring. It's a bit longer. It's the one the Nok Covens used to use when they visited."

"Really? You share the Ring with the Nok? In the past?"

"Indeed, Kaja. Things haven't always been this way, you know. A lot has changed."

"Yes."

They walked along in silence for a while. Despite her small stature, Charlene was very comfortable on a wilderness trail. "Well, fellow freak," she said, "We're assassins now."

"Assassin?"

"We snuck up on others and killed them. That's an assassin."

"You did not mean to kill anyone."

"No, of course not. But I will have to deal with that Nok again sometime. Maybe not in this lifetime, and maybe not in the way I anticipate. But there's no escaping it. I will have to deal with him."

"And me, with all the soldiers in the Hall?"

"Yes. No escape."

Kaja nodded. He lifted his gaze from the trail to the scruffy tough brush growing from under boulders, their dark green sprays shaped by the flowing winds.

"Why did you kill that Nok?"

"Answer me this, first, Kaja. You followed Bwain around that village for two days. If you were going to kill him, why didn't you just do it?"

"I didn't care if he lived or died. I just wanted to use him to get a simple home with Genu. Somehow, I knew, I could use him for that. But how, I did not know."

"Really? That was not what I saw. I saw that you wanted to kill him."

Kaja was quiet for a while. "My way of being, because of the Thurgans. That did change me. I am like them, when I see Bwain follow me. I knew he was sent to kill me. I become Thurgan to live. Again."

Charlene nodded, and they walked in silence for a while. The trees were cool, and the ground was soft, and the aroma of the forest moss and mushrooms comforted them. She asked, "What do you mean, when you say, 'myself?'"

Kaja took a long time to answer. He said, "I no longer know."

"Oh, that's very good, Kaja, very good."

Kaja shook his head. "And you, Charlene, why did you kill that Thurgan to save Bwain?"

"I killed a Nok."

"Yes, that Nok."

"Bwain is the son of one of my Coven sisters. That is why."

"But now he might be poison for your people. Come back a hero—he may be worse for you and yours then."

"Maybe. But I will always protect the children of my Coven sisters. Always."

"I see. They will use that against you."

"How could protecting your young be used against you?"

The true answer to that question is too close to my secret. He said only, "Anything can be used against you, Charlene. Love, especially."

Charlene took her time before replying, "I see."

Kaja noticed a burl at the base of a dead branch. He walked over to it and knocked on it with his walking stick, and then put his weight into the branch. When it broke, Kaja felt the curved wood around the burl and judged the depth of the splintering. He batted the burl against the tree with a small force. To his delight, it didn't crumble. "Do you mind?" Charlene contentedly perched herself on a boulder partially protruding from the ground, and Kaja set to trimming it. "So how did you find me?"

"Oh, Genu and Morgaine came and told me you had been sent away by Sekh and Ogden. We didn't know where, but I found you anyway. You're good, Kaja—it was difficult to follow your trail."

"What mistakes did I make?"

"Well now, I can't reveal all my secrets."

Kaja grinned and held his wood to look it over as a whole. The dawn's light shined on Charlene's cheeks. "I want to go home," he said.

"Me too. But not yet. We have to let Bwain have his moment of glory."

"Won't they know Bwain didn't do it?"

"Oh, Ogden will probably figure it out. But it doesn't matter. If they can use it, they will use it."

"What will happen to the Nok prisoner?"

"I don't know, Kaja, I'm sorry. He'll be dead soon, though. That is certain. And the Nok townsfolk—Ma, I fear for them. Ogden's got his fighting men ready to kill and plunder. Who knows what will happen now."

Kaja scraped patches of bark off his wood with his flint knife. The sky drifted overhead. A linnet alighted on the end of a bowed stem and sang.

After a few days of slow hiking, they came to the Ring of Trees, where they planned to part in the morning.

"I suppose I should tell you a few things to say, Kaja," Charlene said, "so you can fake it better when you get back."

"Yes. Good. I do thank you."

"Since you were sent on a mission, not a proper Spirit Walk, things may be different. But it would be good if you pretended that, after you found the Nok village destroyed, you had some insights. It will be more convincing, since we believe that being alone in the wilderness leads to great wisdom."

"It does."

"Yes, it does. Usually, our people go on several Spirit Walks. The first is early in life, and then, as they feel they want to, they do more as they age. The first one, you take with others— usually with your spirit teacher, and always with one or two other youths and their teachers. If I remember what Morgaine told me of your story, you and your uncle used to do them all the time, when you went hunting or mining. He would teach you your people's stories, and your people's practice?"

"Yes. All the time. Sometimes for an afternoon, sometimes for days. He taught me much and was so patient. He would have kept teaching me my whole life. He told me many times that he would teach me until I to teach him."

"There you are. That's just it. The same sort of thing. Then, someday, you'll go off on your own. That first one should last for half a Moon. You leave when she is new and return when she is full. Each person's is different. But the object is to search for Knowledge—real Knowledge, deep Knowledge of the cosmos, which begins with Knowledge of the Self. It is a long meditation on who you are, and why you are here in this life."

"I would like to know that, I would."

"We all would, Kaja. And we all try to learn the answers, but the quest is more important to some than to others."

"Yes. I have asked Dogen to help me, because he is so intent."

"Indeed he is. If Sekh was a real leader, he would have taken Dogen as his apprentice. But he took Bwain instead, for reasons that have nothing to do with the quest for Knowledge. His choice of Bwain—who is a good boy, really, just in way over his head—was a dark day for all of us in Ogden's realm."

"I see."

"Well, usually, when someone comes back from their first solo Spirit Walk, they gather with their teachers, and they are asked to make some statement about what they have learned. You might be confronted with that."

"Sekh never tires of confronting me."

Charlene chuckled. "No, he doesn't, does he? You are very strong, Kaja, very strong. How you keep control of yourself so well is a mystery to me."

Kaja's brow furled, and he looked away. From his perspective, he felt that all he did was lose control of himself. He loved her for knowing how much he had to contend with, and how hard he tried.

"I miss Genu. That is what I have learned. That would be my statement, that I love her so dearly. And Dogen and Regis and Morgaine and Hypp—all of them. I do love them, and I wish only to be with them always."

Charlene nodded, "And what a fine thing to know about life, Kaja, and why you are here."

In the morning they embraced. Then Charlene took her things—her tiny bed roll, her tiny pack, her tiny pouches and skins—and headed off for her home in Windhollow. Kaja donned his man-sized equipment, and walked off to Ash, ambling slowly in the morning mists.

He circled around the town to come to Hypp's home first, where he found her and the Crones working in her garden. She dropped her tools and ran to him, and they held each other for a long time. Kaja felt like she filled him with power. It came up from the earth, through her, and then from her heart into his, like an ocean wind. His breath deepened, in awe of its force and quantity. He felt like she would give him all the power she had, and that she could always get more from the endless source welling through her Coven.

Arm in arm, they walked to the house, from which poured the rest of the crew. Never had anyone's body felt the way Genu's did then. Her deep blue eyes swam into his, and his hands stroked her long red curls, and their love swelled in them like a spring stream pouring through sunlit flowers.

❧

Bal and Yet came for him not long after. Regis opened the door when he heard the Talon's footfalls, and he and Dogen stood outside to greet them.

"He's coming with us," Bal said, but faltered to see the disdain on their faces.

"Nice armor, Bal. Did you spit-polish your breastplate?" Regis asked.

Dogen smiled serenely. Kaja walked between them and past Bal. "Let's go," he said, leading the Talon to Sekh's lair.

The old wizard sat in his chair, hood drawn, hands clutching the carved owl heads. His unlit pipe sat on a small three-legged table next to him. Ogden was there, too, and, this time, Bwain was not tucked away on the floor with his little magical project. He was sitting on a chair, posing cocky. Ogden motioned for Kaja to sit on a stool, which he did.

"Well," Ogden began, "I'd like to know about the Nok. Do you mind? We'll get to your initiation next. Were you able to find your way?"

"I misread one marker that cost me more than a day," Kaja said.

"Really? With all your skills? Surprises me."

"Yes."

"But eventually, you got there."

"Yes. A disaster had befallen them. A fire. Their Hall had burned, and I believe many of their soldiers were caught inside."

Ogden pursed his lips and pulsed his laced fingers. Now he knew he and Bwain had met in the wilderness and were weaving a lie.

"Bwain," Ogden said, rounding on the boy jovially but with so much energy the apprentice recoiled. "Why would he think many of the soldiers were inside? Didn't you say something about knifing them?"

Sekh did not move, and the boy apprentice felt a cold slither of fear slide down his guts. He focused on the pipe table, and blurted, "They stabbed the roof of the Hall!"

"What?"

"In the fire, to escape, they stabbed the roof of the Hall with their spears. I didn't tell you. The points of the spears stuck out of the top of the Hall, because they died anyway. That's why."

"Liar," Sekh said, freezing the word to shattered crystals in the air.

Bwain began trembling from head to foot. He sought refuge in Ogden.

"Come on now, Bwain. You're a good apprentice." Ogden winked at the boy. "But you didn't do any of that. Why don't you tell us the truth? And then tell us why you lied."

Bwain's throat clogged with gummy spit, and he felt like he was going to puke. "I didn't want to be the apprentice, you know. It's not my fault I have a purple patch on my back."

"But you are the apprentice, Bwain. And, you work very hard. We all see that. Don't we, Sekh?" The wizard was as cold and distant as an ice floe at sea, and still, Bwain clung to him.

The boy is a Thurgan thug, just as possessed, just as beaten, just as obedient. As that thought passed through his mind, Bwain turned on him.

"He didn't attack the Nok alone! Charlene was there!"

His mind is crippled.

"What?" Ogden said, mirth filling his face. "Charlene of Windhollow?"

"He can't do Magic," Bwain said. "She did it."

"Did what?"

"Enough of this dribble, Bwain," Sekh seethed, silencing him with a raised finger. The boy trembled from his core.

Ogden surveyed the lamps atop the poles in Sekh's den, and the bat skeletons hanging from the rafters, and the painted fox skull sitting upon red felt, and the dozens of corked bone jars standing in a pyramid, and said to Kaja, "Why don't you tell us the story. The whole story."

Kaja told it as accurately as he could. At the end, Bwain was petrified, and Sekh's rage was a silent, freezing vapor. But Ogden leaned back and grinned. His smile got wider and wider, until he threw back his head with a mighty laugh.

"Oh, that's rich," Ogden said, "That's just rich. A miniature witch. A tattooed foreigner. And Bwain! The Nok prisoner swinging his head from face to face. He musta been thinking, 'What is going on?' Come on, Sekh, you gotta admit that's pretty funny."

Sekh threw his hood over his head. Kaja did not want to humiliate Bwain to provocation and struggled not to smile. Ogden's laughter tumbled into a decision and an edict. "Kaja, we're going with the version that Bwain's the hero. He did bring the prisoner all the way back, if nothing else. It's better for the realm if this all makes sense. Don't question it, can you do that?"

Makes sense so the Hinge has the power and so the Talon will believe and obey. This is how truth dies. So to protect truth, I lie. Such is this world. "Yes, Honorable Ogden," Kaja said.

Bwain sat up and set his jaw, believing his proud posture looked filial.

And so they birth a hollow hero.

"We have one last order of business here," Ogden said, still smiling. "For your initiation to be complete, we need a statement from you about your… we will call it your manhood Spirit Walk. Can you —"

"Ogden, no," Sekh interrupted, "Kaja will have a proper conference with me to obtain that."

Ogden's mirth iced and cracked. He passed over Bwain and glared at the Hingemen crossly, but said, "Very well, Sekh."

Motioning for Kaja to lead the way out, he rose. Kaja bowed before following his gesture to the door. They walked down the path from Sekh's lair. The canopy closed over them, and purple and pink irises sprouted in patches at the foot of trees. Before they got to the main trail, he waved his hand through the space before them. "Kaja," he said intimately, "I know all of this has been an ordeal for you."

"Yes, Honorable Ogden."

"What is this secret that Sekh wants so dearly? Do you know?"

And still, the secret. No acknowledgement. Just the exchange. "May I speak honestly, sir?"

"Please do."

"The Thurgans had no Magic. I learned none. With fear and violence they ruled. With horses and weapons. I can teach nothing to him."

"I see. But in the Nok village, how did you do it? You used no Magic there?"

"Like a river the ability flowed through me. I had no care, because I feared death was already in me. For Bwain you sent to kill me, did you not?"

Ogden looked away. "I think it would be a good thing for you to live in Windhollow, Kaja. Take Genu there if she wills it. Live in peace."

Kaja looked into his wizened blue eyes, set deep in draping, aged folds. "Thank you, my Liege."

Ogden took a moment in Kaja's eyes before he nodded and walked into the forest alone.

The Music

Not many days after, as the New Moon approached, the townspeople heeded Sekh's call to a public announcement at the Hall that everyone was required to attend the rite at the Hinge.

Hypp had kept Kaja with her, and they were alone. Kaja reclined in his usual spot with his instrument in his lap. He had become possessive of its sound and had managed to keep it secret from all except her. He tuned the strings relative to each other, confident that he finally had it perfect.

While he played scales, Hypp snuggled up next to him. Something about the way she came close but remained alert felt different, as though she needed him. He put his harp in its box, arranged his blanket to cover her as well, and embraced her small frame with one long arm.

"Kaja," she said quietly. "I want you to know how much everything has changed because of you."

"Yes?"

"You fought back, Kaja. That impresses us. It inspires us."

"Not fight. Run."

"That is not what we see. They tried to destroy you in many ways, and despite all that happened to you, you became yourself."

"Myself..."

"I know that's hard for you, Kaja, because 'yourself' includes your family, and the Rishi. You wanted to know yourself through them. Instead, they live through you. None of them is gone, because 'yourself' includes them, and you keep them alive."

Kaja took her hand, and they toyed with each other's fingers.

Hypp went on, "And now, 'yourself' includes some of us as well."

"Yes. All of you."

"I am proud that is true. And 'ourselves' include you, now, Kaja. Your courage has changed my Coven. It has changed my friends. Most of all, it has changed me. 'Myself' includes the Rishi."

"I wanted to become you."

"And so you have, don't you think? To us, you are a fine Ringfolk."

"Ringfolk..."

"Yes. And, you are a fine son."

Kaja held her gently but completely and buried his face in her hair.

"My son, I want you to promise me something."

"Anything."

"Be true to yourself, as a Rishi, and as a Ringfolk."

"I will."

"Help everyone around you be true, too."

Kaja sensed that she was telling him this now for some reason. "I will," he said, and he felt his mind expand and open. The thrill of it strummed his spine like the strings of his harp, and then he felt it, clear and true. The ocean wind blew from his heart and swirled into hers. "Is everything alright?"

She nodded softly under his chin. "It will be. If we have courage."

"Together, we will."

"Yes. Together. In whatever form that takes."

⟪∧⟫

A rumble of footfalls tumbled up the path. The others came inside, carrying a displeased energy full of suspicion that had a distinct source, but no object. They settled into their places, and a moment later, Regis arrived.

"Ma, that Bwain is a gnat!" Cold air clung to him as he poled his parka with one thrust and kicked his boots onto their shelf. "Standin' there, 'Oh, I'm such a hero! I found the Nok village!'" He threw his gloves onto the edge of the hearth and stood next to Morgaine, who put a calming hand on his calf from where she reclined. "'Now I'm a great warrior!'" He took a deep breath and lifted his closed eyes to the rafters and ran his fingers through his long red hair until he switched to stroking his beard, which swiveled his head back to level. "How in Ma's bowels did Bwain ever become the apprentice, anyway?"

"Who knows?" Jinn sneered.

"It shoulda been you, Dogen. It shoulda been you, and everyone knows it."

"Well, now, Regis —"

"I'm serious. This is a mess. Sekh and Ogden making Bwain into a hero. Making a fool of him, really. And he's Sekh's apprentice? If he'd have picked you, like he should've done, none of this would be going on!"

Kaja had never seen Regis agitated like this before. "My people had idea about this, Regis, they did. The teacher must choose his student well."

"Ma's thunder, he should. I almost feel sorry for Bwain, really, I do. He can't count to eleven without taking his shoes off, and Sekh thinks he knows the rites now? What's gonna happen to us when Sekh's gone? There's nothing real about what Bwain does."

"There's barely anything real about what Sekh does," Trawill said. The other Crones nodded in agreement, exchanging knowing smiles before trying to conceal them.

"So what's gonna happen? Hingemen and Talon accomplishing what?"

"I fear it, too, Regis," Dogen said.

"And if only he'd have picked you!"

"Dogen, did you want to be Sekh's apprentice?" Kaja asked.

Dogen preferred to remain quiet at gatherings like this, a benevolent spirit on the fringes of the party, known intimately by each but, through that, known not at all. He was unsure how to respond, for Sekh had become despicable. "Ahh, Kaja. My good friend," he said, fondling his hand. "I don't know what I wanted out of life, I really don't. No profession or mission ever captivated me."

"I know what you want," Kaja said.

Dogen glanced at his fantastic face. What insight had he brought from beyond the known world?

"You want Knowledge, Dogen," Kaja said.

Dogen drew a deep breath and plunged out of his element. "Indeed, that is true. My mother knew I felt this way, and so she taught me how to practice when I was very young. But I have not attained Knowledge. I just live. I just practice as best I can, and live, and I learn what I can in that way. That's all." He made a dismissive motion with his hand.

"That is the true path, Dogen," Hypp said. "Ma's path. And you have learned a great deal. All see it. People respect you deeply, in ways you don't know. I tell you the truth."

"We need the society that would pick him to exist," Morgaine said thoughtfully. "We can't grow by fighting the world. We can only do it in the world, and with it."

Regis reclined next to her, and gratefully took the cup of hot broth Gan gave him.

"Oh, child," Jinn said. "So true. Too long now, we've lived against the Hingemen, letting ourselves slip away little by little."

The Crones were holding hands under their blanket, and they seemed to confer energetically, and to agree.

"We have something to tell you children," Jinn said.

All three Crones landed on Kaja, so clearly he felt it like a touch. *Is that...appreciation?*

"We're going to take it all back at once," Hypp said, illuminated by a quiet, confident smile that spanned the three of them. "We will go on our Spirit Walk. That's what we can do."

The color drained from Regis's face. "What?"

"It's time for my sisters and I to go on a Spirit Walk, Regis. A long one—an endless one."

Regis sat, slack jawed, as conflicting emotions played his face and welled up on his cheeks.

"What do you mean?" Dogen asked.

"In the days before the Hinges, it was customary for Crones to go on Spirit Walks, Dogen. We will go on one, too, to visit with our sisters all across the land. To sit with them, to be with them."

Kaja watched her look around her home, and at her friends. She had only Regis, but Trawill and Jinn had three children each, and their youngest ones had just spread their wings. She admired her giant fan of feathers, and the intricate tile work around the hearth, and the rounded ladder to the upstairs porch. Quip had done much of this work, so her lover's handprint was everywhere on her spot in the world. Could she leave? He said, "Endless?"

"Oh, Kaja, we've given this a great deal of thought. There are dangers, we know. But even if we visit only one other town, only one other Coven, before—well, it will be worth it. Just to show the other Covens that they can do it, too. No one remembers why or when we started talking about Spirit Walks in the past tense. Why, my grandmother used to tell stories of clairvoyants coming from all over the world, all the time, to visit. They would just walk into town and be taken in for a spell. Why did we stop? Why not show the others that we can still do it?"

"Could you imagine," Trawill said, "if at some point we met other Crones doing the same thing? If other Covens began to travel too? What a fantastic effect that would that have on us all!"

"I just want to breathe again," Jinn said. "If only for a little while, I want to walk in Ma's presence as her daughter. As her *free* daughter."

"Where will you go?" Kaja asked, checking Regis, who was stunned.

"It doesn't matter, Kaja, it doesn't matter. We will start in one direction and then change to another. The trails are still there. The Rings are still there. They will guide us."

"Yeah but those trails serve a different purpose now," Regis blurted. "Bandits and traders, if there's a difference, own those routes now. Even the herders will tell you it's dangerous—and they're young and strong."

"We have a different strength, Regis," Trawill said simply.

"And a different youth," added Jinn.

"I know you will worry, Regis. But you are my child. You feel my Spirit within you. While we are Walking, you will feel my Spirit. That will be good for you, as it will be for me, too."
Regis blinked at her.

"I think it is a grand idea," Genu said.

"Me, too," Kaja said. Hypp loved him greatly, and all saw it in her smile. "Breathe and be free, Ma's daughter. Yes. Do it, I say."

"You are a fine man, Kaja."

"You know, it gets really cold out there in the open, Ma. I mean really, really cold. You're so small—how will you stay warm?" They laughed and cried at this, perhaps because Regis had once come out of her and was now three times her size.

"Oh, my son," Hypp said, as tears of happiness rolled down her cheeks. "I am so proud of you, Regis. So very, very proud."

"But. But. How? When will you leave?" sputtered Regis.

"Soon after Kaja's ordeal—I mean 'initiation'—at the Hinge," Trawill said

"So soon!"

"We have been considering it carefully for some time, Regis."

"The Coven knows?"

"Oh yes. They are very happy for us. We hope others will go, too."

"And leave us here with Bwain?"

"And leave you here with our spirits singing Ringsongs to you in your dreams, Regis."

Regis' heart was in his throat. He had lived with his mother his whole life, and even while planning to move to Windhollow he had always known, when the moment came, he would not leave without her. He had never imagined she would leave without him.

"Do you think you can change the world, Hypp, really?" Genu asked.

"We don't know. But we can do this. We can be a story, a tale told in Covens around the island. We can be an inspiration to others. Three old Crones heading out with packs—now it seems an outrageous thought, but for most of our history, it was normal."

"You inspire me," Genu said. "To go on a great adventure near the end of life—what a perfect thing! I respect the wisdom of your grandmother, Hypp. Did she go on a Spirit Walk as a Crone?"

"No, she never did. She talked about it, but she never did. Perhaps she wasn't blessed with companions as I am." Her sisters cuddled her.

"I'm inspired, too," Morgaine said. "But I will miss you so much. You have been so kind to me since…since my mother and my little brother passed away."

"Yes, Hypp, I'll miss you too. You have been a mother to me as well," Dogen said.

"Now, children, children. We will come back now and then. You will see. It is a big island, but not that big."

"We'll see lands we've never seen before," Jinn said.

"And visit people we've only heard of," Trawill said.

"Ma's morning," agreed Trawill.

"Free at last," Hypp said.

⟨∿⟩

"Kaja, let us speak like men," Sekh said as he twitched in his chair.

Kaja stood across from him, delivered by the Hingemen, Phiop and Krev, who stood on the porch outside. He was to reveal what he had learned on his "manhood Spirit Walk," but the wizard's delirious smile alarmed him.

"Yes, High Hingemen. I would like that."

"Good, good. Good." Nodding, Sekh peered into a dark space between stacks of boxes. Kaja waited. "Well. You managed to get your way, Kaja."

"How do you mean?"

"Don't feed me dung," he said, snarling so his gross, smoke-stained teeth showed, and rubbing the owl heads as if to destroy them. "You get to stay. You get my niece. And you gave me nothing for it."

"What can I give you, High Hingemen? Shall I make you an instrument?"

"Enough of this 'sound' crap! There is no sound. I know that now. I don't know what Elrik was driveling about!" Grinding his teeth, he clenched his bony fist so hard Kaja wondered at the depth of his desperation. "So. Then. You won't tell me, will you? Why should you, now?"

"Won't tell you what, High Hingemen?"

"*The secret!* The secret, the secret, the secret! How did the Thurgans do it? How did you take down the Nok and bring home a prisoner? How? That's Magic, Kaja! *I want that Magic!*"

"Oh, you have it, sir."

"Bah! I don't believe it. How did you get Ogden to say the same? That's Magic, too. You have it all about you." His gaze shifted outside of the room and focused on some other realm that Kaja did not know and hoped he never would. The wizard hissed "Tiss!" and slammed his fist down on an owl's head so hard Kaja almost startled, certain he heard a bone break. Sekh did not so much as wince.

"You have it, High Hingemen. You do. The Thurgans ruled with violence and with fear. That is all. They took what they wanted, and when you hated them the most, you were most at their mercy."

"I have known hatred, Kaja."

"Yes?"

"Oh, yes. You would not understand. How could you? I was forced into competition for the High Hingemen apprenticeship. And I deserved it more. Why am I telling you this? Tiss should have picked me. At birth. Before birth, he should have known I was coming. But he made me compete. With Pam. Gentle, contemplative, almost like an idiot. Everybody loved him. For years. Then, on a Spirit Walk we took together, Pam died. A rock fell from a cliff and crushed his skull. We were only eleven. So I never won the competition. I got the apprenticeship because Pam died. That is hatred, Kaja. Do you see?"

"No, High Hingemen. I know about that not at all."

"And then, after decades of faithful service, of first-rate astronomy, and the completion of the Hinge, all these things I have done, my Magic pulls you out of the sea. Even then, even then, they don't really believe it. They don't think it is me. My work. My work!" The cleric trembled so, searching the floor for an answer. "And you, Kaja," he said, fixing a cold, dead gaze and pointing at his face, "You make it worse. All I wanted was your Knowledge. Just the Magic. The Magic my Magic called you to

345

give! That is all! All I wanted! Would you give it to me? Would you? *No!* You make a mockery of my work! You give nothing! *Nothing!*"

Suddenly Sekh stood up, and Kaja recoiled within his body, which remained still and unresponsive. The old wizard shuffled in his heavy, dusty robes. On the back of his cloak was a crescent moon, embroidered with gold wire he had let tarnish. He went to the post, and opened the secret compartment, and withdrew his treasure, concealing it in his hand.

"So now, Kaja. I will ask you one last time." He moved his three-legged pipe table to stand between them. On it he placed a tiny clay figurine. Nana's amulet, the one she had given to Kaja when they were children. The little goddess, with her knee broken off and her face worn smooth, sat meditating on Sekh's table, facing her brother.

Does it still have a trace of Nana's smell? Can I hold it, and feel her touch? May I search it for the imprint of her fingertips? May I know that she once lived, and that my old world is not a dream?

"Do you want this, Kaja?" Sekh's hand hovered over it, ready to snatch it away. His evil smile widened at the sight of Kaja's thoughts. At last, he had the power he wanted.

"Yes," Kaja lifted his gaze to Sekh's, searching for the man in him. "Of my sister, this amulet is all that remains for me. To take it, what would you gain?"

"Oh, I'll let you have it. I'll trade you for it. Tell me the secret. And you can have it. Deny me, and I will destroy it."

The demon calm came over Kaja. "Hingemen," he said, almost paternally. "On your table, see what sits there. For me my sister made it, and to me gave it when I was but a boy. I have lost all of her since then. All my family, my home, my people. If you were me, you would trade anything for it, would you not?"

"The secret, Kaja."

"Now you have it. For the trace of my sister there, I would give you anything. Anything at all. There is no secret, Sekh, for if there was, you would have it now."

"Liar!" Sekh yelled with percussive force, sweeping at the statuette as though to fling it against the wall. But his wrist jerked in pain and he batted the table instead. Its wobble sent the goddess tumbling.

With one swift motion, Kaja caught her just before she hit the floor. He followed the motion to stand. He backed away from Sekh, whose attention bolted from his pain to Kaja. "Give that back!" he shrieked.

"I have no secret to tell you."

"Give that back! I found it! It's mine!"

"I have no secret." Kaja reached for the door.

"How dare you leave without being dismissed! Get back here you black devil!"

"Live in peace, Sekh, live in peace."

"You may never call me 'Sekh!'"

Kaja bowed to the mad wizard and freed himself from his den before striding past Phiop and Krev, who were too bewildered to stop him.

◀◊▶

The morning of his Hingemen initiation, Kaja whispered to Genu, "Come with me." She drew him close. He could feel the soft fox fur pouch hanging over her heart, where he had decided to keep his amulet.

"Where are we going?"

"A surprise."

"Really? I love surprises."

"Yes. Dress warm, we go walking."

She donned her parka, and, holding hands, they strode into the forest. The sky was white, and the high clouds spilled morning light, and the bare branches of the trees trembled with life, as though that day—that very moment—they would explode with blossoms and leaves. The path was no longer mud, but instead had become a stripe of fuzzy green. The gazebo glistened with sunrise dew.

Kaja had her sit where she could see the horizon. The bright blue ocean sent wide, rolling waves to kiss the shore. The gray-green moor was freckled with orange flowers. Genu started to speak, but Kaja put his fingers on her lips, and she became play itself, waiting for her surprise.

Carefully and reverently, Kaja took his harp from the elk-hide box he had made for it and showed it to her. It was an elegant creation, the product of careful, controlled craftsmanship. Kaja sat by her and showed her how the harp fit into his lap, and within his arms, to leave the strings naked and quivering between his hands.

Then he played for her, letting loose a vibration in her mind that she had never imagined. Her hands went to her face, holding her voice, before hovering as though to absorb all that arose from his magical instrument.

A man from another world had brought his music to them. Her inner wisdom awakened, and she intuited the Rishi, and the town that had created Kaja, and the family that had nurtured him.

The Test

Bwain and I will take care of the Nok prisoner," Sekh said.

"He got here as a prisoner, Sekh, but that doesn't mean we have to follow all the rites, does it?" Ogden spoke calmly but surveyed his brother testily.

"Yes, it does. Especially now."

"But why? You should have seen the Nok village when we got there. It was heartbreaking. Burned to the ground. Just about all the fathers and brothers killed in the fire. They gave up on trying to pull them out, and instead just pushed them back in. All the weapons they could find, all the distillery equipment— everything was shoved into the Hall. Then they sealed it off, completely. They were leaving when we arrived. Some to join the herders, others to move to distant towns."

"Yes?"

"Well, I mean, doesn't that have any impact on the rites?"

"Why would it?"

"He's practically the last man alive. It just seems so senseless —"

"To the untrained eye Magic rites always seem senseless. That is why Tiss trained me and not you. Bwain understands. He will be a great wizard someday. This rite is for him. That is what is important, Ogden. Think about Bwain, the Great High Hingemen who will replace me."

"Sure, I understand, but couldn't we —"

"No, we can't. The ceremony will proceed as I plan it. If it doesn't, I am not responsible for the hunt this summer, or the snows next winter. We must do this right, Ogden. We are at a critical juncture. If we fail to fulfill our duties, we will face malice from beyond the grave. We will pay. Tiss knows. Oh, he knows. Kaja knows, too. We must have the strength to carry this through."

"So there's absolutely —"

"No. Enough, brother, please. You vex me, and there is much work ahead of me. Come with the Talon to the Ring. I will show you what to do and when to do it."

Ogden watched while he puttered about his bowls and tinctures. The hunt this summer? Snows next winter? Rage from beyond the grave? Shaking his head, he left conflicted.

"Alright, let's get this over with," Trawill said, standing by Hypp's hearth, looking at her friends. She wore an impish grin, as did Hypp and Jinn. The Crones had stayed at Jinn's home the night before, and something silly or refreshing had happened. The younger people exchanged quizzical smiles around them, wondering and guessing to themselves, but not asking. Even Regis, who still couldn't believe his beloved mother was actually leaving on a Spirit Walk, pursed his wet lips and raised his bushy eyebrows with a merry unspoken hypothesis in his mind.

Genu had given Kaja a beautiful little pouch of red fox fur, trimmed with tiny grey feathers, to hold Nana's amulet. He removed it from his neck and placed it around hers, lowering it slowly into her shirt while holding her gaze with his own, love and lust entwined. She felt the soft fur tickle, and she squirmed a little to enliven Kaja's desire for her.

"'Oh, Ma, I raise this bowl of sacred crud to the spirits of the south!'" mocked Regis. "'And now I walk way over here and raise this bowl of sacred crud to the spirits of the west! And now I'm gonna stand here and think about this sacred bowl of crud for a while, to prove everyone will stand in silence for no reason. And then, zzzzzzzzzzz.'" Regis pretended to nod off to sleep, and the three Crones laughed at his performance.

Gan picked it up, "'Oh, sacred Regis! I'm gonna tag along behind you with my very own sacred bowl of crud! The sun does shine from your asshole, sacred Regis! Ooops!'" he pretended to trip and spill his crud all over Morgaine. "Oh Morgaine, you have been blessed with a shower of sacred crud! Let it dry upon you, for the glory of the stars!'"

"Aren't you proud to be the guest of honor at this?" Dogen said through his laughter.

"I would like to see the sun shining from Regis' behind, yes," Kaja said.

"Oh you children are goofy, just goofy," Hypp said. "Enough now, enough. Or we'll make fools of ourselves giggling."

"I would be proud to be a giggling fool," Jinn said.

"Oh, what am I saying? I want to be one, too!" Hypp said happily.

"We are giggling fools!" Trawill chimed.

"Let's see if we can smile all the way through this!" Gan said.

They called out agreement and made their way to leave. The Crones took up the lead, holding hands and swinging their arms with youthful energy. Unfortunately, the others on the trail didn't share their levity. It seemed clear to Kaja that everyone was prepared to do their duty and be completely bored and intimidated for the evening. It was also clear that there were many more people coming to this ceremony than had come to his real initiation. Every household had disgorged itself completely, and a collective pall had fallen over them. Some of the men and women wore resolute expressions, repelling other's gazes and forcing them to the ground.

The Hinge rose from the horizon as they approached, gigantic and brooding beneath coiling grey clouds. A frigid wind poured over them, as the people of Ash filed into place according to some enforced order. The Crones went to one spot, the women by them, and Kaja stood between Regis and Dogen on the eastern edge of the Hinge.

He surveyed the scene. The Coven blazed in their yellow scarves. Most everyone else wore a distinguishing decoration, too. Some had chest plaques, but with beads of metal embedded to resemble constellations. *Hingemen. And the ones with beasts bearing arms, Talon. Is it reverence that keeps them all so quiet? Is it fear? Is it some other desire, or some other Magic?*

Kaja wondered at the ceremonial setup at the center of the Hinge. There was the platform, which he had thankfully seen before. But atop it sat a pyre of branches, as though to build a fire, with the apex missing. "What are the branches for?" he whispered to Regis.

"Don't know," Regis replied. "We'll find out, eventually."

"Where are our women?"

"Over there," Regis nodded. Kaja squinted, and Genu gave him the little cupped hand again. Kaja couldn't wait until this was over.

A thunderous crashing of drums began without warning, and the assembly jumped as one. The musicians in their white robes and pasted blue hair beat their instruments furiously, and then the flutes screamed like a flock of frightened birds.

Sekh strode through the musicians and into the Hinge, Bwain and Ogden following. The Hingemen wore strange, stilt-like shoes that made them taller, and their heavy black robes fell from their shoulders to the ground. They had their hoods drawn over their heads, but you could see their faces, painted a dull white with red in the sockets of their eyes.

Sekh's hood had a golden crescent moon embroidered with wire, while Bwain's full moon was embroidered with tin. Ogden wore a thick ring of gold around his head. They headed west and walked slowly around the entire circle of the Hinge, and the people covered their faces as they passed. Kaja had never seen people cover their faces as a sign of respect, but when they passed, the Crones dutifully followed suit. So did he.

When the three got back to the musicians, bowls were brought to Sekh led Bwain, but Kaja couldn't capture the fun they had made about this earlier. Ogden moved to stand in front of the musicians. Sekh and Bwain lifted their bowls to the sky and stood for some time at each of the cardinal points. A sense of foreboding clouded the gathering. At the end of their circuit, the Hingemen threw the contents of their bowls into the circle of branches and stood before it.

Sekh put up his hands and walked a tight circle, his mask accentuating the glare of his grey eyes in the fast-fading light. When his hands came down, the thundering, shrieking music fell to silence. Only the wind dared speak, or move.

"Ash!" he screeched.

"Aye!" rose the response in unison, dying instantly. Kaja bristled. The obedience, unthinking and immediate, was Thurgan Magic, pure and vile.

"Today we celebrate a momentous occasion in our history! The Gods have blessed us! Ma has blessed us! Do you hear?"

"Aye!"

"The Hinge foretold a great victory! The Hinge foretold a great hero! The Hinge foretold a great bounty! Do you hear?"

"Aye!"

"Today we celebrate! For our Hingemen Magic has delivered us from danger! Our Hingemen Magic has delivered us from fear! Do you hear!"

"Aye!"

"The Nok who tormented us have been vanquished! Do you hear?"

"Aye!"

"The pasturelands to the north are ours! Do you hear?"

"Aye!"

"No one shall challenge them again! Our herds shall increase! Our wealth shall increase! Do you hear?"

"Aye!"

"The Hinge foretold our victory! Do you hear?"

"Aye!"

"The Hinge foretold a great Hingemen would defeat the Nok! Do you hear?"

"Aye!"

"And so tonight, I present this great Hingemen! I honor our hero! Do you hear?"

"Aye!"

This is how lies become truth. It is happening here.

Sekh took a giant spear, made in proportion to his stilt costume, from a warrior. "This spear is for the Great Hingemen who defeated the Nok! The Hinge foretold our hero would be honored with a spear! Do you hear?"

"Aye!"

"I present to you our great and honorable Hingemen Bwain! Defender of the realm! Do you hear?"

"Aye!"

Sekh stabbed the spear into the sky, and the drumming crashed into the air, and the assembly jumped at screaming demons flying from the flutes. The stone pillars and heavy, dead beams of the Hinge loomed over them. Sekh lowered the spear to touch its flint blade to each of Bwain's shoulders.

When he stood, Sekh handed it to Bwain, who pumped it into the sky, as though attacking the Nok single-handedly. When a few people cheered, everyone followed. Bwain swelled with it before he faced Kaja and sliced the air. The drumming fell silent.

"Ash!" he yelled, his high voice cutting the wind shrilly. "Did you hear that—"

"Aye!"

He paused. "Um, let us honor High Hingemen Sekh, who heard the Hinge speak! Who heard the flower speak! Do you hear?"

"Aye!"

"Let us see the spirit of Ash! Do you hear?"

"Aye!"

Bwain stabbed the sky, and the music roared forth with redoubled force. A pontoon of Talon charged through the musicians, armed to the teeth. They had flint knives strapped to their shins, tin swords strapped to their hips, compound bows slung over their shoulders, huge quivers bristling with arrows, and thick poled, double-edged copper axes. Their hair was pasted into red starbursts, and their faces were painted orange, with black in the sockets of their eyes.

They filled the Hinge, growling and shouting and wielding their gleaming axes. They circled the assembly, baring their teeth and snarling at the folk gathered there. Initial shock found its outlet in whooping for them, and the townspeople joined their voices to the warrior's demon cries and the blistering rhythm of the drummers.

The Talon circled twice before coming to stand shoulder to shoulder around the pile of branches on the platform, facing out, feet spread with their ax blades poised high.

Bwain slashed with his spear again, the music fell silent, and so did the crowd. He shouted, "Ash! High Hingemen Sekh's Magic pulled a man out of the ocean and brought him to us. And now, to prove that he is ours to command, he will demonstrate his allegiance! Do you hear?"

"Aye!"

Bwain pointed with his arm, and the drummers began to beat a methodical, menacing doom. Four Talon came through the musicians, marching to it while shouldering a large bundle of wood. In the gathering darkness, it was difficult to see. But a fifth warrior followed them, illuminating their load with an oily torch. They marched around the circle, leaving in their wake ashen faces of disbelief, or gleeful expectation. Kaja's heart raced.

He watched Genu in the deepening twilight. When the load passed her, horror captured her torchlit face, and she looked at him helplessly. Regis and Dogen moved closer.

"Steady now," Regis whispered as the Talon approached.

They were carrying the Nok prisoner, bound in a sheath of branches. He was crying, searching from face to face to find compassion, to find hope. Kaja breathed deeply to avoid retching, and a crippling weakness spread through his guts. They took the Nok to the platform and secured him in the center of the pile of wood, upright and facing the tattooed foreigner. As they did so, the drumming throbbed with death, the Talon formed a corridor from Kaja to the prisoner, and the wild-eyed in the crowd began screaming for blood.

Bwain's robe lapped in the wind as he watched, silhouetted before the storm clouds in the darkening sky. Sekh came up on Kaja and leaned down from the height of his stilts. "Here is your initiation, Kaja," the wizard sneered, his eyes gray darts. "You want to be a man? Lay with Genu? Then light this fire."

Kaja bored into him. *You have this power. But you do not have my secret. I have failed Ma. But, at least, I have not aided you.*

The torchbearer was Phiop, Krev at his side, and he came forward and held the burning pole where Kaja could take it. He knew that if he refused to kill the Nok, he would be banished, or killed outright. If he executed the Nok, then the Hingemen and the Talon would know that Sekh ruled him. They would tolerate his existence, for they would have humiliated him before himself.

There is no way out. Ma, how much fire must be added to my life before this world will stop stoking it? Will I ever be free to extinguish it?

Dogen leaned into him, "The Nok is already dead, Kaja."

"Just get it over with." Regis said, laying his heavy hand on Kaja's shoulder. "Put him out of his misery. He's been fever and anguish in a wet hole, choking on his own shit. Send him back to Ma."

Shrieking war cries frightened the forest into silence, and the dark moon hid behind a stormy cloud. Kaja nodded grimly. He reached out and took the torch. In the same moment, Dogen strode forward into Sekh. The wizard faltered on his stilts and did not regain his composure for several steps. Kaja watched him. He shouted madly, and waved his staff, but no one could hear him.

The blood thirst he released has overwhelmed his voice. That is worse.

Dogen grabbed the torch with him. Then Regis laid hold of it, too. The three of them walked through the phalanx, carrying it ahead. The drummers caught a vicious beat. The raging Talon held their axes over them and drew their stout flint swords to the level of their throats.

They pushed the burning torch into the circle of branches. Dogen and Regis retreated with their heads down, but Kaja looked up. Sweat flashed on his brow, and his face swelled with terror. The flames quickly rose, and he struggled mightily as his screams soared skyward on the smoke.

Hope

Different messengers came, and they didn't come for Kaja alone. They wanted him and Dogen and Regis. Dogen pointed, and Kaja nodded, getting the box that held his harp. They followed the messengers not to Sekh's din, but to the Hall. Feeling hopeful, they crawled through the low door.

What is this?

The Hall was more beautiful than ever before, perhaps because it was nearly empty. The lamps on the pillars were lit, and the fabulous swirling animals saw the three men enter with their glimmering eyes. Kaja could actually hear them scampering and splashing. A neat fire crackled in the center of the room, and the two red, naked children knelt near it.

At the far end sat their hosts, Ogden and Quinn, dressed in simple-robed elegance. Quinn was radiant. Her blonde locks tossed like a mane, and her youthful eyes shone the blue of the spring sky, surging with enthusiasm and expectation. Ogden, too, seemed especially regal, and his gold ring was polished. His clean, white hair and flowing beard hovered about his calm grin.

"Welcome, welcome," Ogden's voice boomed. The gravely sound carried melancholy, but pride as well. "Come down here and sit with us."

The three friends did so, after lying their parkas neatly by the fur wall hangings. The five of them sat facing each other in a circle for a moment, saying nothing.

"Well, Quinn," Ogden began, "Here they are. Some of our finest, about to move off to Windhollow."

"You will be missed, gentlemen," the young princess said. "Your character is a great asset to our town."

"Well that's a fine thing to say, Quinn," Regis said. "We'll miss you and Ogden, too. Though I expect the simple life will appeal to us."

"I'm sure it will, Regis," Ogden said. "It is good, I think, that you will be removed a ways from our Court. You will not forget us, I hope."

"Good Ma, Ogden, you can walk there in half a day. Not like we're moving to the bottom of the sea or somewhere."

"Why do you say it is good for us to be 'removed a ways from Court?'" Dogen asked.

Kaja had witnessed a change in Dogen that made him respect him even more. Within him, the Nok's pyre burned steadily. He would not forget that he had been forced to kill for love. He would not submit again.

Time gallops to the horizon, tumbling history like the thunder of hooves. Few have the courage or ability to run alongside like a lion, causing it to veer and dodge. Dogen had become one of those few. Kaja didn't know he had this capacity, and it seemed he hadn't known it himself. Now that it flamed in him, his thinking had become clearer, and no one, not even Ogden, would escape his fearless chase.

Ogden sat pensively, and with a slight gesture, showed that he decided to answer Dogen's real question. He sighed, "That was an ugly piece of business, friends. Just so you'll know, I wanted to let him go. The Nok village is probably abandoned by now. They were preparing to leave when we got there. We gave them our food and a good portion of our equipment as well. I wanted to give them that man, too. But..."

"But what?" Dogen said bluntly. Temple veins on his clean-shaven head pulsed, and his eyebrows locked over his penetrating, golden eyes.

Ogden snapped to him, but he saw the man who should be High Hingemen. Pulling rank seemed childish.

Quinn answered for her father, "Dogen, all of you, please accept my personal apology for forcing you into that. My father came to me for council, though I am young and inexperienced. I knew his wishes, and I knew his fears. Sekh believed that we had to complete the rite as foretold by his astronomy, or we risked the well-being of the people, leaving them open to poor hunts and thin harvests. We have prospered for so long, it seemed the life of an enemy was not important. We did not know until it was too late that Sekh's real intent was to torment you. For that, I am truly sorry."

"Quinn, listen, what were you going to do?" Regis said. "My mother and your grandmother go way back. I mean no disrespect, but it's pretty clear to me that Sekh became a little unhinged over Kaja."

"Unhinged?" Quinn said, grinning.

"Well. Perhaps that's not the word..."

"That's exactly the word," Quinn chuckled, and they joined her.

Ogden straightened up and held his palm to Dogen, saying clearly, "I apologize, Dogen. To you and to all three of you. Will that do?"

"Yes," Dogen said. "Though no honorable Ringfolk could ever put it behind them. Where is Sekh?"

Ogden sighed again. "Well, Sekh and I had a rather heated discussion about the rite after the fact. I let him know that sort of thing wasn't to happen again. And I said a few words about Bwain, in whom I have limited faith. So they left. For a while. They're going to a place where they retreat now and then, not far from Elrik. They'll be back. I just thought they needed a little time to get their thoughts together."

"And the warriors? What about the battle you prepared them for?"

Ogden now responded to Dogen's demands without hesitation. "Off to the pasturelands. They're escorting the Yuffs through spring and summer. I gave them orders to build cairns and place plaques marking the pasturelands the Yuffs want as their own. They're training them as warriors, too, and equipping them. The Yuffs are to increase their herds and pay a bounty of wool and meat. The warriors will be occupied for months."

"You'll be a hero out there, Ogden," Regis said.

"Yes, they will be very happy."

"The Talon may learn from the falcons and the wind," Dogen said. Kaja glanced to him, nodding, for they had discussed the Yuff's teachers.

"So you see, Kaja," Quinn said, gently touching his knee, "a measure of good came from all of this."

Kaja smirked crookedly, and they waited, in hopes he would speak. "Quinn. Such a lovely name you have. These trials have weighed heavily upon me. Such a strange life I have led. Through my hands so much of others have passed. Now, to put myself through my hands is what I wish to do. For the Yuffs I am happy, and to move to Windhollow in peace I am happy."

"And so you shall, Kaja. And so you shall. I will personally see to it," said the regal young princess.

"What about when Bwain comes back? He is the warrior's hero now. How will you become their hero, Quinn?"

"We'll make sure Sekh and Bwain help us with that, Dogen," Ogden replied.

"Perhaps we will need your help as well. We shall see."
Quinn appraised him confidently. When Dogen did not take the
edge off his presence, she was unperturbed, as though she expected
no less. To Kaja, she said, "Much has passed through your hands,
Kaja, And still, you are your own man. We shall not forget you,
for you have taught us much. You have taught me much, and I
thank you."

"Aye, me too, Kaja," Ogden said, "I wish we could do more
for you."

"I wish only to see Hypp and the Crones come back safely,
when the day is now."

"What is this about Hypp and the Crones?"

"They're going on a Spirit Walk, Ogden," Regis said. "My
mother, Jinn and Trawill. You remember. When we still
celebrated at the Ring of Trees, some Crones would go off and
travel from Coven to Coven. They're gonna try to revive the
tradition."

"They did not come to me," Ogden said.

"Do not Crones have their own authority?" Dogen retorted
harshly.

"Indeed, they do," Quinn said quickly. "Indeed they do. A
sublime authority. I have no doubt they plan to bid us farewell.
And the three of you—what are your plans? When will you be
leaving?"

"Oh, real soon. Morgaine and I and Kaja and Genu will
take up in her father's house. We're gonna add to it. And Dogen

and Gan found a spot nearby to build a home of their own. We've already made a few trips, carrying things. We'll be there in less than a moon, I'd say."

"And you'll have children in Fall, no doubt," Ogden grinned.

"At least four or five."

"We shall send a big load of wool to you as a gift from the court," Quinn said. "Though your homes will be warm even in the worst blizzard."

"Aye, thank you, Quinn," Regis said.

"That is the least we can do, Regis," Ogden said. "We will do more than that, I promise."

In the pause that followed, Kaja brought the box to his lap. He opened it and withdrew his instrument without comment. Regis and Dogen enjoyed Quinn's and Ogden's expressions. Never had any of them imagined such an instrument. Kaja positioned the harp in his lap. "Here is your gift, Quinn."

He began to play. A graceful, ethereal melody filled the Hall. The animals on the pillars shuffled to stillness, listening, and the two red children, entranced, inched forward to catch it all.

❦

In moving to Windhollow, Kaja had come to a space of peace, where his trials and losses were at a distance. Now, when there was a looming unknown, it was fun.

"He's ours tonight, Regis," Morgaine said, holding onto her lover's hood drawstrings and smiling up at him. "You run off and play with your friends."

"Think they'll feed me?"

"Everyone feeds you."

"Maybe I should visit them one at a time, then."

"Why don't you give it a try?"

"Will you be back tonight?"

"Yes."

"I'll be waiting." He kissed her and waved to Genu and Kaja before leaving.

"Come on, Kaja, come on!" Genu said. She showed him that she had the fox fur pouch around her neck, where Kaja had decided to keep Nana's amulet. She and Morgaine each took one of Kaja's arms, and they strode through cold spring air that tingled their noses with an afternoon drizzle. They walked past houses whose familiarity was still novel. Light green grass grew from everything—the ground, the duff, the crooks of branches, even rooftops. Roses bloomed all around, for the people of Windhollow loved their roses and planted and tended them wherever a spot could be found.

They headed across town, greeted at every turn with smiling faces from porches and gardens. Charlene's odd blue door was slightly ajar, and she squealed with delight when they pushed it open.

"Children, children! How are you? Oh, Morgaine—you look radiant! I think a baby's spirit might find a home in you this month! And Genu, my goodness child, look at you! So strong and wise—I can see it in your stance. Come in! Sit down!" She moved past the girls and held open her arms for Kaja, who leaned down and gave his dear friend a loving embrace. "Kaja, my man. What a noble creature you are. Like a lion. Come on, sit right here next to me. What is that?"

Kaja gave her his package, a fat pork loin wrapped in a thick layer of minty leaves and savory herbs that Genu had artfully prepared. "Oh, you shouldn't have," she said—but her spit was ready, and she skillfully suspended the herbed roast high over her fire, so it would catch all the flavoring. "My goodness, children. How I've looked forward to this! You're all moved in now?"

"Regis has a few more of his mother's things to bring over, but mostly, yes," Genu said.

"Tell me about the Crones!"

"They're almost ready to go, Charlene," Morgaine said. "They've given away most of what they own, and their equipment is about finished."

"It is so exciting," Genu said. "What an adventure! They're going to come visit us first, and then—who knows? They plan to circle the island. Imagine that!"

"Oh, my goodness! The whole island? That is an adventure!"

"They seem to get stronger every day," Morgaine said. "Last time we visited, it was as if they'd all become ten years younger."

"I can feel it, I really can."

"Do you want to go with them?" Genu asked.

"Oh, no, no. I like my life here. Besides, when your little ones come along, there will be plenty to keep me young!"

"That will," Kaja said, his deep voice contrasting with the girl's chatter. The women glanced to each other, as though to remind themselves that he was present.

"Kaja, how's Regis?"

"He is good, Charlene. That his mother leave now, just as he to have family, does bother him. Still, after all we see, the reason why she leaves does impress him. He worries for her, also. Back and forth he goes."

"They will return," Charlene said certainly. "He knows this?"

"He is told this over and over. If he knows it, I am not sure."

"He doesn't know it," Morgaine said. "He gets pretty upset sometimes. And then other times he is so proud he brags as loudly as he can."

"Usually we can keep his spirits up," Genu said. "He likes having high spirits, and it's not hard to get him to go there. I like to ask him about when she returns—that always revives him."

"Oh, yes, I can imagine it would. We'll all be so impressed. And the stories they will tell!"

"I can't wait to hear," Kaja said.

"Well, she's your mother too, Kaja. What about you?"

"To revive this tradition, I can imagine no greater thing. I am very, very proud of her and Jinn and Trawill. Yes."

"Like a lion, I tell you. Genu, you've got a real gem here."

"I know," she said, pulling Kaja closer.

His grin lit the room, and Charlene admired their utterly different appearances, each enlivened with boundless youthful exuberance. The variety of Ma never ceased to thrill her. "So are you going to show it to me or not, Kaja?" she said, as if offended.

"Of course."

Genu took the pouch from her neck and handed it to him. Charlene placed a small, perfectly made, elaborately carved oak wood box on the low table between them. Carefully, Kaja removed Nana's amulet, and placed it on the box, facing Charlene.

Charlene could see immediately that it was made by a child, as in every curve it held a child's unquestioned and unformed faith. The purity of Nana's art moved her, and she fell into a deep silence with the piece. She divined in that instant all she would ever really know about Nana as a woman, and as a sister, so she sat with her distant cousin's spirit a long while, as her tiny head nodded gently. "Such a beautiful person," she murmured.

"She is an incredible woman, wherever she is. She has come to some other community the same way Kaja came to us," Genu said it with such definitive certainty that Kaja accepted it as fact immediately.

"She is very gifted," Charlene said quietly, in thought.

"I picture her in high mountains," Genu said. "I imagine she has spectacular vistas from her town, and that when she sings, her voice rises past the mountain tops."

"A healing path, I think…" Charlene said, still nodding.

"And I know she and I would be great friends. The sort of friends who are always competing because we would be so much alike. She will find love, I know she will. The same way I did— out of the blue, when it didn't seem possible."

Kaja squeezed her ever so slightly, listening with pleasure. Genu had never revealed these thoughts to him before.

"And for some reason I think I even know what her town looks like. Built into a mountain, sort of, with the views from a plaza before their Hall. The houses are not like ours, but are square, and the same color as the mountain. The fields are very steep, but fertile. And there aren't many people. I don't know why I think that, but it's almost like I can see it."

"She knows you are alive, too, Kaja," Morgaine said.

Kaja startled. "Does she?"

"Take a look," Morgaine said.

On the fur rug before her were five Tarot cards, four face down and pointing in the cardinal directions, and the fifth face up in the center. It was the spiral radiating outward from the North Star. "This is the spiral they used to save you, Kaja."

"A strong beginning," Charlene said, commending her student with a thrust of her tiny finger.

Morgaine flipped each of the four pedals with a quiet snap. Three she disregarded, because the south-facing card showed the Water Bird flying in that direction. "To the south. Across the Flowing Sea. She went the opposite direction as you, Kaja, and she made it to safety."

"Where are the mountains there?" Kaja asked.

"I'm not sure, exactly," Charlene said. "But some of the traders might. As they come through in the Spring and Summer, we can ask them."

"Yes," Kaja said. "I would like to know."

A mild turmoil coiled in Genu. Would Kaja someday desire to travel there? Would she go with him? Perhaps her Spirit Walk would be even more fantastic than Hypp's.

"This is a glorious treasure, Kaja," Charlene said. She lifted the amulet gently. "It has tremendous power. So pure. The force of unquestioned faith and love. It astounds me Sekh nearly destroyed it. He is mad."

"There is danger in him for all of us," Morgaine said.

"Though now Quinn and Ogden know, too," Kaja said.

"Let us hope," Charlene said.

"Hypp and the Crones are doing their part," Genu said.

"Indeed they are, child, indeed they are. They are making hope for us." Charlene said.

"We should make some, too," Genu said.

"And you know how to do that, don't you child?"

"Genu knows how to make hope, yes," Kaja said. "Genu does not fear the world. She is not afraid to live, not at all." The lovers regarded each other as a craftsman regards his work, admiring it in the light.

"Charlene," Genu asked, "do the people of Windhollow practice the Spring Rites at the Living Ring?"

"The Coven goes in secret."

"Why don't we invite everyone this year?"

"Sekh's gone," Kaja said.

"Hmmmm, why not? Why not? In truth we don't even know why we stopped. Let us bring it up to the Coven."

"Yes, let's," Morgaine said.

There came a knock on the door. "Morgaine?" Regis' interminably humored voice trilled sillily. Morgaine lit at the sound of it and jumped up.

"Come in, Regis," Charlene chimed.

He entered with a billow of sweet spring air, holding a giant mushroom.

"It just occurred to me as I was walking past —"

"That you might be just in time for dinner?" teased Morgaine.

"Well, that thought had crossed my mind. But I was mostly interested in finding a pot big enough to boil this mushroom."

"And the pots at home?"

"Well that's what I wanted to ask you. Do we have a pot big enough to boil this mushroom, Morgaine?" They laughed merrily at him, as she hugged him and kissed his cheek.

Kaja turned to Nana's amulet, but Charlene had already put it back in its pouch. She put the pouch into the carved box and whispered to him, "The pouch isn't strong enough, Kaja. Keep it in this, someplace perfectly dry."

"Thank you, Charlene. For everything."

She winked. He handed the box to Genu.

Practice

Kaja and Dogen had been searching for a place to build their gazebo, and were sitting on the ground at the best spot they'd found so far. Far off, the ocean horizon shimmered in the sun.

"With such grace and certainty she carries his death," Kaja said.

Dogen nodded, knowing that Kaja was talking about Charlene, and the Nok she had killed. "She was defending the offspring of her Coven, Kaja. That is different."

"Yes. Still, she shot him through the heart, and didn't go to his body."

"Probably part of their tradition."

"So we cannot carry his death same way?" Kaja asked.

"The man posed no threat to any of us."

"We must carry his death, Dogen. Some way. To find the way, we must try."

Dogen scanned the terrain, twirling an oak leaf. The view pleased him. This would be a good spot to practice. He would come more often than Kaja, especially after his children were born. He loved Gan and was thankful for him. Still, in his Spirit Life, he lived alone, and all he ever wanted, even as a child, was a guide. Now he was faced with a far greater challenge, as the very man he had hoped to follow in the Spirit Life had betrayed him to a dark path by forcing killing upon him. There was no clarity there, and no simple understanding was possible. He threw the leaf to the ground. "Yes, Kaja, we must. But how? Where do we begin?"

"Like this," Kaja said.

He matched his breathing to Dogen's. Not quicker, not slower, just the same. His friend had to think this through. He had to put it into some sort of story, something he could believe and explicate. He had to understand how such horror had accomplished itself through his hands. When Kaja could sense this settling in him, he said, "A wise man you too know once said to me, 'Be aware of Ma, and she will speak.' That is what he said to me, and still I believe him. Do you remember, Dogen?"

Dogen recognized his own words. He nodded ruefully, because they sounded shallow now. How could something so vague lead him out of this abyss?

"Do you have faith, Dogen? That Ma will lead you the way?"

Dogen's breathing became more rapid. His face contorted, and tears wetted his cheeks. "He had a family, Kaja. He was one of the only men left. And I...I killed him, because I was too cowardly to refuse."

"You took torch with me, Dogen, because you are great friend. You did not have to move from where you stood."

"That would have been even more cowardly. To let you do it alone. Either way, I did nothing to help that prisoner. Nothing at all."

"Why do you not judge Regis and me?"

"Because I was the only one who could have done anything. I was the only one who had the stature to resist Sekh. What could you have done? They would have killed you and been done with it. And Regis? He sent the man back to Ma, pure and simple. He brings less to it than I. Not that he is simple, just that he is more direct. I am the one who killed him, Kaja. I am the one who killed him because I am the only one who had a chance to save him."

"So then, evil came through you. I know about that, Dogen."

"Evil isn't out there somewhere, coming through me, Kaja. My nature is evil, weak, and cowardly. That is what came through me. I came through me."

Kaja pondered the ocean. What could he do for his friend? It would take a long time. And he would work at it for as long as it took. A new type of calm came over him. Patience. Patience from love, patience from wisdom.

"Once, when I was a little boy, there was a long and wet Winter," Kaja began. "No snow, but much rain, day after day. It went on well into the Spring, and they had to go hunt in driving rain. One day my uncle and some other men went. They come to little stream grown rushing torrent. Across stream lay fallen tree, which was bridge over brush. Usually. Now it was at the water. Across it men walk, careful, the water rushing around their boots. The first two made it.

"But then the third was upon the log, it rolled to side. A branch out of water slid into binding on boot. The man fell into water and struggled to free from tree. The treetop came loose from the far mud, and slowly pointed downstream. The roots held, and top of the tree sank to bottom of the water.

"My uncle and his friends saw the tree push their friend under. He said it happened quickly but seemed very slowly. The fourth man, who was still on first side of the stream, tore off pack weapons boots, dove into water to free his friend. He came back and climb out on log. Friend gone. Disappeared. We find his body until Summer. And so hunters came back to town, their heart pain, to tell his family. That he was dead, drowned in little creek. And never did they forgive themselves for that, Dogen. Though they were not evil."

"That was Ma's work. Ma and Sekh are not the same."

"They are both outside of you, Dogen."

"They are both within me as well. Now, anyway."

"Yes, always they have been inside as well. Yes. And outside, too. You cannot change that."

Dogen stared into the sky. Kaja matched his breathing, and they remained quiet.

"Ma will heal, Dogen. The wise man promised me. Listen well, I too, and we shall hear. Yes?"

❧

Regis and Martin staggered back into Windhollow under huge loads of wooden boxes and collapsed with a crash a hundred paces from Martin's house. Gan, Dogen, and Kaja ran out to help, laughing at the spectacle. What could they possibly need in that load? They had everything already. But this was Regis, who had inherited from his mother the tendency to collect. Each box was big and awkward, and Kaja wondered how they had managed to carry them from Ash in the first place.

"So is this the last of it, Regis, or did you want to carry the house over as well?" Gan asked. Regis was sitting on the ground, his legs splayed out before him, panting and sweating. He gratefully accepted when Morgaine and Genu offered cold juice.

"Can't take the house. Gave it to Quinn."

"You what?" Morgaine exclaimed.

"Quinn wanted it, so we gave it to her. Wall furs, pit jars and all."

"Well, how do you like that!" Genu said. "That will be a fine hello when the Hingemen and Talon return."

381

"Rather poetic, isn't it?" Regis huffed happily, holding up his cup for more.

"Guess what's she's gonna do with a place that big?" Martin asked, also sucking down the cool, sweet elixir.

"What, indeed?" Morgaine said.

"Gonna move the 'next generation' in. What'd ya think o' that?"

"The 'next generation'?"

"That's right," Regis said, juice clinging to his sweaty beard, "Quinn and some of her friends. Children of Hingemen. Children of Talon. Ringfolk of all ages. It'll be a pretty nice place again."

"Are you at peace with it, then?" Morgaine asked.

"Oh, yeah. Hate to see it go to waste. Thought some family would want it, but this is much better.

"The porch upstairs!" Gan said, "that will definitely keep them creative!"

"Ma's truth," Genu said. "No one's ever seen or built anything like it. How's that for a legacy in Ash?"

Regis gave her a broad smile as they all hefted boxes back to Martin's house. Kaja's and Genu's addition was completed, with a door leading into the common garden and a door leading into a new room attaching the two houses, christened the "nursery." The nursery's roof beams were in place—all that remained was framing them and tying on the thick thatch that would keep out the rain and snow. Kaja looked at them, and couldn't help noticing how a porch atop would be nicely sheltered from the prevailing winds...

At twilight, Kaja and Dogen built a fire in the hearth by the swing, placing a pitcher of mead nearby, and they gathered around so the smoke would keep the insects away in the gathering dusk.

"Well, they're on their way, Regis," Martin said after a pause.

"Yeah, that they are."

"When will they be here?" Morgaine asked.

"Day after tomorrow, they said."

"Then that's when they'll be here," Genu said.

"I can't believe it's for real. I mean, when they first mentioned it, it seemed real, but then it sort of faded away. Now it's real again." Regis played with Morgaine's fingers, and she gazed at him tenderly from where she reclined in his arms.

"You alright?"

"Yeah, yeah. I'm fine. It's Kaja I'm worried about."

"I will be alright. I will miss her so. If not for her, I would not be here."

"Funny thing, I could say the same myself," Regis chuckled.

Their conversation meandered from the Crones to plans for the garden to plans for the house to plans for their children and then back to the Crones again.

That night, Genu awoke tight in Kaja's embrace. She could feel his heart thundering, and his legs were entwined with hers, and his strong arms clutched her, and his shuddering breath pelted her neck.

She stroked his dreadlocks, and whispered to him, "I love you, Kaja, I love you. You're home now…"

He held her tighter and began making sounds in his dream. His eyes thrashed wildly behind his eyelids.

"Kaja, Kaja, it's a dream."

Suddenly he inhaled sharply and awoke with a start. He broke out in a heavy, cold sweat from head to toe, and searched desperately for Genu.

"What is it, my love? What torments you like this?"

"Has it happened before?" Kaja asked.

"Yes. Sometimes you awake, but then you fall asleep again, as though dead. Sometimes you do not awake, and I am able to calm you with my voice and my hands."

"You are Ma, alive."

"So are you, Kaja. Do you remember your dream?"

Kaja jerked away from her into darkness. *I remember it perfectly. I cannot escape it. This secret, this horror…*

"Will you tell me?"

"I cannot."

"Why?"

"You will hate me. As I hate myself."

"That is not possible."

"You will never think of me the same again."

"Let me know you, Kaja, let me know all of you."

"The things I have done…"

"When you were a slave?"

"Yes."

"Then it was not really you who did them."

"It became me, because I lived."

"Do not hate yourself for what you were forced to do."

He shook his head miserably.

Genu cradled him. "This secret has too much power over you, Kaja. Tell me, and I will take the power out of it."

"You can do that?"

"I will try."

He was silent for a long time, holding her tightly. Then he pulled back, just enough to search her.

"Things may change between us."

"They won't. I promise."

He was silent again, but his breathing deepened. He pieced it together in her language first. Then he slid to sit against the wall of their room, nearly dark but for a single shaft of moonlight falling across her face.

"Come here," he said.

She moved into his lap, and laid her head on his chest, and listened to his heart. He wrapped his arms around her. As he spoke, her tears pattered his tattoos.

The Journey

The Crones came, just when they said they would. Ringfolk greeted them on the trail and brought them to Martin's house. Kaja held Hypp for a long, long time, and then hung back to watch her while she chatted with the others.

Their equipment was phenomenal. Everything was brand new, made of the finest materials and the finest craftsmanship. Her boots came up to her knee, well packed and waterproof. She wore dungarees that tied tight below the top of the boot, and had a thick insulating felt encircling her kidneys. Her parka fit perfectly, and Kaja had her show him how the hood allowed room for a couple wool scarves but still tied tight around her face without inhibiting her vision. Their wool undergarments—which they were not wearing in the Spring's gathering warmth—were woven so tightly they were wind-proof. The same for their scarves, and their hand warmers.

The question of food came up over and over, but they were confident they could survive on plants and insects they found along the way. They carried nets to catch birds which, for rather small people, would be enough meat. Each also carried an ember chamber as well as stout fire starter kits. They had invented an ingenious lean-to made of three equal pieces, so they could set up a small shelter by the side of their fire to add to the protection of their fitted, double-sided bed rolls.

Kaja and Regis insisted on unpacking their equipment and testing it, as well as confirming the way they loaded their form-fitting, rigid packs so as to allow for unpacking them in tandem with dropping weather. They checked and rechecked the packs themselves, making sure the hoods would shed rain and snow but not freeze shut.

Kaja felt certain that his long and desperate experience in the wilderness would allow him to be of service, but he discovered that they had thought of everything already. He and Regis exchanged shrugs of uselessness, convinced not only that the Crones were serious about leaving, but that they were serious about being on the road for a long, long time.

"No weapons, Ma?" Regis asked at last.

"And who would be afraid of a Crone carrying a weapon? Really, now, Regis. We'll be safer with our sweet smiles and yellow scarves."

"Ma's morning, then. We're relying on the world to be a different place for you."

"It already is, love, it already is."

"The equipment is excellent, Ma" Kaja said.

He had taken to calling her Ma some time ago, but every time Hypp heard him say it, it warmed her heart.

"Thank you, my son. We spent a good amount of time on it. We don't want to go begging for equipment. So it had better last."

"That will not be problem."

"How long do you think you'll be gone?" Regis asked, holding down his emotions.

"We can't really say for sure. It will be several seasons. Perhaps you will hear of us from traders now and then. We're going through the land of the Scotts, though—all the way to the tip of the island."

"Yes. You keep saying that."

❧

All of them, including Charlene, gathered at Martin's house that evening and sat around the porch hearth. Morgaine and Genu had prepared copious amounts of food, and the three Crones did their best to eat, even though their Coven had already feasted them to bursting at Ash.

Late that night, a gibbous moon shone through Martin's tree and wisps of glowing white mist illuminated the valley below. A warm companionship flowed between them, when Genu whispered to Kaja. He nodded. She passed around a fresh pitcher of mead.

Kaja said, "Everyone, I want to tell you the secret that Sekh wanted to know."

With slight motions, they arranged themselves to face him. The three Crones and Charlene sat next to each other, opposite him. The energy of expectation was palpable.

"There is part of story I did not tell in the Hall," Kaja began. "The most important part. I did not tell, because great power it had over me. Now, I want you Crones to know. I want you to carry this Knowledge with you on Spirit Walk. You will use it well."

He paused and wet his mouth with a sip of mead. He rolled the cup between his hands. His friends did not make a sound.

"Sekh knows one Thurgan Magic. He knows the easy one, anyone can see. Torment. Violence. Secrecy. He knows to keep the thing you want, and to make you beg to have. The spell is on your body. You think of it with your mind. But this is not true Magic.

"True Magic, in your soul it comes. In your soul it lives. A demon. The Thurgan knew the way to put a demon in you, so no way to escape it. The art is evil. Violence, yes, but not only. The other ways, to weave the spell, these are worse.

"They began on me when they first threw me to floor of Riversmouth Hall, at feet of leader. Warrior hold my hair, to look up at him. Knee on back, knife at neck. Leader on high chair. Warriors behind. Huge, white face, purple starburst scars from forehead to chin. Mouth deformed. Eyes, danger. He says Thurgan words. I do not know. But I do know what he asks. I say Thurgan words, 'Stop. Go. Honey. Beer. Metal.'

"He gives loud, sharp command. Man on me let go. Leader leans over me. More Thurgan words. I do not know. But I say them back, perfectly. He gives short command, not so loud, and I am given water. I drink all, and they give more. Before I drink, I hold up cup, and say Thurgan word, I think is 'water,' and then drink. The leader smiles. He says one word, and I am given a hard biscuit. Before I eat, I hold it up, and say word. He smiles again.

"He gives long command, and then two men, old, not warriors, come to me. They lift me up, and I go with them. I do not know, but Magic has already begun.

"With two men, I study. All day, into night. I learn Thurgan, and they know of my language. I am kept in small cell, as I told Sekh in Ash Hall. But I am not hungry. I am not thirsty. No. They feed. They give clothes. They give blanket. One day, they give my pouch to me, with my treasure, and I feel gratitude. They destroy life, but give pouch, and I thank them.

"It was like the cart that came. I did not know. If I learn language, if I teach, then I eat, I drink, I have my things. They destroy, I thank. When I do know, it is too late.

"One day, they take me to Hall. Empty, but warriors all around. I learn much of Magic this day. I sit on floor, by the leader. The two old men stand near. Then, doors open, and some of my people come in. I do not know them. They are starving. They are dirty. They wear rags, and their face, full of terror.

"They are led to front, and made to lie on the ground before the leader. They look up at him. They look up at me. Up at me, too. They see I have clothes. They see I have food and water. The old men talk to me in Thurgan. They see that I understand. Then one of the old speaks to my people in my language, but they do not understand. He tries, but does not yet know to say. So he speaks to me in Thurgan again. I am to say the words in my language.

"What do I do? What can I do? I think that I can help my people. I think that if the Thurgan hear my people, then maybe they will be alive. Maybe their dead soul will live again, as true children of Ma. I am ignorant. I am wrong. I do not know.

"From Thurgan, I say to them, no you may not go home. I say to them, no, you may not see your daughters. I say, you must work. I say, if you work, maybe next time. Maybe next time. You see? I become their tool. But I do not know then. I think, 'maybe next time.'

"This is deep part of the Magic Sekh wants. To use hope to destroy. But there is more. Much more.

"Time goes by. I teach the old my language. I say Thurgan words to my people in our language. I have food. I have water. But still, thanks to Ma, I know there is great danger. I tell the truth to Sekh, in the Hall. At night, I dig at my floor. I dig at my wall.

"This is another part of the Magic. I do what Thurgan command, because I hope that tomorrow, it will be new. And it is, but not in way I expect. One day, I am to say Thurgan words in my language, but now, the old men speak instead. And now, they are understood.

"That night, I know that time has left me. What am I when they know my language? I am nothing. I am slave. I am not man, not to them. They can tell that I know. Old men with me still. But warriors now, too. I know why.

"My people have seen me with Thurgan. They have heard me speak for Thurgan. To my people, I am Thurgan. Now, Thurgan must destroy my soul. I have seen their weakness of mind. Once, they needed me, so now, they must destroy me, for all to see. Not to kill me. To kill me would not be enough. My people must see I am destroyed.

"That is when they begin to use torch. When I come before my people, sitting at the feet of the leader, a warrior stands behind me, to hold my head like rock. A warrior before me. He hold torch. When I am to say the Thurgan words in my language, he hold torch by my face. To my eyes. I understand. To them, I do not need to see. I only need to hear, and to speak. Blind, I would still be slave they need. I understand.

"But they do not burn my eyes. If they did, maybe I break. Maybe I fall silent and let them beat me. Maybe I fall silent and let them kill me. But they have that power already. No. The torch burns my soul instead. They want me to be dead soul, like the warrior. This is deep, evil Magic. Not to kill the body, but to kill the soul.

"This is when they bring her. This is how they finish their Magic. I do not know how they knew who she was. I am in Hall, at feet of leader. Warrior behind. Warrior with torch. And they bring my sister, Nana, before me, alone.

"I see her face, right now. She is afraid. She sees what they have done to me. She understands, some. But not all. I understand all. To destroy my soul, they will make me destroy her.

"Leader says words in Thurgan. Warrior hold torch. I must tell her she will go to salt mines. She must lay with Thurgan men there, whenever they want. You must understand this. Women in my people, they gave freely to the men who loved them. Many men, for love. To love is life. All men are lover. All men are father.

"But Thurgan do not want love. Thurgan do not want free. Thurgan want force. Thurgan want fear. Thurgan want take, not receive.

"I am to say, 'your children will be born slave. Boy slave in mine, girl slave like you.' I am to say, 'you will eat, you will drink, like I do, if you let them.'

"I cannot say it. I know I cannot. I see Nana's face. I see her tears. Not for herself. For me.

"And that is when the true Magic happened. I have a choice. That is the worst of the memory. If I refuse, I am blind. Right then. Or, I obey. There is hope still in me. This is why hope Magic came first, so evil hope now. Maybe next time. I hear Thurgan words on my voice, in my language. I send my sister to be slave, and my nephew to be slave, and my niece to be slave.

"At that moment. Deep in my soul, a Thurgan demon came to life. Deep in my soul, they put a demon. I feel what happens. This is Magic that Sekh wants. The demon, how to create. That is the Magic. Evil magic, that takes you away from yourself. This is how it is done.

"Nana cries. They lead her away. But she saves me then. Somehow, she knew how to save. She shout, 'Ma flows in spiral,' two words in my language, and they push her out.

"The Thurgan leader laugh. The warrior laugh. The old men laugh. They know they have worked Magic. They know. They take Nana from me, and I will never have her again. I am Thurgan to her.

"This is secret Sekh wants. A man in body, a demon in soul." Kaja paused and breathed deeply. Genu stroked his hand.

Regis couldn't hold still any longer, and he said, loudly and clearly, "You didn't have a choice, my friend. That's not a choice."

"Yes, it is choice, Regis," Kaja said quickly. "Even to die, a choice. Always."

"No," Dogen said, "no it isn't, Kaja. The little bit of hope you had was not all Thurgan Magic. Some of that hope was Ma's Magic. You chose to fight. Blind or dead, you would have been defeated."

"Only here, in this world," Kaja said. "Not before Ma."

Charlene's high, sweet voice rang out, "That is evil Magic, too, Kaja. Never think that the most important part of life happens after you are dead. You chose to live so you could fight. You made the right decision."

Genu nodded in fierce agreement, and said, "Tell them the rest."

Kaja took a draught and began again. "You are so kind to me. More kind to me than I am to myself."

"Exactly," Charlene said, cheering him with her cup, before motioning for him to go on.

"Yes. The Magic can be overcome. This is what Genu and I want to tell to you for your Spirit Walk. To know how Thurgan Magic, yes, but also to know it can be defeated.

"Nana reminded me of true life. The spiral circles, but never to same place. Yes, demon is real, part of me now. But world spiral, so my true soul not dead. She give me soul, with her prayer.

"I sent Nana to horror. She save me. Forever, this to be true between us. That night, I escape. I chew wood with teeth. I dig with fingers bloody. With feet. The opening not big enough. I push naked through, I tear skin and rip joints. I pull clothes behind me. I run to forest.

"As I run, demon changes. With me, yes. But without the leader, without demons in warriors and old men, with me alone. The demon is rage. Blind, like I would have been. But now, the demon knows if I die, it cannot move to another. If I die, it dies.

"I make demon myself. When I need to kill, or steal, or force my brothers to take me on boat, I am demon. Every time I do, demon gets stronger. More of me to become it. And when I am alone, when I dream, the demon torments me. Tries to kill my soul and to own me. To be me, all. But no. I am still there, and I fight back to it, always.

"Sekh understands. He could know this, somehow. His flower, his nature, his soul, somehow he knows the how. He tries to help the demon win."

"Oh, exactly," Regis said. "Just like the old bugger. Brings out the worst in you."

"Yes. I tell Sekh, 'you know Thurgan Magic,' and this is what I mean. He feeds demon. He wants demon in you. Not you."

Kaja shifted forward, and his long locks swung towards the Crones, and the flames burned in his black eyes, and his voice became resonant. "This is how you stop him. You give power to soul. Kindness to me, and my soul has strength. Demon cannot win, even when Sekh helps to win. You are Ma, and so you stop them both.

"I always think, since the ocean put me here, that Ma was to test me. To see if I can kill demon and live a good man. But not just me. No. She tests us all.

"One night, I tell Genu, and she holds me. Her great kindness is to understand. Together, souls destroy the demon with love. Now, gone.

"That is how. Your Magic is strong. On your Spirit Walk, tell the Covens, so they will know."

The stars flew behind the swelling moon, and her light soared along the treetops below them, and flocked above the waves of grain on the verdant valley's floor. An owl hooted from the pristine forest up the trail. The fire whispered and cracked. Deep into the night, their soft voices comforted each other, and they dreamed of a world where Ma never had to fight for souls but had them all.

❧

The next morning, the entire town of Windhollow gathered at the Oak to bless the Crones.

Kaja and Regis held Hypp snuggly between them. Over and over, they said, "Come back here, come back to our home."

The Crones were joyful. Their hope filled the crowd as they bid their last farewells and headed down the trail together. It meandered playfully through a meadow bursting with golden mustard.

Charlene followed them a short way. She called, and when they turned to wave, she threw Bwain's seeds high into the air. They twinkled as they drifted down, free to grow as they would.

The Crones pressed their palms together, and bowed to her, in the fashion they had learned from Kaja. Charlene, and all the townspeople, bowed back the same way.

Kaja watched them go. Their yellow scarves blazed against the blue sky, and they held hands as they dropped below the horizon, skipping like children.

Please join my email list:

tombast.com

Special offers and updates.

⋘⋙

Also by Tom Bast:

The Underground

Sinister oppression.
Epic revelations.
Ferocious rebellion.
Apocalyptic stakes.

Printed in Great Britain
by Amazon

87671804R00231